ABOUT THE AUTHOR

Nancy Carson lives in Staffordshire and is a keen student of local history. All her novels are based around real events, and focus on the lives of the people of the Black Country.

By the same author:

Poppy's Dilemma
The Railway Girl
The Dressmaker's Daughter
The Factory Girl
A Family Affair
Daisy's Betrayal
The Lock-Keeper's Son

NANCY CARSON

Rags to Riches

avon

This novel is entirely a work of fiction.
The names, characters and incidents portrayed in it are
the work of the author's imagination. Any resemblance to
actual persons, living or dead, events or localities is
entirely coincidental.

AVON

A division of HarperCollins*Publishers*
1 London Bridge Street,
London SE1 9GF

www.harpercollins.co.uk

This paperback edition 2017

First published in Great Britain by
Hodder & Stoughton in 2000 as *Love Songs*

This edition published by
HarperCollins*Publishers* 2017

Copyright © Nancy Carson 2017

Nancy Carson asserts the moral right to
be identified as the author of this work

A catalogue record for this book is
available from the British Library

ISBN-13: 978-0-00-819189-4

Set in Minion by Palimpsest Book Production Limited,
Falkirk, Strirlingshire

Printed and bound in Great Britain

RAGS TO RICHES

Chapter 1

'Living in the same house as Stephen Hemming for two years hasn't exactly been the most inspiring thing that's ever happened to me,' Maxine Kite admitted philosophically to Lizzie, her mother. Maxine had never spoken to her before about her love life but right now, companionable together on this special day in this unfamiliar scullery with its clean whitewashed walls, she felt a compelling need to talk.

'So what's wrong with Stephen?' Lizzie asked, wringing water from a sheet she was rinsing in the deep, stone sink.

'Oh, I'm not so sure that Stephen's the problem, Mother. It's me.' Maxine stared reflectively at the brass tap that was fixed to the wall, dripping water. 'I can't stand his eyes following me at every turn. He makes me feel uncomfortable – as if he's mentally undressing me.'

'You poor soul, our Maxine. I sympathise. I can only imagine what it must be like. And yet he seems such a nice, gentle chap.'

'Oh, he is, Mother. He wouldn't hurt a fly. He thinks the world of me, I know he does . . . And I like him – as a friend – he's a good friend. But I'm not in love with him. I know he'd like me to be, but I can't help the way I feel about him. And I don't like him looking at me the way he does, either.'

'But that's just men,' Lizzie remarked. 'You're a nice-looking girl, our Maxine. You've got lovely dark hair, a lovely trim figure. Men like pretty girls, and they'll always turn to have a good look at those they think are worth looking at. You must expect it. Be thankful for it, our Maxine.'

'But it's when he sits down opposite me . . . I'm sure it's only so he can look up my skirt . . .'

'Men will always try to look up your frock whether or no.'

'Yes and I daresay some girls like it when they do, if it's somebody they fancy who's having a peep – but I bet they wouldn't be so keen on Stephen doing it. Whenever I go to my room to change, he always seems to be hovering – as if he's trying to peer at me through the crack in the door. Even when I practise my cello I have to wear a long, flared skirt to hide my legs. It's laughable really.'

'It's because he fancies you, our Maxine. It's been worrying me, you and him living under the same roof,' Lizzie declared frankly. 'So I take it there's been no hanky-panky.'

'With Stephen?' Maxine scoffed. 'Mother, you cannot be serious. I just don't fancy him that way. I'm not especially fond of him touching me. And that's the trouble. In any case, his mother and father are always around. I'm lodging with *them*, remember. Not him. The fact that he lives there as well is by the by.'

Maxine perceived the relief in her mother's expression at her blatantly honest response; she knew Lizzie had always worried about her precious daughters; no doubt she always would. After all, a pretty daughter and a hot-blooded man did not always create a favourable combination.

'You don't think you're imagining all this?' Lizzie queried sceptically, treating the sheets to another immersion in water so cold that it was making her bare hands tingle.

'No,' Maxine replied. 'I'm not imagining it. Pansy's noticed as well.'

'You mean he looks up his sister's frock?'

'No, Mother.' Maxine started to giggle at the unthinkable absurdity. 'Pansy's noticed he's like that with *me*. He doesn't give *her* a second glance. She's his sister, for goodness sake . . .

So . . . let's hope I pass this audition with the City of Birmingham Orchestra. It'll give me the perfect excuse to get away from him.'

'Have you told him yet as you're likely to be leaving?' Lizzie added some hot water from the gas geyser and looked up from the white cotton sheets as she kneaded out the last trace of suds.

'Well, not yet. I *want* to be straight with him, Mom, but I haven't plucked up the courage yet.'

'Then it's time you did, our Maxine.'

'I know . . .' Maxine replied guiltily. 'I'll tell him tonight.'

'And what do you think he'll say?'

Maxine shrugged. 'It's not up to him to say anything.' She felt suddenly irked that Stephen should be considered important enough to even warrant a say in the matter. 'It's my decision, not his.'

'But he'll have an opinion, Maxine. Allow him that.' Lizzie said, wringing a sheet now.

'Course he will. But he doesn't own me. Okay, I know he wouldn't want me to give up lodging at his family's house, but it'll be a lot more convenient living here if I get that job. Besides, I don't want to live in the same house as him any longer.'

'I take it you're not thinking of getting married then?'

'Me, married? I'll never get married, Mom. It's not something I desire. I'm married to my music. I'd never marry Stephen anyway.'

'Never say never,' Lizzie counselled gently. 'You just might change your mind.'

Maxine shook her head resolutely and folded her arms as she leaned against the cupboard. 'No. I'll never change my mind about Stephen.'

Maxine stared forlornly across the shimmering expanse of water known as Rotton Park Reservoir, which kept Birmingham's canals topped up. A team of ducks, and the more exotically coloured drakes that accompanied them, sailed importantly some distance from the edge. Moorhens shepherded a waddle of tiny black chicks that bobbed in the radiating rings of a fresh-cast fishing line. It was as pleasant a view, through the yellow-flowered curtains that framed the imperfect panes of the scullery window, as you would find from the rear of any terraced house. Soon, it might be her new home.

Of course, she could return to live with her mother in Dudley but, rather, Maxine was inclined to accept her sister's offer of accommodation here. She had tasted freedom and relished it. Going back to mother's she would lose that precious independence. In any event, her self-esteem would not allow her to return home.

Maxine was pinning all her hopes on the audition. It would mean regular work, money in her pocket. But most importantly, it would allow her this much-needed breathing space from Stephen. No, she was not in love with him. Trouble was, he was too fond of her, too protective. He was suffocating her. And this house here in Ladywood, the home of her sister and brother-in-law, was far more convenient for the Town Hall and the CBO's rehearsal rooms than having to lug her cello to and from his folks' house in Smethwick, especially on those occasions when she had to make the journey by tram. The trouble was, there had been talk of moving from Ladywood back to Dudley; and that meant Smethwick would be more convenient again. Still, she wouldn't mention that to Stephen yet; he would only try to get her to stay.

'I should've thought the chances of anybody making a living playing a cello in Birmingham would be a bit limited to say the least,' Lizzie commented and Maxine detected the same sad scepticism she'd heard a hundred times before. 'It's not as if they want a celloist on every street corner.'

'The word is *cellist*, Mother,' Maxine corrected, amused that her mother had got the word wrong. 'But I can play piano as well, remember . . . and I can sing. If I don't get this job in the CBO I'd be quite prepared to play piano and sing – in a pub even.'

'Over my dead body.' Lizzie wrung the sheet more animatedly

and tossed it into a wicker washing basket with the other, ready to peg out. 'I'm not having you singing in a public house like some wailing old music hall tart. I'll see you back home first. You're not twenty-one yet, remember . . . Struth, it's been bad enough worrying over our Henzey up there these last few years, not to mention our Alice. Now I worry about you as well.'

'You needn't worry about me, Mom. I'll be okay.'

'Famous last words . . .'

The kettle on the gas stove started to bubble and boil and Maxine applied herself at last to making the pot of tea she should have organised a while ago.

'I'll go and hang these sheets out,' Lizzie said. 'Don't forget to pour me a cup of tea before you take some upstairs to our Henzey and Will.'

When she climbed the stairs carrying the tea tray, Maxine thought she heard her name mentioned. The door to Henzey's and Will's bedroom was ajar. She pushed it open gently with her foot.

'Tea!' Will Parish exclaimed chirpily, and held the door open for her. 'Thank the Lord. We thought you'd got lost.'

Maxine placed the tray on the dressing table. 'Sorry I've been so long. Actually, I forgot.' She uttered a little laugh of self-mockery. 'Telling Mother about Stephen. Then I had a lecture off her.' She rolled her eyes. 'So how are you feeling now, Henzey? Tired, I bet.'

'Tired, but content.' Henzey ran her fingers through her dark hair and smiled happily. She looked pale but she was entitled to, having just endured childbirth, even though it had not been protracted. Henzey leaned over towards the crib at the side of the bed where the new baby lay. 'Isn't he beautiful? Who do you think he's like, Maxine? D'you think he's like Will?'

Maxine peered into the crib where the new baby was sleeping. 'Mmm,' she murmured indecisively. 'He's got your colouring, our Henzey . . .'

'But his features are Will's, don't you think?'

'Oh, he looks like himself, Henzey,' Will protested, half amused at speculation he considered pointless. 'How can you say who he's like yet? He hasn't been born more than a few hours. With a newborn child, I don't see how you can possibly tell who he's like. In a week or two you might be able to say. But more often than not, children tend to look like their grandparents.'

'In that case,' Henzey declared, 'he's bound to be like my father, his hair's so dark. He was dark, as well, with blue eyes. And tall. Oh, I wish he were here now to see him.'

'Yes, he's a bit like our dad, Henzey, now you mention it,' Maxine conceded, handing a cup and saucer to Henzey.

'I wish I'd known your father,' Will said in all sincerity, accepting his cup of tea from Maxine. 'Thanks, chick . . . A real character by all accounts.'

'A gentleman,' Henzey uttered nostalgically. 'Honest and forthright. He used to love to hear Maxine play the piano . . . Remember, Maxine?'

'It seems so long ago . . .' At the mention of her father Maxine peered out of the window into the back garden, seeking her mother. 'Mother's pegging out your sheets, Henzey. I'd better go and help her. It looks freezing out there for April.'

'Don't let her stay too long, Maxine. She's worked hard all day. I don't know what we'd have done without her.'

'We'll just clear up, Henzey. Then we'll be off. Can I come and see the baby tomorrow? I'd love to hold him. Oh, I'm dying to hold him, Henzey. He's so beautiful . . .'

Henzey smiled contentedly. 'Course you can. Come as soon as you're ready.'

Maxine's audition for the City of Birmingham Orchestra fell on 30th April 1936, a Thursday. The large rehearsal room with its high ceiling, its tall, Gothic windows and its sawdusted, wood-block floor, looked and smelled like a school hall. Musical instruments stood or lay haphazardly, unattended, alongside utilitarian metal music stands and the printed scores of Elgar.

6

Leslie Heward, the conductor, asked Maxine some questions about her musical training and she confirmed that she'd spent the last three and a half years at Bantock's School of Music studying her instrument.

'Show me what you can do, Miss Kite,' he said. His demeanour was kindly, maybe to ease her nerves.

'May I play *The Swan* from *Carnival of the Animals?*'

'Of course. Let me hear it.' Leslie Heward smiled generously. *The Swan* was no surprise.

The long hanging notes of a haunting melody, as poignant as a love song, poured from Maxine's cello like tears. The rich timbre of the instrument, the emotion in her playing, her instinctive grasp of the composition's spirit, and the visual grace with which she played, all conspired to work positively for her. She was aware of other musicians, including the principal cello, listening intently from the rear of the rehearsal room.

'That was excellent, Miss Kite. You seem to have a natural empathy with your instrument. I'm impressed.'

'Thank you, Mr Heward.' She smiled demurely.

'What else do you know?'

Maxine had swotted up Dohnànyi's *Konzertstück* for cello and orchestra, but Mr Heward heard her play only a part, evidently satisfied already with her ability. He pulled out a volume of music from a pile beside him and asked her to sight read. It was a section from Elgar's First Symphony. She performed that with expertise too and Maxine knew she had been successful when Mr Heward turned and smiled to one of the musicians sitting at the rear of the hall, who nodded his approval.

'Congratulations, Miss Kite,' he said pleasantly. 'You'll be receiving official notice to play in all the orchestra's concerts this season. We'll be doing Sibelius's Seventh Symphony soon. Are you familiar with Sibelius's work?'

'Some, yes, Mr. Heward.'

'Excellent. And we're doing Beethoven's Fifth, the 'New World', Shostakovich's First, and Tchaikovsky's Fourth . . . and lots of Elgar, of course.' He smiled steadily. 'Doesn't scare you, does it?'

Maxine smiled back; her usual shy smile. 'No, sir, it doesn't scare me at all.'

'Splendid! That's what I like to hear. Thank you, Miss Kite. Rehearsals will start for you here next Monday at ten. I shall look forward to your contribution to the orchestra.'

'Thank you, Mr Heward.' She beamed, her delight evident in her eyes that were the colour of her cello. 'Thank you so much.'

Mr Heward shook her hand and left Maxine to put her cello away while he sought the company and comments of the principal cellist.

While she smiled to herself, so relieved and so pleased that she had got the job she wanted so much, another man, much younger than the conductor, walked up to her. He was in his late twenties she estimated, tall, confident and oh, so good-looking.

'I think you surprised our lord and master,' he said amiably, adjusting his fashionable paisley tie.

Maxine regarded him with interest. 'Do you think so? How did I manage that, I wonder?'

'I think he was expecting to hear somebody of average ability. He wasn't quite prepared for somebody with such a pretty face to play quite so well.'

Maxine felt herself colour up at the compliment. But she was at a loss for a suitable reply, apart from a sadly inadequate 'thank you'.

'I'm Brent Shackleton, trombonist in this aspiring orchestra you've just joined.' He held his hand out. 'Nice to meet you. I really enjoyed listening to you.'

Maxine shook his hand. It was cool, dry and smooth but his grip was lingering. She smiled readily. 'I'm Maxine Kite. I'm still in a bit of a daze to tell you the truth. I can't believe I just got into the CBO.'

'I shouldn't worry, Maxine. I daresay you'll soon get used to the idea. Smoke?' He proffered a silver cigarette case.

'I don't, thank you.'

He took one and lit it. 'I've been with this outfit nearly five years now. It keeps me in these . . . Just about . . .' He tapped the cigarette case nonchalantly and she was not sure that she admired his indifference. 'Where do you live, Maxine? Are you local?'

'Ladywood,' she replied, anticipating her new lodging arrangements. 'With my sister and her husband.'

'Ladywood? That's almost walking distance from here, isn't it?' He exhaled a cloud of blue smoke.

'It's very convenient.' Her cello was back in its case. She closed the lid and picked it up. 'Well, I'd better be on my way. Nice to meet you, Mr Shackleton.'

'Call me Brent. It is all right if I call you Maxine, isn't it?'

She smiled and lingered a moment. There was something appealing about him after all; the way he looked at her. His dark eyes were focused only on her, piercing, making her feel decidedly self-conscious. But not the way Stephen did. Definitely not the way Stephen did.

'I'll see you at rehearsals next week, I imagine,' she said affably.

'Shall you come to the concert on Sunday evening?'

'The concert? I could . . . I suppose I *should* really, shouldn't I?'

'You should. Come and say hello afterwards. I'll introduce you to some of the team.'

Stephen Hemming was a quiet, practical, but very determined soul. He was twenty-six, unmarried, living at home with his parents and Pansy, his younger sister. Pansy had introduced him to Maxine Kite when the two girls were attending Bantock's School of Music together. Stephen fell in love with Maxine on sight. He could not resist her. She seemed so vulnerable and he wanted to protect her, especially since he was predisposed to girls like that. But her apparent vulnerability was not her only attractive feature; she was inordinately lovely with lips that for many sleepless nights he yearned to kiss and creamy curved

9

breasts he longed to caress. And her ears were so delicate, translucent, like finest Dresden china . . . He was mesmerised that her forearms lacked any of the soft down that every other girl seemed to have. Yet, she was totally unaware of her silky sensuousness. It never ceased to astound him how he managed to keep his hands off her. But she did not allow him such liberties.

Stephen loved art, in its broadest sense, and thus anything artistic and creative. So he saw in Maxine's musical ability a gift that he wished to see flourish. And she arrived in his life at the right time three years ago when he was languishing over a girl to whom he'd been engaged. Maxine certainly diverted his mind from that trauma.

Stephen designed jewellery in Birmingham's Jewellery Quarter and he was good. His talent was being sought by several manufacturers since he understood all the manufacturing processes, the techniques and the skill of the people who made the products; and he took account of all this in his designs. He was seriously considering starting his own design house, specifically aimed at serving the abundance of businesses in the area that produced adornments ranging from cheap buttons to creations on a par with the Crown Jewels. His lack of capital, however, was impeding any such progress.

Yet he had made himself afford a car; a 1935 Austin Ten-Four Lichfield. It was bigger than he needed, but it could accommodate Maxine's cello across the back seat – and that had been the deciding factor. It had set him back one hundred and fifty-two pounds; money he could have used to set up a business. But since he realised he was not extravagantly handsome, owning a car set him apart from other young men and gave him an advantage; in Maxine's eyes especially, he hoped. Yet, so far, it had done him no good. So far, all that his gallantry had achieved was delivering her, her cello and the rest of her belongings further away from him, to the home of her sister and brother-in-law.

He drove her into Daisy Road in Ladywood and pulled up outside the end of terrace house that was her new home.

'You can't imagine how upset I am that you're leaving us, Maxine,' he said, making a final attempt to get her to change her mind. 'The good times, the laughs we've had . . .'

'It's not as if I've emigrated to Australia, Stephen,' she replied pragmatically.

'But you won't be there when I get home from work, or when I get up in a morning. I'll miss you, Maxine. I'll miss you like hell. Pansy will miss you as well. So will my mother and father.'

'Pansy understands, Stephen. Knowing what it takes to lug my cello about, she appreciates that living here will be far more convenient. Your mother and father understand, too. It's not as if I've upped and left without discussing it. I wouldn't. And I shall visit them when I can. They've been very kind to me while I've been lodging there.'

'Because they love you – like a daughter,' Stephen commented, trying desperately to invoke greater feelings of guilt in her. 'But sometimes I get the impression, Maxine, that it's me you're trying to get away from.'

'Oh, I'm not at all,' she fibbed, affecting indignation, for she was anxious not to hurt his feelings. 'How can you think that? But seeing each other less often, we might appreciate each other the more. Anyway, thanks for taking the trouble to bring me here. I really appreciate it.'

'I'll help you with your things, shall I?'

'That's very nice of you, Stephen.'

'I'll expect a kiss for my trouble.'

'And if you don't get one?' she asked, half-serious.

'Then I'll leave your things at the side of the road.'

Of course, he did not mean it and she smiled to herself as she alighted from the car. She opened the rear door and attempted to get her cello off the back seat herself, knowing full well that he would gently move her out of the way and do it for her. As he did so, with his predictable chivalry, she leaned towards him, gave him a token peck on the cheek and smiled to let him believe she'd been teasing.

'Is that it? My kiss?' he queried, his disappointment obvious. 'Each day that passes they're rationed the more . . . So, shall I see you on Saturday night?'

'Best not this Saturday, Stephen. I'll have so much to do. But Sunday, if you like. If you feel like going to the CBO concert with me.'

'Okay, I'll take you.'

'Say seven o'clock. The concert starts at half past. That'll give us plenty of time. But come in and have a cup of tea now you've come this far, Stephen.'

Chapter 2

That Sunday, Stephen arrived promptly at seven and parked his Austin behind Will's maroon motor car, a Swallow SSI. He walked up the path and knocked at the door.

Will Parish invited him in. 'I imagine she'll be ready in a minute or two, Stephen. Come and wait in the sitting room.'

'Hello, Stephen,' Henzey greeted affably, fastening a napkin on the baby who was lying on the settee next to where she was sitting. 'Sorry if it pongs a bit in here. I've just had to change him.'

Stephen spotted a soiled napkin on the floor near Henzey's feet and tried not to breathe in too deeply lest it offend him. 'One of the joys of having children,' he commented.

'One of the drawbacks. Oh, he's as good as gold . . . aren't you, my little cherub?' she cooed, slipping the baby's waterproof pants over his napkin. She lifted him, holding him against her bosom. 'There . . . that's better, isn't it? Now you feel all nice and comfy again.'

'Have you decided on a name for him yet?' Stephen asked conversationally.

Henzey looked at Will for permission to reveal it. He nodded his assent with a smile.

'Aldo,' Henzey said.

'Aldo?' Stephen queried, uncertain as to how he should react.

'Well . . . Aldo Benjamin, really. But we shall call him Aldo.'

Maxine appeared at the sitting room door. She wore a simple

13

dark-green dress with a flared skirt, belted at the waist, and carried a black leather handbag that matched her shoes.

'So, now you know the baby's name, Stephen.'

'Yes. It's, er . . .'

'Awful?' Maxine suggested wryly. 'Is that the word you're looking for?'

'It's lovely,' Henzey said, clutching Aldo to her. 'Isn't it my little pet? It's a beautiful name for a beautiful little boy.'

'It's a frightful name,' Maxine countered with a gleam in her eye, and Will chuckled again at the minor controversy this choice of name was causing. She carefully took the child and cradled him in her own arms lovingly while Henzey took the soiled napkin to the scullery. 'Whatever possessed them, eh?' she said in baby talk. 'Fancy calling a lovely little boy like you Aldo, you poor thing. Fancy calling you Aldo when they could have called you something decent, like Robert, or Peter . . . or David . . . or even Stephen.'

'Oh, Even Stephen's a good one,' Will mocked good-naturedly. 'Why don't we call him Even Stephen?'

'Because we've already got one Even Stephen,' Maxine answered flippantly.

Stephen felt flattered, hopeful even, that by implication he was one of the family . . . almost.

Once in the car and on their way, Stephen said: 'Are they serious about calling the poor child Aldo?'

'I know. Isn't it just too awful?'

'How are you settling in, Maxine? D'you think you'll be happy? You know you're more than welcome back at—'

'It's nice,' she interrupted. 'They haven't even noticed I'm there yet with the baby to occupy them, and that suits me . . . Anyway, I'm really looking forward to the concert, aren't you? It seems ages since I've been to a CBO concert.'

'You went to a couple last year. I took you.'

'But, like I say, it seems ages ago. I should have gone to more.'

'Seems like you will in future, doesn't it?' He turned to look

14

at her as he changed up a gear. 'I wonder what they're playing tonight?'

'Mozart's "Prague" for one, somebody told me. Sibelius's Second and . . . oh, I can't think of the other.'

In no time they were pulling up into a space outside the Italian Renaissance style Council House in Colmore Row. Birmingham Town Hall and its colossal columns faced them, predominating like the Roman Temple of Castor and Pollux as it overlooked the weathered statue of Queen Victoria and New Street.

Stephen got out of the Austin and, to Maxine's annoyance, immediately rushed round to the other side to open the door for her. Why did he persist in doing that? She could just as easily open the door herself and save time, too. It seemed he was putting her on a pedestal when she did not want to be on a pedestal. She did not deserve it. She had nothing to give in return.

They found their seats in the auditorium and, as the orchestra tuned up, Maxine grew more excited at the prospect of playing with these musicians. She wanted tonight's concert to be a triumph.

She turned to Stephen. 'I'm getting quite nervous, you know.'

'But you're not even playing.'

'I've got the jitters for the orchestra. I do hope it goes well.' Just then, the audience began to applaud and Maxine looked up. 'Look, that's Leslie Heward, the conductor,' she exclaimed in an excited whisper. 'The man who auditioned me.'

The audience fell quiet and Leslie Heward raised his baton. Suddenly the place was charged with the first explosive chord of Mozart's Symphony number 38 in D major – the 'Prague' Symphony.

No sound is as rich, as full, or as emotive as the sound of a full orchestra playing Mozart, Maxine reflected, moved – except maybe Beethoven. Such an extraordinary, exciting sound. No wonder its appeal had spanned centuries. She wallowed in it, savouring every note, loving every familiar twist and turn in the score, every interweaving of the instruments, every development of every theme.

But, halfway through, it surprised her to discover that she was paying scant attention to the cellists, the bassists, or any of the strings. For some time, her eyes had scarcely moved from the handsome trombonist sitting in the brass section. Brent Shackleton seemed to play with more panache than his colleagues. He was more animated, more of a showman, bursting with confidence. His hair was attractively unruly, inclined to flop to one side as he played, causing him to push it back with his fingers when the score allowed him the opportunity. But then, he was younger than any other member of the brass was. He was certainly worth looking at.

In those rarer moments when she was not concentrating on Brent Shackleton, Maxine also tried to envisage herself playing in this brilliant orchestra. The thought of actually being a part of it thrilled her, especially the notion of being broadcast on the wireless, of being recorded and able to hear the performance on record forever after, knowing she would have contributed.

When it was all over and the applause had died she remained in her seat, while the rest of the audience drifted outside into the chilly May evening.

'Shall we go?' Stephen suggested, 'Or are we going to stay here all night?'

'What time is it?'

He looked at his watch. 'Ten past ten. I have to be up in the morning.'

'But I've been asked back to meet some of the orchestra. Do you mind?'

'No, course not. Who invited you? The conductor? You never said.'

'Oh, just one of the players,' she answered dismissively.

'Well let's make our way to the side of the stage. Some of them are mingling there already, look. You'd best go first – they won't know me from Adam.'

Maxine got up hesitantly from her seat. 'D'you reckon they'll think I'm a bit pushy?'

'Not if you've been asked.' He felt an urge to hug her. Her reticence was typical.

'But it was only a casual invitation. Maybe I—'

'Come on, let's get it over with. It'll be good for you to make an acquaintance or two before you actually start working with them. Somebody familiar to talk to when you actually get there.'

She sighed guiltily. 'Okay.'

Hesitantly, she led the way to the side of the stage. Some of the players were sharing a joke, accepting the plaudits of friends and relatives. A hefty middle-aged man with grey hair saw her and smiled as she approached.

'Hello, Miss,' he said, over the shoulder of a colleague. 'Are you looking for somebody?'

'Oh, nobody in particular. I'm, er . . . joining the orchestra next week as a cellist. I was invited to meet some of the members after the concert.'

The other man turned around to look at her. 'Joining the team, eh? Well, we could do with a pretty face among this bunch of sourpusses, that's for sure. Cellist, did you say?'

She nodded.

'What's your name, by the way?'

'Maxine Kite.'

'Nice to meet you, Miss Kite.' They shook hands. 'Jim Davies, first violins. And this is Bill Roberts. Second violins.'

She shook Bill's hand too. They seemed a friendly lot so far.

'I was impressed with the performance tonight,' Maxine remarked. 'The 'Prague' Symphony was brilliant.'

'Well, you can thank Mozart for that, m'dear,' Bill suggested dryly.

She introduced Stephen and, as she did so, spotted Brent Shackleton. As he looked in her direction she involuntarily put up her hand and waved. He acknowledged her and made his way towards her.

'Good to see you, Maxine,' he said. 'You made it, then.'

Unwittingly she turned away from Stephen and the others. 'Yes, I made it.' She was aware she sounded breathless.

'Enjoy the concert?'

'Yes, it was grand.'

'We played well,' Brent said. 'It's a fairly safe repertoire for the Sunday concerts.'

'I suppose that's what people come to hear . . . something they're familiar with . . . something they know.'

'I reckon so. Are you looking forward to joining?'

'I can't wait. You can't imagine.'

'Is that your young man talking to those two fiddle players?' She resisted the urge to turn around and nodded dumbly, wishing profoundly that she could deny Stephen. 'I think he's trying to catch your attention. Is he a musician as well?'

'Oh, no. He designs jewellery. He's actually very good.'

'Jewellery, eh? Did he design that brooch you're wearing?' She nodded.

'Quality piece,' he commented approvingly. 'Very elegant . . . You look very elegant yourself, Maxine, if you don't mind me saying so. I love your dress.'

'Oh! Thank you.'

Her delight showed in her eyes, but Brent did not have time to notice it. His attention was suddenly drawn beyond her, beyond Stephen, and Maxine thought she saw him acknowledge someone. It was a woman, possibly in her mid-twenties; statuesque, beautiful, exquisitely dressed, her dark hair sleek in a style straight out of *Vogue*.

'Sorry. I have to dash, Maxine.'

'That's all right.'

'See you at rehearsals.'

As Brent walked away she turned and rejoined Stephen who was labouring over his conversation with the two violinists.

'I see you've already met our Brent, then,' Bill said.

18

'Brent, yes. I'd quite forgotten his name. He introduced himself after my audition.'

'He should've introduced you to Gwen. Come with me, young Maxine. Let me introduce you to Gwen. You'll be playing alongside her. Brilliant cellist, is Gwen . . .'

'Maxine, can I ask you something?' Stephen said, breaking a silence that was disproportionately long for the short drive back to Ladywood.

'What?'

'Will you marry me?'

He'd sussed that she'd earlier avoided admitting that Brent Shackleton had been the one to suggest going to meet some of the orchestra after the concert, that he was the one she'd really gone to see. He'd seen her acknowledge Brent too eagerly and turn her back on everybody else. He'd witnessed her sparks of interest for Brent, sparks too bright for her own good, too bright for his own good. He must prevent them flaring into a full scale inferno, and the only way he could think of doing that was by escalating her interest in himself. He had not caught sight of Brent's beautiful companion, so this was a radical strategy which, in all probability, would not work anyway. But desperate situations required desperate measures. And Stephen was desperate. He was also desperately celibate.

'Did I hear you right?' Maxine replied, surprised and disappointed that he should offer marriage.

'You did. I'm asking you to marry me.' He flipped the indicator switch on the hub of the steering wheel and they turned right into Reservoir Road.

'Oh, Stephen . . .' She sighed, full of sympathy for him in his foolishness. 'In God's name, why? What on earth for?' She turned to look at him. The meagre light falling from the street lamps as they drove past momentarily brightened his face so serious, so intense, as if he already knew her answer.

'Because I love you,' he answered straightforwardly. 'Why else?'

19

Maxine felt sorry for him and his self-inflicted vulnerability, and was silent for a few seconds, stalling as she decided how best to answer him.

'Oh, Stephen . . .' she responded at last, not wishing to sound exasperated, although she imagined she did. She should, after all, be flattered. But whatever words she chose in refusing him would hurt him. She did not want to hurt him. He was her friend; one of the most reliable friends she'd ever had. 'I . . . I've just got this new job, Stephen . . . and . . . well, I really prefer things the way they are right now.'

'I love you, Maxine, and it's driving me mad the way things are.' He slowed the car and turned left, then right into Daisy Road.

'How do you mean, driving you mad?'

'I would have thought it obvious.' He looked at her but she didn't answer. He pulled up under the gas lamp outside the house and switched off the engine and the headlights. 'It drives me mad when I'm alone with you, when I can touch you like this . . .' He stroked the silky smooth skin of her forearm under her sleeve. 'But I'm never allowed to make love to you.'

'But we sometimes kiss goodnight, Stephen.'

'Occasionally you allow me a quick goodnight kiss, Maxine, but that's all. That's not making love. It's never passionate, never lingering. I want more. I want to lie with you in bed, naked, and feel your warm, soft skin pressing against mine.'

'Stephen! What a thing to say!'

'Well it's true. I want to kiss you all over your body, I want to caress every inch of you, and . . . oh, you know what I mean.'

'Stephen! If you did that with Evelyn, you're not doing it with me. Lord above!' She shuffled in her seat, affecting righteous indignation. 'They say men are only interested in one thing. Is that all you want to marry me for? So you can . . . so you can do *that* to me?'

'No. Of course not. I want to look after you. I want to provide a home for you, give you security. I want us to have children.'

'I'd want children too, Stephen. But the world's not fit to bring children into if you ask me. Not the way things are. You only have to look at what's happening in the world ... Unemployment, poverty, the Depression, Hitler, Mussolini and all that. Why, every day in the papers you read about some lunatic thing somebody's up to. Everybody says there's going to be war sooner or later. Will reckons there's going to be a war again.'

'He's got a child now,' Stephen argued logically.

'That doesn't mean I should have one yet. I don't want to bring children into a world riven with war.'

'All the more reason to let me look after you, Maxine. Anyway, there might not be a war at all. It's only speculation.'

She shrugged. Of course, she could not be sure. Nobody could be sure.

'Look, Maxine, I'm going to start my own business soon. I shall do well. I shall do very well. I know I shall.'

'Well, I hope you do,' she said sincerely. 'I'm sure you will. But I don't want to get married, Stephen. Really, I don't. I don't want to be tied down by marriage. Not yet at any rate. I've got my career to think about. It's only just beginning. I want to exploit it. I want to get the most out of it. I've just been presented with a once-in-a-lifetime opportunity. You don't begrudge it me, do you, Stephen?'

'I don't begrudge it you at all, sweetheart,' he replied earnestly. 'You know I don't.'

'It sounds as if you do.'

'Rubbish. You can still do all that even if we get married. Marriage wouldn't stop you.'

'Says you now. What if I found myself having a baby?'

'You wouldn't, Maxine . . . I wouldn't . . . I mean, I wouldn't let you get pregnant if you didn't want to. I'd be careful. I'd be very careful. It wouldn't interfere with your career. We'd only think of starting a family when you were ready.'

Maxine sighed. What madness had suddenly seized him to

make him think of marriage? Why did he have to spoil everything by wanting to tie her down?

'Do you want to think about it?' he asked.

'Oh, Stephen . . .' With the utmost sympathy she took his hand and gently stroked it. 'I don't deserve such consideration. I'm not ready yet for marriage. I'd be no good for you, my love, because I don't feel the same way you do. I've got so many other things to do in my life I couldn't give you even half the devotion you deserve. Ask me in another three or four years. Ask me when I've got all this out of my system.'

He sighed heavily. 'Oh, I think I could wait forever if I had to, Maxine. You're worth waiting for . . . It's just that I prefer not to wait, that's all. In the meantime, we could get engaged,' he suggested brightly. 'What do you say to that?'

She sighed again, but with exasperation. 'What's the point? If you're engaged, you're still promised to be married . . . You're still spoken for.'

He shrugged. 'I know. That's the idea. But, like I say, we needn't be married till you're ready. But at least you *would* be spoken for.'

'Stephen, I don't want to be spoken for. If I ever decide I want to get married, that's when I'll get engaged . . . You can't be seriously engaged and not name the day, can you? It makes a mockery of engagement. It belittles it. Don't you see?'

'No, I don't agree. I want to be engaged to you, Maxine. I want the world to know how I feel about you . . . And I had this smashing idea for a ring.'

'Stephen, the whole world doesn't need to know by virtue of a ring. It's a promise between two people – no ring required really. If we're still friends in a couple of years' time, ask me again. Who knows, I might feel different then. I'm too young to think of marriage yet.' She summoned a smile of sympathy. 'What do you say? Agreed?'

He shrugged, profound disappointment darkening his

expression. She had won this round. She had wriggled out of it tonight. But next time she might not wriggle out of it quite so fast.

'All right,' he said. 'But I'm not giving up, Maxine. You'll be mine one day – one way or the other. You'll see.'

'One day, maybe,' she said, happy to concede that point for now. 'Are you going to come in for a nightcap?'

He peered at his wristwatch by the scant light of the street lamp. 'Much as I'd like to, I'd better not. I've got to be up. When shall I see you?'

She shrugged with indifference. 'I don't know. Come round Wednesday night, if you want.'

'Not till Wednesday? What about before that? What will you be doing tomorrow night . . . and Tuesday night?'

'Practising my cello, I expect. I have to practise, Stephen.'

'I could listen. You know I love to hear you play.'

She shrugged again, irked at his tedious inability to face reality. 'Come round Tuesday night then.'

'What about Monday night?' he persisted.

'Stephen, I can't see you every night. And I don't want to see you Monday night.'

'Just Tuesday then.'

'Just Tuesday.'

'. . . A kiss?'

She pursed her lips in the least romantic way she could and he pressed them with his own. At once breaking off, she opened the car door, wiped her mouth with the back of her hand and, before he had chance to open his and come round to her side, she was gone. As she thrust open the front door of the house she heard him start the car and drive off.

Inside, while she hung up her coat, she heard Henzey and Will talking in the sitting room. Henzey called, and Maxine answered.

'The kettle's just boiled if you want a drink,' Will said. 'Had a good night?'

23

Maxine smiled enigmatically. 'Yes, and no.'

Henzey looked up from folding clean napkins on her lap, instantly curious. 'Tell us, then.'

'Well the concert was smashing. The orchestra was brilliant. And I met one or two of them afterwards . . .'

'But?'

'But . . .' Maxine sighed dramatically and shook her head. 'On the way home Stephen asked me to marry him – of all the stupid things.'

'I take it you don't want to marry him,' Will said.

She slumped down on the settee, disconcerted. 'I'm too young, Will. This new job. I'm not ready for marriage. I don't want to be tied down. There are too many other things in life I want to do first.'

'You could do a lot worse, our Maxine,' Henzey commented. 'You could do a lot worse than marry Stephen Hemming.'

'Oh, I know, Henzey. He's as good as gold. But I'd be no good for him. He's just a friend. It wouldn't be fair.'

'Then let's hope he doesn't get tired of waiting.'

'If he wants to wait that's up to him, but there are plenty of other fish in the sea for him. Maybe *I* ought to swim around in it a bit and meet a few more. Just think what I might be missing.' She got to her feet again. 'I think I'll make myself a cup of cocoa. Anybody else?'

'No thanks,' Will said.

'Not for me, either,' Henzey said. 'But, hey – I nearly forgot . . .'

'What?' Maxine stood poised at the door, ready to take off into the kitchen.

'Will came up with the idea of all the family getting together and going along to see your *maiden concert*, as he called it, then all coming back here afterwards for a celebration. For your twenty-first. What do you think?'

Maxine grinned happily. Her widest grin that night. 'Oh, that would be smashing. Oh, isn't that husband of yours kind,

Henzey?' She looked at Will. 'It's a lovely idea, Will. Thank you. Thank you ever so much.'

'And tomorrow,' Henzey added, 'I'm going to buy the tickets for the concert.'

Chapter 3

It was with some nervousness that Maxine took her place by her beloved cello on the stage at Birmingham Town Hall that second Saturday in May 1936. She looked bewitching in a new black evening dress she'd treated herself to, and her eyes shone with expectation. Along with everybody else she checked her tuning, at the same time peering into the audience, trying to locate family and friends who had come to both support her and celebrate her twenty-first birthday afterwards. Gwen Berry, at her side, nodded her encouragement as she adjusted the music score on the stand in front of them that they were to share.

Before Maxine knew it, they were into the first elegant phrases of Mozart's Clarinet Concerto in A Major. John Ball, the soloist, whom she had met briefly, was the orchestra's own clarinettist. At rehearsal Maxine had been impressed with his ability.

It was a glorious feeling playing with other musicians. The music was like a magic carpet flying them all to exotic places. The tempo was the speed of flight, the melodies the delightful undulations in it, each trill the carpet's frill rippling in an ethereal breeze. It all seemed unstoppable. Not that she wanted it to stop. It was addictive. Maxine likened it to riding in Stephen's car; moving was infinitely more agreeable than not moving; stopping was inevitably a disappointment. But all too soon the music was at an end. All too soon the magic carpet had landed.

After the applause they took off again on another ride: a fairly recent piece by Ravel, called *Boléro*. Leslie Heward controlled the emotion in the music skilfully, building the tension almost imperceptibly. At first it was coquettish, provocative like a frivolous woman tantalising an admirer. Halfway through, their mutual arousal was already obsessive, ascending steadily to an orgy of compelling passion till the last, loud, staccato chords brought it to a shuddering, juddering finish like sated lovers spent of their last drop of energy.

Applause was immense and sustained and Maxine turned to Gwen, smiling with satisfaction, proud to be a part of this orchestra. So profound had been her concentration that, at the interval, she felt drained. Yet still to come was Beethoven's Fifth Symphony. Backstage she joined the queue at the trestle table that supported a pile of cups and saucers and a huge urn containing enough tea to refresh the orchestra with at least two cups each.

'How's it going, Maxine?'

She turned to see Brent Shackleton standing behind her and her heart skipped a beat. 'Oh, hello.' She smiled brightly as she would at an old friend and hoped he could not detect her nervous reaction. The opportunity to speak to him had not presented itself since after last Sunday's concert, even at rehearsals, and she wondered if he had deliberately avoided her. Well, he was not avoiding her now.

'So? How's it going?' he asked again. 'Are you settling in all right?'

'Oh, fine, yes, thank you.'

'Good. I spotted you in *Boléro*. Kept you busy towards the end, didn't it?'

She laughed awkwardly. 'You, too. I saw you had plenty to do as well.'

'I'm still breathless.' He wiped his brow with the back of his hand. 'Good, though, wasn't it?'

'Great.' They shuffled towards the head of the queue together.

'You can hear the jazz influences in *Boléro*, can't you? The sliding trombone and all that.' He offered her a cigarette which she declined, and lit one himself. 'It's not so stuffy as some of the music we play.'

'I suppose not. Still . . .' She shrugged, hesitant, not sure in what vein to continue the conversation, anxious not to disagree with him. 'To tell you the truth, I love it all.'

'Mind you, some of these so-called modern classics are a bit pretentious. You know . . . Mahler, Scriabin . . . stuff like that.' He deeply inhaled smoke and seemed to hold it in his lungs for ages. 'In my opinion.'

'I know what you mean,' Maxine said inadequately. They had reached the trestle table, so she picked up a cup and saucer and held it under the tap of the urn.

'Not like jazz,' he remarked.

She moved away from the table when her cup was full. 'You like jazz, then?' she asked when he'd rejoined her.

'Oh, I love jazz.'

'I like jazz as well,' she replied truthfully and sipped her tea. 'I used to listen to jazz records all the time. The people I used to lodge with – before I went to live with my sister – have a daughter who was a keen jazz fan. She used to get hold of some obscure records from America. She's a musician as well and we used to play it together, mimicking it – just for a laugh, me on the piano usually, she on clarinet. I don't get the chance to hear much now. Occasionally I hear a snatch on the wireless. Yes, I quite like jazz.'

'You play piano as well?' He sounded surprised.

'I started out on piano.'

He nodded his approval. 'Oh, it's great, jazz. It's not so contrived as this stuff we play here, is it? You know where it comes from?'

'America, I suppose.'

'Africa.' He drew on his cigarette and paused long enough for this gem of information to register. She saw his probing eyes, steady upon her, awaiting her response.

'Africa?'

28

'Missionaries.' Now he took a gulp of tea.

'Missionaries?'

'Missionaries. Missionaries achieved Africanisation of their own hymnbooks, you know, when they were converting the natives to Christianity.' He sounded pat, as if he'd held the same discussion many times before.

'I'm not sure I understand.'

'Well, African tribes interpreted our Christian hymns their own way, using the influences of their own music. That's what I mean. You know . . . their own ritual music – chants, tribal songs – stuff like that.'

'And that was jazz?'

'Not yet. It was just the beginnings.' He was laughing. She had not seen him laugh like this before; he always seemed so serious; a touch preoccupied maybe.

Maxine lifted her cup and sipped her tea again, still drawn to his penetrating eyes like a beautiful moth drawn to a night-light.

'You see,' he went on, 'African music developed in a way totally differently to our European music. It was less abstract, less aesthetic – do you know what I mean?' Maxine nodded her increasing understanding. 'It was more practical, more of a language – a way of communicating – and they could alter its meaning or emotion just by altering the pitch of a note, or changing the inflection in the voice.'

'So it was more functional than music for mere art's sake?' She was glad that her interest in his explanations was genuine. 'Is that what you're saying?'

'Yes, and more rhythmic. Much more rhythmic. They used what they could lay their hands on for percussion instruments. A stick to beat out a rhythm. On a hollowed out tree trunk, for instance.'

'Yes, of course.' Maxine had never seriously pondered the roots of jazz before. It was quite intriguing. Brent Shackleton was certainly intriguing.

Brent puffed more smoke into the room, then drained his cup. 'Then, when those poor Negroes became victims of the slave trade, these songs – these hymns if you like – evolved into work songs with lyrics to suit the situation. The slave owners encouraged them to sing such songs – apparently they improved the work rate. They weren't daft, you know. When the slaves were freed, the more musically inclined of them that could afford it got hold of proper instruments. Some got to be brilliant and, because of their own Negro influences – you know, using complicated rhythms and altering notes and sounds by pitch and inflection – jazz evolved.'

'I never realised,' Maxine said. 'I thought somebody just invented it.'

'Well, there you are. You learn something every day . . . Fancy another cup of tea?'

She leaned over to the trestle table to return her empty cup and saucer. 'Oh, I'd best not, thank you. Any more and I'll be plaiting my legs,' she remarked self-effacingly.

'And you can't play the cello with your legs plaited.' His eyes met hers directly with a candour that prompted her colour to rise at what she imagined he implied though, to her surprise, she did not mind. 'Anyway, what are you doing afterwards, Maxine?'

'After the concert?' Her heart fluttered while she sipped tea again, her eyes down, lids lowered, in an effort to conceal her intensifying blushes.

'There's this club I go to . . . I wondered if you'd like to come.'

She managed to stifle the urge to choke. 'I can't,' she said, surprised at the depth of her disappointment. 'Sorry. Not tonight at any rate. But thanks for asking.'

'Some other time, maybe?'

'Yes . . . I'd like that.' She felt guilty for encouraging him, because of Stephen. But what was wrong with a half-promise to go out with Brent at some other time? It was a vague agreement anyway. It might never happen . . . And yet why shouldn't it?

She was not married to Stephen. She was not even engaged. Nor ever likely to be.

'Is it because of your young man that you can't come?'

'No, not just him,' she said. 'My whole family is out there. There's a celebration afterwards. It's my twenty-first today, you see.'

'Your twenty-first?' Brent turned round. 'George, d'you hear that? It's Maxine's twenty-first today.'

It seemed that all the rest of the orchestra heard it, too, and at once Maxine was swamped with congratulations from all directions.

'Your first concert with the band on your twenty-first birthday, eh?' somebody said. 'You'll never forget that.'

Maxine flashed a polite smile.

'Does the boss know?' another person asked.

'We'll make sure he does,' yet another replied.

Maxine looked with amused bewilderment from one to the other, thanking each well-wisher. What had she done to deserve all this attention? She looked at Brent and shrugged.

'Will you excuse me, Maxine?' he said.

Someone else stepped up and began talking to her, then another, and another. Before long, she was the centre of an animated group. They spoke as if they had known her all their lives and she felt easy with them. But afterwards she could not remember a word any of them had said; her mind was awhirl with Brent's offer to take her out and her regret that she'd had to refuse. But she did have Stephen to consider after all. She could hardly dump Stephen on a whim and take off with Brent.

But what about the beautiful girl she'd seen Brent with? Surely she warranted some consideration too? Besides, how could she compete with a girl like that? How could any man want anybody else when he already had a girl as beautiful as that? A girl with those looks could have her pick of men. Why would Brent be interested in dull Maxine Kite? These questions plagued her till she sat down at her cello for the second part of the concert and for some minutes into it; until she made herself pay attention lest she made any embarrassing mistakes.

Her embarrassment, however, came at the end of the performance. Everyone, including Leslie Heward the conductor, had taken their final bows when he held out both hands to Maxine and gestured for her to stand up. Bewildered, she obliged. But she was even more bemused to receive a round of applause and some cheers, not only from the auditorium, but from the orchestra as well. Still reeling from the shock of it all she turned around and saw that Brent Shackleton and George, his fellow trombonist, were holding up a huge poster for all to see, evidently hastily cobbled together, that proclaimed in huge letters, 'Maxine – 21 today'. To her embarrassed delight, he and George then led the singing of 'Twenty-one today'.

Almost at once, the audience was good-humouredly joining in and, when that finished, there rose the inevitable strains of 'Happy Birthday to You'.

At any concert of classical music there are always huge bouquets of flowers ready to be presented to soloists, leading musicians and so on. So it was a surprise to nobody, except to Maxine, to find herself being presented with such a bouquet from Leslie Heward, who shook her hand and stepped forward to afford her a fatherly peck on the cheek. She grinned with delight, said thank you and bobbed a neat curtsy, which had the combined effect of invoking more cheers.

'I can't believe all this,' she said in an aside to Gwen Berry.

'It's not every concert when one of our members is twenty-one,' Gwen replied. 'Most of them are at least twice that age. Make the most of it, my girl.'

Three motor cars and a motorcycle, conveying family and friends, all jovial and lively, left Birmingham Town Hall after the concert and travelled in convoy to Daisy Road where Mrs Fothergill, the next door neighbour, had been babysitting for Aldo.

'Glorious concert, young Maxine,' Jesse Clancey, her step-father, commented.

'Oh, it was brilliant, Jesse. I couldn't believe it when everybody sang "Happy Birthday".'

After they had discussed the concert a while longer, Henzey said, 'And this is Stephen's sister, Pansy, I presume?'

Henzey and Pansy had not met before but they greeted each other like long-lost sisters and Pansy's green eyes creased into a warm smile. She was about the same height as Maxine, slim and pretty, with a mop of thick, titian hair. There could be no confusing her and Maxine; they were so different.

Meanwhile, Will was welcoming others, taking their coats and hats and guiding them to the parlour where mounds of sandwiches and cakes graced the table.

'You must be proud of your youngest daughter, Lizzie,' Will said. 'I thought she did very well tonight. She seemed to fit in well.'

'Oh, I'm proud of her all right, Will,' Lizzie answered, taking a dry sherry from him and nodding her thanks. She raised her glass. 'But Jesse can take some of the credit. He's encouraged her as much as anybody – paid for her to go through music school. He's been like a father to her . . . to them all.'

Jesse joined them, clutching a pint of beer. 'Can I just say, Will, how grateful we are to you for holding this party here. We'd intended holding one at the dairy house, o' course, but with Maxine suddenly landing this job and all . . .'

'You're welcome, Jesse. It just seemed more logical now she's living here.'

'Behaving herself, is she?'

Will laughed and patted Jesse on the back. 'What do you think? I've got no complaints.'

'Lizzie tells me you're moving house, Will. To Dudley. Do you intend Maxine to lodge with you still? I mean she'd be welcome to live at the dairy house.'

'It's up to her, Jesse. I'm content for her to live with us if that's what she wants. Like I say, I've got no complaints.'

In the front room, somebody was thumping out tunes on the piano.

'That'll be Joe, Lizzie's brother,' Jesse chortled. 'He don't half love to play the piano at parties. He'll have us all singing at the tops of our voices in no time. Mark my words.'

'They're a lively lot, aren't they?' Pansy remarked.

'You just wait.' Jesse turned to Will. 'Anyway, Will, we've all brought something for Maxine. Can I count on you to bring everybody to order later, so's we can present 'em to her?'

Will nodded. 'Leave it to me, Jesse.'

Before long, after he had already shepherded everybody into the front room, Will was trying to attract their attention, his hands in the air like a politician fending off hecklers. 'All right, everyone! Would everyone please listen?' The piano playing, the singing and the talking stopped. 'Now, we all know why we're here, and I hope you're all enjoying yourselves . . . Well it's time to wish Maxine, my very talented sister-in-law, a very happy birthday.'

The cheer from the family turned into a rousing chorus of 'Happy Birthday to You', then more cheers and shouts of '*Speech!*'

'Twenty-one is a person's coming of age,' Will went on after his further request to be heard had been heeded. 'It's that time in a young person's life when she is considered an adult, considered to be of an age, at last, when she can be independent. She can come and go as she pleases – within reason – which is why she is traditionally handed the key of the door . . .'

'She's already got the key to our door,' Henzey remarked.

'It is a time when she doesn't have to seek permission from her parents to get married, if marriage is on the agenda. It is a time when she can sign up to any legal binding contract. In short, it's a time of freedom from the constraints of parental discipline. However, I have got to know Maxine a little better since she's been living here with Henzey and me, and I believe she is not one to abuse such freedoms. She's sensible, level-headed . . . and, incidentally, far too modest about the exceptional talent she has. So . . . before we all shower her with gifts and congratulate her, let's make her sing for her supper . . .' Will grinned roguishly. 'Maxine, I'm well aware that your cello playing has done you proud recently, but some of us here consider your piano playing worth a listen. So would you like to take the stool and play?'

Maxine blushed, giggling with embarrassment while Joe moved clumsily away from the piano. 'What on earth shall I play?' she asked as she sat down.

'How about "Clair de Lune?" Henzey suggested. 'That's one of my favourites.'

'Okay. There's this nice romantic passage . . .'

Debussy's inspired music flowed easily, melodically through Maxine's fingers, while everyone listened in attentive silence. She played the section tenderly, demonstrating an accomplishment beyond her years. It never crossed her mind to wonder if anybody knew how difficult it was; the long hours of practice needed to play well; the dedication. Yet, it was clear for all to see that Maxine had a natural gift since she could play two instruments with such apparent finesse.

'Play something modern,' Herbert, her brother, cried when the piece was finished. 'We've had enough classical for one night.'

'You and Pansy play that Fats Waller thing,' Stephen suggested.

'Oh, yes. I know,' Maxine replied, glad of a prompt. ' "Whose Honey Are You". Come on, Pansy. Will you play on this one?'

Pansy took the piano stool and began to play. Immediately, the compulsive rhythm had everybody's feet tapping. But even more of a surprise than the piano playing of either girl, was Maxine's singing as she leaned against the piano. Nobody had ever heard her sing before.

'Do "Stormy Weather",' Stephen called. 'You know – that one by Ethel Waters.'

Pansy played the introduction and Maxine launched into the song, using the same soft vocal technique, mimicking the style of Ethel Waters. This American music was unfamiliar to most of them, since few such records were available and they listened to few on the wireless, but everyone was stunned silent by Maxine's vocal dexterity.

'More, Maxine!' Will called when it was finished. 'That was great. Do you know any more?'

'They could go on half the night, I daresay,' Jesse answered.

'Isn't that enough?' Maxine asked at the end of it, effervescing with her success and enjoying the attention she was getting. 'Can't I have my presents now?'

'One more,' Herbert called.

'Yes, one more,' Will echoed.

'*Then* can I have my presents?'

They all agreed she could.

'Okay. Well here's one for Jesse. Mom would have asked me to play it, I know . . .'

Pansy vacated the piano stool when it was obvious that Maxine wanted to accompany herself this time. She launched into a compulsively rhythmic, 'My Very Good Friend the Milkman'.

'Oh, very appropriate,' Jesse the dairyman remarked to Lizzie with a wry grin.

'Cheeky madam,' her mother declared, watching and listening with profound pride. 'She told me she'd get a job playing piano and singing in a pub if she had to,' she whispered to Jesse, 'but I never realised she'd be this good. She's come on a bundle since she left home.'

It was obvious that most of the folk present would have allowed Maxine to play and sing for them all night, but Will brought the impromptu concert to a close.

'Maxine,' he said, and raised his glass. 'God bless you and your wonderful talent. Here's to your future success and happiness. Congratulations and many happy returns of the day.' He drank, and everybody followed his example. 'Now . . . I understand that one or two of us have gifts for you . . .'

Henzey stepped forward before anyone else. 'Congratulations, our Maxine. Many happy returns.' She took her youngest sister's

36

hand and kissed her on the cheek before pointing to the large but beautifully wrapped parcel lying on the floor that had puzzled Maxine since their return. 'That's from Will and me.'

'Am I supposed to open it now?'

'Of course.'

She stooped down and fumbled with the wrapping, to reveal a portable gramophone. She gasped with genuine delight, stood up and kissed Will, thanking him profusely, then Henzey. 'I never imagined . . .'

'Consider yourself lucky,' Henzey said good-humouredly. 'I would have bought you a vacuum sweeper so you could help with the housework, but Will thought a gramophone might be more appropriate.'

When she'd unwrapped a gold watch, a leather writing case, a silver-plated photograph frame and an elaborately carved wooden music stand, Stephen stepped forward. Maxine was expecting an item of jewellery he'd designed. He handed her a small thin case that she guessed must contain a necklace of some sort and, when she opened it, saw that it was indeed a string of pearls with matching pearl earrings.

'Thank you, Stephen,' she said with obvious delight and kissed him on the cheek. 'But you shouldn't have done.'

'I . . . er . . . I have this as well, Maxine,' he said unsurely, and handed her a small cube, wrapped in fancy gilt paper.

She looked at it apprehensively. It could be a ring but she dearly hoped it was not. He'd already said he'd had an idea for a design. Warily she regarded him, hoping that she was wrong.

She said, 'Thank you, Stephen. I think I'll open this one later.'

'No, you must open it now, Maxine,' Henzey chided. 'It would be very ungracious not to open it now.'

She was aware of somebody else saying, 'Yes, you must,' and she hesitated.

'Please open it, Maxine,' Stephen said softly, earnestness brimming from his eyes.

She looked at him again, a look that was a mix of compassion

37

and admonishment, and fumbled as she tried to locate the join in the wrapping. Perhaps it was only a dress ring – nothing to get worked up about; or just another pair of earrings. She removed the wrapping paper, screwed it into a ball and gingerly opened the ivory coloured box. At once she shut it again, unsmiling. She was disappointed, angry and embarrassed simultaneously and Stephen was watching for her reaction, looking apprehensive.

After her initial silence, some pressed her to tell them what it was.

Stephen obliged them. 'It's a ring,' he announced.

'An engagement ring?' somebody queried.

He shrugged, unsure of himself. He had intended it as such.

'Congratulations, Maxine,' her brother peeled. 'You must be thrilled.'

She wanted to say *I'm not thrilled at all*, but she could not. She wanted to say that Stephen had got a real nerve trying to pull this off in front of all her family; that it was all a big misunderstanding and she was not engaged. But she could not utter a word. She could neither defend herself, nor leave Stephen open to embarrassment by an outright refusal. As her confusion mounted along with her uncertainty as to how she ought really to respond, the congratulations began to flow along with pats on the back, hugs, kisses and best wishes for their future happiness.

But significantly, not from her mother. Nor from Henzey.

And then, overwhelmed by it all, Maxine rushed out of the room trying to hide the tears that all at once were stinging her eyes. Lizzie watched anxiously, then followed Maxine upstairs to the bathroom.

She tapped tentatively on the door. 'It's me, Maxine. Let me in.'

But Stephen had also followed Lizzie. 'Where is she? What's the matter with her?'

'Leave her to me, Stephen,' Lizzie advised gently. 'She seems a bit overcome. I'll talk to her.' So Lizzie tapped the door again. 'Maxine, open the door.'

'Is Stephen still there?' a little voice queried. 'I just heard him.'

'He's gone back downstairs.'

The door opened and Lizzie saw tears running down Maxine's face. She joined her daughter inside and closed the door behind her. 'What is it, my flower?' She handed Maxine a clean handkerchief and put her arms around her.

'Him. He's such an idiot.' Maxine mopped up her tears. 'I could kill him. I could, really.'

'*Is* it an engagement ring?' Lizzie asked.

'Yes, the damned fool . . .' She sighed with exasperation, tears ebbing now. 'Only last week he asked me to marry him and I told him I didn't want to. I told him I wasn't ready for marriage – that I didn't love him.' She dabbed her eyes again, sniffed and blew her nose. 'I don't love him, Mom and I haven't asked for this. I haven't said I've wanted to get engaged. I refused that as well when he mentioned it. I don't *want* to be engaged.'

'Then if you've already told him that, he's very naughty to do this now. It's as if he's trying to railroad you into it. But it's not the end of the world, our Maxine.' Lizzie gave her a motherly hug. 'Don't let it spoil the night for everybody else. Say nothing for now and, if folk congratulate you, just thank them and smile graciously.'

'I know . . . I don't want to embarrass Stephen, Mom. He means well.'

'Well this way you won't. But later when you're by yourselves, or tomorrow if you see him, you can talk it over with him quietly. Leave him in no doubt that you can't accept it . . . Quick, though – let's have a look at it before you give it him back.'

Mother and daughter grinned cannily at each other and Maxine opened again the small cube to show Lizzie the ring.

Lizzie gasped. 'My God, it's a great big amethyst . . . and in a cluster of diamonds. Oh, it's beautiful, our Maxine. It must have cost him a fortune. Put it on and let's see what it looks like . . .' It fitted perfectly of course. 'Oh, it's absolutely beautiful.'

Maxine sighed. 'What a pity . . . I can't keep it, can I? . . .

Should I keep it, do you think, Mom?' She smiled, seduced by the magnificence of the ring adorning her long, slender finger. 'I mean, it doesn't mean I'm going to get married, does it?'

Lizzie gave her a knowing look. 'You can't have it both ways, my flower. Engagement is a serious betrothal – a binding promise to marry. If you don't intend to marry the lad, you mustn't accept his ring.'

'But I think I'll keep it on to show everybody. It *is* beautiful, isn't it? He's such a good designer.'

'If you show it to everybody, they'll take it as you're engaged. Then they'll want to know if you've named the day. You'd best make your mind up if that's what you really want, our Maxine.'

Chapter 4

After the party, Maxine accompanied Stephen when he drove Lizzie and Jesse back home to the dairy house where they lived in Dudley. The ride was distinguished by the stilted conversation. Jesse had already been discreetly advised that Maxine's 'engagement' was not entirely in accordance with her wishes and this inhibited any mention of it; but now, all other topics seemed like laboured small talk. So it was with some relief that Maxine parted company with Lizzie that night, with of course, the customary kiss and mutual instructions to look after themselves.

On the way back to Ladywood, Maxine and Stephen remained unspeaking for some minutes, till Maxine decided this problem should be sorted out, and the sooner the better; and that she should get in the first thrust.

'Why did you give me this ring, Stephen, when you knew perfectly well I didn't want to get engaged?' she began calmly. 'It was so embarrassing. What did you expect me to do?'

'It was a calculated risk,' he answered honestly, avoiding her eyes by fixing his on the glinting tram lines that sometimes made the car veer one way then the other if the narrow tyres became tracked by them. 'I risked my hand believing you wouldn't make a fool of me by handing it back – not in full view of everybody, at any rate.'

'Well you were right about that. But, Stephen, I can't believe it. We only discussed all this a week ago. I told you then that I

41

didn't want to get engaged. Do we have to go through it all again? What do I have to say to make you understand?'

'Oh, I do understand, Maxine,' he replied, and stroked her knee affectionately with his left hand.

She didn't like that but she tolerated it, as long as his hand did not presume to wander higher. Why did she not enjoy being touched by Stephen? And he wanted her to marry him and do all those disgusting things he'd mentioned?

'So why did you do it?' she pressed.

'Because I want to make you my own. I thought that if you didn't refuse it then, then you would have accepted it – full stop – in the eyes of everybody there. I thought you would have committed yourself by not refusing it. Do you understand what I'm trying to say?'

'But it can't work like that, Stephen. I have to agree to it. Don't you see?'

'I just thought you would. I just thought that giving you the ring openly, with everybody watching, would sort of . . .'

'Coerce me? . . . I think that's the word. But coercion won't work with me, Stephen.' She took the ring off her finger and slipped it into the top pocket of his jacket. 'There. If you're that keen on getting engaged offer it to somebody else.'

Stephen was angered by that. He stopped the car abruptly and switched off the engine.

'Maxine,' he said indignantly, 'I want *you*. Nobody else. Now I'm sorry if I've embarrassed you with my offer of marriage, but it was sincere. I can't help being in love with you. I can't help the way I feel.'

'But you seem to have no understanding or appreciation of how I feel, Stephen. Is that why you lost the last girl you were engaged to? By not considering her feelings?'

That struck a chord, Maxine could tell. He'd never offered any explanation as to why his previous entanglement with Evelyn had failed, and she had never pressed him for one. It seemed irrelevant to *them*.

'I'm sorry, Maxine,' he said quietly, and sighed like a football being deflated, as if resigned to the situation at last. Perhaps he saw that if he persisted with this he was going to lose her altogether. 'No more talk of engagements then, eh?'

She shrugged indifferently. 'I'm not even sure that I want to carry on seeing you.'

'Maxine!' He felt a cold shiver run down his spine in his panic. He couldn't lose her. He mustn't lose her. 'Maxine don't say that. Please don't say that.'

'Well it's true, Stephen. I'm not in love with you. I don't think I'll ever fall in love with you.'

'That doesn't matter.'

'Of course it *matters*.'

'No,' he said resolutely. 'It doesn't matter at all, because love will come. In time, you *will* come to love me. Such things happen all the time. I can wait. I'm quite happy to wait.'

'I think you'll be waiting for ever.'

'Don't say that, Maxine. Look, let's just go on as we were, eh? I promise I won't mention marriage or getting engaged again.'

She sighed, a heavy, frustrated sigh; Stephen was not going to be easy to shake off. 'I don't know . . . Do you want to know the truth, Stephen? I feel trapped with you. You don't give me any space. You don't allow me any time to myself, or time with any other friends – even with Pansy, your own sister. You want to see me every night of the week when I don't want to see you. You don't give me time to practise my cello even, when I need to practise on my own. When I need to stay in and practise you still come round. What do you think I'm going to do when you're not there? Run off with somebody else? It's as if you don't trust me.'

'Of course I trust you.'

'You don't . . . because you assume I'm like you. You're judging me by your own standards.'

'Maxine, I never realised . . . I never knew you felt that way,' he said, shaking his head. 'If that's what you want, that's all right by me. I won't see you every night.'

'So let's make it just two nights a week.'

'Three,' he pressed.

'Two, or nothing at all . . . And I choose which two.' She could not help but smile to herself. She knew he had to agree or lose her. She had no wish to hurt him or belittle him but she needed space; more now than ever before; and if it cost her his friendship, then so be it. 'Oh . . . And no more opening the car door for me. Or any other damned door for that matter. I can do that on my own – if you don't mind.'

'Agreed . . .' He sighed, and hesitated, as if to say something else.

'Go on . . . What were you going to say?'

He felt in his pocket and withdrew the ring. 'This . . . Give me your left hand.'

'Stephen! I don't believe what I'm hearing.'

'Hear me out, Maxine . . . Give me your left hand.'

'No.'

'Just give me your left hand.'

He was smiling mysteriously, triumphantly. What sort of silly game was he playing? She gave him her hand tentatively.

'I'll only take it off again,' she warned.

'It's no longer an engagement ring, Maxine,' he said seriously and positioned the ring perfectly on her third finger. 'It's no longer an engagement ring. It's just a ring . . . Any sort of ring. A ring of friendship. A dress ring. Anything you like.'

'But it's not an engagement ring?' she queried, seeking reassurance. Then, more assertively: 'It's not an engagement ring.'

'I just said so. It's not an engagement ring. I conceived it and designed it just for you . . . to have, no matter what. I want you to have it, Maxine. Wear it, or don't wear it, as you fancy.'

'As long as it's not an engagement ring.'

'Not any more. How many times must I tell you?'

Maxine admired it on her finger again. The magnificent amethyst shone, amplifying the paltry light it picked up from the gas street lamps. It really was beautiful. Stephen certainly knew his job.

'Okay,' she said, satisfied. 'Thank you. Now can we go?'

He drove her home, content that whilst she no longer regarded it as an engagement ring, everybody else would.

Rehearsals that week were hard work. Sibelius's 6th Symphony was scheduled for its Birmingham airing in two weeks, and nobody, even the conductor, was familiar with the score. But they battled through it, and after the third effort, everybody felt more comfortable with it. *Roméo et Juliette*, from Berlioz, was also on the agenda, universally popular with the players, and Maxine enjoyed its honest melodic drama.

All week Maxine had been puzzled and disappointed that Brent Shackleton had not taken time to come and chat to her, neither during breaks nor at lunch times. Even when they had finished and it was time to go home he had stayed chatting to his fellow brass. His lack of attention intrigued her. Maybe he had noticed from a distance the new ring she was wearing and, perceiving it as an engagement ring, decided discretion might be better exercised. Maybe if she took it off when she was coming to rehearsals . . . That would be sensible anyway.

But things took a different turn the following Monday. An evening rehearsal had been arranged so that the CBO could team up with the amateurs of the Festival Choral Society, to practise Beethoven's mammoth Mass in D. It was the first time Maxine had been involved with choral music.

Rehearsal finished shortly after ten o'clock and a further orchestra-only rehearsal was scheduled for the following morning. Thus, Stephen need not collect her and her cello since she could leave it packed away in the rehearsal room ready for the next day. Whether Brent had sussed this had never crossed her mind, but he ambled over to her, carrying his trombone case.

He was smiling, which negated any notion that he'd been

45

deliberately avoiding her. 'You're looking well, Maxine. Pretty as a picture, as usual.'

'Thank you.' She blushed instantly and felt her heart start pounding like a kettledrum. She did not understand why she reacted to him in this way. It was such a nuisance. She did not enjoy blushing; she felt such a fool. Suddenly she was aware of the ring on her finger and tried to avoid showing her left hand.

'If you don't fancy going straight home, I'd love to take you to that club I know.'

Lord! He wanted to take her out. 'I'm not exactly dressed for clubs, Brent,' she said excusing herself but with bitter disappointment. She was wearing a full navy skirt of a length sufficient to afford some modesty when she was playing her cello, and a white blouse that she felt must be grubby after a whole day's wear.

'Oh, you're dressed fine, Maxine. It's only a jazz club.'

'A jazz club?' Her eyes gave away her interest.

'Yes.' It amused him that she seemed to repeat everything he said, but phrased as a question.

Of course, she would love to go to a jazz club. It would be a change to hear jazz. 'I'd love to,' she admitted. 'The only problem is, they'll be expecting me back home soon.'

'Haven't you got a key?'

'Oh, yes, I've got a key.'

'Well then . . . Why keep making excuses not to come?'

'But what about your young lady?'

'What about your young man?' he countered.

'Stephen? He's not coming tonight.'

'Neither is my young lady, as you call her.'

'So what should I call her? What's her name?'

'Eleanor.'

'Won't Eleanor mind? You taking me to a club, I mean?'

'I shan't ask her whether she minds or not. I shan't tell her anyway.'

Her smile of approval confirmed her collusion. 'Actually, it's

46

no business of Stephen's, either . . . If you're sure I'm dressed okay? I could go home and change. It's only up the road.'

'You're fine, Maxine. You look ravishing.'

She thrilled at his compliment, sincere or not. 'I bet you say that to all the girls.'

'I might, if they deserve it. Come on, then, let's go. I don't want to be late.'

She grabbed her handbag and the navy cardigan that had been draped over the back of her chair and hurtled after him, finding it hard to keep up.

'How far is it?' she asked when they were outside in the street.

'Not far.'

'Do you have to walk quite so fast?'

He hesitated. 'Sorry. It's just that I should have been there fifteen minutes ago.'

'Why? What's all the rush?'

'I'm due on stage. I play in a jazz band.'

'You play in a jazz band?'

There she went again, repeating his words. 'Yes. I'm a musician, remember. I have to earn money somehow. The CBO doesn't pay enough. Here . . .' They had arrived at a car; a very smart, curvy looking car; a Mercedes Benz, black, big, flaring with chromium plating. It sported enormous headlights perched on the front wings and a spare wheel nestling in the side sweep. He unlocked the door and threw his trombone and case in the back. 'Hurry up.'

She let herself in and recognised the rich, dark smell of leather. He fired the engine and they shot off like a hare sprung from a trap. Maxine silently approved of his showing off in this expensive motor car. Yet their journey was short; incredibly short. They had travelled no more than four hundred yards when he pulled into a side street off Broad Street, the main road west out of the city, and stopped outside what looked like an old warehouse. Maxine stepped out of the car and while Brent retrieved his trombone from the rear seat she caught a glimpse of a canal basin harbouring a random fleet of narrowboats tied up for the night.

'This way,' he called. 'Look, do you mind if I go on ahead and see you inside? Silas will let you in. Just tell him you're with me.' He dashed off, leaving her to find her own way.

She decided then not to rush. Let him get on with it and indeed, she would see him inside, when she got there. She entered by the door that he had not held open for her and pondered with wide-eyed amusement the very novelty of it. The reek of stale beer, body odour and cigarette smoke was strong, even in the small lobby she found herself in. A man was sitting at a table, and she knew the body odour was wafting from him.

'One and six to get in,' he mumbled.

'How much?' Now that *was* inconsiderate of Brent. She fumbled in her handbag.

The man drew asthmatically on a crinkled cigarette that was wet with spittle at one end. 'Am yarra member?' he asked, in a thick Birmingham accent.

Maxine could hear the buzz of people laughing and chatting inside, the chink of glasses and the unmistakable plinks of a banjo being tuned.

'Sorry, no,' she replied. 'Do I have to be? I'm with Brent Shackleton, that chap who came in before me with the trombone. He's in the band.'

'Wharrim?' His look suggested both scorn and a suggestion that he did not believe her. 'You'm a fresh un, in't ya?'

She shrugged. 'Fresh as a daisy, me.'

'Goo on, then, young madam. Gerron in. I'll believe ya. Thousands wun't.'

Maxine shoved the door open. She had no preconception of what the inside of this jazz club might be like. It bore no resemblance to the ultra smart jazz clubs in America she'd read about: the Cotton Club in New York, the Sunset Café in Chicago. Bare light bulbs hung dimly from ceiling rafters rendering a sleazy, Spartan atmosphere. Drifting cigarette smoke and the blend of feminine perfumes failed to mask the underlying mustiness that caught the back of her throat like the pungent stink of a damp dog. A few shaky tables furnished the place, acquired from house clearances by the looks of them, and rickety old chairs of similar origin that some people were rash enough to sit on. But most folks remained standing; including the young girls; *too* young, some of them. The stage, a makeshift affair, was constructed of beer crates supporting sheets of plywood, but Maxine could see several instruments on it, and one or two players getting ready to perform.

Brent located her in the dimness. 'Oh, there you are. Let me get you a drink.'

'A glass of lemonade, please.' She was relieved that he'd taken the trouble to find her. 'What time do you start playing?'

'In about five minutes. Arthur's split the reed on his clarinet. He's just gone to get another.'

'Where's he going to get a reed from at this time of night?'

'He reckons he's got a spare one in his car.'

'In his car?' she jibed. 'Not in his instrument case?' It seemed inconceivable that a clarinettist should not have a spare reed immediately to hand. It was akin to having no spare strings in her cello case. Unthinkable.

Brent turned away from her and addressed the barman. Next thing, she was clutching a half-pint of beer.

'I asked for lemonade,' she said, amused that he'd got it wrong.

'Never mind. You'll enjoy that. Do you good . . . Look, Arthur's back. See you later.'

As he hurried towards the stage, she smiled to herself. Stephen would stifle her with attention if she let him, but Brent was the sort of person who needed space himself, so would never restrict her. She could scarcely believe that two men could be so different. And yet this Eleanor, whom she had seen but not met . . . Where did she fit in? Was Brent married to her, or was she just a casual girlfriend? Already, Maxine perceived that Brent was not the sort to tie himself down in marriage; she felt they had that in common.

The band struck up, interrupting her thoughts. They were

playing a thing called 'Tiger Rag'. She'd heard it before on a record by the Original Dixieland Jazz Band – a record that Pansy had acquired. Her feet started tapping and a few couples started dancing. Arthur came in with a clarinet solo that Maxine did not consider very enthralling. The trumpet player followed – he was good; he was very good. Then it was Brent's turn on the trombone and he shone, using a plunger mute and growling his notes with great panache. When it was the turn of the piano player Maxine at once noted his lack of competence, as if his fingers could not work the keyboard fast enough. But the banjo player was brilliant, as were the double bass player, and the drummer. Funny, she thought, how being a capable musician enabled you to pick out the flaws in other musicians' performances, irrespective of the instrument they played.

When they finished the piece a smattering of applause flecked the background murmur and Arthur announced their next number, 'Fidgety Feet'. Maxine was familiar with that one as well. A tall young man, smart, wearing a Fair Isle pullover the like of which she had seen on photos of the Prince of Wales, asked her to dance and she felt guilty at having to refuse him. She preferred to listen to the band.

This jazz was so informal, so improvised that it allowed for some ineptitude, she pondered, as she watched the pianist's fingers stumble over the keys. The odd wrong note wasn't that noticeable and mostly didn't matter. The music was full of discords anyway, intermingling of instruments that at times sounded chaotic even though a firm underlying matrix was always present. So why did this pianist stand out as being so ill fitted to his job? The tempo changed slightly and Maxine recognised a tune called 'Empty Bed Blues'. Arthur, clutching his clarinet casually at his side, sang a couple of triplets – incongruously, since the lyrics were meant to be sung by a woman – then proceeded to give another less than sparkling clarinet solo.

Then it struck her. The pianist. He wasn't using syncopation.

He knew what notes to play, but it seemed that he had not fathomed out how to stress the weak beat, the offbeat. The very elements of jazz, she thought, pitch, texture, melodic and harmonic organisation, all those bent notes, are woven around provocative rhythms. The way this man played he might just as well have been pounding out a hymn in a Methodist mission hut. Maxine felt pleased that she had diagnosed this ailment in what was otherwise a reasonable, tight sound.

Having sorted out the piano player, Maxine regarded Brent. His expression was earnest, eyes closed, sweat dripping off his brow as he slid his trombone through intricate passages in 'Twelfth Street Rag'. This was evidently his preferred world, his preferred music.

At this point she asked herself what she was doing here; what she hoped to gain in this seedy, musty old warehouse that was hazy with cigarette smoke. Had she accepted Brent's invitation because she wanted to listen to the music? Or was it because she fancied her chances with him? Accepting his invitation was a way of being with him, wasn't it? But she wasn't actually with him. He was on the stage sweating buckets over the one thing that possibly mattered more to him than anything else, while she was standing eight feet from the bar, watching, listening, being asked to dance by strange men in whom she had no interest, sipping beer she did not enjoy. She was not actually talking to Brent; she was not getting to know him any better. Neither was she discovering about Eleanor and the depth of his involvement with her.

Maybe she was wasting her time. Why would Brent Shackleton bother with Maxine Kite? In any case, he was inconsiderate. Look how he'd hurried off without her, leaving her to her own devices to gain admittance to the club. Totally, irritatingly inattentive. The absolute opposite of Stephen's irritatingly superfluous gallantry. Both were as bad as each other. As soon as Brent came off stage she would make her excuses and go home. Besides, it was getting late. Henzey and Will would think she'd been abducted.

Yet, he must be interested in her. He'd asked her to this club, hadn't he?

As she stood watching, thinking, listening, wavering between one emotion and another, she was aware that a man was standing at her side, but she avoided looking at him.

'Excuse me,' he said half apologetically, 'would you mind very much if I talk to you?'

At least his approach was straightforward, even if he was a bit shy.

'Why me?' she asked, curious. 'The place is full of girls.' But her smile broadened in direct proportion to her appreciation of his handsome face and the kindly look in his soft eyes that were framed by wire-rimmed spectacles.

'Because you look like the sort of girl who might have something to say,' he answered with a warm but tentative smile. 'The others? I doubt it. I'm also intrigued as to why a girl so attractive should be standing by herself.'

She chuckled amiably. 'Oh, spare me the flattery. Attractive? Dressed like this?'

'To tell you the truth, I've been watching you for some time, trying to pluck up the courage to come over and speak to you.' He was about twenty-eight, she judged, clean and well groomed, but with an unruly mop of dark hair that gave him an appealing schoolboy look. 'Howard Quaintance.'

'Excuse me?' They were having to speak in raised voices to be heard over the sound of the jazz.

He smiled pleasantly. 'I'm Howard Quaintance . . . Now you're supposed to tell me your name.'

'Sorry. Maxine Kite . . . How do you do?' She felt that, for the sake of good manners, him being so polite, she ought to offer to shake his hand.

He stood there holding a glass, his other hand in his pocket, casual, unassuming. 'Delighted to meet you . . . er . . . *Miss*? . . . Kite.'

'Miss, yes,' she affirmed strenuously, amused by his unsubtle way of checking her marital status. 'Call me Maxine. I'm quite happy to dispense with formality.'

He took a swig of beer. 'Well, Maxine, what *is* such an attractive girl doing, standing all on her own in a den of iniquity like this?'

'Actually, I'm with one of the band.'

'You don't say? Might I ask which one?'

'The trombonist.'

'You don't say . . .' Maxine thought he sounded inordinately surprised. 'A good musician. Not bad band, either, wouldn't you say?'

'Not bad,' she concurred unconvincingly. 'Between you and me, though, I'm not so sure about the pianist.'

'Interesting you should say that,' he remarked, focusing on the piano player.

'I've been watching him and listening. If only he would syncopate they would really swing.'

'Mmm . . . Interesting you should say that.' He took a thoughtful slurp from his pint. 'It doesn't surprise me, though. I'm certainly no musician, but what you say doesn't surprise me at all. *You're* not a musician, are you, by any chance?'

'I am a pianist,' she confessed, to justify her comments. 'But I play cello in the CBO.'

'The CBO? Hey! You're a classical musician. That explains your being hauled here by Brent.'

'You know Brent?'

'Nodding terms only, I'm afraid. Friend of a friend. Look, can I get you a drink?'

She looked at the barely touched glass of beer with distaste. 'Would you mind?' she replied. 'This beer is too awful. I'd love a glass of lemonade . . . If it's no trouble?'

'Absolutely no trouble at all.' He quaffed what remained of his pint and turned for the bar.

Great! She had a friend to talk to while Brent was busy. And he was easy to talk to. He seemed nice. She smiled cheerfully, uplifted now. It was pleasant to make new friends. What had he said his name was? . . . Howard? Yes. Howard Quaintance. Difficult to forget a name like that. In no time he returned and handed her the glass of lemonade. She took a mouthful eagerly to destroy the lingering, bitter taste of the beer.

'So, how come you and Brent are on nodding terms?' she asked.

'Through one of the other members of the band, actually.'

Maxine felt herself go hot. Of course, this Howard was going to tell her it was the piano player, she could feel it coming with the certainty of an express train hurtling down a track to which she was tied and unable to escape. She put her hand over her eyes, and cringed.

'Don't tell me it's the pianist, Howard. *Please* don't tell me it's the pianist!'

He guffawed aloud, his eyes sparkling behind his spectacles with unconcealed delight at Maxine's gaff. 'Oh, I'm afraid it is.'

'Oh, God!' She wanted the ground at her feet to open up and consume her. 'Me and my *big* mouth.'

Still howling with laughter, he touched her forearm and she felt his hand, warm, reassuring as he squeezed it.

'Don't concern yourself, Maxine,' he said gently. 'Old Randolf would be the first to admit he's no jazz musician. Actually, he's a church organist, you know. Jolly good he is too, as choirmaster, at playing Wesley and Stainer. Does an intoxicating "All things bright and beautiful". Took this on as a challenge. For a hoot. A tad out of his depth I think.'

She breathed a sigh of relief. 'Thank God for that. I've gone all hot.' Then she chuckled at her *faux pas*. 'Maybe I'm too honest.'

'Never ever say that, Maxine. *Make thine honesty a vice . . .* Shakespeare . . . *Othello*, you know.'

She shrieked with laughter. 'Really? Shouldn't I make it a *virtue?*'

He laughed with her at his own gaff.

'So what do you do for a living, Howard, that makes you quote Shakespeare out of context? Are you an English teacher, by any chance?'

He chortled again and took a mouthful of beer, all the time looking straight into her eyes. She held the glance and recognised an untainted, well-brought-up look.

'I'd rather not say. I don't want to sound presumptuous, Maxine, but I rather like you and if I tell you what I do for a living you might not wish to be as affable as you are.'

'Affable, am I?'

'Definitely. I find you easy to talk to and hugely amusing. I also find you very direct. I like that. It's refreshing in a girl . . .' He hesitated. 'On the other hand, we may never meet again, so there'd be no harm in telling you anyway. But, I won't.'

She laughed at his indecision or his teasing; she wasn't sure which it was. 'God! You're infuriating. Why won't you tell me what you do?'

'It's of no consequence – really . . . But hey, I am thirsty.' He took a long quaff from his beer, finishing it off.

'Well, you're drinking that rather quickly,' she commented.

'Good God! You're not in the Band of Hope, are you?'

'Certainly not. More like the band of no hope, me.' Her tone, she was aware, must have sounded melancholy.

'How can you possibly say that?' he asked. 'With all the musical talent you must possess?'

'I wasn't thinking about musical talent particularly.'

'Oh? What, then?'

It was her turn to shrug, unsure as to how much she should tell him. 'Oh . . . Men. I find men are a pain in the neck . . . Oh, I don't mean you, Howard – I don't know you – but some at any rate. I mean it's either all or nothing with them. At least that's my experience – which is a bit limited, I hasten to add – just in case I've given you the wrong impression.'

'Is that an engagement ring you're wearing, Maxine? You must have captured somebody's heart. But that's hardly surprising.'

She brought her hand up so he could inspect the ring in the dimness. He took off his glasses to better see close to and slipped them into the top pocket of his jacket.

'Very impressive,' he remarked.

'But it's not an engagement ring, Howard.'

'No? Well that's a blessing.'

She explained in some detail about her relationship with Stephen. How he wanted more than she was prepared to give, how she did not enjoy his caresses, even though she liked him as a person; how he'd tried to trap her into saying she would marry him. She was surprised at the consummate ease with which she was pouring out her doubts and fears to Howard, as if they'd been bosom pals always.

'But everyone will think it's an engagement ring, Maxine, and your Stephen knows that,' Howard advised her. 'Don't you see? *I* thought it was an engagement ring, actually. Why don't you wear it on your right hand, if you're still keen on wearing it? Then there can be no misunderstanding. It tends to put off potential suitors, you know.'

Maxine looked at him with wide-eyed admiration. 'Why didn't I think of that? That's brilliant, Howard! That's absolutely brilliant.'

'Here. Let me do it. I've never removed a ring from a finger before.'

She gave him her hand, thinking it a strange thing for him to say. He put his glass down on a nearby table and touched her slender fingers. Deftly, he slid off the ring.

'Now, give me your right hand.' He put the ring on the third finger. 'Does it fit?'

She nodded coyly, aware that her heart was beating fast with the unanticipated intimacy of the moment. To her surprise, being touched by someone who was not Stephen was surprisingly pleasant and, for the first time in her life, Maxine felt that maybe she was not destined to be unresponsive forever. It had to be Stephen. She felt new hope. Physical contact might be pleasurable after all, and she wondered what her reaction would be if Brent touched her.

'There. That's all there is to it. Problem solved.'

'Thank you.' She felt herself blush; though in this dim light it barely mattered.

'Is that why you're here tonight with Brent Shackleton?'

'What do you mean exactly?'

'I mean, are you trying to seek some reason to justify discarding this Stephen?'

He had a point.

'Maybe. I don't really know. I hadn't analysed my motives particularly. Brent's a fellow musician. A colleague. To tell you the truth I was ready to go home before you came talking to me.' But suddenly she saw her chance to find out more about Brent. She must sound as casual as she could. 'Anyway, I don't really know Brent that well. What can you tell me about him? I've seen him with a girl after CBO concerts. A really beautiful girl. Is he married or anything?'

Howard looked bitterly disappointed. 'Why don't you ask *him*, Maxine?'

Outside it had started to rain. Maxine had not anticipated rain tonight. She pulled her cardigan over her shoulders and ran behind Brent as they headed for his car. He threw his trombone onto the back seat. Once inside he unlocked the passenger door for her.

'Bloody weather,' he murmured. 'Which way?'

'To the top of Broad Street, then turn right into Ladywood Road.' She shuffled her bottom on the seat to get comfortable, Howard's presence still with her.

He turned the car around and drove off. 'Well? Have you enjoyed tonight?'

'Yes, I've thoroughly enjoyed myself, thank you. The band's good. I'm impressed. Have you got a name for yourselves?'

'The Second City Hot Six.'

57

'The Second City Hot Six? . . . But there are seven of you.'

'Arthur doesn't always play. His wife won't let him out all the time.'

'Lord, I can scarcely believe that!' she scoffed. 'He's not that brilliant anyway, is he?'

'Not really. But most of the time we haven't got him. When we have, he's a bonus.'

'A liability, more like. He plays that clarinet as if it were a piece of lead piping. The pianist too – he's the same – worse, possibly.'

He chuckled at her directness. 'This stuff's not serious, Maxine. It's for fun. It doesn't really matter how good or bad we are, so long as we enjoy playing together. It pays reasonably well, anyway. *That's* a bonus.'

'I suppose so. But I tend to be a perfectionist, Brent. I couldn't stand to play jazz – or anything else for that matter – unless I was doing it as well as it was possible to do it.'

'Does that apply to everything you do?' he asked provocatively.

'Of course it does.' His innuendo was lost on her, however. 'I see you were talking to Randolf's chum.'

'You mean Howard? He was nice. Easy to talk to. I liked him.' The same glow she'd felt when he held her hand lit her up again as she recalled the moment. After a pause, she said: 'I asked him about you.'

He snorted with laughter. 'I bet that impressed him.'

'I asked him if he knew whether you were married.'

'Oh? And what did he say?'

'He said to ask *you* . . . I think I upset him. So I'm asking. Are you married, Brent?'

He hesitated, and she knew he was debating with himself whether to tell her a lie. 'Why? Is it important?'

'It might be.'

'Yet you didn't ask before you accepted my offer to take you out.'

'Nevertheless, it had occurred to me.'

'Nevertheless, you accepted my invitation.'

She felt her colour rise. 'I suppose I did.'

'Which suggests it isn't relevant.'

'It would be relevant if I had designs on you,' she said, trying to make it sound as if she hadn't.

He grinned to himself in the darkness. 'And *do* you have designs on me?'

'Certainly not. Especially if you're married. So? Are you married?'

'I might be,' he teased. 'And then again, I might not.'

'Sorry, Brent. Turn left here, please.'

'Left? Hold tight.' He braked hard and turned the car into the corner.

'Now right.'

'Okay . . . Now where?'

'Just here will do . . . Thank you, Brent. Thanks for taking me to listen to the Second City Hot Seven.'

'Hot Six.'

She smiled enigmatically as she clambered out of the car. 'See you at rehearsal in the morning.'

Chapter 5

Orchestra rehearsals for Beethoven's Mass in D went well. By five minutes past ten everyone had tuned up and was playing. Leslie Heward was not content with some of the passages in the final movement, prompting various discussions and one or two individuals practising certain phrases privately and spontaneously before going over it again together. They broke for lunch at one o'clock.

Maxine, who had avoided looking in the direction of Brent Shackleton, was surprised when he sidled up to her as she spoke to Gwen Berry on a point of interpretation on the cello score.

'Sorry to interrupt, Gwen. Do you mind if I steal Maxine off you?' he asked courteously. 'Have you got a minute, Maxine?'

Maxine excused herself and stood up.

'Last night, Maxine . . .' he began seriously. 'Look, do you mind coming with me to The White Hart for a drink? There's something I want to talk to you about. It's probably best done over a drink.'

'Okay,' she said, surprised at the prospect of being in his company again so soon. 'What do you want to discuss with me?'

'I need some advice. Something you said last night.'

About the question of him being married? 'Let me grab my bag.'

She trotted alongside him to the exit. 'Horrible last night, wasn't it? The weather, I mean.' She smiled appealingly to confirm she really did mean the weather.

In Chamberlain Square the pigeons were out in force, strutting earnestly in the sunshine, flapping boisterously as crumbs and crusts landed among them. Lunch time was an engrossing time of day for pigeons, for on fine days such as this the providers of all these scraps of bread, the city's office workers, took to the Square to enjoy sandwiches and flasks of tea among the splendour of some of Birmingham's grandest Victorian architecture. Office romances budded and blossomed as workers sought relief in the sunshine from the tedium of eye straining paperwork in poorly lit rooms.

Maxine and Brent walked briskly through this urban springtime lunch hour, forcing conversation, for both were aware of how strained their tenuous relationship had become overnight. Brent ventured a remark on the progress of Amy Johnson's solo flight to and from South Africa, and Maxine replied how brave she must be to attempt it. Then he told her it would be his dream to play jazz on the *Queen Mary* when the liner made her maiden voyage to America at the end of the month.

He was nicer today, not dashing off in front. She didn't have to struggle to keep up with him. He was more attentive. In fact, he was beginning to sound rather charming.

They arrived at The White Hart. It was busy, noisy with conversation and laughter.

'What would you like to drink, Maxine?'

'Lemonade, please . . . Brent – no beer this time, thank you.'

He grinned. 'Okay. Lemonade. What about a sandwich? They do decent sandwiches here.'

'No thanks.' She had taken her own sandwiches as she did every rehearsal day. They were lying in her basket next to her cello; to be eaten alongside her cello usually. Besides, she could never countenance buying sandwiches when they were so cheap and easy to make at home.

Brent returned with their drinks. 'There's nowhere to sit.'

'Then we'll have to stand.' She took the glass from him and sipped it. 'So what do you want to discuss with me?'

'The Second City Hot Six.' He took a long draught through the foam on his beer.

'Oh? How do you think *I* can help?'

'Well, you're a musician, Maxine. You listen to jazz. You reckon you play it yourself occasionally . . .'

'But only for fun. Never seriously. I've only ever played it with my friend Pansy. She's brilliant, mind you. Completely wasted.'

'Cigarette?'

'I don't smoke, Brent. You know I don't smoke.'

'I forgot. Sorry . . . Something you said last night, Maxine, made me think. You said there was no point in doing something – playing jazz for instance – if you didn't do it right. You said you're a perfectionist.'

'I suppose I am. I can't stand music to be played slapdash.'

He lit his cigarette. 'After I dropped you off I thought about that. And you know, you're spot on. I want to earn my living playing jazz. It's all I've ever wanted to do. You made me realise with that comment of yours that if that's what I want, then I have to do it properly to achieve it. Why shouldn't I be the best? Why shouldn't the band be the best? It's the only way forward.'

'Quite right,' Maxine agreed, wafting unwanted smoke away with her hand.

'I *want* to take it more seriously, Maxine. You know, there's good money to be made playing jazz. I could earn a lot more than I do playing in the CBO and, believe me, I could do with it. So I need some guidance from a self-confessed perfectionist. You heard us last night, Maxine. What should we do to get the best out of what we've got? How can we improve, do you think?'

'By hard practice, I should say. By disciplined practice. It's no good turning up for practice and fooling about. If there's something to be rehearsed, rehearse it. Rehearse it till it sounds as good as you hear it in your imagination. And then keep on rehearsing it till playing it is second nature – till you don't have to think about it.'

'But everybody else in the band has to be of the same mind.'

'Course they do. A half-hearted musician will stick out like a sore thumb amidst really serious ones – and spoil what they do.'

'The one bad apple that spoils the whole bag, eh?'

'Yes. So, it requires hard work and very serious commitment. But, Brent, I tell you straight. You'll get nowhere with that pianist. I don't mean to be unkind but he's next to useless. He's an organist and choirmaster, for God's sake, and that's all he knows how to play. Even Howard said he was no good playing jazz.'

'Oh yes. I forgot you and Howard are big chums now.' His comment seemed tinged with cynicism, Maxine thought, but she hoped she was mistaken.

'You need a decent clarinettist besides. Somebody dedicated. It's no good having one whose wife won't let him out at night. That's just too pathetic. You have to be professional about this if you want to be a professional – all of you. In any case, he hasn't got the ability either to play jazz. He doesn't *feel* the music. I told you . . .'

'Yes, you did . . . So will you help us? Will you come to some of our practices and try to put us right? Will you come and guide us where we're going wrong? Help us get things right? I'm too close to it to judge properly. It needs a fresh ear. I reckon you could do it. You know what to listen for. Make any comment you reckon is warranted.'

'I'm flattered that you've asked me,' she replied with a broad smile that revealed her even teeth and put a sparkle in her eyes again. 'I'd love to help. When do we start?'

'How about tonight? I'll pick you up from home at half past seven.'

It had not occurred to Maxine that the jazz club might not be open for business that night. The Second City Hot Six had assembled to practise, and they had the place to themselves except for Nat Colesby, the owner and licensee. He was cleaning beer lines, restocking shelves, cleaning up, and on hand to serve beer to the six or seven musicians as they worked up a thirst.

The band practised here most Tuesdays. Although the rest of them had noticed Maxine the previous evening with Brent, he introduced her tonight. He outlined his ideas and aspirations and explained how he thought she could help.

'So what happens about Arthur?' Kenny Wheeler, the drummer asked. 'The chap's woman-licked. You can't count on him to be that dedicated.'

'That I know,' Brent replied. 'We'll have to find another clarinettist.'

'Ain't there nobody in the CBO?' Charlie Holt, the slightly tubby double bass player enquired.

'Nobody who'd want to join us,' Brent remarked.

Maxine had already considered that Stephen's sister, Pansy, would be an admirable replacement but it was not up to her to suggest it. It might sound too pushy if she did. But if they found nobody quickly, she could perhaps drop a hint. After all, Pansy could do with the work. She was dissatisfied working in the pit orchestra at the Hippodrome. On the other hand, maybe they wouldn't want a girl in this band.

George Tolley, the banjo player who answered to Ginger, took his instrument out of its case and began plinking, tuning it up. 'Where's Randy? He's late. So do we bugger off home or get cracking on something then without him?'

'Randolf's not coming,' Brent informed them.

'Bloody typical. So bang goes this new commitment before we even start.'

'I've sacked him, Ginger. He just isn't good enough. And Maxine agrees. That job's up for grabs as well. So we'll have to start without a pianist.'

'Christ. Who is considered good enough?' Kenny asked. 'Are all our jobs shaky in this line-up? I'd like to know in case I need to look elsewhere.'

'You're not going to be sacked, Kenny,' Brent said. 'Nor anybody else. Those of us here are first-rate musicians, well capable of playing the sort of stuff we're likely to encounter.

Arthur and Randy are not up to it. Deep down we all know that and odds are they'd admit it themselves. I want us to be the best jazz band in the Midlands – in the country – so we need chaps capable of getting us there. As of now, we look for a new clarinettist and a new pianist . . . I'll put an advert in the paper in the next day or two . . . Right. What shall we start with?'

'"Alexander's Ragtime Band",' Jimmy Randle suggested with a mischievous smirk. Jimmy was the trumpet player and better known as Toots.

'Oh, anything but that, Toots,' Ginger pleaded. 'I hate it. Let's do "My Sister Kate".'

Brent stood up, poised to play his trombone. 'Right. "I Wish I Could Shimmy like my Sister Kate" . . . One, two, one two three four . . .'

And they were away.

Maxine listened intently. Some things that could be improved were evident immediately and she could not imagine why they had not put them right before. Maybe it was because a stranger's ear can detect weaknesses that those most closely involved are deaf to. Wood for trees. But they were all competent musicians.

'So, what d'you think, Maxine?' Brent asked when they had finished running through the number.

'Well . . . It seems as if you're all trying to outplay each other – as if you're all trying to do a solo at the same time. Try to play *for* each other. Be more together, as one unit, not six separate ones. It all needs tidying up, too. The stops should be cleaner . . . Kenny, when you're supposed to have a rest for a few beats, don't try and fit in a drumroll to fill the gap. Stay silent till you're due to come in again and let the melody instruments and the singer have their glory. Those little rests are for emphasis, for effect. It's what makes Jelly Roll Morton great. It'll make your music more effective as well. Otherwise it sounds all ragged and undisciplined.'

'Kenny likes to turn every number into a drum solo,' Charlie

Holt remarked, and Maxine detected his frustration at Kenny's overly enthusiastic drumming. 'He thinks he's Gene Krupa.'

Maxine's eyes creased into a smile. But she had to be honest. She had to take this seriously. That's why she was here.

'Same applies to you, Ginger, really,' she continued. 'The banjo is a rhythm instrument as well. Try playing *with* the drummer, not as if you're in competition. Generally, when Kenny has a few beats break, you stick to the break as well . . . Why don't you try it again doing just that?'

Brent counted them in once more. At the first point where Kenny was supposed to stop, he did so and the effect was significant: it all held together more tightly, more eloquently. The musicians looked at each other and Maxine could see satisfied grins passing from one to another at the immediate improvement. She was relieved, for she was not certain how these hard-nosed males, with vastly more jazz experience, were likely to view advice from a much younger person – even worse, a *girl*. Doubtless one or two would resent it unless she had something positive to say, something that really worked. Musicians, she had learned already – male ones especially – were a race apart: hard-nosed, uncompromising; usually hard drinking as well, just to add to their volatility.

'It sounds better already,' Toots Randle admitted.

'Just one little point that improves the overall quality,' Maxine confirmed. 'It demonstrates much more musical discipline as well.'

'Let's try something else,' Toots suggested.

'How about "Tiger Rag"?'

Brent counted them in.

The same principles applied, of course, and the band again signalled to each other their approval as their instantly cleaner, more refined music pleased everybody.

'Something's still missing,' Charlie Holt complained. 'I grant you it all sounds tighter playing it how Maxine suggests, but it's lacking something . . . Soul, for want of a better word.'

'Rhythm?' Maxine suggested.

'We've got rhythm,' Kenny said. 'I provide the rhythm.'

'Some of it, I agree,' Maxine countered, afraid that she sounded like a know-all. 'But you don't want lifeless, mechanical rhythm like a metronome. Jazz needs more than that. It needs to swing easily. It has an inner rhythm that you either feel or you don't feel. And if you *feel* it, you can turn it loose. Try to be more relaxed about your playing – everybody. Loosen up a bit. Each instrument should have its own rhythm.'

'We're missing the piano,' Brent said. 'That's what's lacking.'

'Yes, that'd help,' Kenny agreed. 'Can't *you* play piano, Maxine? Just to give a bit more body to the sound. Just to fill it out a bit. It don't matter if you play a few wrong notes. Just to give us the *feel.*'

'I could try.' She stepped up onto the stage. 'What key is this in?'

'B flat.'

'Oh, Lord!' she laughed, rolling her eyes. 'Can't you play it in C?'

'I can play it in any key you want,' said Kenny with a smirk as he ostentatiously twirled his drumsticks in the air.

'Okay.' Self-consciously she made herself comfortable on the rickety chair. 'When you're ready.'

'One, two, one two three four . . .'

Twelve bars into the piece, Brent and Kenny signalled each other with a look that gave complete approval to the difference Maxine's piano playing made. They all felt and heard something that none of them had felt or heard before in the Second City Hot Six: real syncopation; slick, smooth, well-oiled syncopation that insinuated itself into their own individual performances, improving the quality of the whole out of all proportion.

They were enjoying the difference so much that they didn't finish the number where they normally finished it. By a tacit understanding that regular musicians acquire, they continued to play, swept along on the rising tide of enthusiasm and joy that playing something well engenders. Brent took a solo, improvising, sliding and growling his notes like he'd never done before, followed by Toots whose trumpet sounds sparkled like the polished brass his instrument was made from. The next verse and chorus they all played together, followed by Kenny's promised drum solo. At Kenny's signal they all came in together again for another verse and chorus, then Ginger excelled with a banjo break that Maxine thought must surely end up with his right hand flying off his wrist. And finally, although she'd been dreading it, there came an impromptu piano solo from Maxine. She'd never had to improvise like this before, but clinging tenaciously to the principles of syncopation she worked around the basic structure of the piece – the main chords – and delivered a creditable performance that made her perspire.

Then, suddenly, by a nod and that aforementioned tacit understanding, the others stopped playing. She had not seen any signal from Brent and, for a few bars, she carried on. She turned around as soon as she realised she was playing by herself and saw them all laughing. Her first thought was that they were mocking, so she stopped – embarrassed. But they applauded. They were definitely not mocking.

'Where did you learn to play like that, Maxine?' Ginger asked.

'Yeah. Brent said you played the flippin' cello.'

'Was it all right then?' Maxine shoved a wisp of hair from her face with the back of her hand. 'Did I do all right?'

'All right? That was great,' Toots enthused. 'Sign her up, Brent. Sign her up.'

Brent placed his trombone on the floor, took out a cigarette and lit it. The others took their cue from him.

'You played that really well, Maxine,' he said. 'It made a world of difference, I have to admit.'

'A girl as good-looking as Maxine would be a big asset to this band,' Kenny commented with enthusiasm. 'She'd be a hell of a novelty. Folk would come and pay to see us just to get a look at her. God, she's bloody lovely . . . She can really play as well.'

'She might not be interested in playing with us.' Toots suggested. ' So why don't we ask *her* first?'

She was blushing again, not only at the compliments, but because she was causing so much controversy all of a sudden. 'I'd be happy to play in the band as long as it didn't interfere with the CBO. I'd love to play.'

'Brent? It's up to you, mate. But I think we're all for her joining.'

'I reckon we'd be bloody stupid to turn down the opportunity,' Charlie said. 'She'd be a brilliant attraction. We could double our booking fees *and* get twice as much work.'

'Without doubt,' remarked Toots.

That clinched it for Brent. The possibility of commanding more money was too great to resist. At once, he saw the potential in having a lovely looking girl in the band, especially a girl with real talent.

'Okay,' he said. 'Maxine, welcome to the Second City Hot Six. If you can put up with us, we can certainly put up with you.'

'Thanks. I'll do my best.'

'Are there any more at home like you, Maxine?' Kenny asked.

'Never mind him, Maxine,' Toots said. 'He's married. Not that it makes any difference. So watch him.'

'As regards the CBO, it won't interfere, Maxine,' Brent assured her. 'I don't let it interfere. We don't make bookings for when the CBO are playing or rehearsing. We couldn't have them missing a cello *and* a trombone, could we? Okay, now that's settled, what shall we have a go at next?'

'Let's ask Nat for a beer.'

'I don't know that one. Is it a blues number?' Maxine enquired, and looked surprised when the others roared with laughter.

Chapter 6

With hardly a breeze to disturb it, Rotton Park Reservoir mirrored the yellowing flare of the western evening sky and its wrack of orange cloud in its cool stillness. The air was gentle and mild and the trees, casting long, springtime shadows, wore their fresh green coats vividly in the low, brassy sunshine, hardly waving. At the water's edge three schoolboys dipped their fishing nets and one whooped with glee as he scooped out a stickleback. Stephen took Maxine's hand, which she accepted without enthusiasm, as they set off clockwise around the reservoir for a stroll.

'You been all right?' he asked.

'I've been fine.'

'Rehearsals going okay?'

'Fine.' Of course, he meant the CBO. 'We're rehearsing with the choir again on Thursday evening. Beethoven's Mass in D. It'll be the last practice before we perform it.'

'I'll pick you up after. You'll need a lift with your cello.'

'No, it's okay, Stephen. I'll get a lift.'

'Oh? Off who?'

'Off Brent Shackleton.'

'Brent Shackleton? Why him? No, I'll meet you. I'll bring you home.'

She was tired of this. She stopped abruptly, breaking the idyll. She slipped her hand out of his and turned to face him, her eyes ablaze with the fire of the sky. 'Stephen, there's something I have to tell you. I don't want you to collect me, because after rehearsal I'm going somewhere with Brent.'

'You're what?' he taunted. 'Over my dead body.'

'Listen, I've been asked to join a jazz band as pianist and I've accepted.'

'A jazz band? As if you hadn't got enough to occupy you.'

'Yes, a jazz band, Stephen. And we're practising like mad to get everything right. Thursday night, after CBO rehearsals, Brent and I are going to the jazz club to practise. He's the trombonist in the band as well, see?'

'No, I don't see, Maxine. Why couldn't you have told me about it sooner? I reckon there's something going on between you and that Brent Shackleton.'

'There's nothing going on, Stephen.' *Worse luck*, she felt like adding.

'I won't let you do it, Maxine. It's not fair. I won't let you.'

'Stephen, it's all fixed,' she rasped, hot with indignation. 'You won't stop me, either. If you try and stop me I'll stop seeing you anyway. You don't *own* me. You can't tell me what I can and can't do. What a damn cheek!'

'I don't like it, Maxine,' Stephen said sullenly. 'I don't like it at all.'

'Then you know what to do. Give me up, for God's sake. Forget me. It's not going to work anyway with you following me everywhere like a lapdog. I need to be free, Stephen. I need freedom to pursue my own life. You don't seem to appreciate that. You've never appreciated it.'

He sighed. She was right. Their romance had no chance of succeeding while she was only half-hearted about it. But what could he do? He wanted her. He wanted to be with her. Always. But what was the point of banging your head against a brick wall?

They ambled on, unsettled, their business unfinished. A hundred yards behind them, the three little boys had lost interest in their fishing and hooted with laughter as now they skimmed stones across the lake to see who could achieve most bounces. Before them, the trees and houses on the opposite side took on a dark grey hue, silhouetted against the deepening evening glow.

'Are you sure there's nothing going on between you and Brent Shackleton?' Stephen asked at length.

'Nothing at all.'

'You give me your word?'

'God!' she exclaimed, exasperated. 'On my honour!'

'So where do I fit in with this jazz band? It seems as if I'm superfluous to requirements.'

'Oh, I suppose you'll be lurking somewhere. Anyway, I want Pansy to join the band as well.'

'Oh, well, I bet Pansy would jump at the chance,' he said brightly.

Maxine smiled to herself at his sudden change of mood and imagined him asking Pansy to be his spy. Not that it would do him any good; Pansy would only tell him what she wanted him to know. But it could work against her; if he delivered Pansy to gigs he would still be around when she really wanted to see less of him.

'Will you ask her to meet me on Friday night at that jazz club in Gas Street when she's finished at the Hippodrome?' Maxine requested. 'We're playing then and I'd like her to meet the others.' She thrust her hand into the pocket of her skirt. 'Will you give her this letter? . . . It explains everything. We really do need a good clarinettist. Hearing us play might just whet her appetite.'

'All right, leave it to me,' he said. 'I'll see she comes along. I'll bring her myself.'

By half past ten on Friday night the Gas Street Basin Jazz Club was heaving with people. Cigarette smoke drifted in fat blue clouds into the high, timber ceiling, swirling lethargically around the nicotine stained light bulbs that lent the requisite amount of sleaze. Men drank pints of warm beer, as did some of the women, though most girls were sipping drinks considered more elegant. They were smart, chic in fashionable summer dresses, laughing, openly enjoying themselves.

Brent Shackleton had brought Eleanor along and she sipped gin and Italian with a practised finesse. She was beautifully dressed in a long, black, backless, figure-hugging evening dress that left little to the imagination. Yet she wore it with such dignity and elegance that Stephen, who was mesmerised at the sight of her, felt as if he was prying if he let his eyes linger. However, that did not stop him. With a girl like Eleanor around it was apparent that, where Maxine was concerned, he had nothing to fear from Brent Shackleton. It was obvious where Brent's attentions would naturally be focused. The first thing Maxine sought on Eleanor was a wedding ring; and she found one. Confirmation, if any were needed, that Brent was indeed married to her.

'Brent tells me you've made a difference to the band already, Maxine,' Eleanor said when they'd been introduced.

'Thank you for saying so,' Maxine replied graciously. 'But I'm so nervous about playing tonight.'

'I'm looking forward to hearing you. Brent says I'll be pleasantly surprised. I don't come out to hear him and his jazz very often. Actually, you're the only reason I've come tonight. He said how . . . how appealing you are – to look at – that people will come to hear the band just to get a peek at you.' Maxine perceived that Eleanor spoke grudgingly. 'I was curious to see for myself.'

Maxine smiled, gratified none the less to learn that Brent found her looks interesting.

'He really wants to succeed in jazz, Maxine,' she continued. 'I hope that, with your help, he will.'

'I suppose we all want to succeed, Eleanor – at whatever we do,' Maxine said, slighted at the implication that she should be merely a tool by which Brent's aspirations should turn to reality. 'Everything I do, I put my heart and soul into. Trouble is, we've not had much time to practise together yet, so I hope you'll make allowances. In a few months, though, we'll be really slick, so judge us then and not now.' She smiled pleasantly. 'Anyway, it's nice to meet you, Eleanor . . . If you'll excuse me. They're getting up on stage now, look.'

Maxine joined the lads on stage and took her seat at the piano. With no introductions they went straight into a King Oliver number – 'Rhythm Club Stomp'. It did not take long for the audience to realise there was something different about the Second City Hot Six. Almost at once they had everyone's attention and a spontaneous round of applause at the end of the first number. Without waiting for the applause to die down Brent counted them in for 'Royal Garden Blues', Bix Beiderbecke style, followed at once by 'Tiger Rag'. It was then that Brent introduced Maxine to the audience as the band's new pianist, at which she smiled coquettishly and waved, to a roar of approval and a barrage of wolf whistles.

Maxine kept looking to see whether Howard Quaintance had turned up. But there was no sign of him. Doubtless, without Randolf, his piano playing organist pal, he had no reason to be there. Pity. From time to time, she tried to catch Pansy's expressions to gauge whether she was enjoying the music and approving of it all. Pansy was sitting listening intently on one side of Stephen. Eleanor was on Stephen's other side, listening intently to him.

Just before the break Arthur split the reed of his clarinet. Evidently, he hadn't got a spare, so he sat out what remained of the session. This was exactly the chance Maxine had hoped for. During the break she grabbed Pansy and they both followed Brent to the bar, waiting patiently while he got served and took the compliments of one or two club members.

'Brent, can I introduce you to Pansy Hemming?' she said, giving him no chance to move further.

He was carrying three pints of beer and inevitably spilling some. 'Hello, Pansy. Forgive me if I don't shake your hand.'

'Pansy's a clarinettist,' Maxine said. 'I think I've mentioned her before.'

'A clarinettist? Hey, that would be convenient,' Brent said, flashing her a knowing look. 'So what are you suggesting, Maxine?'

'That maybe you could let Arthur go home to his dear wife and let Pansy fill in for a few numbers,' she said. 'Fancy not having a spare reed, Brent. I can't believe it. His lack of any professionalism at all makes him a liability. Not to mention his awful playing.'

Brent chuckled. 'Oh, I know what he's like . . . But could you do it, Pansy? Could you fill in at such short notice?'

'Course,' she replied as if such an activity were an everyday occurrence. 'I can play jazz – this sort of stuff. My clarinet's in Stephen's car. It wouldn't take a minute to get it.'

'Go on, then, get it, Pansy. I'll just take these pints over and have a chat to Arthur. I'll have to tell him what we're doing. I don't suppose he'll be that bothered, though. Then we'll have a chat as to what you can do.' As Pansy went in search of Stephen and her clarinet Brent flashed Maxine a perceptive look. 'If I didn't know you better I'd say you'd got this planned, Maxine.'

'Planned? Me? Listen, I know a good clarinettist when I hear one.' Maxine tagged close to Brent as he delivered the glasses of beer, talking to him all the time. 'She's brilliant, Brent. Wait till you hear her. She's stacks better than that Arthur.'

'That shouldn't be difficult. But she'll have had no rehearsal. Don't you think it's a bit risky letting her loose with no rehearsal?'

'Not half as risky as having Arthur in the band. She can improvise like nobody else I've ever heard. She can make that thing talk.'

He put the beer on the table where the other band members were in conversation. 'Lads, we've got a new clarinettist coming to have a blow with us next half.' He shrugged, as if to suggest he'd been railroaded into accepting it.

'Who?' Kenny Wheeler asked after supping the froth from his beer.

'Another girl, can you believe? A friend of Maxine's called

Pansy. She's just gone to get her clarinet . . . Look, I'll be back in a minute.'

'Christ, we'll be an all-tarts band at this rate,' Toots commented, and nudged Ginger Tolley. 'Me an' you am the wrong sex for this outfit, Ginger.'

'Oh, I don't know, Toots. I think I'd look quite nice in a frock.'

'Not as nice as that Pansy,' Kenny assured him. 'She's a beaut. Beautiful shock of red hair, nice legs, nice arse, nice tits. Bags I have first go.'

'Sod off, Kenny, you're married.'

Within a minute or two Brent returned and took the vacant seat next to Eleanor. 'Maxine reckons this Pansy's good,' he said, 'and I trust her judgement.' He took out his cigarettes and offered one to Eleanor.

'Pansy's not just a good clarinettist,' Maxine plugged, 'she's good on the piano and she sings as well. Don't you see? It means we could double up on things – make things more interesting to watch. It means we'd also have two girl singers in the band, as well as Toots and yourself, Brent.'

'Useful,' Toots agreed.

'It also means we'll have to change the name to the Second City Hot Seven,' Ginger said.

'Er . . . I've been thinking about the name,' Maxine said, looking at Brent apprehensively. 'I think we should change it to something more stylish. I mean, are we going to want to play this New Orleans stuff forever? Everything's changing . . . going to Swing. Maybe we should consider doing some Swing. It's more sophisticated, more modern.'

'But that's big band stuff, Maxine,' Kenny said.

'Not necessarily. We could play it with our line-up. Jazz is evolving. All I'm saying is that we should evolve with it.'

'It's something we should think about,' Brent concurred. 'Look, Pansy's back . . .'

When the introductions were over they compared repertoires

and it seemed Pansy was familiar with most of the pieces the band was to play.

'And if I don't know it well, I'll improvise,' she said.

As they sat talking companionably, all drinking, some smoking, it was evident that each member of the band was fired with enthusiasm for the promise of what was to come. The rapid changes would be for the better. They were at a watershed, and Maxine, a classically trained musician, had a clear vision of what was needed to make their jazz outfit really succeed. She had shown them, in the very short time she had been involved, that she had an unerring musical ear, a talent that was undeniable. Maybe she also possessed the enviable gift of being able to predict musical trends. Certainly, she had a knack of getting her own way since Brent Shackleton, their undisputed leader, allowed her to manipulate him. Maybe he recognised that Maxine had something he himself needed to be successful in jazz. Anyway, something fresh was stirring in the wind. Everything was going to be different. Everything was going to be better.

And when Pansy played it *was* different. The difference that Maxine alone had made was significant. Now that difference was doubled. Pansy played with a confidence and ability that none of the other musicians had ever seen. It surprised them totally, because this assured, creative thread of clarinet playing was coming from a *girl*; and she was no more than twenty-one years of age.

It manifested itself in the first number after the break – 'Royal Garden Blues', and Pansy handled the clarinet solo with such astonishing flair that her flamboyance and joy elicited an uplift of effort and poise from each of the others. People stopped dancing just to stand and watch. The mood of the band now was infectious; their newfound competence made them smile and project themselves to their audience with even greater panache. They were great to dance to, brilliant to listen to, but even better to watch. They had presence.

Next came a bouncy version of 'Dippermouth Blues', a King

Oliver number, which was a bit of a risk because it had an extended clarinet solo. But Pansy handled it magnificently, and even the band applauded her after it.

Brent was enjoying himself more than he could ever remember. When Maxine turned to get her timing from him he winked at her and she felt a warm glow when she saw the gleam of contentment in his eyes. She had done the right thing in introducing Pansy. It was a feather in her cap. After a few weeks of dedicated rehearsals, who knows what great sounds they might be producing, what great songs they could be performing?

'So how much money can we expect to make each week from playing in the Second City Hot Six, Maxine?' Pansy asked from the rear seat of Stephen's Austin Ten as he drove towards Daisy Road. 'I'd love to give up playing in that pit orchestra.'

'I haven't the foggiest idea, Pansy,' Maxine replied, turning her head to see into Pansy's sparkling eyes. 'Not a great amount yet, I don't suppose. But the way we played tonight . . . and *that* without a practice. If we play like that all the time we'll be getting bookings all over the place. I'm really excited.'

'And would you give up playing your cello in the CBO, Maxine, if this jazz thing really took off?'

Maxine shrugged. She loved her cello; she loved the classical music she played on it. 'I don't know, Pansy. This jazz is . . . well, it's fun but . . . I suppose there's more money to be made playing jazz than there is playing classical music, but I don't know.'

'More than playing in the pit orchestra at the Hippodrome. What do you think, Stephen?'

'Oh, I'm all for it, Pansy. I think you'll do well – very well. Eleanor was mightily impressed, and she's heard a few jazz bands.'

'What did you think of Eleanor, Stephen?' Maxine asked with genuine curiosity. 'I thought she seemed a bit snotty.'

'Snotty? Maxine you do say some things. She wasn't snotty at all. I found her very nice . . . very easy to talk to.'

'Easy to look at, too, eh?' Pansy teased. 'She should have been arrested wearing that dress. It looked as if it had been painted on – like her red nail varnish.'

'Don't exaggerate, Pansy,' Stephen said, irritated by his sister's criticism. 'I agree it was . . . well, revealing, but she wore it with such style.'

'Well I wouldn't wear anything like it. Would you, Maxine?'

'Well, let's face it, you couldn't carry it off – either of you,' Stephen responded curtly, without giving Maxine her chance to reply.

'Don't be daft, Stephen. Maxine's figure is equally as good as Eleanor's. So's mine for that matter. It's just that we're not interested in flaunting ourselves like she is.'

'Because you couldn't carry it off. Eleanor can. There's a subtle difference.'

'She's got no inhibitions if you ask me,' Pansy persisted. 'That's why. I don't see that as something to be proud of, our Stephen.'

Stephen smiled smugly to himself as he stopped the car outside the end terrace that was, for the time being, still the home of Henzey and Will and Maxine. He kissed Maxine cursorily on the lips as he bid her goodnight.

'Goodnight, Stephen. Goodnight, Pansy.' She squeezed her friend's hand in appreciation. 'You were brilliant tonight, Pansy. Absolutely brilliant.'

'Thanks, Maxine. Goodnight . . . Hey, Maxine! Do you know whether Toots, the trumpet player, is married or anything?'

'Toots?' Maxine grinned. 'I haven't a clue. I barely know him. Fancy him, do you?'

Pansy shrugged, and the darkness hid her blushes. 'He seems nice.'

Chapter 7

Stephen Hemming stopped his car behind Brent Shackleton's outside the Gas Street Basin Jazz Club and bid cheerio to his sister Pansy and to Maxine as they left him for another evening of band practice. 'See you about eleven,' he called as the two girls turned to wave before they entered the club.

'Thank God for this new business he's started,' Maxine commented. 'At least it's keeping him out of my hair.'

'I can see *you* don't mind.' Pansy said.

'Mind? I'm glad. He was driving me mad a while ago. Wouldn't let me out of his sight. At least it's taken his mind off me. Gives me a chance to get on with my own life for a change.'

Pansy opened the inner door to the club. The others were there, tuning up, fooling around. 'To be honest, I don't know how you put up with him, Maxine – how you've put up with him for so long. I wouldn't fancy him for a boyfriend. He's too self-centred.'

'Well, while the cat's away . . .' She winked at Pansy devilishly. 'I think he's losing interest anyway. I won't let him have what he wants.'

'I don't blame you, either. I can think of much nicer men to play hanky-panky with.' Pansy smiled at Maxine, reflecting her contentment as she fell into the welcoming arms of Toots Randle. 'Hello, sugar-lips,' she greeted, kissing him briefly. 'Sorry we're late. Stephen was late collecting us.'

She placed her clarinet case on a chair and went back to

Toots's arms. In the month since Pansy had joined the band, a vibrant romance had blossomed between them; a romance that did not hide itself but which was open and honest, for all to see. Both had been unattached, neither seeking romance, but suddenly it had hit them and they were enjoying it. It was reflected in their playing too. A musical rapport was blossoming between them that manifested itself in some clever and often seemingly spontaneous interplay between trumpet and clarinet.

But spontaneous it was not – at least, not always. The band had been practising intensely and the musicians, especially Pansy and Toots, had got to know each other's play better than ever. Each probed the abilities of the others and they pushed themselves and each other to the limit of their capabilities. This required many practice runs at the same piece, and a new riff that was improvised one moment, when considered worthy by the others, would become standard play in that number. But even to an experienced musician who might be listening, it seemed spontaneous.

'What's on the agenda for tonight?' Maxine asked Brent.

'Something a bit different. For a change. A friend of mine just came back from the United States. He picked up a record in New York that he reckons is a big hit there. He thought we'd be interested in playing it before anybody else cottoned on. I brought it along to listen to.'

'What is it?'

'A swing number – a bit of a novelty really. Called "The Music goes 'Round and Around". It's ideal for a seven-piece band.'

'Let's hear it then.'

Brent called everybody to order and placed the record on the turntable. He wound up the gramophone, placed the needle in the groove and they all sat in silence while they listened, Pansy on Toots's lap, her arm round his neck.

'So?' he asked, when it had finished.

'Let's hear it again,' said Kenny.

Brent played it again.

'I like it,' Pansy said. 'It's got some lovely riffs.'

'But who's going to sing it?'

'Well. It describes the course of a note travelling through a trumpet, so maybe Toots should sing it,' Brent reasoned.

'Better if Pansy sang it,' Maxine suggested logically, 'then Toots could be blowing his note while she's singing about it.'

'I don't like this new stuff,' Ginger complained. 'It's not proper jazz, is it? And we are supposed to be a jazz band after all.'

'It's swing,' Brent said.

'Like I say, it's not jazz.'

'Swing is what jazz is evolving into, Ginger. Why should we be stuck in the style of New Orleans? This new music is more varied – you get novelty songs like this for instance – beautiful love songs as well, but you still need skill to play them. It's no less taxing on your ability.'

'It'll be taxing on Ginger's,' Kenny remarked pointedly, adjusting the height of his high hat. 'There's no banjo in it. It's all guitar – amplified at that.'

'I can play guitar as well,' Ginger protested. 'Amplified or not.'

'Huh! Says you. How come we've never seen your guitar?'

''Cause we play jazz. Jazz requires a banjo.'

'Well from now on it's gonna require a guitar as well if we're to progress,' Brent advised. 'So I suggest you brush up on your guitar and bring it next time.'

'D'you think Django Reinhardt will have anything to fear?' Kenny wisecracked.

'Have we got the sheet music to this, by any chance?' Charlie asked, tuning his double bass.

'Sorry. Just this record. Let's listen to it again, eh?'

They listened once more, and took the first faltering steps in trying to play the number by ear. It was to take many hearings before each became familiar with his or her own part, but by the end of the evening they had it more or less right. Brent was happy, and Maxine was happy. The more they performed it the more comfortable they would be with it and the better it would get, meanwhile acquiring the characteristics of their own developing style.

So, at the end of the evening, they were content that their hard work had achieved something worthwhile. They talked together about this and that while they packed their instruments away and made ready to leave, a time for banter.

'Anybody want a piece of chewing gum?' Kenny asked, tossing a chicklet into his mouth nonchalantly. Pansy accepted and so did Toots. Then Kenny reached into one of the cases of his drum kit and splashed toilet water over his face.

'Off out now then, Kenny?' Toots enquired.

Kenny grinned. 'I gotta smell nice. I'm seeing a bit o' stuff. Picked her up here a couple o' Sundays ago. A right little goer. Hotter than cayenne pepper.'

'Well let's hope your missus never finds out.'

Pansy rolled her eyes at them and turned to Maxine. 'Toots is taking me home, Maxine. Do you want us to wait with you till Stephen comes?'

Maxine looked at her wristwatch. It said ten past eleven. 'No, he'll be here in a minute. You go.'

'I'll wait with you, Maxine,' Brent offered. 'We can wait in my car.'

Maxine thanked him and followed him outside, and they all wished each other goodnight. Brent got into his car and unlocked the passenger door.

'I thought that number went well, considering,' he said, lighting a cigarette when Maxine was sitting at his side.

'So did I. I'm all for trying these newer styles of jazz. I think it's got more appeal than straight, traditional jazz.'

'There's no doubt, Maxine . . . And I've been thinking . . . I want the band to have more visual appeal as well. We've proved the sound is better – that we're an accomplished band already. Now, you and Pansy are really good-looking girls. I think we should exploit that to the limit. I think you should both wear really slinky dresses that show up your every curve – something to get the men's pulses racing a bit. This swing stuff is more sophisticated, more in line with that image. Would it bother you . . . doing that?'

'Wearing a slinky dress?' She hooted at the thought. 'It's not really me, but no, I don't mind – on stage. Maybe I could borrow Eleanor's.'

He chortled impishly at her irreverence. 'It wouldn't fit. She's bigger than you.'

'I wasn't serious, Brent. I'd buy my own.'

'Great. You'll do it then?'

'If you think it's for the good of the band . . . Talking of which, what are we going to do about the name? The Second City Hot Seven isn't exactly inspiring.'

'Not in keeping with what we're trying to achieve, I agree, Maxine.'

'As I see it, Brent, the name has to reflect what we're trying to achieve. It has to do with the concept we're trying to put over.'

'Well, you two in your slinky, revealing frocks could give us a clue. How about Wayward something or other?' He looked at her admiringly and, in the half-light, she discerned a gleam in his eye. 'I wish you were a bit wayward, Maxine.'

'You could have fooled me,' she replied coolly. 'Anyway, I think we should try and project sophistication . . . Something adult. Our music is getting more sophisticated, so why shouldn't we aim at a sophisticated audience? Adults, who know their own mind, who live life as they want to live it – even in sin, if that's what they want.'

'Sophisticated Sinners?'

'Too much of a mouthful.'

'Syncopating Sinners?'

'No. I like the Sinners bit, though.'

'Swinging Sinners.'

'No, too ordinary . . . How about Sinful Swingers?'

'God, no. That's terrible.'

'Sinful Syncopators?'

Just then, Stephen's car pulled up alongside them. Maxine opened the door to let herself out. She turned to Brent. 'Wayward Swingers.'

He sniggered out loud. 'What? Sounds rude to me.'

She smiled patiently. 'Goodnight, Brent. Thanks for waiting with me.'

'Hey, Maxine. I've got it. The perfect name. The Rhythm Seekers.'

'Yes, that's good,' she replied. 'That's very good.'

'No, Maxine. On second thoughts, what has *seekers* got to do with jazz?'

She closed the door again and sat back. This brainstorming of ideas should not be rushed. 'Honey Seekers. That's got a nice ring to it. And it's jazzy. Remember "Whose Honey Are You" and "Honeysuckle Rose"?'

'How about Honey and Plenty of Money?'

She tittered irreverently. 'Wrapped up in a five-pound note, you mean? Are you serious?'

'Why not? It's from "The Owl and the Pussy-Cat". At least it has a familiar sound. "The Owl and the Pussy-Cat went to sea in a beautiful pea-green boat. They took some honey and plenty of money wrapped up in a five pound note" . . .'

Outside, Stephen hooted the horn of his car with impatience.

'The Owls and the Pussycats,' they said in unison, almost as if it had been rehearsed, and burst out laughing.

'Brilliant!' Maxine exclaimed.

'That's the one,' Brent agreed. 'The men are the owls, you girls are the pussycats – of course. It couldn't be better.'

'I'd better go, Brent. Old Face-Ache outside will be upset if I keep him waiting any longer. See you tomorrow. Thanks for waiting with me.'

'My pleasure, Maxine . . . really.'

Brent was becoming ever more aware that Maxine was no

ordinary band member. She was a woman and he was warming to her inexorably. He'd always considered her beautiful in a demure way. And that virginal demureness attracted him, especially now she was going to buy a slinky, revealing dress for their stage shows. He was really looking forward to it; to seeing her dressed to kill. The transformation from demureness to out and out glamour promised to be stimulating, and he was reminded of how it had been with Eleanor; a blossoming, innocent schoolgirl suddenly transformed into a bewitching young woman. If Maxine's complexion was anything to go by, her skin beneath her clothes would be sensational.

At each rehearsal nowadays, whether it was with the band or the CBO, Brent found his eyes always seeking hers, fishing for her warm smile. Undoubtedly she was attracted to him too, but she was evidently uncertain about him, because of Eleanor. Maxine was so talented, too; so talented that she could do wonders for his own career, and for his bank balance, which was permanently in a precarious state these days.

It was not good sense to park his car directly outside the house of the woman with whom he had commenced an affair, so he pulled up in a side street about fifty yards away. It was not normally good sense to conduct such extra curricular activities in her marital home either, but he knew that tonight it was safe enough so long as they left no trace. As he walked furtively from his motor car, his heart was pounding at the prospect of what he knew was to come. This adventure had given him a new lease of life, had put the world in a much brighter light. His hard-tolerated celibacy was at an end, for the foreseeable future at any rate. This woman was so strikingly beautiful and so anxious to let him partake of it, that even thinking about her aroused him beyond his wildest fantasies.

He tapped on the door. Almost immediately she opened it and his heart leapt with joy at the sight he beheld. The hall was in darkness, to avoid light spilling onto him outside, which neighbours might see. Yet, sufficient light enabled him to see she wore merely a glistening, diaphanous, white nightdress that buttoned down the front. She closed the door quietly behind him.

At once they were in each other's arms, seeking eagerly each other's lips before any words passed between them. As he held her, his hands roamed over the thin film of silky material that was between him and her smooth skin. He detected no underwear beneath. Urgently, he undid the buttons at the front and treated himself to a handful of breast, firm, warm and luxurious. As he kneaded one, her nipple hardened and he was excited even more by this response. She, in turn, unfastened his belt and the buttons of his fly with expertise and he felt his trousers fall and lie around his ankles.

He opened the flimsy nightdress fully, dived inside and cupped her firm small buttocks in his hands as he pressed her hard against the newel post. While their mouths were hungry for each other, tasting, tongues exploring, she thrust her hands inside his underpants and he sighed with pleasure as she withdrew him and held him as if she were fondling a priceless treasure. Then, without further ado, she parted her legs and gasped with delight as he slid easily into her.

She threw her head back, sighing, savouring the wonderful sensations, while his mouth explored her, his teeth scratching the tight, smooth skin of her neck. They slumped onto the stairs in their passion and found only minor comfort, she in the support the hard staircase afforded, he in the purchase it provided. They rocked erratically, frequently lying still to try and prolong the ecstasy. But all too soon he had to withdraw, unable to contain himself any longer, and he pumped his semen over her belly.

'I'm sorry,' he breathed. 'I'm a bit out of practice.'

She hugged him, but with bitter disappointment. 'It's hardly surprising, I suppose.'

'Give me half an hour.'

'What do you expect me to do in the meantime? Read?'

It troubled him that she sounded impatient. 'I'll do better next time . . . but not here. Can't we go to your bed?'

She shook her head slowly, deliberately. 'The sitting room. The sofa's fine.'

He rolled off her and tried to stand but his trousers, still around his ankles, ensured that he lost his balance when he moved, so he stumbled, falling back onto the stairs.

'Oh, Stephen,' she chuckled. 'You are funny. Why didn't you take them off first?'

He laughed with her, acknowledging how silly he must seem, and sat beside her on the stairs. 'I forgot I still had them on,' he muttered, untying his shoelaces. 'I'm not used to all these shenanigans.'

'Are you suggesting that *I* am?'

'No, Eleanor, certainly not.' He kicked off his shoes and reached down to remove his trousers from around his ankles. 'It's just that I've never found myself in a situation like this before. Not in a hallway as soon as I walk in.'

'Then maybe you'll have to get used to the idea,' she said with a gleam in her eye. 'Come on, let's go into the sitting room. I've opened a bottle of whisky.'

She stood up and held her hand out to him. He gathered his trousers and his shoes in one hand and took her hand with the other, allowing himself to be led into the sitting room. It was not particularly tidy and the furniture, he knew from previous visits, was past its best and shabby, though comfortable enough. The only light was from a small table lamp standing on a whatnot in the curtained bay window that lent an ambience of intimacy. Eleanor poured him a measure of whisky and leaned over to hand it to him. As she did so, her nightdress fell open, exposing herself.

'Thanks, Eleanor,' Stephen mumbled, his eyes first catching a tantalising glimpse of the dark triangle of hair between her legs, then her long smooth flanks. He gulped with disbelief. God above, was this real? Was he really so privileged as to be bedding this beautiful girl so soon after they'd been introduced; this girl who had fascinated him from the first moment he saw her? Was he really to be so privileged after all this time of celibacy trying to wheedle the knickers off Maxine Kite? The effort of all that, compared to the lack of effort required to achieve the same result with Eleanor, was unbelievable. That two girls should be so different, should take such different attitudes to sexual contact, was thoroughly confusing. But thank God for it.

Eleanor sat beside him, leaned against him and he put his arm around her. 'Why don't you take the rest of your clothes off and kiss me?' she suggested.

He felt like a god. It could never get better than this, surely?

'All right,' he breathed and nonchalantly took a sip of whisky before removing his jacket, tie, and shirt.

'Don't forget your underpants,' she said. 'And your socks . . . By the way, I hope you brought some French letters with you this time.'

He fished an unopened packet from his jacket pocket and showed her proudly, amused that she had given him no chance to use one when he first arrived, that she found him so utterly irresistible that she couldn't keep her hands off him. As he divested himself of what remained of his clothes, she shifted so that she was lying down on the sofa, then squashed up to its backrest to make room for him. He lay beside her, opened her nightdress and entertained himself with her breasts while he kissed her.

'I wonder what Maxine would say if she could see you now?' she remarked, trying to stir some life again into his nether regions with delicate fondling.

'I wonder what Brent would say if he could see his dearly beloved spread-eagled almost naked across his own sofa?'

'It's not *his* sofa,' Eleanor replied. 'It's mine. Such as it is . . .'

Stephen had a mental picture of Eleanor in the stunning dress she wore the first time he'd noticed her at the jazz club. Who would believe she had such a fine dress while her furniture was so threadbare? Such incongruity. Brent's fabulous Mercedes Benz, too, belied the impoverished state of their home.

'Surely you don't have to put up with it,' he suggested. 'Buy some new stuff.'

'What with? Brent doesn't earn enough to keep us in fine furniture.'

'But look at that car he's got. It must have cost a fortune. And those beautiful dresses you wear.'

'We had money once . . . and you have to keep up appearances . . . That's why I hope he'll do well with this rejuvenated jazz outfit and make some more money at last. At least we'll have your prissy Miss Maxine to thank for that.'

He kissed her on the lips briefly and ran his hand over her buttocks as she lay on her side. 'I hope so as well. At least while they're out playing and practising we can get on with the serious business of making love.'

'If you ever get this thing hard enough again,' she said cruelly, and felt between his legs again to check on its current state.

'Oh, it'll soon be there,' Stephen promised self-consciously. 'Why don't you tell me about Brent, Eleanor?'

'Why, will that do the trick, d'you think?'

He chuckled at her sarcasm. 'Hardly. I just wonder about him . . . about you. I don't know anything about you.'

'Why do you want to know about Brent? *He's* not very interesting.'

'Do you think he's interested in Maxine?'

'Romantically?'

'Well . . . yes.'

'I doubt it,' she said, dismissing the notion. 'He's only interested in her because of what she can do for the band and consequently his bank balance.'

'Ah! So you think he's using her?'

'He says she knows what she's talking about when it comes to music. She'll improve the band, he believes. So in that sense, yes, I suppose he's using her.'

'Where do you come from, Eleanor? You're not Brummies, are you?'

'God! Do we *sound* like Brummies? We come from the Cotswolds.'

'The Cotswolds? Fancy. Did you live there when you were first married?'

She sighed impatiently. 'Oh, Stephen, do shut up and kiss me.'

He was about to ask Eleanor why they had moved to Birmingham, but, slightly miffed, he did as she bid and kissed her. She responded eagerly, parting her legs to accommodate his thigh as he pressed it against her. While his hands explored her body once more he felt the stirring in his loins that had seemed to be eluding him, and yet which was actually recurring after a commendably short time. He reached for his jacket, acquired the packet of French letters, but knocked over the glass of whisky.

'Damn!' he cursed, unable to believe his ill luck and stood with the intention of mopping it up with something.

'Oh, never mind that,' Eleanor said impatiently, and held her arms open for him. 'Sod the whisky. Put the damned thing on before he goes limp again.'

He looked down at her, at her naked body so smooth, firm and inviting, at her outstretched arms entreating him to enjoy her. He knelt at the side of the sofa and commenced by briefly kissing her toes. Then, he licked his way up her long legs with tantalising slowness, lingering deliciously at her dark triangle of hair. Her navel he left wet with kisses, and her breasts he bit gently before teasing a nipple with his tongue; and she let out a little cry of pleasure as he entered her again at last, like a salmon wriggling up a stream.

From the moment Stephen collected her from the jazz club that warm Friday night Maxine could tell something was amiss. Strangely, his indifference seemed greater than before he delivered her there. She'd never known such a cold arrogance about him before, and she did not like it.

'You're quiet, Stephen,' she said, half chastising, but trying to strike up a conversation; they were already nearing Daisy Road. 'Is anything wrong?'

'No more than usual,' he responded off-handedly.

'Have you had a busy night then?'

'Very.'

'Obviously too busy to stay and listen to us,' she said.

He sighed impatiently, looking directly at the road ahead. 'But not too busy to come and fetch you to take you home. I made time for that, didn't I?'

'Well, please don't think I don't appreciate it. But you needn't have bothered if you had something that needed doing. Brent will always give me a lift. He won't let me wait on my own for long.'

'Oh, Brent, Brent, Brent! Brent will always do this, Brent will always do that.'

'He's already offered. It would save you the trouble. I think it's decent of him.'

'You would. What d'you think he's after?'

'Oh, don't be so childish, Stephen. I was thinking about how busy you are. So was he, if only you could bring yourself to acknowledge it. Far be it from me to interrupt your work by you having to come and fetch me. Don't think I can't imagine what it's like setting up a new business.'

They pulled up outside the house, but unusually Stephen left the engine running. 'Maxine, I . . . I, er . . . I don't really know how to say this . . .'

'Say what?' She sighed with exasperation. 'Just say it – whatever it is.'

'It's just that . . . I don't think I'm going to see you any more. I think it's for the best. I don't see any point in us carrying on, frankly. So, I've decided to . . . to stop seeing you.' He shrugged for lack of more appropriate words.

'Oh.' She sounded genuinely disappointed.

'Actually, I thought you might be pleased,' he said, self-deprecatingly.

'Pleased? Why should I be pleased, Stephen?'

He shrugged again. 'Well, you never show me any great affection. There's never any passion between us. In fact, you've never yet let me near you.'

'That sort of thing doesn't interest me, Stephen. You know that. We've talked about it often enough.'

'Well it interests me, Maxine. It interests me a great deal. Frankly . . . if you want to know the truth . . . you're too much of a cold fish for me.'

'So you want to be free to find someone who isn't. Is that it?'

He shrugged again, avoiding her eyes. 'If I meet somebody, all well and good. As you say – *you're* not interested.'

'If that's what you want, Stephen . . . If I'm such a cold fish . . . If it's that important to you I can't do much about it, can I?'

'No, I don't suppose you can.'

'If you meet somebody you like better than me, fine. I don't mind awfully, I suppose . . . So, thank you for telling me. I wish you the best of luck.'

'Thank you. So you're not upset?'

'I'm surprised, Stephen. And maybe a bit disappointed, yes. But I'll get over it.'

'Well . . . there you are then. I must say I've enjoyed our . . . our times together. It has been nice. It's been very nice.'

'Oh, don't be such a hypocrite, Stephen. And don't patronise me.' She sighed for want of something else to say. She felt sad that it was over. It was the end of an era, an important part of her life. 'I'd better go,' she said flatly. 'We're moving house tomorrow, remember, and there's still stacks to do.' She had her hand on the door handle ready to leave him, but she hesitated. 'Er . . . Do you want the ring back . . . to give to your next lady friend? You can have it back if you want it.'

'No, Maxine, it's yours,' he said impatiently. 'It was meant for you. I want you to keep it.'

'I think you should have it back. I really do.'

'It doesn't matter.'

'No, Stephen, you must have it back. I can't keep it now. The more I think about it . . .' *Especially since I'm such a cold fish.* She wrenched it off her finger, leaned over and slipped it into the top pocket of his jacket. 'Goodnight, Stephen. Thank you for the lift. Thank you for everything.' She felt a tear tremble on her eyelash then trickle down her cheek. So that he shouldn't see she turned away and opened the car door.

'I hope we can still be friends, Maxine,' he said.

Her automatic reaction was to turn to him. 'Were we ever not friends?'

'We were always *good* friends. I hope we always shall be. I'd like that.'

The glow from the street light glimmered off her tears, and when he saw he knew that she was hurt.

'Maxine! . . I . . .'

'Oh, I won't hold it against you, Stephen, if that's what's worrying you,' she said and stepped out of the car. 'I'll always be your friend.' She closed the door and walked away with as much dignity as she could muster, not looking back.

She was sad, but not filled with sorrow. Another side of her emotions told her she was greatly relieved but, truly, she had never expected this. If anybody was going to finish the relationship, it should have been her. She was the one in control of it, not Stephen. What a nerve! What had come over him?

She opened the front door and went in. Henzey and Will were still packing tea chests ready for the move as they had been most of the day. Will was methodically writing down the contents of each one as they filled it.

'You're up late,' Maxine commented. 'Shall I put the kettle on?'

'Ooh, please,' Henzey answered. 'I'm parched.'

Having put the kettle to boil Maxine returned to the sitting room, the hub of the action. She sat down, still in a state of shock.

'You'll never guess what.'

'You've decided to marry Stephen.'

'Henzey! He's given me up. He doesn't want to see me again. I can't get over it.'

Henzey stopped what she was doing and looked openmouthed at her sister. 'But he doesn't mean it, Maxine,' she said consolingly, believing her to be upset. 'I bet he doesn't mean it.'

'He does.'

'So what happened?'

'He just told me he doesn't want to see me any more. He wants to be free to chase other women. Women who'll let him have his wicked way . . . He says I'm a cold fish.'

'Sounds to me like he's already found another woman, Maxine,' Will said, looking up from his labours. 'Sorry to sound so cynical, but I bet it's true. Otherwise there'd be no point in giving you up, would there? Not till he'd actually found somebody . . . Just you think about it.'

'Gosh, Will. Do you think so?'

'It stands to reason.'

'The rotter! And he reckons he's been working hard trying to get his new business off the ground. I bet all the time he's been off with somebody else.'

'The crafty monkey,' Henzey said.

'The dirty devil,' Maxine concurred.

'He's a dark horse, our Maxine. I always had him marked down as a dark horse. Are you *very* upset?'

'I'm surprised more than anything. And disappointed. I'm not upset particularly.'

'Oh, it's a terrible thing, infidelity,' Will remarked. 'Emotional incontinence, that's what it is. Anybody who embarks on the ship of infidelity deserves to go down with it.'

Henzey looked up at Will. 'That's a bit profound,' she remarked.

'It's true, though, Henzey,' Maxine said. 'A sign of moral weakness, isn't it, Will? I could never do that to anybody. I might think about it, but when it came right down to it, I couldn't do it. I know I couldn't.'

'I've seen so many people come to grief over their infidelity,' Will said. 'At least you're not married, Maxine. At least you don't have the prospect of a ruined marriage ahead of you . . . Children . . . Divorce. Thank your lucky stars for that.'

'But only a few weeks ago he was asking me – begging me to marry him.'

'Fickle,' Will said, with great scorn. 'I've got no time for fickle folk. Good job you found out about him now and not later.'

'I bet the kettle's boiling,' Henzey said, getting up from the sofa where she had been wrapping oddments. 'I'll go and make the tea. Then I'm off to bed. We have to be up early in the morning.'

'What are the arrangements for tomorrow, Henzey?' Maxine enquired. 'Do you want me to come with you first thing, to help you put the curtains up and that?'

'No, no,' Henzey replied. 'I can cope. I want you to stay here and keep an eye on Aldo while Will takes me to the new house first. I can hang the new curtains and do a last clear up before you and the removal van arrive.'

Chapter 8

Maxine listened in awe to Boris Szewinska, the solo violinist who was appearing with the CBO, and his impassioned interpretation of Brahms's Violin Concerto. In parts she and her cello were unoccupied, and in these quieter moments she marvelled at the soloist's dexterity. Some of those passages seemed impossible, yet he not only played them with apparent ease, but also eked out emotions that sent shivers up and down her spine. Such fervent emotion. Such staccato fire. And yet, such poignant tenderness. If only she could play like that. If only she could summon passion profound enough to enable her to play like that.

Maxine had been mulling over Stephen's ditching her a fortnight ago in favour, obviously, of another girl. Why had she been unable to show him any affection? Was she really so frigid that she could feel none of the emotions that other, normal girls, evidently feel? Would ardent love, true desire, elude her forever? Indeed, would she ever recognise it if it stared her in the face?

And then, for no accountable reason, she remembered Howard Quaintance. It was during a quiet passage when the solo violin was soulfully singing a song of lost love, piercing in its plaintiveness, agonising in its intensity. Maybe she could feel these things for Howard Quaintance if she ever met him again, if she was ever blessed with the opportunity – if, indeed, he could even remember her. But she remembered him all right; how she felt when he touched her hands to swap over her ring from one hand to the other. She remembered his closeness, his unassuming geniality, the lovely manly scent of him, and the thrill of it returned bringing a lump to her throat. Maybe she *could* feel emotion. Maybe she was not such a cold fish after all. Maybe it was just that Stephen had never brought it out in her. Maybe only music could make her feel like this. Maybe she could feel nothing unless potent music was present to urge it on.

Maybe she never would.

With a deft swoop of his baton, Leslie Heward, the conductor, collected the whole orchestra into a rich swell of sound and Maxine was right on cue. The soloist, for a few bars, became just another player intermingling with the other instruments till he soared away again on another flight of extraordinary complexity and fervour. Funny, Maxine thought, how even when you are concentrating on your music your mind still considers other things; funny how Howard Quaintance had sprung to mind.

Before she knew it, Boris Szewinska was taking his bows. He took a beautiful bouquet of summer flowers that somebody handed to him, bowed again, and left the stage, showing no inclination to perform an encore. The applause continued, Boris returned and turned to the orchestra and conductor, happy for them to take a share of the acclaim.

On the way back to the dressing rooms, Maxine stopped when she saw Brent Shackleton barging his way over to her.

'When you're ready, Maxine, I'll give you a lift home,' he said.

'Oh, thank you,' she replied. 'I only have to change. I'll be a minute, no more.'

In the ladies' dressing room, she doffed the black evening dress she wore for concert nights and put on her normal Sunday attire. It was thoughtful of Brent to always give her a lift to and from concerts. To lug her cello all the way to Dudley now, alone on the tram, then walk all the way to Oakham Road and the new house, would be no mean feat especially late at night.

'Can you manage that?' Brent asked gallantly as they left the Town Hall. 'Let me carry it.'

98

'I can cope. It's no weight. Besides, you'd have two instruments to carry.'

'The piccolo player's got the best job when it comes to transport,' he quipped. 'You should have taken up the piccolo.'

'Or the triangle.'

He laughed generously. 'I'm only thankful we don't have to lug a piano about. At least the jazz club's got its own . . . Talking of which, do you fancy going there now for an hour?'

'But we're not playing tonight . . . Are we?'

'*We're* not, but another band is. The Brummagem Hot Stompers. Ever seen them?'

'No. Are they good?'

'Not bad. In any case, it's always good to evaluate the competition occasionally.'

That did it. It was reason enough. 'Okay, let's go then. You won't get into trouble with Eleanor, will you? Being late home, I mean.'

'Oh, sod Eleanor,' he said with feeling. They reached his car, parked on the street outside. He opened the door and took Maxine's cello. 'She's been a bit off lately. It'll serve her right to be on her own.'

'Maybe that's the problem, Brent,' Maxine suggested as she watched him place her cello on the back seat. 'Maybe she spends too much time on her own. Maybe you should go home sooner. You should bring her to more concerts.'

'She's not interested in concerts,' he said looking at her over the roof of the car. 'She's not interested in anything except herself. When I get home she'll most likely be in bed, fast asleep. She's probably already in bed now.' He got in the car and unlocked the passenger door. Maxine got in and made herself comfortable. He lit a cigarette, turned the key, and the big powerful engine burst into life. 'So let's go, eh?'

They had travelled about a hundred yards when Maxine said: 'You know, Brent, I feel guilty going to the jazz club with you tonight if you're not on the best of terms with Eleanor. Perhaps you should take me home.'

'What the devil for? It's nothing to do with Eleanor. In any case, I'd rather be in your company than hers.'

Maxine smiled with tenderness, flattered that Brent should make such an admission. She looked at him as he drove, the moving street lights reflected in his brooding eyes.

'It's nice of you to say so,' she said. 'But my concern is that Eleanor might get the wrong idea.' She shrugged. 'You know . . .'

'I don't care if she does.'

'But I care, Brent. Spare a thought for me. I don't want her maligning me for something I haven't done.'

'So you'd rather go home?'

'Unless you promise you won't tell her you've taken *me* tonight.'

He smiled to himself. 'Oh, count on it, Maxine. I've no intention of doing that.'

'Good. Thank you, Brent.'

They arrived outside the Gas Street Basin Jazz Club. Brent pulled on the handbrake, stopped the engine and drew heavily on his cigarette. 'By the way, there seems to be a lot of outside interest in the band all of a sudden. I've got bookings for the Tower Ballroom for a few Saturday nights, starting the week after next, and if they like us it could be a resident spot. As well as others. What do you think of that, eh?'

'That's smashing,' Maxine said inadequately, but with a wide grin of satisfaction. She showed no intention of getting out of the car, happy to learn of the band's increasing success.

'I've had enquiries, too, from further afield. Some wanting to book us up for Christmas and New Year. We can put our fees up for then, especially New Year's Eve. We can virtually name our own price.'

'Brilliant.'

'You're gorgeous in that slinky new dress, you know, Maxine.' He gave her a grin as indiscreet as his thoughts.

'Well thank you,' she replied.

'I've been thinking, Maxine. I think we should feature your singing more. I want you to be the band's main vocalist. Leave the piano sometimes and stand stage front. You've got a great jazz voice – different – but you look the part as well. We must exploit it. So, think of some more songs you'd like to sing.'

He leaned towards her, almost imperceptibly, and she could have sworn he was going to kiss her, so she tilted her head tentatively to offer her mouth. But he did not take advantage and she felt a pang of disappointment when he opened his door to get out. At once she opened the passenger door, her disappointment turning to embarrassment, for he must have noticed her intention to submit. What if he thought it too obvious? Think of something to say, quickly, to distract him.

' "Where or When?" '

'As soon as you like. At the next practice if we can.'

'No,' she exclaimed, a peal of laughter concealing her embarrassment. 'I mean can I sing the song called "Where or When"?'

'Oh, that. Sure.'

The CBO was busy with the summer season and The Owls and the Pussycats had a rapidly filling schedule too. After the Saturday promenade concerts, Maxine and Brent had to dash to the Tower Ballroom for their new series of gigs. They were booked to play a couple of forty-five minute spots, alternating with the resident dance band who, like all self-respecting musicians, welcomed the break as an opportunity to consume more beer.

But increasingly, the regular dance band were foregoing their extra beer to listen to this outstanding new seven-piece outfit. Maxine and Pansy, in their new, slinky, shiny, clingy dresses, drew wolf whistles galore, but everybody had to admire the music they were creating, and that manifested itself in loud and prolonged applause.

When Maxine sang her favourite new love song, 'Where or When?' the couples who were dancing fell into an embrace and shuffled together slowly on the dance floor, but most also had an eye on the stage, watching her. She had presence. She had style. Oh, she had everything.

Rehearsals saw them attempting more of the new swing music that was coming from America. From a specialist source in New York that Brent knew, called the Commodore Music Shop, they were able to send for records and musical arrangements. They acquired records by Jack Teagarden, Django Reinhardt, Louis Armstrong, Benny Goodman and Duke Ellington that were not available in Britain. And, as they enlarged their repertoire and their music became more sophisticated, so the booking enquiries flooded in. Would they play at this wedding, that society function? Would they give an outdoor concert in Canon Hill Park? Would they play at this town hall, that hotel?

Certainly. They would play as many as they could. Brent wanted the money. And as they played further afield, more and more people were hearing their name.

'Have you heard that new band called The Owls and the Pussycats? They're great! They're fantastic! They're wonderful!'

Word spread.

Word spread like fire in a bone-dry forest, fanned by a strong breeze.

However, Brent Shackleton's growing elation over the band was offset somewhat by a discovery he made at home late one afternoon in July. Returning from a CBO rehearsal, he went upstairs to get changed. He took off his cufflinks and went to place them in the small glass dish on his tallboy where he always left them, when he noticed Eleanor's jewellery box there too. It had been left open inadvertently. She was not overly endowed with fine jewellery, but one piece stood out among the other trinkets. It was a ring, with a huge amethyst set in a cluster of diamonds. Brent picked it up. He had seen this ring before. A ring as distinctive as this he could not be mistaken about. This ring he had seen on Maxine Kite's finger. It was her engagement ring, later transferred to her right hand. What in God's name was it doing in Eleanor's jewellery box?

After Saturday evening's CBO concert, Brent was already waiting backstage for Maxine to leave the ladies' dressing room.

'Maxine,' he said, and his cool brown eyes manifested a look of disquiet. 'I'll give you a lift to the Tower, but I can't play tonight. Something's cropped up.'

She looked at him with concern. 'Oh? What?'

'I can't say. It might be nothing. On the other hand, it could be significant. I can't say yet.'

'Well I hope it's something easily sorted out,' she said sincerely. 'But how shall we get on tonight without a trombone player?'

'Oh, you'll be okay,' he assured her. 'Nobody will miss my line. You'll cope fine.'

They walked to his car, and he drove her to the Tower Ballroom. 'The manager is supposed to let us know tonight whether he wants to book us for a resident season,' he said as he pulled up outside. 'Talk to him, Maxine, and explain that I can't be there. I'll leave it to you to sort out. But don't go below that figure we said. If they want us they've got to pay.'

Maxine nodded. 'All right. I'll see you Tuesday at practice. I hope you get it settled, whatever it is.'

He smiled ruefully and held up his hand as a departing gesture.

Funny how Maxine Kite had grown on him. Three months ago he hadn't been that interested. Nowadays, though, he considered Maxine a prospective conquest. But Eleanor alone was enough for any man. His relationship with Eleanor was strange, obsessive, and he could not help himself where she was concerned. Ever since she'd coyly let him glimpse her first adolescent triangle of soft, pubic hair, they'd been lovers and their secret had fuelled their greater ardour for each other over the years. The curious and inexpert fumblings of youth, the unexpected, uncontrived sensations they experienced together, all gathered momentum and escalated into an ardour so intense that there had been times when they simply could not get enough of each other; when they would stay in bed all day. And this prolonged, frenetic lovemaking would render them sore and exhausted for days afterwards.

But their relationship was strained at present. A couple of times in the past Eleanor had been aloof, indifferent towards him. He had grown suspicious then that she had been interested in another man. Whether or not it had amounted to anything, he did not know, short of asking her. Yet, he would not ask her for fear of learning the truth. The same suspicions had drawn him home early tonight. Something was wrong and he needed to find out what.

As Brent drove on through the poorly lit streets of Bearwood towards Handsworth where he and Eleanor lived, he thought of the other women he had had; women who had failed to divert him in the way Eleanor evidently became diverted. They meant nothing; merely conquests; food for the ego.

His thoughts quickly returned to Maxine Kite. He understood that it would be ungallant of him to try and ensnare Maxine in a sexual relationship, but only because he perceived she was forthright and had some honour; he could not reasonably expect her to be willing because of Eleanor. All the same, she was eminently beddable; and gallantry had never been his strong point anyway. Each time he looked at her he discovered something new; a different expression, a tiny mole on her arm he had not noticed before, how the light glinting off her lush dark hair reflected some other unexpected colour. She was his equal when it came to conversation, knowledgeable enough to discuss any topic. She was bright, intelligent, fun, not given to tantrums or selfishness. She would be bright, intelligent and fun in bed, too. Sooner or later he would bed her. He always got what he wanted. And he had no other competition now that Stephen was gone.

At that moment, Brent saw Stephen's car parked in Arthur Road, a side street close to his house in Grove Lane. What the devil was he doing here? This could explain the ring. Unless he was visiting somebody else close by. Brent knew few of his neighbours; by choice he did not socialise with them, so he did not know who lived where Stephen's car was parked.

But Eleanor's recent indifference and his finding Stephen's ring spelled it out, shouted it louder than any megaphone could. Of course, the crafty monkey was visiting Eleanor. Brent's mind flickered back to that evening at the jazz club when Eleanor first met him. They had chatted easily and for quite a while, but not sufficiently to arouse any suspicion. Stephen was the last person he would have considered to be of interest to Eleanor. The man was too insipid, too ordinary and too dull for somebody as vibrant and discerning as Eleanor.

Brent sat staring at Stephen's car for ages, deciding what he should do for the best. He did not want to enter the house for fear Stephen was there with Eleanor. It would be counter-productive to confront them or find them in a compromising situation. First, in any case, he *should* make sure. So he reversed his car into Mostyn Road, another side street where it was out of view and hid behind the school gates from where he had sight of Stephen's car and his own front door. One thing was certain; if Stephen was up to no good with Eleanor, he would take great pleasure in his revenge. And what more fitting revenge than to bed Maxine Kite when Stephen had manifestly failed to do so? What more satisfying conclusion than to induce her to fall in love with him? That would prove beyond any doubt that he was much more of a man than Stephen.

He lit a cigarette and waited . . . and waited.

At the Tower Ballroom, all was going well. Despite Brent's absence, The Owls and the Pussycats were giving a good account of themselves. Only they seemed to know that somebody was missing from the line-up. As far as the dancing couples were concerned, everything was fine. When they had finished their first spot they headed thirstily for the bar. Within a couple of minutes a man approached them wearing a dark suit that badly needed pressing.

'Who's the leader of your band?' he asked, addressing all of them and nobody in particular. 'I'm from the *Evening Mail*. I wondered if I could interview your leader.'

'Maybe I can help?' Maxine responded.

'But you're never the band leader, are you?'

'I am when he's not around,' she answered steadily.

'But you're a woman. Who is the recognised leader?'

'Brent Shackleton,' she said, keeping calm. 'He's not here. And when he's not around I look after anything that might crop up.'

'Okay,' the man conceded. 'I reckon you'll have to do. I daresay you're a sight prettier than this Brent Shackleton, anyway, eh?'

'But *he* can be quite charming when he's a mind to be.' Maxine responded, indignant at the man's attitude but maintaining her polite smile.

'Can I get you a drink, Mister?' Toots said, his arm as always around Pansy's trim waist, even while waiting to be served at the bar.

'Thanks, pal. That's the best offer I've had since I've got here. Pint of Ansell's . . . My name's Bill Brighton, by the way. I'm the music critic for the *Mail*.'

'Oh, I've read your column lots of times,' Maxine said, over-looking her indignation, recognising the need to exaggerate the truth in the cause of flattery and what it might buy them in free publicity. 'I always enjoy reading it.' At this, Bill Brighton's attitude visibly softened. 'So what do you want to know about us, Mr Brighton?'

'Well, word has got to us about the band. Some pretty impressive comments over the last few weeks. I wanted to come and hear you for myself.'

'Pity we're short of the trombonist then,' Toots commented. 'Trust that to happen when you come along.'

'I've heard enough,' the reporter said. 'I've been mightily

impressed . . . The name of the band, though . . . The Owls and the Pussycats? Who thought that one up?'

'Brent Shackleton and me,' Maxine answered, recalling their brain storming a while ago.'

'Borrowed from Edward Lear, eh?'

'Well, we didn't think he'd mind.' She took her drink from Toots and thanked him.

Toots handed the reporter a beer. 'Thanks . . . So who plays the runcible spoon, eh?' he roared.

'Nobody in this band, Mr Brighton,' Maxine replied straight-faced. 'The owl and the pussy-cat *ate* with a runcible spoon.'

Everybody burst out laughing.

'Oops, sorry, Miss,' Bill Brighton said, discountenanced. 'An easy mistake. And I thought I knew that poem by heart. Anyway, listen. I really like your music and I like the way you play. I reckon you've got a big future ahead of you, and I'll tell our readers that. Good bands are hard to come by. Are you professional?'

'No, we all have other jobs,' Toots replied raising his glass.

'Cheers. Do you hope to become professional?'

Nobody answered, only an exchange of uncertain glances between the band.

'Some of us would love to be,' Maxine said. 'But I don't think it will happen. Some of us are professional musicians already. I play in the CBO. So does Brent Shackleton. Pansy here plays in the Hippodrome pit orchestra. We'd have to be mighty successful to give up our regular jobs and depend solely on The Owls and the Pussycats for our bread and butter.'

'For your mince and slices of quince, eh?' Bill Brighton suggested, jeopardising his credibility with another risky witti-cism, which everybody ignored.

'I'd give up my other job tomorrow,' Pansy remarked. 'I'd love it just playing in this band.'

Bill Brighton had many more questions. Finally, he said he'd got enough information to give them a write-up in his newspaper and asked when he might send a photographer to take some pictures. Brent Shackleton would organise that, Maxine said. Brent would be in touch with him early next week.

Brent Shackleton drew earnestly on several more cigarettes before he saw his front door open and reveal a dim column of light. A tall man was momentarily silhouetted – Stephen Hemming. Brent watched him leave, turn and wave to Eleanor. His pulse raced with bitter resentment. The cheek of the man. Just how long had this been going on? He tried to calm himself down as he watched Stephen furtively cross the road to his car in the darkness. What was the sense in getting up tight about this? What sense was there in creating a fuss? Creating a fuss would achieve nothing. He would confront Eleanor, but calmly. He must not get angry like the last time. The trick was to remain reasonable. In any case, why try to compete? If she wanted him, she could have him. No amount of animated cajoling would win back her favours.

He waited till Stephen disappeared then drove his own car unhurriedly to the front of his house. Breathing deeply in an effort to maintain his calm, he locked the car and slowly walked up the path to the front door. As he opened it, he caught sight of Eleanor at the top of the stairs, floating across the landing in her dressing gown.

'Eleanor!'

She did not answer.

If they had been to bed the bedclothes would still be strewn about. He rushed upstairs and walked into their bedroom, expecting the worst. But the bed was untouched, exactly how it had been when he left home earlier; his Fair Isle pullover was still on the counterpane where he had left it. Stephen and Eleanor had evidently not been to bed. Maybe he was wrong about Stephen. Maybe he was wrong about Eleanor. Perhaps it had been merely a social call.

Eleanor was in the bathroom. He sat on the bed, his head in

his hands. Still agitated, he stood up again and walked downstairs to the sitting room. Everything was neat and tidy. Every cushion was where it should be. No used cups and saucers lay about, no dirty drinking glasses, no articles of clothing, no carelessly discarded underwear, no unwitting clues that might hint at any extracurricular sexual shenanigans. No, Eleanor was too artful to be caught out like that. Except that maybe the place was too tidy.

In the kitchen he boiled the kettle, ground some coffee beans and made himself a drink. He grabbed his half-full bottle of cheap French brandy, poured a generous measure into a tumbler and sat down with both drinks at the kitchen table, sipping the hot one, alternately gulping the one that caught the back of his throat. Why *had* Stephen Hemming been to this house? What was the creep up to?

Eleanor left the bathroom and Brent called her. This time she answered: no, why should she come downstairs? She was going to bed. She was tired. Just because he was home early didn't mean she had to sit up with him.

'I've just seen Stephen Hemming,' he called, trying to stay calm, trying to sound casual, that it was of no consequence. 'What was he doing here?'

'Stephen?' she commented as if it was news to her.

'Yes, Stephen. I saw him leave here a few minutes ago. His car was parked in Arthur Road. Why was he here?'

He heard Eleanor padding down the stairs and he lit a cigarette.

She appeared at the kitchen door looking apprehensive. The pleasant fragrance of her toilet soap was like an aura around her.

'Yes, Stephen was here,' she said evenly. 'I'm helping him with his new business.'

Brent exhaled smoke in a great gust and took another slug of brandy. 'Helping him do what?'

'Helping him get organised. He's got no idea of office routines, accounting – that sort of thing.'

'So how are you helping him, Eleanor? You know as much about office routines and accounting as I know about the inside of Hitler's trouser legs. What's going on?'

'What *could* be going on?' she asked, her sham resentment purporting innocence.

'I dread to think.'

'With Stephen? You can't seriously suggest — Nothing's going on, Brent, for God's sake. Jesus Christ, why do you think anything's going on?'

'Because I know you.'

'Are you accusing me of something, Brent Shackleton? If so, you'd better be careful. You'd better be very careful.'

'Then why are you in possession of his engagement ring? The ring he gave to Maxine Kite?'

Eleanor gasped with trepidation. 'That was *not* an engagement ring, Brent,' she answered, affecting to appear unfazed. 'Stephen would never have got engaged to *her*.'

'You reckon?' Brent slurped his coffee. 'That's not what she said. So why have *you* got it?'

'It's a sample . . . a sample of his work . . . It's a brilliant design and he's a brilliant designer. I'm going to do some canvassing for him . . . in the Jewellery Quarter. Then he wants to sell it to raise some capital.'

He studied her keenly as she answered, looking for evidence of lies. But her explanation was plausible.

'So why didn't you tell me, Eleanor? Why didn't you let me know you were trying to help him?'

'Because you would have got the wrong idea – like you did. I didn't want a row . . . again.'

'Well next time he comes, tell him he needn't park his car round the corner where he thinks I won't see it. Next time he comes tell him, if he's got nothing to hide, not to be so damned sneaky . . .'

Chapter 9

'Lord knows why you couldn't have this child baptised at St John's on Kates Hill, our Henzey,' Lizzie remarked. 'It'd have saved May and Joe their tram fares and no mistake.'

They were standing in the warm evening sunshine outside St John's church in Ladywood, awaiting the rest of the family for Aldo's christening. A peal of bells, contrasting resonantly with the family's muted chatter and laughter, melded occasionally with the whine and clatter of a tram in an abstract symphony. Already inside were Will's sister-in-law Eunice in her wheelchair and his brother, Neville, who was to join Herbert as godfather and Maxine as godmother.

Henzey chuckled generously at her mother's flippant comment. 'It's time Jesse bought a car, I should say. Then you could have brought May and Joe with you. Why don't you get him to buy a car, Mom?'

'Why would I need a car?' Jesse chipped in. 'A van, maybe, for the business, but not a car.'

'But then you'd have no need to worry about trams. Fancy having to rely on trams at your time of life, Mother.'

'You talk as if I'm on my last legs, young lady. I'll have you know I've never felt better.'

'And you look wonderful. Nobody would guess you're forty-six.'

'I would have said thirty-five,' Will said, gleefully buttering up his mother-in-law. 'You look no more than thirty-five at most, Lizzie.'

'Oh, you're a charmer and no two ways, Will.'

'It's true. If I didn't know, I'd say you were about the same age as myself.'

'Shall I hold the baby for a bit, our Henzey?' Lizzie suggested. 'I bet your arms could do with a rest.'

Henzey handed over the baby. 'Thanks, Mom. He is getting a weight.'

Will watched a tram turn from Icknield Port Road into Monument Road. It stopped outside the church and family members alighted, all in their Sunday best.

'I think maybe we should go inside and take our seats,' he suggested. 'The others are here now, look.'

Together, they tiptoed up the centre aisle. Soft, mellow music drifted over from the organ as Maxine, Will, and Henzey, holding the baby again, filed into a pew. Behind them sat the others, including Will's family. The church was well attended most Sunday evenings but, since it was the beginning of the holidays and many people were due to have gone away, a smaller congregation was expected tonight. Promptly, at half past six, the door to the nave opened and the choir and clergyman emerged in procession, headed by a chorister carrying a cross.

Maxine looked a picture in her wide-brimmed straw hat and new summer dress with a floral print. She did not heed the procession as she stood up, conscientiously trying to find the first hymn in her hymnbook. The choir shuffled into their stalls and the clergyman took his place behind them on the decanal side.

Maxine turned to Henzey. 'You're not going to change your mind about calling him Aldo?' she whispered good-humouredly.

Henzey shook her head and smiled serenely.

'We shall sing hymn number three hundred and sixty-two,' the preacher intoned, his voice ringing clearly through the beautiful 19th-century church.

Maxine thought the preacher's voice, his warm, rounded accent, sounded familiar. Curious, she glanced towards him and at once her heart started thumping good and hard. She focused her eyes on him then turned in disbelief to Henzey who was oblivious to her incredulity. She looked again at this man whose voice she was certain she recognised, peering at him intently. There was absolutely nothing the matter with her eyesight; she could not be mistaken.

It *was* him, as large as life and just as lovely.

She could never mistake Howard Quaintance.

In his dog collar, his cassock and surplice, he looked so different to how she remembered him, and far too boyish to be wearing such vestments. Her mind raced back to that May night when she first met him. He looked and acted like no preacher then, drinking his pint of beer in the jazz club like any other young man. Except that, unlike any other young man, he had succeeded in igniting something within her that only lately was she beginning to understand. But he was a clergyman . . . Or, maybe he was just a lay preacher. Yes, a lay preacher. That must be it.

Maxine could not remember singing the first hymn, although she joined in with the congregation. She could not recall the psalms either, nor the prayers while her eyes were transfixed on the young man who was leading the service so adeptly. It was only after the second lesson that she started to come to terms with the situation, when the ministration of baptism was about to take place. The family, and Howard Quaintance, assembled at the beautifully ornate font.

'*Hath this child been already baptised?*' He looked from one to the other of the godparents, and was visibly shaken when he saw, and immediately recognised, Maxine Kite, holding the child in her arms.

They all, except Maxine, answered, 'No'.

She was still too dumbfounded to utter any response. His eyes were hypnotic upon her and she coloured up with excitement. He hesitated, stumbling on his words. Reluctantly, his eyes left hers as he searched for his place in his prayer book.

'Er . . . *Dearly beloved* . . . ahem! . . . *Forasmuch as all men are conceived and born in sin . . .*' Occasionally, as he recited the ritual, his eyes left his prayer book to seek Maxine. '*I demand therefore . . . Dost thou, in the name of this Child, renounce the Devil and all his works, the vain pomp and glory of the world, with all the covetous desires of the same, and the carnal desires of the flesh, so that thou wilt not follow, nor be led by them?*'

They were supposed to answer '*I renounce them all.*' Maxine's eyes met Howard's again and, obviously possessed of the Devil, she privately made no effort to renounce her own covetous desires. Deep, deep inside, she wished that Howard could interpret her silence in the way she wished it to be interpreted, and hoped the Lord would forgive her this one sin. How could she renounce these carnal desires of the flesh, neither follow nor be led by them, when she was already being led so strongly by the very presence of Howard Quaintance? How could she renounce these carnal desires, her heart thumping mercilessly inside her chest, banging against the baby who was sleeping peacefully in her arms, when she did not yet know what the full implications were? Surely these sensations could not be so wicked when, all at once, desire felt so suddenly alive and so exhilarating within her.

'*Dost thou believe in God the Father Almighty, Maker of heaven and earth? And in Jesus Christ, his only begotten Son our Lord? . . .*'

Maxine watched Howard's lips as he tried to concentrate on what he was doing. She hoped he felt as excited as herself, but he was conducting himself with admirable poise. He still kept raising his eyes to catch hers and once she was certain he flashed her a secret smile. Next time he looked at her, she would smile back.

'*Wilt thou be baptised in this faith?*' he asked the godparents.

Maxine dispatched a dazzling smile. '*That is my desire.*'

'*Wi—* Er . . . ahem! . . . excuse me . . . *Wilt thou then obediently keep God's holy will and commandments, and walk in the same all the days of thy life?*'

'I will.' *With you, Howard, I think I would.*

'*. . . Regard, we beseech thee, the supplications of thy congregation; sanctify this water to the mystical washing away of sin; and grant that this child, now to be baptised herein, may receive the fullness of thy grace, and ever remain in the number of thy faithful and elect children; through Jesus Christ our Lord.*'

'Amen.'

'*Name this child.*'

'Aldo William Neville,' Maxine said with emphasis, trembling as she handed the baby over to Howard Quaintance.

'Aldo?' the clergyman evidently wished to verify, to Maxine's amusement.

'Aldo William Neville.' Their eyes lingered a second more than they need have done.

'*Aldo William Neville, I baptise thee In the Name of the Father and of the Son, and of the Holy Ghost. Amen . . .*'

When Howard handed the child back to Maxine their hands touched and they lingered too, and the chemistry between these two was unmistakable. She felt her heart pound the more at his closeness. She thought she was going to faint. But she must not. She was holding the child. She took a deep breath and tried to gather herself together, garner her thoughts. But this was a heady moment, and her mind was awhirl with happiness and the intoxicating realisation that she might indeed be capable of love and even healthy, hard desire, after all her cold fish self-doubt. So she held on, stoically remaining upright and, at the end of the ministration, walked back to the pew, her legs weak and shaking. Henzey asked if she was all right.

'Do you remember me telling you about a man I met at the jazz club?' she whispered, almost breathlessly. 'Howard Quaintance?'

Henzey's eyes opened wide. 'Vaguely,' she answered. 'The one who swapped your ring over to your right hand?'

'Yes.'

'You're not going to tell me that's him? The vicar?'

Maxine nodded dreamily. 'Isn't he lovely?'

Henzey smiled knowingly and sat down next to Maxine. She took from Maxine the placid Aldo who slept on, having hardly stirred when Howard Quaintance intrusively doused his forehead with cold water and mopped it dry.

Maxine remained in a trance, a reverie enhanced by the choir's rendering of Sir Charles Villiers Stanford's anthem 'Ye Choirs of New Jerusalem'. Normally, she would have relished the sound of serious music performed by serious performers, music with which she was not familiar, but to her, this evening, it was just a pleasant background to some pleasant thoughts.

Howard Quaintance preached a brief sermon and in no time, it seemed, the service was over. When the congregation filed out through the main door, each member shook hands with the visiting clergyman who knew none of these parishioners, but they thanked him nonetheless for standing in at short notice.

Will was the first of their party to express his thanks for the way the christening had been executed. He shook Howard's hand and said how ably he had conducted the service in Canon Gittins's absence.

'I do hope he will recover soon,' Howard said.

Henzey, too, shook the hand of Howard Quaintance. 'I believe you've already met my sister,' she remarked mischievously, to Maxine's surprise.

'If you mean Maxine, then indeed, I have. Under rather different circumstances.' His eyes twinkled behind his spectacles and Henzey understood why Maxine was so attracted to him. He turned next to Maxine and, though he shook her hand formally, she thrilled to the warmth in his eyes that told so much.

'You know, Reverend,' Henzey said experimentally, 'we're having a small family gathering at home to celebrate Aldo's christening. If you have no other plans for tonight, you're very welcome to join us.'

Howard grinned like an overgrown schoolboy. 'That, I would

welcome with all my heart. Thank you. But you'll have to give me directions how to get there.'

'Oh, we can wait for you. I imagine we can find a space for you in one of the cars.'

'Well, actually, I, er . . . have my own car. I could follow you.'

'In that case,' said Henzey, seizing the opportunity, 'why not let Maxine travel with you? She could show you the way.'

Howard looked delighted. 'That sounds a very practical arrangement.'

'Good. Then I'll get her to wait outside for you while I go on with my husband and the rest of the family to prepare things.'

Maxine nodded biddably, more than content to go along with this surprising development.

'That's great,' agreed Howard. 'I'll only be five minutes. If Maxine could wait for me outside . . . I must express my thanks to the rest of the congregation.'

'So we'll see you later,' Henzey added.

When they were outside in the warm evening air, Henzey turned to Maxine. 'You didn't mind me playing Cupid, did you?'

Maxine smiled coyly. 'No, course not. I just don't know how you've got the nerve, our Henzey.'

'It's not a question of nerve. *You* could hardly ask him, and he could hardly ask you with all the parishioners looking and listening, however much he might have wanted to. Anyway, it's polite to ask the vicar to a do after a church ceremony, isn't it, Mother?'

'Only right and proper,' Lizzie concurred. 'Why? What's going on?'

Henzey grinned and nestled the baby comfortably in her arms. 'I'll tell you on the way home.'

Maxine tilted her lovely face towards the reddening sun while she waited for Howard and felt its summer warmth. She pondered her own nervousness that was increasing inexorably at the prospect of being alone with Howard so unexpectedly. Fancy him being a clergyman! No wonder he didn't want to tell her what he did for a living when they first met. And fancy him being here this evening to conduct the christening. It had to be fate. It just had to be.

A tram rumbled past, breaking her idyll, clanking and scraping as it slowed down to turn into Icknield Port Road. The last of the congregation bid her good evening as they headed for home in their precisely pressed Sunday best outfits and she happily returned the greeting.

Howard took no longer than the five minutes he'd promised. She saw him exit the vestry and scan the street for her. He waved and hurried towards her, his vestments over his arm like a mackintosh.

'Maxine! I really can't believe it's you,' he said brightly.

'Me neither.'

'You look absolutely smashing. How are you?'

'Oh, I'm well, thank you, Howard. It was such a surprise to see you. You can't imagine. Everybody was expecting Canon Gittins. Is he ill or something?'

'Taken with appendicitis last night, apparently. And, true to form, the resident curate is away on holiday. So they asked me to step in . . . Lucky, that, I should say . . . My car's over here . . . Where are we going?'

'Dudley.'

They reached his car. He first placed his vestments carefully on the rear seat, then let her in.

'It's jolly decent of your sister to invite me back,' he said as she made herself comfortable. 'I really appreciate it. So what's been happening in your life? Are you still going to that jazz club with Brent Shackleton?'

'In a way, yes,' she replied ambiguously, and was pleased to note the disappointment in his eyes. 'I play in his band now.'

'The cello? You're joking.'

'Fancy you remembering I play cello,' she said, beaming at him.

'I remember everything about you.'

'Well, I play piano in the band – and sing as well. I took over from your chum.'

He started the car. 'Oh, Randolf. Yes, he told me he'd left the jazz band. I was beginning to wonder why I failed to get invitations to go with him any more, so I took the liberty of asking him. So you took his place? Fancy that . . . Hell, I can't imagine you in a jazz band, Maxine. Hardly seems a sufficiently ladylike occupation for a girl like you.'

'Well, it's not an out-and-out stomp band like it was before. It's changing. We play more American swing nowadays, more blues. More sophisticated. Less of the old traditional, stomping stuff. Even Ginger Tolley, you remember, the banjo player? He plays mostly guitar these days.'

'Who'd have thought it, eh?'

'We've changed the name of the band as well. It's no longer the Second City Hot Six. It's The Owls and the Pussycats.'

'Hey, that's a smashing name. And you're the PussyCat, I take it.'

'One of them. My friend Pansy is the other. She plays clarinet and saxophone.'

'So you're not the only girl in the band? That's good . . . It really is a smashing name for a band. Who thought of it?'

'Brent and me.'

'He's a big influence on you, is he?'

'I wouldn't have said so, Howard, but we are friends. We have to be.'

'Of course . . . I, er . . . I came to a couple of the CBO's concerts at the Town Hall, you know . . . after we met.'

'Really?' She sounded and looked surprised. 'How long ago?'

'Oh, two or three weeks after we met. I hoped I might see you afterwards, but it wasn't to be.'

'You should have sought me out, Howard . . . If I'd known you were there I'd have loved to have seen you. What a shame you didn't.'

'Well, I had no idea whether you would have wanted to see

119

me. I tend not to push myself, Maxine. Anyway, I wanted to hear you play. I wanted to see you in the orchestra. You don't mind, do you?'

'Mind? No, I'm flattered. But look at you . . . I can't believe you're a clergyman. It's the last thing I would have expected you to be.'

'I know . . . Sorry. Am I a great disappointment to you? Hell, I must be—'

'Of course you're not a disappointment, Howard. Not at all. But it is a surprise, yes . . . We have to turn left here.'

He slowed and changed down a gear. 'It really is brilliant to see you again, Maxine. I often think about you, you know. Wonder what you're doing. Somehow I imagined you'd fall victim to Brent Shackleton.'

'Victim? To Brent? Good gracious, no. As I said, we're friends. Anyway, he's married.'

'Ah, so you found out? I remember you asked me if I knew whether he was married.'

Maxine put her hands to her face in horror as she recalled it. 'Gosh, so I did. I really do apologise for that.'

'Apology accepted. Deflated me completely, you know.' He laughed generously. 'I swore I'd never forgive you. But I have – seeing you again. You were having boyfriend trouble, too. I've forgotten his name, though. I swapped a ring onto your wrong hand so nobody would be confused . . .'

'Oh, that was Stephen. He's gone,' she added dismissively. 'I'm not seeing anybody nowadays.' She held out both hands to show they were free of encumbrance.

'Well, Maxine, I can't say I'm sorry. But I expect you have enough to occupy you anyway with the band and the CBO, without having the distraction of a boyfriend.'

'I keep busy, Howard, but I could still find time for somebody I really wanted to be with . . .' She hoped she did not seem forward.

He asked her about Stephen and she told him at length what

had happened and how she felt about it. Before they knew it they had arrived at the new house in Oakham Road in Dudley.

'Look, here we are. That house there, where the maroon car is parked.'

'Didn't take too long, did it?'

Not long enough, she thought. 'Well now you'll have the chance to meet my mother properly.'

'Willowcroft', as Will had decided to call their new home, stood in its own mature grounds in Oakham Road, a desirable area of Dudley in which to live. You could easily be fooled into thinking you were in the countryside, since the factories' red brick chimney stacks were out of sight and the clang of metals was out of earshot. Compared to the modest end terrace they occupied in Daisy Road in Ladywood the house was salubrious with its four ample bedrooms.

The first time Maxine stepped inside it her voice echoed in the emptiness, she recalled. Despite the warmth of the summer weather it seemed cool in this house. Its residual aroma filled her nostrils, and it was strange. It smelled of the previous occupants; their lives, their loves, their fears, their happiness, their sadness, and not least, their cooking. It had a garage that used to be a stable, and a tiled bathroom with a separate toilet. For this was not a newly built house, but late Victorian. The previous owners had emigrated to America, seduced by the promise of greater wealth from relocating the manufacture of their precision pressings there, to serve a bigger, rapidly expanding market.

This bright evening, on this day of Aldo's christening, Maxine led Howard through the hall and into the sitting room overlooking the rear garden. Some of her family were already ensconced enjoying their usual banter. She introduced Howard to them all in turn and he stood chatting for a while with Lizzie and Jesse while Maxine went to help Henzey in the kitchen, doling out sandwiches, slices of cake and cups of tea. When

Howard rejoined her in the kitchen the others tactfully left them to be alone.

'I can scarcely believe that Lizzie is your mother, you know, Maxine,' Howard said. 'She must have been very young when she had you.'

Through the brightly curtained window she looked between the houses in the near distance and caught a glimpse of the pleasant, undulating landscape falling away into a valley before rising again at the Clent Hills on the horizon.

'She was always a bit of a bobbydazzler, by all accounts,' Maxine replied. 'Men falling at her feet.' She chuckled, like all young people making light of their parents once being young, beautiful and eminently wooable, as if such things were highly unlikely.

'Well, I can see where you get your good looks from – all of you.'

Maxine smiled demurely. 'Thank you, Howard. So you approve of my mother?'

'A lovely lady.'

'I think she approves of you, as well.'

They chatted for ages alone in that kitchen, easily, never stuck for something to say. There was a visible incongruity between them, however; he in his white dog collar, she the young, raven-haired beauty with alluring brown eyes. But any incongruity was merely in the eye of the beholder. As far as Maxine and Howard were concerned, no paradox existed.

Eventually, he looked at his watch. 'I hate to say this, but I really should be going. It's past eleven already and I have a very early start tomorrow.'

'Would you like another drink before you go?' Maxine asked, trying to detain him a few minutes longer.

'Thanks, but I'd best not.' He looked at her appealingly. 'I really do have to be up early.'

'Well, I hope you've enjoyed yourself tonight.'

'I really have. More than you know. I wouldn't have missed it. It was so unexpected and everybody has been so kind – so hospitable.' When he smiled she detected a look of sadness in his eyes. 'I suppose I'd better say my goodbyes.'

'I think they're all leaving, look. Well, I expect they all have to get up for work in the morning as well – the men at any rate. Jesse has to be up at about four o'clock. Why don't you wait till they've gone?'

They moved out of the kitchen into the hall where the families were reassembling. Lizzie opened the front door, stepped outside and stood waiting for Jesse to join her. On the doorstep a brief conference decided there was no need for Charles and Alice to give Lizzie and Jesse and Richard a lift as they were happy to walk back home with May and Joe as companions. Howard also offered to transport them but they declined and Maxine was not sorry. At least she would have him to herself for a moment or two longer.

'Go inside, Henzey, why don't you,' Maxine bid her sister, 'while I just say goodnight to Howard.'

'All right, I'll leave the catch off for you,' Henzey said compliantly. 'Goodnight, Howard, and thanks again for everything.'

'You're more than welcome, Mrs Parish, and thank *you*.' Henzey closed the door and he turned to Maxine. 'Are you too cold to walk with me to my car?'

'No, course not. It's a lovely night . . . Just look at the stars. They're beautiful.'

'Well, they look beautiful enough from here. Inhospitable places to be though, I imagine. Either millions of degrees hot, or so cold they'd freeze you solid in a flash.'

'Not like the heaven that you preach about then?' she commented wryly.

He chuckled at that. 'Hardly like heaven, even if they might occupy some of its space . . .' He took her hand, which surprised her, and she allowed herself to be led to his car, parked in the road. He said, almost in a whisper: 'Maxine, I realise you're a busy girl, but are you too busy to let me take you out one night? I'd love to see you again.'

'I'd love to,' she breathed, delight in her eyes. 'When?'
'When are you free?'
'Oh . . . Wednesday night?'
'Perfect. Shall I collect you from here?'
'Or I can meet you.'
'No, I'll pick you up here. Is eight o'clock all right?'
She smiled happily. 'Perfect.'

Chapter 10

The photographs for the *Evening Mail* were shot, appropriately, in and around the circular bandstand at Birmingham's Botanical Gardens. Birds sang from the trees with summer abandon, intoxicated by the warm, fresh smell of new-mown grass and flowers in full bloom. For the photographs the men wore their black tuxedos, white shirts and red bow ties and the girls their slinky, clingy, shiny red dresses that panchromatic film and newsprint would render a dismal grey. The photographer said with a wink that for a small consideration he would be happy to take some extra pictures on the side, for publicity purposes, to which they all agreed. So, when the photo session was done and everybody had changed back into normal day clothes, Brent and Maxine, with Pansy and Toots, decided to take a leisurely lunch together at the cafeteria. The others would return grudgingly to their jobs; except Kenny, who said he had a house call to make.

'You mean you're seeing a woman?' Charlie Holt suggested.

Kenny grinned waggishly.

'I thought I saw you chatting to somebody on Saturday night. Little blonde piece,' Toots said. 'That the one?'

'Married,' he replied in a whisper – for effect. 'Husband's a matelot. He's in the middle of the Atlantic Ocean at the moment. You have to make the most of these opportunities . . . See you tomorrow night, eh?'

That July day was hot with the sort of lazy, hazy sunshine that accompanies an atmosphere so humid that your clothes seem to stick to you. Maxine had changed into a light, loose-fitting summer dress that rendered her youthful loveliness ever more bewitching. Together, they sat out on the terrace soaking up the summer warmth and the sunshine, breathing in the scents of brilliant exotic flowers that wafted over from the hot houses.

'What would you like to drink?' Brent asked the others, detaching his eyes from Maxine.

'Something cold,' Pansy replied emphatically.

'A Vimto or something, please,' Maxine suggested.

'I'll get 'em, Brent,' Toots said. 'Anybody want sandwiches as well?'

'Oh, ham or cheese,' Pansy answered with enthusiasm. 'And a nice jam doughnut if they've got any. D'you fancy a jam doughnut, Maxine?'

'Ooh, yes please. I'll settle up with you afterwards, Toots.' Toots was always so obliging.

'I'll come and give you a hand,' Brent proclaimed.

When the men were out of earshot, Pansy shuffled up to Maxine and said, in little more than a whisper: 'Listen, I've been dying to tell you, Maxine – Eleanor Shackleton is working for our Stephen. I don't suppose Brent has mentioned anything?'

Maxine gasped. 'Eleanor? Working for Stephen? Never!'

'Has been for a couple of weeks now. She's going round all the jewellery firms canvassing for work for him.'

'Does Brent know?'

Pansy shrugged, her green eyes wide. 'I imagine he must.'

'He can't *not* know, can he?' Maxine reasoned. 'He hasn't said anything, though . . . Hey, I wonder if him going off early the other night when we were at the Tower had anything to do with it? You remember? He said he had something at home to sort out.'

Pansy gave Maxine a look that told of her growing suspicion. 'Do you think there's anything going on, Maxine?'

'Crikey, how should I know? But, hey, I wouldn't be surprised. Look how he dropped me all of a sudden. Will reckoned he must have had somebody else already to have done that.'

Momentarily, they paused their gossip, allowing this snippet to sink in. A bee, drawn by Pansy's perfume, hovered conscientiously over a bright printed flower on her cotton dress; then, discerning no profit, hummed discontentedly away, to her relief.

'Oh, Maxine, isn't Stephen a complete twit if he's having an affair with Eleanor? God, that's all we need. Mind you, heaven knows what she sees in him if it's true. I wouldn't fancy him.'

'Well, Stephen is your brother, Pansy. Whoever fancies their own brother? I certainly don't fancy mine – even if he weren't, I wouldn't.'

Pansy chuckled impishly. 'Oh, your Herbert's nice, Maxine. I quite fancy *him* anyway.'

'And you're welcome as far as I'm concerned. I'd fix you up, except that I wouldn't wish him on anybody.'

Pansy giggled at Maxine's flippancy. 'Oh, Toots is as much as I can handle.'

'Hey, *I've* got a date tonight, Pansy . . . with somebody *I* really fancy.'

Pansy's green eyes widened with curiosity. 'You dark horse! Why didn't you tell me sooner? Is it anybody I know?'

Maxine shook her head and smiled mysteriously. 'No, it's somebody I met a while ago – before I joined the band. I saw him again the other day.'

'Well, aren't you going to tell me who he is?'

'Tomorrow.' She grinned. 'I'll tell you tomorrow . . . Look, the lads are back. Don't mention it to them. I don't want anybody else to know yet – especially Brent.'

Brent and Toots appeared, each carrying a tray laden with sandwiches, doughnuts and drink.

'How much do I owe you, Toots?' Maxine queried as he laid the tray on the table and began handing out their lunches.

'Nothing,' Brent replied. 'I'm paying for yours.'

'No, you're not, Brent. You're always buying me drinks. It's time I paid.' She turned to Toots again. 'I'm paying for Brent's as well, Toots. Tell me how much I owe you.'

Toots shrugged. 'Call it two bob.'

Maxine picked up the handbag that was lying at her feet and retrieved her purse. She took out a florin and handed it to Toots.

'Thanks, sweetheart,' Brent said. 'But you don't have to.'

'Yes I do. I like to pay my whack. I don't expect you to pay for drinks for me all the time. Especially not sandwiches. I mean, it's not as if we're . . .'

'Not as if we're what, Maxine?' He looked her straight in the eye.

Maxine thought she detected a shadow of dejection in Brent's eyes and, because of what she had just learnt, she felt a strong compassion for him. She wanted to take his hand and console him. She wanted to say how sorry she was that maybe all was not well where he and Eleanor were concerned. But she could not. Of course she could not. So she bestowed on him an expression that conveyed all the sympathy she felt and said, 'I mean, it's not as if we're going out with each other.'

'Well, that sort of luck is reserved for the Stephen Hemmings of this world, wouldn't you say?'

At once Maxine and Pansy flashed apprehensive glances at each other.

'I don't know what you mean by that,' Maxine said, a mite embarrassed. She avoided his eyes, not really knowing what to say for the best. 'Stephen and I haven't been seeing each other for ages now.'

'So I believe . . . Even so, Maxine, you seem a million miles from me.' He took a bite out of his sandwich.

'You're married,' she reminded him crisply.

He shrugged. 'Either way . . . Married or not.'

'Is something the matter, Brent?' Maxine enquired plainly. 'You seem depressed. Is there something you want to get off your chest?'

He shrugged again, clearly feeling sorry for himself. 'Why should there be? Just because you're so bloody lovely – in or out of that frock – that's no reason for anything to be the matter,

128

is it? But why should I be any different, just for fancying you? A thousand men must fancy you. Those chaps that come and watch the band every week must all fancy you . . . I just joined the queue.'

Maxine raised her glass to take a drink and glanced again at Pansy over the rim. 'I don't know whether I'm being flattered or blamed,' she said, feeling helpless. 'Should I feel flattered or blamed, Brent? Tell me, please.'

'Flattered,' he said and his smile was warm as the day again. 'You're young and fresh and desirable. Of course I fancy you. What man alive wouldn't?'

'I expect it's the heat,' Pansy commented flippantly.

'For goodness sake, can we change the subject?' Maxine asked.

It was twenty-five minutes past three when Brent dropped Maxine outside Willowcroft.

'Do you want to come in for a cup of tea or something?' she asked, opening the door, glad to get out of the stifling heat within the car to the less stifling heat outside.

'It's okay, Maxine. I'll see if Eleanor's back yet. See you tomorrow morning.'

She watched him turn around and drive off, glad, as ever, of the lift home. But her overriding concern was his evident anxiety over Eleanor and his life at home. Brent had not mentioned her on the journey back, but if Stephen was having an affair with her, no wonder he was so unsettled.

Maxine was surprised that his interest in her seemed to be escalating and she wondered how much the one situation was influencing the other. Brent's increasing regard and attention was having a disturbing influence upon her; an influence that she truly did not desire now, because of Howard.

'Yoo-hoo! I'm back,' Maxine called as she entered the house that seemed so invitingly cool inside. She headed for the kitchen with the intention of having a long, cold drink. From the new refrigerator she took out a bottle of home-made ginger beer and poured herself a glass. Then, in a swirl of cotton frock, she swept out of the kitchen into the hall and ran upstairs. It was time for some cello practice; there would be no opportunity tonight since she was seeing Howard. And she wanted to visit her mother later that afternoon.

'How come you'm 'ere, our Maxine?' Alice, her older sister, said. Alice had recently returned home from work. Edward, her young son, was on her lap eating a jam sandwich. 'I never expected to see you.'

Maxine shrugged. 'Just thought I'd call and see how you all are.'

'Am yer stoppin' for your tea? Oh, careful, Edward. I don't want jam all over me frock. It was clean on today. And Aunty Maxine don't want it all over hers, neither.'

'No, I shan't stay for tea, Alice. Henzey will have got mine ready.'

'Why don't you? You can phone Henzey and tell her you won't be back.'

'But I've got a date tonight. I'm seeing somebody. I have to change into some fresh clothes.'

'Borrow something of mine,' Alice suggested. 'We're the same size. Anyway, is it anybody we know? . . . Oh, I bet I know – the vicar. Is it that vicar you'm seein'? . . . Stop that, Edward.'

Maxine nodded but had no wish to pursue that topic. 'How's Charles? Is he all right?'

Alice shrugged indifferently. 'I don't want to talk about *him*. Anyway, I heard you'd split up with Stephen. What happened?'

'It just didn't work out. We've got different interests. He thought it best that we stop seeing each other.'

'Shame really. He seemed to think a lot o' you, our Maxine. Edward, I shan't tell you again . . . So, you'm seein' the vicar now then, eh? It's different anyway, goin' out with a vicar, eh?'

'I'm going out with him tonight for the first time.' She shrugged. 'It might be the only time.'

'He's got a motor, ain't he? Is he comin' to fetch you?'

'Yes.'

'Why don't you phone our Henzey and ask her to send 'im 'ere for you? Then you can have your tea 'ere with us.'

'I suppose he wouldn't mind . . . If you'll lend me a dress.'

'Course. Then you can tell us how the jazz band's comin' along. Mom says you got plenty bookings.'

'It's going well.'

'I can see you being famous, our Maxine. Don't forget us when you'm rich an' famous.'

'Me famous? That'll be the day. Why don't you ask Charles to bring you to one of our bookings? It'd be a change for you. You'd both enjoy it. You like dancing, don't you?'

Edward heard Richard yelling to him from outside, so he slipped off Alice's lap and ran off to join him in the back yard.

'Mind what you'm up to!' Alice called. 'And no plaguin' the 'orses . . . Yes, Maxine, I'd love to. Where's the best place?'

'The Tower at Edgbaston is as good a place as any. Everybody dresses up for the Tower dance.'

'Mmm,' Alice said thoughtfully. 'I wouldn't mind goin'. It's been ages since I went dancin'. I've just had a lovely new frock an' all . . .'

So Maxine telephoned Henzey and stayed for tea; and yes, she would redirect Howard when he came to collect her; she would draw him a map. After tea they talked around the table for ages and Maxine decided it was time to strip off and have a good soak in a cool, cool bath. It had been so hot today, so humid, and she felt horrible and sticky.

She lay there for ages, wallowing in the tepid water that was so refreshing. Her thoughts drifted from Howard Quaintance to Brent Shackleton and she tried to imagine the anguish plaguing him. Maybe he needed Eleanor more than he was prepared to let on.

There came a knock at the bathroom door.

'Maxine, are you in there?'

'Yes, Mom.'

'Henzey's just phoned to say that young vicar's on his way.'

'Already?' Maxine was out of the bath as if she had been forcibly ejected from it, water dripping from her naked body. 'He's early. Tell him to wait,' she answered earnestly. 'Tell him I'll only be a minute.'

In a frantic hurry she towelled herself dry. With some droplets of water still clinging to her, she wrapped the towel around her and scurried to Alice's bedroom. She put on a clean pair of Alice's knickers and rummaged through her chock-full wardrobe for a pretty summer dress. Having found one, she stroked a brush through her hair a few times before hurriedly applying some make-up. She checked herself in the mirror. After putting on her shoes, she made her way downstairs with a calmness that belied her haste.

'Here she comes now,' she heard Jesse say as she turned at the bottom of the stairs.

When she entered the sitting room all eyes were on her and she felt embarrassed. 'Hello, Howard, I hope I haven't kept you waiting,' she said apologetically.

'Not at all, Maxine. I'm early if anything. My! You look very nice.'

'Thank you.'

'She was in the bath a minute ago,' Lizzie offered.

'It hasn't taken you long to get yourself ready, though, Maxine, eh?' Alice said, then mischievously added: 'By the way, I love my dress. It really suits you.'

Maxine gave her sister a withering look. 'I'm ready when you are, Howard.' She turned to him with a smile that instantly melted his heart and at once headed for the door so he should not mistake her intention to leave at once.

Chapter 11

'Do you like funfairs?' Howard asked, effecting a neat three-point turn in the narrow confines of Cromwell Street.

'Sounds smashing. I haven't been to one for years.'

'Good.' He pushed up his spectacles to sit more comfortably on the bridge of his nose and the thrash of the car's engine reverberated off the terrace of houses opposite. 'There's one at Lightwoods Park in Bearwood. Roundabouts, chair-o-planes, all sorts of things.'

'Oh, I saw it as I came back home this afternoon.'

'I thought we might enjoy that together. Should be fun.'

Maxine stole a glance at him. Tonight you would never know he was a clergyman, informally dressed as he was in an open-necked shirt and light-beige sailcloth slacks, ready for a pleasant summer evening. His eyes bore that boyish twinkle that she found so appealing. It was hard to believe she was out on a date, alone with Howard Quaintance at last.

'It's been so hot today,' she commented. 'What have you been up to?'

'I'm happy to say I had the day off.'

'You had the day off?' She looked at him impishly. 'I thought every day but Sunday was a day off for you.'

'Ooh, you're mocking me, Maxine.' She saw he had a gleam in his eye. 'People really believe that, you know – that we only work one day a week. They don't realise there's so much else to do. Services every day, not just Sundays. There are christenings, marriages, burials, confirmation classes, meetings with couples who want the banns read, visiting the sick, the elderly, new mothers, the bereaved. Because I'm only a curate still, the vicar tends to use me as a bit of a lackey. It never stops, Maxine, believe me.'

She picked up on one of the things he'd mentioned. 'New mothers, eh? Have you got lots of new mothers in your parish then?'

'Well, making babies seems to be an eternally popular pastime, you know. And once they've arrived it's our job to see they're welcomed into the church and baptised.'

'So what have you done on your day off?' she asked.

'I went to see my folks.'

'That's thoughtful. Where do they live?'

'Warwickshire. Near Solihull, actually. Far enough away to make my visits less than frequent.'

They drove past Willowcroft and Will's maroon Swallow SSI looked elegant parked on the gravel drive.

'Do you have any brothers or sisters, Howard? You never said.'

'I have an older brother and a younger sister.'

'Both married?'

'My brother's married, but not my sister.'

'So how come you're not married? I would have thought you were a rather eligible bachelor.'

'I suppose I am eligible now you mention it. But I don't think it would be every girl's dream to be married to an impoverished clergyman. Do you?'

She shrugged, not sure how to answer that one, aware of his eyes on her. 'I imagine it could be quite interesting. Especially if you're a sociable sort. Especially if you're well educated and know how to talk to people – how to mix with people. Bishops and suchlike, I mean.'

'Bishops?' he chuckled. 'Hardly ever see a damned bishop.'

'But I suppose *you* have to be well educated – the clergy, that is – to be able to become bishops?'

'Yes, to some extent, I suppose. Many come from the . . . how shall I put it? . . from what we tend to call the upper classes . . . the educated families . . . the old families.'

'You mean the wealthy families?'

'Wealthy in days gone by certainly. Not so wealthy these days, I think.'

'But you've been decently educated, Howard?'

'I've been lucky, but please don't think I come from a wealthy family. I should hate you to harbour that impression.'

She wanted to say it would make no difference. 'Or even an old family?'

'My grandfather's old,' he answered breezily. 'So's my grandmother.'

Her laughter was like a bell tinkling and he turned to her, smiling generously. It was so good to be with her again. After he'd said goodbye to her that first night they met in the jazz club, he never really expected to see her again. Oh, he could have turned up there at any time seeking her, but to what advantage? He was not prepared to see her on Brent Shackleton's arm, nor anybody else's, for that matter. So he had left well alone, as he saw it, except for his experimental visits to the Town Hall to listen to a couple of CBO concerts. By doing that, he'd seen her again, but only from a distance. To see her at that christening last Sunday, however, and discover that she was gloriously unattached . . . *That* had been a gift from heaven.

'So what about your family?' Maxine asked. 'Tell me about them.'

'Not much to tell really. My father's a school caretaker, my mother helps him. The house they live in belongs to the school. It's in the school grounds, actually. It's a boarding school – private. So, because my father was caretaker, I was educated there for free – one of the perquisites of his job.'

They had just driven past the Dudley Golf Club to an elevated point, overlooking Birmingham to the east.

'Pity it's not clear,' he said, glancing around. 'When there's no haze I bet you can see for miles . . . So how are The Owls and the Pussycats doing?'

She told him how they'd had their publicity photographs taken that morning, and he said he would look forward to seeing them. Then she mentioned briefly what Pansy had told her, about Stephen and Eleanor, and how Brent Shackleton seemed unsettled by it. She was careful not to mention, however, that the tide had turned and he was now showing an interest in her.

'People do create problems for themselves, don't they?' he remarked.

'I suppose what they do is their own business,' she answered dismissively. 'Anyway, why don't you come and hear us play one night? See how we've come on. Saturdays are good at the Tower Ballroom.'

'Is that an invitation?'

'Yes, if you like.'

'Thanks. I'd like to. I think I *should* get away from my tread-mill.'

'No burials that day, nor new young mothers and babies to visit? . . . Nor your parents?'

'Well, I do usually get Saturday evenings off.'

She smiled happily. 'That's settled then.'

They drove on, conversing easily about this and that, and soon arrived at Lightwoods Park.

'Look, here we are. I think I'll park right here . . .' Once he'd manoeuvred the car into position he stopped the engine.

'So what's your favourite ride at the funfair, Howard?' Maxine asked as she opened the passenger door.

'The g-g-g-ghost-train,' he said, giving a mock scared look.

As they stepped out of the car they could feel the energy from the funfair; the throbbing of generators, the rumble of rides, the screams of adolescent girls as they whizzed high through the air in swing boats, the delighted shrieks of children. And the low sun in the western sky was bleeding orange ink into the fleece of cloud.

136

'You caught the sun today,' Howard remarked, taking her hand, leading her towards the action.

'I think I did,' she agreed. 'I must remember to rub some moisturising cream over me tonight to stop my skin drying out.'

The thought troubled him.

'Yes, you, er . . . you have lovely skin.' He longed to touch her bare shoulders, to feel her warm silkiness. 'You must look after it.' He lifted her hand to examine it more closely, rubbing his thumb over the back of it. 'Your hands, too. They're so soft.'

'Thank you,' she answered, aware of this sudden intimacy and welcoming it. 'But please don't inspect the ends of my fingers where I press the strings down on my cello.'

Of course, he did. He could not resist. 'Just hard skin,' he said dismissively.

'I know. It's awful.'

'The price you pay for that talent you have, Maxine. Everything has its cost, I suppose. But that's nothing, surely.' He looked into her eyes, wide like pools of sherry with the descending sun reflected in them. He could so easily drown there. He looked at her lips. He wanted to kiss her. He wanted so much to kiss her.

Holding hands they turned and walked towards the centre of the action, and Maxine felt the sort of contentment she had never experienced before. She wanted to skip and jump and laugh and run, because she felt so carefree.

'Tell me about your music,' Howard said. 'I mean, how you became interested in it.'

'It began as a child,' she answered with a glorious smile. 'We had an old piano that was all out of tune, but I used to love to tinker on it. Then, when my father saw I had an aptitude for it, he decided to get it tuned. Old Ezme Clancey – one of our neighbours – used to give piano lessons in those days and I used to go there every week. She was a stickler as well. Every week she would give me a piece to learn and, if I couldn't play it without a mistake next time I went, there would be hell to pay. Anyway, her son, Jesse – the one now married to my mother

137

– remembered there was a cello in their attic and he gave it to me. I fell in love with it on sight. Then, when I heard the sounds it could make, oh . . . such rich, mellow, weepy sounds . . . It's such a romantic instrument you know, Howard. You can make it weep if you want to. Trouble is, it makes me weep too.'

He looked into her eyes again and saw the tears of sincerity well up, but she was still smiling. Yes, he could so easily drown in these eyes.

'So which do you prefer now, the piano or the cello?'

'I love 'em both. They're so different. The cello is really just for classical music. The piano is more versatile. I mean, you couldn't use a cello for jazz, could you? Well you *could*, but . . . But I enjoy playing the piano in the band just as much.'

'And if you had to choose, Maxine. If you had to choose a career either in classical or in jazz, which would you choose?'

'Everybody keeps asking me that. I'm very serious about classical music and my job in the CBO. I look on the jazz as fun. But why shouldn't I enjoy both? Why shouldn't I enjoy the best of both worlds?'

'Would money influence you?'

'I haven't thought about it. I'm just content doing something I love. Look, Howard! Can we go on the swing boats? They're just coming to a stop.'

'All right,' he said.

They walked towards them, more pace in their step, to where a man was collecting money for the rides. When the people coming off had cleared, they climbed the steps and sat in a swing boat opposite each other, waiting to start.

'I've never been on one of these before,' she confessed.

The other swing boats filled up, mostly with couples, and eventually they were given a push to get them started. It took only four or five swings to get the hang of it and soon they were soaring and dipping to howls of delighted laughter. Maxine had never experienced before the sensation in her stomach as she came down in a great arc, forwards, then backwards. She felt that they would surely hurtle in a full circle over the top of the arm that suspended them if they pulled any harder on the ropes, and she screamed with the anticipation of it.

Howard watched her, laughing, relishing her every whoop of excitement. It was an added bonus how the forward velocity opened the front of her flimsy skirt like a parachute when she swooped forward, to reveal tantalising tracts of creamy thighs; though to his credit, he tried hard to avert his eyes.

Breathless, they finished the ride and sought another. It was a roundabout, and it was fast. Maxine screamed as the centrifugal force urged them towards the outside of their seat and he held her tight so she would feel safe from falling out. Next was the chair-o-plane and it was the sensation of flying that appealed, banking high over the fairground.

The cakewalk was different, but a pleasure no less, especially for Howard who loved it when a sudden gust of wind from the grating below blew Maxine's skirt almost over her head. She screamed, with both delight and embarrassment at revealing her legs – and possibly her knickers – to all. Then it was the dodgem cars and the shrieks as somebody crashed into you. Afterwards, Maxine checked her arms and knees for bruises, for she thought she must surely have collected some.

The last daylight was fading from the sky; the lights from Pat Collins's fair were bright, however. A cacophony of sounds filled the air; the rumble of gears meshing, of flat driving belts, of rubber-tyred wheels whizzing over glassy wooden tracks, the throb of traction engines, the excited squeals of laughter, the scratchy sound of amplified music, a barrel organ.

'Look. There's your ghost train,' Maxine proclaimed. 'There's a queue, though. Let's go and wait in it.'

'Hang on. Let me see if I can win you a teddy bear first.'

He nodded towards the coconut shy and dug in his pocket for coins as they ambled over to the stall where a man handed him six wooden balls. Intently, he hurled one at a coconut that was deeply embedded in sawdust atop a wrought-iron stand, but missed. He weighed up his target again and threw the ball hard. It struck the target this time but the coconut refused to budge.

'How many times do I have to hit the coconut to win a teddy bear?' he enquired of the man in charge of the stall.

'Three times. But you have to knock it off the stand for it to count.'

One or two folk were gathering round watching Howard's efforts, but he was not conscious of it. His only intention was to win a teddy bear for his lovely companion and his mind was focused on that.

'Is there much chance of that?' he asked evenly. 'Those coconuts are stuck fast to the stands.'

'Well, you've got the same chance as everybody else, mate,' the man replied.

'Maybe so, but it would be fairer if the coconuts were made easier to dislodge.'

'Then everybody would win and I'd be a bloody pauper,' the man scoffed. 'These teddy bears cost money, you know. I can't afford to give 'em away to every Tom, Dick and 'Arry what comes along.'

Undaunted, Howard hurled another ball. It also hit the coconut, but the coconut would not be shifted.

'Yo'm roight, mate,' a voice at his side said. 'A bloody 'and grenade wunt shift them. It's a fiddle if y'ask me.'

Howard looked benignly at the man who had spoken. 'Well, I've hit two out of three so far. Let's see what the last three will do . . .'

Another hit. The coconut remained sitting.

'Yo've gorra good aim, I'll say that for yer.'

'Thanks. But some use it is if the damn things won't budge.'

'I bet any money they'm nailed on, them coconuts,' the onlooker said. 'Hey, mate – am they nailed on, them coconuts?'

The man in charge of the stall lifted one from its bed of sawdust. 'There y'are. Course they ain't nailed on. That wouldn't be fair, would it? Nailed on!'

Howard missed the next altogether. 'Damn.' One to go. Try a different coconut; the one next to it is sitting higher in its cradle. He threw as hard as he could – so hard that he thought it would impede his ability to aim accurately. But with an almighty crack the ball struck and rebounded off. The coconut teetered on the edge, then fell to the ground to a huge cheer from the sizeable group that had now gathered.

'There. Told yer they wasn't nailed on.'

'If I wanted to buy a teddy bear, how much would it cost me?' Howard asked.

'One o' these?' the man pointed to one of his selection. 'Seven an' six.'

'And what about that one there? The bigger one.'

'Ten an' six.'

'Ten an' six?' the other man gibed. 'I could buy a decent pair o' shoes for that.'

'Tell you what,' Howard said. 'Since I've already hit four coconuts and only one fell, how about if I give you seven and six and you hand me the big teddy bear? Does that sound fair?'

The stall holder shook his head. 'Can't do it, mate. Sorry.'

A murmur of disapproval rippled through the growing crowd.

'So it's no use any of us havin' a go then?' Howard's ally suggested to the stall holder. 'Not if we got no chance o' knockin' any o' them coconuts off. Christ, it's hard enough just to hit the bloody things, then, if they won't budge, what's the point?'

'Dead right, mate,' somebody else muttered.

The crowd murmured their agreement.

'So we might as well all bugger off then, eh? What's the sense in payin' good money for summat that's a fiddle? I *was* gunn'ave a goo meself to try an' win a teddy for our bab, but where's the sense? No good throwing good money after bad, is it? I'd be better off buyin' one from Lewis's.'

The man in charge of the stall, realising that his chance of profiting at all from this was rapidly diminishing, decided it was

141

time to try and win back some of the goodwill that was draining away. He said to Howard: 'Go on, then, give me seven and six and you can have the big teddy.'

'Thanks,' Howard said gratefully, and from his back pocket pulled out a ten-shilling note. The deal was done, and he turned to Maxine with a big grin and handed her the teddy bear.

'Oh, Howard, thank you,' she said. 'But you went to a lot of trouble and expense.'

'Come on, let's go,' he whispered over the hubbub, of which he was the cause. 'Let the rest sort it out between themselves. I got what I came for.'

'The ghost train now?' she suggested.

The ghost train, she reckoned, was sufficiently frightening for her to huddle to Howard for protection. He cheerfully cocooned her in his arms while she screamed with joyous horror at the skeletons and disgusting witches that swooped and clawed at her, and the sham spiders' webs that slithered over her face and through her hair, sending cold shivers down her spine. She was both glad and sorry when they re-emerged into the warm night air and the bustle of the fairground.

'Are you hungry?' he asked.

'No, I'm not hungry, Howard. Why? Are you?' She'd been enjoying herself too much to think of her stomach.

'Do you fancy a drink? We could go to a pub. Personally, I could murder a pint.'

'Okay. Let's go to a pub.'

So they walked hand-in-hand, content in each other's company, towards a public house called 'The Dog'. Howard came back from the bar clutching a pint of bitter for himself and a half-pint of shandy for Maxine. He set them on the table and sat beside her.

'I love this teddy,' she said enthusiastically, her eyes sparkling, holding it to her like a little girl hugging a rag doll. 'He's beautiful. Oh, I'll always love him . . . Will you christen him for me, Howard?'

'Gladly.' He took the bear from her as if it were their child. 'Name this teddy bear,' he said, parodying the Christian ritual.

'Maldwyn,' she grinned.

He laughed joyously. 'Maldwyn? Why Maldwyn?'

'I think it suits him.'

'Okay.' Howard dipped his fingers in his beer, trickled a couple of spots over the teddy bear's forehead and said, 'Maldwyn, I baptise thee in the name of Atkinson's Ales,' before handing it back.

'Thank you, Howard.' She chuckled and gave Maldwyn a hug. 'You know, I thought that man at the coconut shy was going to get funny with you.'

'Oh? I don't think so. He could see everybody was siding with me and he was likely to lose business. He had to make some offer to save face. Anyway, I'm content. I reckon I had a bargain.'

'I can see you're a bit hard-headed for a clergyman. I'll have to watch you.'

He quaffed his pint long and hard and licked his lips. 'Not hard-headed, Maxine. Not at all. But I hate to be taken for a fool. It was so obvious those coconuts couldn't be moved.'

'Except for the one.'

'Yes, the token one.'

'I've really enjoyed the funfair, Howard. Thank you for taking me.'

'The night's not over yet, Maxine, is it?'

'I hope not.' Maxine sipped her shandy and put her glass back on the table pensively. 'Do you disapprove of people having illicit affairs, Howard?' she asked.

'Excuse me?' He regarded her curiously. 'That's a strange question. What makes you ask that?'

'Well, you know Brent Shackleton? We think his wife is having an affair with Stephen Hemming. You remember me telling you about Stephen? The one who wanted to be engaged to me. The one whose ring you took off for me. You remember?'

Howard nodded. 'Of course I remember. But who's to approve

or disapprove? Who knows what they feel for each other? If they are so strongly attached, something draws them. Who am I to suggest that exquisite feelings between two people shouldn't exist? When two people are ardently in love, all other considerations are forgotten.'

'What if it's only sex that draws them?'

He laughed in admiration of her clear-sightedness . 'You mean lust? Oh, it'll burn itself out pretty soon, I imagine.'

'By which time the damage to her marriage will be beyond repair.'

'I imagine so.'

'What's the Church's view on adultery, Howard?'

'Simply, that *thou shalt not commit adultery* – that marriage was ordained as a remedy *against* such behaviour . . . that – and I quote – "*such persons as have not the gift of continencey*" – that is, those who cannot keep their hands and other parts of their anatomy to themselves – "*might marry and keep themselves undefiled members of Christ's body*".'

'And do you believe that?'

'Yes, I do, Maxine. The principle of it at any rate. Marriage is for life and the married partners should remain faithful.'

'But what if a couple have made a mistake marrying each other? What if their marriage turns out to be a hell on earth?'

'Is Brent's marriage a hell on earth?'

'I've no idea. But I wasn't meaning them specifically. People fall in love with someone else along the way sometimes, don't they? Someone other than the person they're married to.'

'Of course. It happens. Sometimes people can't help feeling something for one person that they don't feel, or have ceased to feel, for another . . . And people change. They change their views, their interests, their priorities. Married partners likewise change, and often in different directions. That's when the problems start. But society, if nothing else, applies the pressure of respectability, Maxine, so most couples end up putting up with each other for the sake of it.'

'With one, or both, having a bit on the side.'

Her terminology amused him and he chuckled. 'Quite possibly, I suppose, if they feel they can get away with it . . . if their consciences allow them to do it.'

'So you don't altogether disapprove of someone having a bit on the side?'

'I can understand it in certain marriages, but I don't condone it, Maxine. There's absolutely no substitute for a stable marriage partnership. Of that, I'm convinced. It's the best way to rear children. It's the best way to bring children up as responsible citizens.'

In the smoky atmosphere of the pub Maxine was suddenly conscious of someone approaching from behind; a perception that cut through the general hum of conversation. She decided not to turn round to see who it was but a tall, slender woman walked past her, her figure striking in the elegant dress she was wearing. Maxine recognised her at once and bent her head so the girl could not see her face if she turned around. A man followed her; Maxine saw a familiar pair of brown brogues and grey flannels as he brushed past her. Then she caught a whiff of the girl's perfume. She couldn't help but look up and watch them make their exit. The man's hand went to the small of her back to guide her gently through the door in front of them, then he pressed his hand intimately against her backside. Maxine caught her breath, but her very pause from conversation spoke volumes to Howard who caught her look of astonishment.

'You look as if you've seen a ghost. Was that somebody you know?'

'That was Stephen and Eleanor.'

'Talk of the Devil . . .'

'Oh, poor, poor Brent!'

'Poor Brent indeed, Maxine. But at least, he's not your worry.'

'Yes . . .' she replied, but without conviction. Somehow, she thought he might well end up her worry, although she did not like to say as much.

145

Chapter 12

'I've really enjoyed tonight, Howard,' Maxine said. Her voice was breathy, intimate, little more than a whisper, enjoying the privacy of his car.

Howard smiled, grateful for the confirmation, and she could just discern in the darkness the delightful curl of his lips. 'It hasn't exactly been a chore, Maxine,' he replied.

'I'm glad.'

'I'd love to see you again. Do you still stand by what you said about going to the Tower Ballroom on Saturday?'

'Yes, course,' she breathed.

'Then I'll see you there, if that's all right. What time do you normally arrive?'

'Not until after the CBO concert's finished at the Town Hall. About half past ten, maybe quarter to eleven . . . But why don't you come to the CBO concert as well?'

'You know, Maxine, I'd love that.'

'I could get you a ticket. Then I could meet you before the concert and hand it to you.'

'Great idea. But let's go one better. Let me collect you from here and take you.'

She hesitated. Brent would be expecting to collect her. He might think it ungracious of her to break that routine. But if Brent collected her as normal and she returned with Howard, wouldn't that seem even more ungracious? Oh, damn Brent! She could not live her life for *him*.

146

'I don't mind,' she agreed. 'As long as you don't mind carting my cello as well.'

'Mind? It'll be a privilege.'

Pausing, he took off his spectacles and looked at her intently. The catchlights from the lighted windows of the house glistened in her soft, soulful eyes as she held his gaze with an unmistakable expression of admiration.

'I can see better close to without my glasses,' he announced. 'I can see your hazel eyes better now.'

'I can see yours better too . . .'

'Maxine . . .' Something in his voice made her heart skip.

'Yes?' she answered expectantly.

'Would you mind awfully if I asked to kiss you? I . . .'

'No, I wouldn't mind at all, Howard . . . Not at all.'

'Good . . . Then, may I?'

Her leaning towards him and tilting her head was consent enough. His arms went about her and their lips met at last.

Instantly, the feel of his lips on hers was exotic, delightfully soft, accommodating. Such lips were meant for kissing . . . and then, even more kissing. She could not break off. She did not want to break off. To break off would be the most difficult thing in the world. How long they kissed she did not know, for she was not timing it but, when eventually their lips parted, she sighed heavily as he squeezed her with a great hoard of affection.

'Oh, Howard,' she breathed, delighted. Never had she believed she could enjoy a kiss so much. She felt released from her fears of being a cold fish. Physical contact was going to be repulsive no more. This she enjoyed. She longed to feel his kiss again. It awakened so many other sensations, heightening awareness of her own tingling sexuality. 'Mmm, that was nice. Would you mind kissing me again?'

The expression on her lovely face was so intense and he gladly obliged. As their lips met a second time he stroked the back of her neck, and a tremor ran down her spine in response; a shiver of pleasure.

'Oh Howard . . .'

'Yes?'

'Kissing you is really nice.'

'You sound surprised.'

'I didn't mean it like that. Sorry.'

'Well, you enjoyed it no more than I did.'

She had discovered so much about herself in these fleeting moments. And it was because of him. 'I'm really glad you kiss so nicely. You don't know how important it is to me . . .'

He kissed her again. His right hand rested at her waist and he was aware of the soft warmth of her body so inviting, so damnably inviting.

For the first time since his ordination, Howard Quaintance wished he were not a man of the cloth. To be an ordinary Joe, unshackled by the religious expectations of morality that bound him to a state of celibacy before marriage, would be much, much preferable right now. If this affair progressed further – and later he intended to offer a private prayer to the Almighty that it would – he knew he would be too weak-willed to abide by those religious expectations. He was a man, first and foremost. He was flesh and blood and at the mercy of all the natural desires the Almighty bestowed on man. He was driven, as is every man, by a pounding heart and that irrepressible surge of blood to his loins that is the engine of all man's desires. His religious calling could not gainsay that. Even as he kissed those soft, succulent lips, as he held her in his arms, he made a decision: he would not struggle with his conscience where Maxine Kite was concerned if this affair progressed that far. There would be no mental conflict between what she or the Church required. *Maxine* would be his priority. *Her* emotions, *her* expectations, *her* desires, would always take precedence.

Brent Shackleton had gone to bed with a large glass of brandy and an inkling that his world was about to cave in. Through several cigarettes, he pondered his situation with growing unease. Sitting up in bed, he finished his brandy, damning Eleanor's liaison with Stephen Hemming. Eleanor had taken to going out at night quite regularly – something she had not done before – but even more disturbing was the hours she was keeping. Everything pointed to a growing involvement with Stephen. It was just so obvious.

Yet something surprised him; he was not angry. He should have been hopping mad but he was not. Oh, he was saddened by the whole thing; surprised that she had involved herself with such a nonentity as Stephen, and particularly concerned about what she might divulge. But angry? No.

In a way, he was relieved. He fancied the taste of new flesh and Eleanor's actions could free him to pursue Maxine Kite more earnestly, whom he needed now perhaps more than he needed Eleanor. In truth, his thoughts lately had not been entirely focused on Eleanor; much of the time he'd been thinking about Maxine, taking advantage of the time he spent with her, trying to turn her head. Recently she had given him no reason to feel encouraged. Their relationship depended on their music, existed because of it. Not so long ago she had shown more than just a spark of interest in him, but the discovery that he was married had deterred her, and would no doubt deter her still.

The brandy was finished, the last cigarette stubbed out. Brent switched off the light and settled down, warm under the single sheet. His thoughts meandered on, about Eleanor, about Maxine, the CBO, the band. He could not sleep. Outside he heard the rattle and thrum of a car engine, a voice raised in anger – Eleanor's voice – followed by the slamming of a car door, hurried, defiant footsteps, the key turning agitatedly in the front door lock.

Well, well! They had had a row.

He would pretend to be asleep. He would pretend he had not heard.

She opened the bedroom door and entered quietly. In the darkness he heard the rustle of her clothes as she undressed – perhaps for the second time tonight for all he knew – and the sound of her going out again to the bathroom. He peered at the clock and could just discern that it was half past one in the morning. Five minutes later she lifted the sheet and slid into bed beside him.

She was naked. Because of the heat.

Inch by inch she snuggled closer. Her arm came across him tentatively at first, gently caressing, trying to ascertain whether he was asleep, and he could discern her minty toothpaste breath near his face.

Maybe it was not because of the heat.

He felt himself harden.

'Are you awake?' she whispered.

He feigned a yawn and stretched. 'I am now. What time is it?'

'I don't know. What time did you come to bed?'

'About half past eleven,' he said.

'And how long have you been in bed?'

'God knows . . . an hour?'

'Then it must be about half past twelve,' she suggested, confident she would get away with it. 'Put your arm around me and kiss me, Brent.'

'Where have you been till now? It's way past that time.'

'Oh, do shut up, Brent.'

She snuggled up to him and found his lips, giving him a long, probing kiss that sent him a message he had certainly not been expecting to receive that night. Her hand reached between his legs and stroked him sensuously. She pressed her moist, lightly perspiring body against him and he rolled on top of her, her breasts yielding as his own chest pressed against them. Almost at once he entered her, surprisingly easily, as if she had been ready for this, and he revelled in the familiar luxury of her slippery softness.

But too soon he had to withdraw. To prolong the ecstasy he had to withdraw.

'Don't stop already,' she hissed, her disappointment obvious.

'I had to,' he groaned.

'By God, Brent, you're bloody useless . . .'

'Sorry . . .'

'Oh, don't put one of those damned things on. It'll be all right now – this time of the month.'

'If you're sure . . .' His tongue left a wet trail between her breasts, down past her navel and over her belly before it was swallowed up in a warm crop of dark, damp curls.

Next day, Eleanor and Stephen pulled up outside a detached house at Selwyn Road in Edgbaston. The elegant dwelling, overlooking Rotton Park Reservoir, was to let and Stephen already knew how much it would cost in rent. Realistically, it was beyond his means but, in his eagerness to impress Eleanor, and especially since their tiff last night, he was prepared to make himself afford it. There had, after all, been a great deal of interest in his new jewellery-design venture and already commissions were abundant. He had sold the ring he'd designed for Maxine for a handsome price and, in three months' time, he would be making so much money he would not even notice the rent. He might even be looking to buy a house.

He switched off the engine and turned uneasily to face Eleanor with a smile that begged both forgiveness of his trespasses and approval of his lofty aspirations.

'Nice, isn't it?'

'Quite *bijou*, I suppose,' she answered, affecting some disinterest, justifiably, she believed. 'I'd like to see inside before I make any further comment.' She looked around her condescendingly. 'It's a fairly good area, I suppose. At least it overlooks the lake. What time did that chap say he would be here?'

Stephen looked at his watch. 'About now. I told you last night what time.'

'Well, maybe I wasn't listening.'

'Listening! You weren't speaking either.'

'You know why I wasn't speaking. I don't want your prissy Maxine Kite mentioned again.'

'She's not *my* Maxine Kite. She's nothing to do with me any more.'

'So why were you so damned concerned who she was with when we saw her last night? If she's nothing to do with you any more what the hell does it matter?'

'Just natural curiosity, Eleanor. Nothing more. It doesn't matter . . . Let's not argue about her any more.'

'I'm getting out for a breath of air,' she said, underscoring her annoyance. 'My clothes are sticking to me like I don't know what in this too awful car of yours. I'm going to wander along the road and take a peep at some of the other houses along here. Some of them look *very* nice.'

Stepping out of the car into the hot summer sunshine, he followed wordlessly.

'Is he coming by car – this chap?' Eleanor asked as Stephen joined her on the pavement and obsequiously took her arm.

'Haven't a clue.'

'Didn't you have the gumption to ask?'

'I never thought.'

'Then how will you know him?'

'Eleanor, I just assumed we'd know each other by dint of actually meeting here. That's obvious, I would have thought.'

'It might be obvious to you, Stephen, but I like things more cut and dried.'

'Well, you can't get it more cut and dried than that. Here, look. I bet this is him now . . .' They watched a man striding towards them expectantly. 'Good afternoon . . . You must be Mr Paisley.'

'Indeed.' The man smiled vigorously. 'Mr Hemming? Very pleased to meet you . . . Mrs Hemming . . .' he held out his hand and they shook it in turn, catching each other's eye to acknowledge the man's incorrect but forgivable assumption. 'Have you been waiting long? Sorry if I've kept you waiting.'

'Not at all,' Stephen said affably. 'We were enjoying the sunshine.'

'Yes, it's a beautiful day again.'

'This is quite a nice area,' Eleanor remarked to Mr Paisley. 'I've not been down here before.'

'Oh, very select,' Mr Paisley responded with great assurance.

'Reflected in the price of the rent, of course,' Stephen commented wryly.

'But an excellent property, Mr Hemming. And elegantly furnished. Of course, it represents an excellent opportunity to take advantage of this delightful neck of the woods, so convenient for the city. Do let me show you the property . . . After you, Mrs Hemming.'

They turned and headed for the front door. As they walked up the short gravel drive, Mr Paisley delved into his trouser pocket, withdrew a set of keys, and thrust one into the lock. They entered.

'Oh, very imposing,' Stephen remarked approvingly. 'Just look at that staircase, Eleanor. The handrail itself is a work of art.'

'The carpet feels lovely and soft under my feet,' she conceded.

'Moving along the hall . . .' Mr Paisley said, 'here, we have a cloakroom . . . That door there is to the drawing room, and the one over there is to the dining room. This door here . . .' he gestured to a door under the staircase, 'leads to the cellar, which is exceptionally dry, clean, and with ample wine racking. My client is a connoisseur of fine wines, you know.'

'Might he have left some in the cellar, by any chance?' Eleanor enquired, tongue-in-cheek.

Mr Paisley shook his head and smiled. 'Unfortunately not.'

'Pity. I'm very partial to a glass of champagne.'

'Obviously a woman of exquisite taste.'

'A woman of expensive taste, Mr Paisley,' Stephen said frankly. They followed Mr Paisley as he led them through this door and that. Then, as she entered the dining room, Eleanor gasped. Never had she seen such furniture. The highly polished cherry-wood table, chairs and sideboard were positively regal, compared to what she was used to. She imagined a brilliant, silver cande-labra adorning the table laid with a sumptuous feast for important guests. An Italian marble fireplace distinguished the room, and an elegant Art Deco lamp standard, the likes of which Stephen had never seen but admired enormously, stood sublimely in a corner.

'Are you allowed to tell us who your client is, Mr Paisley?'

He shook his head. 'Suffice to say, Mr Hemming, that the family have emigrated to one of the Carolinas – health reasons – the lady of the house, you understand. If, after two years, they decide to stay there, which in my humble opinion is likely, then this house is to be sold. Meanwhile, it is available for rent on a two-year lease as I discussed with you. My client is keen that the lessee should be a professional gentleman – preferably, er . . . without children . . .' He looked from one to the other apologetically. 'Someone with some empathy for the fine furnishings, you understand. Someone who will nurture the place, who will care for it. I take it you are a professional man, Mr Hemming?'

'Oh, indeed, yes, Mr Paisley. I am a jewellery manufacturer.'

'Indeed. Ah!' Approval.

'This is certainly a fine room, Mr Paisley.'

'I'm certain the whole house will impress, Mr Hemming, Mrs Hemming . . . Let's move on, shall we?'

When they had seen the rest of the house, they descended the impressive staircase in procession, led by Mr Paisley. Eleanor turned to Stephen and silently signalled her approval of the house by raising her eyebrows.

'So, Mr Hemming,' Mr Paisley said, 'the choice is yours . . . I think you'll agree it is an excellent property.'

'And liable to be up for sale in a couple of years,' Stephen reminded himself. 'Mmm . . . I'll take it, Mr Paisley. I'll take it.'

'Excellent . . . Er . . . Do you have children, by any chance, Mr Hemming? Mrs Hemming?'

'Oh, no,' Stephen answered with finality. 'I think we qualify nicely on that score.'

Brent Shackleton, relieved that his relationship with Eleanor seemed to have taken a turn for the better, was even more confused and frustrated when she returned home early that evening, having evidently reverted to the former aloofness that was all too symptomatic of her affair with Stephen Hemming. So, last night's lovemaking had been just her way of getting back at Stephen after a row. Nothing had really changed. And when he analysed his feelings in more depth, apart from the resentment he harboured at having been used, he found he was still as indifferent to her as he had been before.

Tchaikovsky's Symphony No. 6 seemed the perfect choice of music for a humid summer's evening. Despite the clammy heat, Howard Quaintance imagined easily the glistening frost of a heroic Russian winter invoked by the bewitching melodies and glittering blend of instrumental sounds. It was a musical feast enriched by the sight of Maxine, at one with this great orchestra. Frequently she would glance his way and the warmth and admiration for him in her look as she caught his eye made his heart leap. Never had he witnessed such feminine grace, such fluidity of movement as he saw now in her playing of the cello. She was mesmeric, yet so lacking in awareness of her sensuality, oblivious to the effect she had on him. He wanted her, oh, God, how he wanted her. He remembered her lips last Wednesday night, cool, succulent, like lush petals unfurling from a bud; chastity and sexuality existing within her symbiotically. Now, he was drifting on a tide of sensuous recollection of those luscious moments as well as anticipation of more.

The interval came, and Howard remained near the front of

the auditorium while many around him headed for a frantic drink at the bar in the short time allotted. He thumbed through his programme absently, imagining the moment when Maxine would be at his side once more, when he would be able to hold her and tell her with his eyes how much he was already in love with her. He wanted her to know, but it was too soon yet to actually say the words. He wondered fleetingly whether she might appear from backstage and stay with him for a minute or two, but she was evidently unable to. So he sighed and waited, with ultimate patience, for the second half of the programme when she would appear again.

Rimsky-Korsakov's *Scheherazade* was the perfect finale to a programme of more modern Russian music. Howard pondered the creativity of the Russian composers; the vitality, originality and emotion that seemed to explode like brilliant beams of dazzling sunshine from behind dense black clouds.

Soon enough the concert ended, overrunning its time by nearly fifteen minutes. It meant having to dash with Maxine to the Tower Ballroom, encumbered by her cello. On the way, she asked Howard how he'd enjoyed it.

'Immensely.'

'Then you should come to every performance,' she suggested. 'I can always get you a ticket.'

'Count me in,' he responded happily.

'Not for August, though. There are no more concerts in August.'

'You mean you have a holiday?'

'From the CBO and two weekends clear of bookings for the jazz band. I'm looking forward to the rest.'

They got out of his car and Howard took the overnight case in which Maxine always transported her slinky, clingy dress that she wore for jazz bookings. When he had locked each door she took his hand with such endearing familiarity, as if it were the most natural thing in the world, that his heart rejoiced at the spontaneity of it.

Inside the ballroom, Maxine met the others and introduced Howard.

'I know you, don't I?' Brent said brusquely. 'You're a pal of Randolf who used to play piano with us.'

'That's right,' Howard admitted affably. 'He's the organist at my church.'

'Being a church organist is about his level. How is he? Seen him lately?'

'I see him every Sunday.'

'Tomorrow's your lucky day then, eh, vicar?' Brent remarked acidly. 'But, hey – no need to give him my regards.'

'God, no. We wouldn't want to upset him unduly.' This cynical response was warranted, Howard felt, for he could not condone Brent's anti-social attitude. The man might be suffering emotional turmoil over his woman, but his curtness took Howard aback.

Brent turned away, acknowledging neither him nor Maxine further.

With a frown she nudged Pansy. 'What's up with him?'

'He's jealous,' she whispered.

'Of who?'

Pansy gave a sideways glance at Howard who was laughing at something Toots had said, and Maxine understood. But she was disappointed in Brent's attitude if jealousy really had instigated it. He had no right to be jealous. He had no call on her, no prior claim. Besides, he was married, and just because his wife was having a fling with her own previous boyfriend, that was nought to do with her. She would tell Brent not to be so churlish.

'I have to go and get changed,' she said, turning to Howard. She warmly gave him a peck on the cheek. 'We're on in five minutes. See you later.'

Pansy followed her backstage and into the dressing room they shared with the other band members. It was customary by now for the men to turn away tactfully while the girls stripped to their underwear to change their dresses, and tonight was no exception. It did not take more than a moment for both girls to

157

wriggle into their stage dresses and fasten each other's hooks and eyes.

'You're a dark horse,' Pansy said conspiratorially. 'I know you said you had a date in the week, but he's a bit tasty.'

Maxine turned and smiled contentedly. 'I know. He's not bad, is he?'

'You keen on him then?'

'Yes, I like him,' she said demurely. 'Very much.'

'Brent called him "vicar". He's not really a vicar though, is he?'

'No,' Maxine replied, applying a layer of fresh lipstick. 'He's a curate.'

'Honest?' She laughed with incredulity. 'He's a curate?'

'What's wrong with that?'

'He'll probably end up being the Archbishop of bloody Canterbury,' Brent interjected. 'His sort always do.'

'Oh, shut up, Brent.' It was the first time Maxine had ever spoken to him as sharply. 'What right have you got to complain?'

'No, I won't shut up, Maxine. You'd better watch him. He reminds me of that Stephen Hemming.'

'He's nothing like Stephen Hemming.'

'Says you. Whether he is or not, I'll lay odds you'll come to a sticky end with him if you don't watch it.'

Maxine made her eyes wide with mock astonishment. 'Mmm. Brent makes it sound rather exciting.'

She glanced at Pansy and they burst into peals of laughter.

The following day, Brent Shackleton received a telephone call from somebody called Dan Robertson. He was the photographer who had taken their pictures at the Botanical Gardens the previous week. The proofs were ready and could they meet so that Brent could see them and tell him which and how many he wanted? Brent suggested meeting at The Woodman at twelve-thirty.

Dan was already standing at the bar, talking to another man

when Brent arrived. They recognised each other and shook hands.

'Nice to see you again, Brent. What would you like to drink?'

'I'll have a pint of pale, please.'

'You've met Bill Brighton before, haven't you?' Dan asked. 'The reporter who did that feature on the band.'

'No. I think we missed each other when you came to listen to the band,' Brent said. 'We spoke on the phone though, a day or two later.'

'Which band's this?' Bill queried.

'The Owls and the Pussycats. I'm the one who wasn't there the night you came to listen to us. Had I known you were coming, of course . . .'

'Well, there's a turn-up for the books!' Bill Brighton offered his hand and Brent shook it vigorously. 'The Owls and the Pussycats. Great outfit. I like your sound. Even without the trombone you were good.'

'Well, you gave us a good write-up. Thanks very much for that.'

'Credit where it's due. Those girls are good, aren't they? Where did you find them? Lovely-looking girls, as well.'

'Yes,' Brent agreed. 'We're lucky to have them. They're a big asset.'

'Two big assets, eh?' Bill suggested bumptiously, nudging Brent on the arm and winking. 'Two big assets apiece . . . eh?'

Dan Robertson handed Brent his pint. 'Cheers.'

'Cheers!'

'I've got those photos of 'em here, Bill.'

'Why didn't you say? Let's have a squint at 'em.'

From a briefcase at his feet, Dan withdrew a large brown envelope and took from it a sheaf of full-plate photographs.

Brent quaffed his beer, then handed his cigarettes round. While they lit them, Dan handed over the photos to the journalist.

'Superb,' Bill Brighton said. 'Lovely-looking girls. You should go far with those two . . . I know one thing – I wouldn't mind going all the way with either of 'em.'

'Who wouldn't?' Brent agreed.

'That redhead! Cor! I love redheads.'

Brent did not wish to be drawn into a bawdy conversation about his two female colleagues and thought a change of tack might be appropriate and do the band some good. 'Why don't you come and hear us again, Bill? Come and hear the full line-up. If you thought we were good as a six-piece, you'd be more than impressed with the full line-up. And we've worked on some newer material since.'

'Actually, I'd love to. If only to get a look at them madams again.' He guffawed at that. 'I expect they're already fixed up?'

Brent nodded.

'Ah well. Never mind. I'll come anyway. It should be an aural as well as a visual treat, eh? . . . Tell me, Brent – have you got much work on?'

'Pretty fair. Two nights a week regular. Occasionally three.'

'I expect you'd like to turn professional?'

'I already am. I play in the CBO as well.'

'But there must be stacks more money playing jazz.'

'If you get well known. If you're in demand. If you broadcast. If you make records.'

'That's a lot of "ifs", Brent. I get to know quite a lot of people. Influential people. There's one chap it might pay you to get in touch with. Tell him about the band, the sort of stuff you play, your aims. Send him a couple of those photos. Let him see what beautiful girls you've got playing with you and stress how talented they are. I mean, Brent, an outfit like yours could be a really big draw in London as a show band.'

'So who is this chap?'

'Seth Cohen. He runs an entertainment agency in London. He books bands like yours for shows and big important dos. Get in with him and you could be made.'

Brent drew deep on his cigarette, looking pensive. 'But just a letter and a couple of photos might not be enough to tempt him – enough to offer us anything. I mean, he'd want to hear us.'

'Yes, I imagine he would. He'd want to see you performing.'

'Well, he's hardly likely to trek all the way from London on the strength of a letter from its leader.'

Bill Brighton mused over the photographs again. 'You know . . . for a small favour, I might be able to pull some strings.'

'What sort of favour?' Brent queried.

'Fix me up with one of those girls. The redhead.'

'She's spoken for, Bill. Well and truly.'

'The dark-haired one, then. The sharp one. I ain't that fussy.'

Brent pondered Howard Quaintance and his intense dislike of the man. 'Mmm. Leave it to me, Bill,' he answered with a wink.

'Sounds all right to me.'

'So what sort of strings can you pull?'

'When I get back to the office I'll telephone Seth Cohen for you. I'll give him the name of your band as a hot tip. I'll tell him how good you are. I'll tell him where you're playing regular . . . Where are you playing regular by the way?'

Brent told him.

'Okay. I'll tell him he ought to come and see for himself, else he could lose out. I'll tell him another agent's interested but I reckon he should get in quick. I'll tell him you're going to send him some photos . . . The dark-haired one, eh? . . . Mmm . . . No, leave it all to me. I'll send him the photos as well. Coming from me, it'll be better. You're right, he might not take so much notice of a letter from you. After all, you're biased.'

'Well thanks, Bill. I'll see as you're fixed up with Maxine . . .'

They shook hands.

'I always had the feeling us two could work something out, Brent.'

Chapter 13

At practice the following Tuesday, the band learnt 'I'm Gonna Sit Right Down and Write Myself a Letter', the vocal taken by Maxine. Then they perfected a bright, zippy number that had recently come from America called 'Just One of Those Things', composed by Cole Porter for the Broadway show *Jubilee*. Brent dreamed up a sparkling trombone solo to be complemented immediately afterwards by Pansy soloing on clarinet, then Toots on trumpet. It promised to be one of their standard numbers. Maxine polished a love song she had been practising at home called 'He's Funny That Way'. She insisted that it be done in a very plaintive way, with only her own piano accompaniment, incidental rhythm guitar, and double bass. The rest of the band had no objection; they could disappear from the stage for a drink while it was being performed.

While they were running through 'He's Funny That Way', Brent took advantage of his rest by studying Maxine. She was, without doubt, the most talented person he had ever met. Her instinct for knowing how to interpret a song never ceased to astonish him. Many a time at rehearsals they would have discussions, sometimes heated, on how a particular song should be performed, but he almost always had to concede that hers was the better way. He usually consulted her nowadays over any musical arrangements he was writing. The upshot was that the band was developing a style and sound of its own. Even though the numbers they played were by other artists and generally well known, they put their own stamp on them, rendering them unmistakably theirs.

Maxine halted progress of the song to establish with Ginger Tolley when he was to come in with his amplified guitar. It did not seem appropriate to introduce the guitar too early.

'What's wrong with me coming in right from the top?' Ginger asked.

'Because it enhances the song and the arrangement to come in at the beginning of the verse after the chorus,' Maxine said. 'Let's try it.'

So they tried it again, with just piano and bass to start and her vocals, of course. At the point she wanted Ginger to start playing, she nodded to him. The mellow jazz chords melded perfectly with the two other instruments, and yet were exquisitely understated. Its effect induced beams of approval from the others.

At the end of the song, Maxine turned to Brent. 'Wasn't it classier done that way?'

'I have to admit, it adds to the overall effect. It's a quiet, serene sort of number done this way. Maxine's right, Ginger. We shouldn't overcook it. It sounds better now. Let's hear you go through it again . . .'

Brent watched Maxine's hands as she played the introduction on the piano, her right hand deftly trickling semiquavers, her left hand accompanying with soft, sustained jazz chords. She had beautiful hands; elegant, eloquent, smooth and gentle; to put rings on those slender fingers would be to spoil them. His eyes travelled over her tanned right forearm and he noticed how flawless her skin was. He would love to see her with no clothes on. God, he would love to finger all that lovely warm skin, feel it writhing passionately against his own. He watched her mouth. Her lips were even more succulent, even more beautifully animated as she sang. Why had he not seen long ago how sensual her mouth was? He tried to imagine kissing her. He watched her lightly tanned bosom rising and falling with every controlled breath. Her breasts were pushing against the thin cotton material of her low-cut summer dress, nipples nudging tantalisingly against the bodice. Then he allowed his eyes to roam over her skirt to witness how it outlined so tormentingly the contours of her thighs as she sat. Hopefully, her liaison with Howard Quaintance would not last. But why not try and turn her head anyway?

'That was great, Maxine,' he said and began applauding. The others did likewise. 'Brilliant. I think you've got that one off to a tee now. Are you happy with the double bass part, Charlie?'

Charlie said he was.

'Okay, so let's run through the other songs again – then we'll call it a night.'

When they had finished and packed up their instruments, Brent stepped over to Maxine.

'Do you want a lift, Maxine?'

'Please, if it's no trouble.'

They left the building and walked to his car. When they were aboard he fired the powerful engine and they were on their way.

'That number you did tonight, Maxine . . . It was superb. You really know how to put that stuff over.'

It was how she felt, she wanted to say; she was in love, that's why she could put it over so well. It came from the heart. But she merely thanked him for saying so.

They discussed their practice. It had been a fruitful night and they were both pleased with the results. They were travelling past the hangman's tree when Brent said what he really wanted to say.

'Maxine, I've been thinking about you a lot . . . On a personal level . . .'

She turned and looked at him apprehensively. 'Oh?'

'I'd love to take you out one night. Let's go out and have some fun together, you and me. We get on well, we have similar interests.'

'We do, I agree.'

'And I fancy you like hell, Maxine . . .'

'You said so before,' she replied trying to sound modest about it. 'Brent, I'm really flattered . . . but . . . but already I'm seeing Howard and I'm very fond of him. He's fond of me, too . . . It wouldn't be fair. And besides, you're married. You know I wouldn't dream of going out with a married man.'

'Maxine, if you knew how I felt about you, you wouldn't turn me down quite so heedlessly.'

'Well, you just said you fancy me,' she replied. 'So what? I suppose you fancy lots of girls. You won't exactly be heartbroken if you can't have me.'

'But I'm aching inside for you. I have been for ages. And to watch you become taken with another man is painful, Maxine. Very painful.'

'I'm sorry.'

'And anyway, I don't think he's any good for you. I think he's the wrong sort . . . Too serious . . . Hell, Maxine, he's a vicar. He'll try and put a stop to your going out nights and playing in the band.'

'Let me be the judge of that, Brent.' She did not appreciate his comments very much but was touched that he should appear concerned.

'I care about you,' he said persuasively. 'I want you. I want to look after you. I want to be your man . . . As regards Eleanor, I'll give her up – gladly – today if you want me to. Just say the word.'

They pulled up outside Willowcroft and Brent tugged at the handbrake. His arm crept around the back of her shoulders.

'Why now, Brent?' she asked.

'What do you mean – why now?'

'When I first joined the CBO I would've fallen at your feet. I think you know I was quite taken with you . . . before I knew you were married, that is. Why choose now to capitalise on it? Why choose now when I'm already seeing Howard Quaintance?'

'I wasn't certain of my feelings then. I am now.'

'Oh, Brent . . . Don't. I'm not worth it, believe me. I'd be no good for you. I'm not sexually experienced or anything like Eleanor must be . . . I'm not even sure I want to be. I just want to play my music. I don't want a complicated life.'

'Just say you'll go out with me, Maxine.'

'I *can't*,' she said decisively. 'You see me often enough – mornings and evenings. God, we must spend more time together than the average married couple. I can't be involved with you more than that, Brent.'

He shrugged and took his arm from round her. 'I won't give up, you know, Maxine. I might retreat now, but I won't give up. So be warned . . . And remember – all's fair in love and war.'

'I'll bear it in mind,' she replied.

Over the next few weeks, Brent did not allow her to forget it. Although he was never gushing, she was affected by his persistent declarations of his feelings. The trouble was, she was never quite sure why he really wanted her; never quite sure whether what he felt was good honest lust or plain jealousy over Howard. It seemed certain that whatever he felt was exaggerated by Eleanor's obvious lack of devotion, so maybe he was just lonely and needed a shoulder to cry on. She felt sorry for him and felt the necessity to humour him a little, but not sufficiently to give him the wrong impression.

And all these confused emotions began to percolate into her relationship with Howard. She loved Howard. She knew it was love, because she always looked forward to the next time they were to meet; she missed him terribly when they were apart and hated it when he left her at night. But, with all these distractions from Brent, she wondered how Howard perceived her strength of feeling; did she seem sufficiently committed in his eyes? Could he discern her distraction? In their tender moments, she had already whispered that she loved him, and she meant it, but was she sufficiently convincing? She wanted Howard to be under no illusion and her guilt began to fuel her need to compensate. She must prove her love beyond any doubt.

She saw she was about to get the chance one morning at the end of August when she and Henzey were having breakfast after Will had gone to work.

'Are you enjoying your holiday, Maxine?' Henzey asked.

'I'd be enjoying it more if Howard and me could go away to the seaside or something for a week. Look at the weather – it's beautiful.'

'You'd be talked about scandalous, our Maxine. Word might even get to Howard's church.'

Maxine buttered a piece of toast and nodded. 'I know. We've been out on day-trips here and there but it's not the same.'

'Are you going out Saturday night?' Henzey asked speculatively.

'We've got nothing planned. Why?' She bit into her toast.

'Will and I have been invited to dinner with Neville and Eunice. We need a babysitter . . .'

'That's all right, Henzey,' Maxine replied, at once appreciating the potential. 'Me and Howard would be happy to stay in and baby sit.'

'Are you sure?'

'Course I'm sure.'

'Thanks, Maxine. Will can let him know tomorrow. We do appreciate it.'

'I wish I could do it more often, Henzey. You seldom seem to go out. Any night we're free Howard and me could baby sit.'

'I didn't like to ask before.'

'I'm quite happy to baby sit with Howard.' She gave Henzey a knowing look. 'You won't be home too early, will you?'

Henzey chuckled at what her sister was implying. 'Far be it from me to spoil your fun, Maxine . . . So why don't you make a real evening of it and cook him a meal? You could light some candles and make it really romantic.'

'Yes, a nice, romantic dinner by candlelight . . .' Maxine smiled joyously. 'Hey, that's a smashing idea. I could buy a bottle of wine. Any ideas what I could cook for him?'

'Oh, we'll think of something . . .'

Maxine sipped white wine from one of Henzey's crystal goblets, then peered over the top of it. Her eyes, sparkling like brilliant, full-cut brown topaz in the candlelight, met Howard's with a jubilant smile.

'And what did you say it's called, this dish?' he asked.

'Chicken Marengo.' She spelled it out. 'M-A-R-E-N-G-O.'

'I'm impressed.'

'With my spelling, you mean?'

He hooted with laughter. 'That as well.'

'Do you know where it comes from – the dish?'

'Marengo? – But that's just a wild guess.'

'Stop mocking, Howard.' She tittered then sipped her wine again. 'Well, I'm going to tell you. After the Battle of Marengo in eighteen hundred, which Napoleon won in Italy – against the Austrians, by the way – he sent some men to forage for food for his supper and all they could find was chicken, tomatoes, onion, garlic and a bit of smoked bacon. So they mixed it all together and cooked it in wine. Better that than let their glorious leader Napoleon starve, they thought. As it happened, it turned out quite tasty and, by all accounts, it became one of his favourite meals. He always referred to it as Chicken Marengo.'

'So there's garlic in it?' Howard queried.

'Some. There doesn't have to be but there is in this. Don't you like garlic?'

'You won't want to kiss me.'

'It won't matter if we've both eaten it. Like with onions. Have some more wine, Howard . . .' she picked up the bottle and topped up his glass.

'You'll have me drunk.'

'What are you like when you're drunk? . . . But I bet you don't get drunk, do you, being a clergyman?'

'It has been known, Maxine. Especially when I was a student at theological college. We're not all saints, us clergymen. Not by any means. And certainly not at college.'

'Have you ever been drunk on communion wine?' she asked, replenishing her own glass.

'Once or twice – but not at church. Mind you, I have heard tales about some of our more elderly brethren toping on the stuff. Anyway, finishing off what's left after Holy Communion gives you an appetite for your Sunday lunch.'

'How come when I take Holy Communion, the vicar only ever allows it just to touch my lips? Why am I never allowed a good swig? It isn't fair.'

'I just told you. He has to save it for himself for later. I'd let you have a jolly good swig, though, Maxine. I wouldn't be stingy.'

Love radiated from her eyes that seemed extra large by candle-light. She reached over the table and put her hand on his momentarily. 'You're kind, Howard . . . I'm really pleased you've enjoyed my cooking. It's not something I do often. Now, let me clear these plates away and we'll have some pudding.'

'Pudding? You're spoiling me. What sort of pudding?'

'Apple pie, laced with cinnamon – and lashings of thick cream.'

'Sounds inordinately wicked.'

'Mmm, I hope so.' Their eyes met and held. 'It's about time we started to be wicked.'

She collected the plates and took them into the kitchen where she slipped them into a bowl of sudsy washing-up water to soak. Two minutes later she returned to the dining room with the apple pie and cream.

'How big a piece can you manage?' she asked.

'Big,' he replied assertively. 'I do have a weakness for apple pie.'

She cut him a piece and spooned dollops of thick cream over it. 'I made the pie myself.' She handed it to him and watched him, her elbows on the table, her face in her hands. 'Go on, tuck in.'

'Aren't you having any?'

'I'll burst if I eat anything else yet. I might have some later.'

'Mmm. It's delicious.'

'Good . . .' She watched him a moment or two longer, then said, 'It's funny how we enjoy fruit, isn't it, Howard? Why don't we eat flowers, I wonder? Some flowers look as though they might be really tasty, don't you think?'

'Such as?'

She shrugged. 'Well, daffodils for instance. They look all buttery. And roses look as though they'd be all sweet and syrupy with maybe just a hint of tartness. I bet they'd make a lovely pudding.'

'I imagine they'd be tasteless,' Howard ventured. 'Like grass.'

'Have you eaten grass?'

He burst out laughing. 'You are a treasure, Maxine. Of course, I haven't eaten grass. It's just an impression.'

'You must think I'm mad,' she said.

'Deliciously so.' He pushed the empty dish away from him and leaned back on his chair. 'I think you're the loveliest, most amusing, most delightful girl in the world and I love you for it . . . I think I'm very, very lucky.'

She finished the wine in her glass and poured herself another. It was going to her head but so what? The moment was already heady.

'I think I'm lucky, too, Howard,' she whispered, sincerity oozing from her eyes. 'I can't imagine life without you now.'

'Maxine,' he whispered and his voice was loaded with emotion. 'I daren't even try to imagine life without you now. Life, before you came along, was just . . . so dull, so uninspiring. But not any more . . .' He finished off his pudding and pushed his dish away, then raised his glass to her. 'Here's to us, Maxine. Here's to the future.'

She raised her glass and drank with him.

'I've got a song I want to sing for you,' she said, getting up from the table. 'Let's go in the sitting room to the piano.'

They got up from the table and she took his hand as they strolled into the next room, stopping for a moment to listen for any sound from Aldo. All was quiet.

She placed her glass on top of the piano and sat at the stool. He watched her from an armchair. For this very special evening, she was wearing a long black evening dress in the latest fashion, pencil slim and elegant. It enhanced every curve of her body, but tastefully. If he had not been aware of it before, he could see now how perfectly proportioned was her figure.

She ran her fingers over the keyboard. 'Tell me what you think of this,' she said. 'It's a beautiful love song.' She began the introduction, and then she sang 'He's Funny That Way'.

Howard could not help but be moved by it. 'Is that a new number in the band's repertoire?' he asked when she'd finished.

'Yes. I've been practising it a while. Do you like it?'

'It's beautiful. Did you write it yourself?'

She smiled as she walked over to him, perching herself in his lap. 'God, no. I wish I could write a song like that. Brent got the record and the sheet music from his contact in New York. I just embellished the piano part a bit.'

'It should go down well . . . Snuggle up to me.'

She snuggled up to him and raised her head to look into his eyes. 'I'll always think of you when I sing that song. I'll always think of this night. Oh, Howard, I love you so much.'

He gave her a squeeze. 'Thank God you do.'

'I do. With all my heart . . . Kiss me . . .'

They kissed.

'You're right,' he said when they broke off, 'you can't taste garlic on somebody if you've eaten it yourself.'

'How romantic! Here's me, trying to be all lovey-dovey and you start talking about garlic.'

'Sorry, sweetheart.'

'Let's try again.'

They kissed again, but it was too contrived and they ended

up giggling. Maxine got up, fetched her glass of wine from the piano and took another drink.

'It's this wine,' she said. 'It's making me feel all gooey.' She placed it on the floor at the side of the chair and nuzzled up to him again.

'I like you all gooey,' he breathed and ran his hand from her waist over her hip.

They both made a determined effort to wring as much enjoyment out of the next kiss as it was possible to do. She felt his hand running up and down her thigh gently, which made her heart beat fast and she wished with all her heart that he would slip it up the inside of her skirt and into her knickers. Maybe she should have left off her knickers tonight. He might have noticed. He might have taken the hint.

'Shall we get on the floor?' she suggested.

'If you like,' he replied, his pulse suddenly quickening. 'I'll just take my coat off.'

Maxine reached up for a cushion to put under her head, and lay down seductively. She extended her hands out to him and, when he lay alongside her, they wrapped their arms about each other in a warm embrace. Their lips met again and he pressed himself against her. It was beginning to look very promising, until they both heard Aldo cry out. They waited a few seconds, hoping he would drop off to sleep without further ado, but he continued crying.

'I'd better go up to him,' she said, reluctantly dragging herself away from Howard. 'I won't be long.'

It was unusual for Aldo to wake once he'd been put to bed, but trust him to do it tonight, of all nights. She picked him out of his cot and held him to her gently, cooing softly. Of course, Aldo knew his Aunty Maxine and was quite used to her, but it seemed he did not want to settle. For a long time, it seemed, she was rocking him in her arms, but he persisted in crying. She thought maybe he had wind and put him over her shoulder, but that made no difference either. Then, she had an idea and called Howard to come and hold the child.

He rushed upstairs and carefully took the child from her.

'Just rock him gently in your arms,' she said. 'I'm going to try another way to get him back to sleep.'

Howard stood, rocking Aldo in his arms, speaking softly to him while he waited for Maxine. In just a few seconds she returned with her cello and her bow, hitched up the skirt of her dress – which gave him a tantalising view of her legs – and sat down to play. She played *The Swan* by Saint-Saëns; the piece she'd performed for her CBO audition.

Howard was mesmerised. It was not just the sight of her long legs either; the haunting melody, the rich mellow tone of the cello, the emotion that poured from it, and Maxine's feminine grace as she played, all contrived to affect him. He ached to take her in his arms and smother her with love. She deserved all the love he could give.

She came to the end of the piece and looked up at Howard with misty eyes. He smiled lovingly. The child in his arms had ceased to cry and was settling down.

'It's working,' he whispered. 'He's nearly asleep. Please play that again. It's a beautiful piece of music.'

She put her bow to the strings once more and repeated the performance. Overwhelmed by the tenderness of the moment, Howard felt tears fill his eyes and he blinked hard to push them back. Here he was, holding a helpless child, a gift of God; the woman he loved was with him, playing the most beautiful music imaginable. How could such a combination fail to touch his heart? He would always remember this moment. He would always remember this melody. He would never forget the effect it was having on him. Maybe some day they would be married and, like this, he would be holding his own child by Maxine while she tried to get him to sleep with this same potent magic. It was certainly a dream worth striving for.

She finished playing and looked questioningly at him again.

'He's asleep,' Howard said softly. 'Your magic spell has put him to sleep. I'll put him in his cot while you put your cello away.'

Maxine nodded and silently withdrew with the instrument. In her own room she put the cello in its case and looked at herself in the long mirror on the wardrobe door. A thought struck her. A wicked thought. A wanton thought. What would be Howard's reaction if he saw her naked? Tonight, she felt she had the nerve. Tonight, she knew she could do it . . . It was the wine, of course.

Surprised at her own brazenness, she kicked off her shoes, took off her black dress and hung it up, then put her underwear and stockings in the laundry basket. Standing as naked as the moment she was born she left the door ajar and softly called Howard.

A few seconds later he tapped it gently.

'Yes, come in,' she answered. She made no attempt to hide her nakedness but grabbed her nightdress as if she had been about to put it on. She stood coquettishly, posing with her back towards the door but, twisting her torso, she turned to watch Howard enter. His expression, when he saw her, thrilled her.

'Maxine! I'm so sorry. I had no idea . . .' To his credit, he tried not to look at her but found it impossible. His eyes fastened on to the smooth contours of her skin, tanned where the sun had caught her, pale where it had not. 'I'll come back when . . .'

'No . . . No, Howard. I want you to stay. Close the door. I'm not embarrassed a bit. Not with you.' She went to him, trying her hardest to hide her nervousness.

'Honestly?' he gulped.

'Honest,' she whispered. 'Never with you.'

He threw his arms around her and kissed her full on the lips. Her arms went about him in turn while his hands lingered at the small of her bare back, caressing the skin he'd fantasised about while he enjoyed this most promising of kisses. Slowly, tentatively, he allowed one hand to rise from her waist so that it came round and cupped the curve of one cool, firm breast

174

and he thought his head would explode from the throbbing of his heartbeat. Breaking off from their kiss, Maxine took the belt that was around his trousers and unfastened it, all the time looking into his eyes, challenging him to stop her. She unbuttoned his fly and gently thrust her hands inside.

'Do you think I'm brazen, Howard?' she asked earnestly. She was tingling in places she was not aware could tingle. 'I can't help it. I just want you . . . Have you known other girls like this, Howard?'

He shook his head. 'Never,' he croaked.

'Oh, Howard, come to bed with me.' She put her head on his chest. 'I don't see the point in waiting any longer. Not if we love each other.' His trousers fell around his ankles and she ran her hands over his buttocks inside his underpants. 'There is no point waiting . . . is there? Tell me you agree. You want me, don't you, Howard?'

He hugged her tighter. 'Oh, Maxine . . . If only you knew . . . If only you knew how long I've wanted you, how *much* I've wanted you . . .' He looked up to heaven and closed his eyes momentarily. 'God above knows how much I want you.'

'And I want *you*. Here, let me . . .' She helped him off with his shirt and tie, and calmly moved away from him to hang them up on the hook at the back of the door. He stood watching her; entranced, watching how the soft feminine muscles of her slender thighs moved in concert with her neat buttocks.

'I can't take my eyes off you,' he said apologetically. 'Maybe you should turn out the light.'

'It doesn't matter.'

But in the darkness she felt more at ease. Although Howard no doubt believed all this did not unnerve her, inside she was shaking. Thankfully, the darkness allowed her some modesty, for to pose like she had done and then call him to her room, had been pure impulse. Had she stopped to think about it she would never – could never – have done it.

'Are you going to take off your underpants and your socks?'

'Maybe I should.'

Maxine pulled back the sheets and nipped into bed, instantly moving over to make room for Howard. She found Maldwyn, her teddy bear and moved him out of the way. Howard slid in beside her and the feel of his skin on hers as their bodies touched was like nothing she had ever imagined. His warmth, the firmness of his smooth body pressing against her own slender form lit her up in a way she'd never anticipated. And she loved the way his fingers stroked her, how his lips felt so gentle gliding over her skin, sending shivers up and down her spine.

'Oh, Howard,' she breathed. 'Don't stop. Please don't ever stop.'

His lips were on hers again, one hand cupping her breast as her own hands explored the smooth hard skin of his back and his buttocks. She felt her nipples harden, a sensation she had only ever been aware of when she was cold or when Howard kissed her. Then he lowered his head and kissed her breast. He licked her nipple and she sighed at the utter pleasure of it. His hand went to the soft warm place between her thighs and she felt his fingers, kind, gentle, and oh, so sensuous, deliciously probing that most secret place, and she was amazed at how much she liked it. In fact, the longer he did it, the more pleasurable it seemed to get.

Then, at long last, she welcomed his manly weight upon her.

'My darling,' he said softly and kissed her closed eyelids and the delicate skin beneath her eyes.

Her hands squeezed his buttocks, urging him to enter her and, when he did, it was like the stab of a knife, but so exquisitely beautiful. She arched her back to greet his body like a wife welcoming back her long absent husband from a gruesome war. At each sharp, pleasurable pain as he moved in her, she uttered a little gasp of joy that settled into a gentle rhythm that hurt no more.

*　　*　　*

176

Howard was asleep but, as she lay in his arms, sleep eluded her. Never had she felt such happiness as she felt now, and she smiled with utter contentment. All she could feel was his warmth and an exquisite inner peace. All she wanted now was to go to sleep in his arms and wake up when he woke her. She relived every magical moment, every mesmeric movement inside her. She had not really known what to expect from lovemaking. Girls had boasted how their insides seemed to glow with toe-curling pleasure but she had experienced nothing quite so dramatic. Just a feeling of profound happiness and joy that she had given herself, and a priceless tingling sensation where she had been so well loved. She adored Howard now even more than she had before. And she was certain he loved her equally. It felt strange how girlhood was suddenly behind her, how all at once she was a woman.

Eventually she fell asleep, rousing only when Howard shifted. She opened her eyes. The light was sufficient to see him clearly. She gazed at his face with deep affection and raised her head so that she could kiss his mouth and fondle his dark hair with wordless pleasure. Instantly, he awoke. For a second or two he looked about him, disoriented. Then he smiled lovingly at her.

'Maxine . . . Gosh, am I still here? I must have fallen asleep . . .'

'If you have a care for my reputation . . .' she said and laughed as if it didn't matter at all.

'Maybe I should go,' he said earnestly. 'Do you know the time?'

She turned and peeped at the clock with the luminous hands on her bedside table. It was nearly eleven o'clock.

'Maybe we should get up now,' she said.

He kissed her bare shoulder, lingering . . . lingering . . . Her warm flesh against him was too strong an attraction to dismiss easily; far too compelling to walk away from so soon and return to his own cold, empty bed. He nuzzled her hair, ran his fingers over her smooth belly and down to her triangle of silky hair, then looked into her eyes, so beautiful in the half-light, so wide.

Their message was clear. Their lips met again with soft, gentle touches, then more ardently as they snuggled down in the bed together. Once more, they made love before Howard silently, contentedly departed Willowcroft.

Chapter 14

Saturday nights at the dairy house had changed over the years, but not greatly. Instead of Lizzie and Jesse going out to the Shoulder of Mutton, nowadays they were content to stay at home minding their young son Richard and Alice's son Edward. Alice, meanwhile, usually went out with Charles Wells, the young man she worked for, while Herbert was out on his motorbike courting Elizabeth Knight. This Saturday night in the middle of September was one such. Alice had donned her best dancing frock and looked delicious enough to eat, and in the ten minutes or so before Charles was due to call she tucked Edward up in bed and read him a story. Motherhood had not been the easiest thing for Alice to come to terms with but, with Lizzie's coaching, goading and fine example, she had more or less got the hang of it and Edward was none the worse for it.

Punctually – you could normally set the clock by him – Charles arrived at eight. In his usual gushing manner, he greeted everyone and gave Alice a peck on the cheek, then told her how nice she looked.

'Off anywhere special tonight?' Jesse asked, swilling out an old whisky bottle that was to be refilled with beer at the out-door.

'Yes, we're off to the Tower Ballroom to hear The Owls and the Pussycats.'

'Our Maxine's band?' Lizzie queried. 'You never said, Alice.'

'Why do I have to tell you everythin'?' Alice complained.

'I wasn't informed either till last night,' Charles said defending her. 'Still, I don't mind. It'll be a nice change. I rather like jazz.'

Once in Charles's car, Alice said, 'Why did you tell me mother "I wasn't informed till last night"?' she asked sourly, mimicking Charles. 'Anybody would think we only ever do what I want to do.'

Charles shrugged. 'It was meant light-heartedly, Alice.'

'Blimey, all we ever do is sit in the Dog and Partridge. We never go to the pictures or to a dance. You used to take me roller skatin' once in a while but even that's stopped now. No wonder *I* decided we should go dancin' for a change. A girl likes to dress up every now an' again an' show herself off.'

'And you look very nice, Alice. I already told you.'

'I 'eard you the first time . . . Do you know the way to the Tower, by the way?'

'Of course I do.'

'That's a wonder.'

'It's close by where Henzey and Will used to live.'

Charles was a solicitor and Alice worked for him. Yet, while he was still as enamoured of her as the day he met her, this daily and nightly familiarity for Alice had bred some contempt and she was not one to hide it. At first, she was taken with him. He amused her with his irreverent quips and little jokes, but now she had heard them all so many times they were not so scintillating any longer. At first, she had intended mending her wanton ways and settling down, wishing to be wooed like a lady. She was wed at sixteen with a child already in her belly, but now she and her husband had separated she aspired to effect some mystique and be no longer a woman of easy virtue. However, such an objective was totally out of character and it had not taken her long to shed her knickers for Charles. Yet even that exercise had become so uninspiring with him as to be entered into with little enthusiasm these days. When it did occur, she demanded great carefulness from him, for she did not intend getting pregnant again out of wedlock.

180

Alice was way ahead of other girls her age when it came to worldly ways. Since adolescence she had been man mad. It had been her vocation in life to find out as much about sex as she could and what she discovered exhilarated her. At fourteen she knew more about it than most married women and, at sixteen, had indulged in it in more fanciful ways than most ever dreamed of. Alice went out and did what they dared not even think about. Many would have been disturbed to know how wantonly she behaved, others might even have applauded and admired her, envying her absolute defiance of rigid convention. But to Alice it was sheer recreation.

The trouble was, Charles was intending to act for her in her divorce and it would cost next to nothing. So, for the sake of thrift, she was loathe to dispense with him. In fairness, he was doing his best within the limitations of the law since his just reward, he believed, would be her hand in marriage. But, to Alice, it seemed to be taking an age, even pleading special circumstances. Neither was she bothered about giving her hand in marriage. She fancied a change already.

Many a young woman would jump at the chance of marrying a well-off young man, especially as he was presentable and had an assured future in the family law practice. It would be a wonderful opportunity to step up in the world and *be* someone, to indulge yourself with almost everything you wanted. However, for the time being, Alice's priorities lay elsewhere.

On the way they spoke little, except to communicate what she wanted to drink when they stopped at a pub in Smethwick. Typically, too, she asked how much it cost. Charles was not stupid, and it was plain to him that their relationship was not as vibrant as it used to be. However, he patiently endured Alice's sullenness as just being part of her nature, and looked forward to the next time she would deign to allow him access to her sylph-like body, for the promise of these exotic activities, which she performed *par excellence,* sustained him through the dry times.

They finally arrived at the Tower shortly after nine o'clock. Few folk had arrived by this time, but the Bob James All Stars were playing a sequence of quicksteps, though nobody was dancing yet. They made for the bar. There they stayed, talking little, mostly watching other people. Alice was fascinated by a petite blonde girl with a pretty face and a neat figure about the same age as herself, but who wore a wedding ring and a printed cotton summer dress that looked home-made. It had a loose skirt and a tight bodice with a recklessly low neckline which, Alice reckoned, made her look common and sluttish. And although Alice often acted like a slut, she never ever dressed like one.

Shortly after ten o'clock, Maxine walked in with Howard.

'Alice!' she greeted. 'What a surprise. I never expected to see you tonight. Hello, Charles. You've already met Howard, haven't you?'

Charles stood up, extended his hand and they shook.

'You'm cutting it a bit fine, in't yer, our Maxine?' Alice suggested. 'What time yer on? I din't think you was comin'. We've been sittin' 'ere like mawkins, waitin'.'

'We don't go on till half past ten.'

'Blimey! Not till then?'

Charles asked them what they fancied to drink. Presently Pansy arrived with Toots and the conversation expanded. Brent Shackleton arrived, smoking and, in five minutes, the rest of the band were present. Alice was intrigued to see the common blonde girl she'd been watching make a beeline for one of the band members; the one Maxine had introduced as Kenny Wheeler, the one with the wicked smile. Now the girl was hanging possessively onto his arm as if he would make an involuntary exit skywards if she let go. So blatant a display of possession annoyed Alice. Besides, he was far too classy for *her*; far too handsome. Kenny introduced her as Rose, but it was evident by the wedding ring and her demeanour that she was somebody else's wife.

By now the bar was full and noisy with the sound of conversation and laughter, and you had to speak up to be heard even by the person next to you. Saturday-night-out perfume vied for precedence with the smoke that crept through every cubic inch of the atmosphere. At twenty past ten, Maxine and Pansy excused themselves; they had to change ready for the show. Howard continued chatting with Charles while Alice, intrigued, insinuated herself into Rose's conversation with Kenny.

Unfortunately, Rose did not particularly welcome the intrusion, for Alice soon started to garner Kenny's attention. Rose flashed withering looks at her, which Alice noticed but defiantly ignored, for she had set herself a mission. Kenny himself was married and not averse to a bit on the side by the looks of things. He could make an ideal candidate with whom to conduct an exciting casual affair, someone to whet her own sexual appetite, someone with whom she could pep up her own flagging sex life. She need not become emotionally involved. The overwhelming appeal of his masculine good looks and convenient circumstance created an ache for him in her groin.

'How long have you played in this band, Kenny?' Alice asked, in another deliberate attempt to annoy and oust Rose.

'Two years I reckon. How long have you been Maxine's sister?'

She smiled coquettishly, pleased with his response. 'That'd be tellin'. If I told you that you'd know how old I am.'

'Thirty?' Rose suggested snidely.

'Look in the mirror if you want to see somebody thirty,' Alice replied, scorning the girl further. Kenny seemed amused by the exchange. She turned to him again, eyes brim full with sparkles. 'What's your day-time job then?'

'I work for the Post Office.'

'The Post Office? Mmm! You can stick a letter in my letterbox anytime.'

Rose seemed to grow bigger with her increasing annoyance. 'He ain't a postman, then see. He works for the telephones.'

'He can phone me then,' Alice retorted incisively and flashed another dazzling smile at Kenny as much to further belittle Rose as to intrigue him. 'I'll give you my number . . . later.'

As she walked away she heard Rose say, 'Cow! . . . And stop gawping after her.' Knowing that the eyes of both were upon her, she swung her slim hips provocatively – an undeniable talent she possessed – as she walked away to rejoin Charles. She was pleased with her sortie. She was sure she had achieved her objective.

A few minutes later she was aware that the others had gone to take their places on stage. 'Come on, let's go and watch our Maxine's band,' she said to Charles and Howard.

It was the first time either Charles or Alice had heard The Owls and the Pussycats. They stood for a long time, watching, though Alice's eyes seldom strayed from Kenny.

'Dance with me,' she suggested to Charles.

Charles shrugged at Howard with a look of resignation and stepped onto the dance floor with Alice. He was not a brilliant dancer but he did a passable quickstep before the band slowed the tempo. As she and Charles shuffled across the floor in a clinch Alice manoeuvred them near to the stage where she could easily watch the band over Charles's shoulder. Kenny caught her looking at him. She lowered her eyelids feigning coyness and he winked at her, making a big show of twirling his drumsticks into the air. When she looked up again he was still watching her and she mouthed her telephone number. 'Two – four – three – one.'

He repeated it back in an exaggerated mime and she confirmed it with bright eyes laden with devilment, before Charles turned her round and pressed her firmly to him.

Maxine invited Howard in as usual for a drink before he went back to Quinton. She made a pot of tea and, while it steeped, they both made innuendo, probing to see whether the other thought it appropriate to make love when it was so late. But that night fell into the pattern that had been evolving ever since the end of August; when the tea had brewed, they each took a mug into the sitting room and quietly closed the door. And the tea went cold while they made love in the dark with ever increasing devotion and expertise, lying partly dressed on the three-seater settee in front of the fireplace.

They had discussed, of course, the possibility of being compromised if either Will or Henzey came downstairs. It hadn't happened yet, and Maxine was confident it never would. Henzey had already intimated that because her sister was in love she needed privacy and a place to express it. Her hearth was infinitely preferable to the back seat of Howard's old car or the damp grass of some cold meadow, for he, of all people – a man of the cloth – could ill afford to be discovered by some over-zealous vigilante of public morality who might happen on them.

The other of the Kite sisters to indulge in lovemaking that night was Alice. It took place on the back seat of Charles's car overlooking the reservoir in Edgbaston. New and novel locations always seemed to lift their encounters, but the cramped and unladylike contortions she had to endure rather took the edge off it. However, Alice was somewhat motivated by another factor; Kenny was but a short distance away in his Post Office van – with Rose. Having left the ballroom at the same time, Alice brightly called goodnight to him and waved as he stashed first his drum kit into the back of the van, then Rose into the front. Whilst she was anxious to see whether Kenny's windows would steam up, she could hardly linger herself without creating some reason to stay. So Alice took the initiative, made amorous advances to Charles and they eventually clambered into the back of his car. The logic behind all this was that Kenny would see, would know what they were doing, and receive notice that she was not averse to such nocturnal activities. From her supine position on the back seat, she contorted herself agonisingly to raise her head, turn and wipe the window to see whether the windows of Kenny's van were steamed up. From his vastly more convenient elevation, lying on top of Rose across the two seats of his van, it was easy to raise his head and peer through his own window to return the compliment. Simultaneously, Alice tried to live out the fantasy that it was Kenny who was applying himself to her with such dedication.

One person who was not quite so fortunate was Brent Shackleton. Brent arrived at Handsworth that night to a house in darkness. As usual when he came home, he poured himself a drink and went to sit at the kitchen table, intending to scan the evening newspaper. As he turned on the light he saw an envelope standing against an empty milk bottle on the table. It bore his name in Eleanor's handwriting. His throat went dry as he opened it. It read:

> *Dear Brent,*
> *I don't imagine it will surprise you after all that has happened to learn that I've gone to live with Stephen. I know this is the coward's way of letting you know, but Brent I am a coward and I couldn't stand a blazing row. I hope you'll forgive me. Please don't come after me asking me to come back because it will do you no good. I've gone for good.*
> *I have taken everything I own, except the furniture. If I find I have forgotten anything I still have my key so I can come back for it when you're out.*
> *Our relationship was never right and you know it, so please don't think too harshly of me for taking this opportunity to make a new life for myself. It was inevitable. I wish you well and I hope you do me, too. When the dust has settled a bit I hope we can be adult about it and that you can accept it.*
> *Whatever, I shall always love you,*
> *Eleanor.*

Chapter 15

When the CBO's season of concerts had finished, Maxine had cultivated the habit of going by bus to attend Evensong at Howard's church. Occasionally, he was allowed to preach a sermon and when that happened she would gaze at him fondly from her pew, listening intently and pondering how extraordinarily fortunate she was to have the love of this kind, gentle soul.

He was everything she had ever dreamed of. She adored his easy-going ways, his calm, stable nature. It was not his style to endow Maxine with flowers every time they met, nor could he afford to, but he never failed to surprise and delight her with little flourishes of romance, whether by deed or by word. He was sensual, loved touching her and she, responsive to it, was often reminded how months ago she hated it when Stephen Hemming used to touch her. Things were so different now.

They had not talked of furthering their relationship; the subject of marriage had not cropped up. However, she knew he was as serious about her as she was about him. Marriage, she had no doubt, would be on the agenda at some point. And she was happy not to press for it. It was still too soon – much too soon. She still relished the freedom to pursue her music, and certainly Howard would never shackle her with constraints. Let marriage approach in its own good time . . .

So, as the service ended that Sunday evening and the choir and clerics trooped out to the vestry, Maxine edged her way to the end of the pew and joined the queue that was moving slowly down the aisle to exit into the dusk of this cool September. Peering round the heads of the departing parishioners she saw that already Howard was at the door at the rear of the church, shaking hands and saying goodnight. She marvelled at how he could manage to get there so quickly. But when Maxine's turn came Howard was talking to somebody, so to save holding up the queue and making her partiality for the curate obvious, she shook the vicar's hand instead and waited for Howard outside.

When he finished he whisked her back to the vicarage where he had to change, for he could hardly patronise the Gas Street Basin Jazz Club wearing a dog collar and black shirt. So Maxine, as usual, waited in the car while he scurried off inside.

When they arrived at the club, bustling, noisy and smoke laden as always, Brent Shackleton put down his pint and made a beeline for Maxine.

He acknowledged Howard as if he'd conceded that Howard was a valid consideration in her life now. However, he looked straight at Maxine. 'Can I have a word – in private?'

'What is it?' Maxine responded.

Howard discreetly nodded his consent. He still felt this cold resentment from Brent. He would never speak privately to Maxine in front of him.

Maxine moved to one side and Brent followed. 'What's the matter, Brent?'

'It's Eleanor ... She's gone ... Left ...' He shrugged to emphasise his lost look and the hopelessness of his situation.

'Oh, Brent, I'm so sorry ... You mean she's gone with —?'

'With that bloody Stephen Hemming. She's gone to live with him. I rue the day those two ever met.'

He looked upset and Maxine felt sorry for him. She felt the urge to draw him to her and comfort him, but she resisted it. Instead she put her hand on his arm and squeezed it reassuringly.

'She'll come back. I bet you anything she'll come back. If it's any consolation, Brent, I don't know what she sees in him. When did it happen?'

'Last night when I got back from the Tower. She'd left a note.'

'A note? That was considerate. Couldn't she tell you to your face?'

He shrugged. 'Evidently not.'

'Do you want her back – after what she's done?'

His reply, a second or two coming, was considered. 'She's made her bed. She can damn well lie in it.'

'I wonder if Pansy knows? Stephen is her brother after all.'

At that moment, Pansy and Toots arrived. Maxine called Pansy over and Howard took advantage of the moment to enquire what Maxine wanted to drink.

'Did you know about Stephen and Eleanor?' Maxine asked Pansy.

Pansy looked bewildered, not knowing how she was supposed to reply. Maxine realised her friend's dilemma; whether she should let on that she'd known almost from the beginning that they were having an affair.

'I mean, did you know that Eleanor had left Brent and gone to live with Stephen?' Maxine said.

'Gosh, no! When?'

'Last night,' Brent answered.

'She left a note,' Maxine said scornfully. 'Can you believe that?'

'If it's any consolation, Brent, I don't know what she sees in him.'

Brent forced a smile. Strange what could amuse you in times of distress. 'That's exactly what Maxine said, Pansy.'

'Well, he's such a nonentity. I have to admit it, even though he's my own brother.'

'I get the impression his new business has got off to a good start.'

'So he says. Last time I saw him he said how well he was doing already. He reckoned he'd got lots of work. He's started off a manufacturing business as well now. Did you know that?' Brent shook his head then rolled his eyes. 'That's where he'll make a lot of money, he says. He must be coining it in already. That great big house he's renting . . . And he's bought a posh new car, you know.'

'A new car?' Maxine queried. 'He must have borrowed a fortune from the bank.'

'Or pinched it from the Mint,' Brent said derisively. 'Anyway, I reckon that's what the attraction is – money. Eleanor's money mad, you know. Knowing her as I do, she's seen Stephen as her best chance to get into the money. She's realised it's too hit and miss waiting for me to make money from music. She must believe she's got a better chance with him . . . But I'll show her. I'll show her who's capable of making money . . . Big money . . . I'll show her. Mark my words. We just need a lucky break.'

The Owls and the Pussycats had played four numbers, the usual warm-up type of stuff that went down well in the jazz club – traditional, stomping music. Then, through the darkness, standing at the other end of the room close to the bar, Brent spotted Bill Brighton, the music critic from the *Evening Mail*. He was with another man, small, slightly built, grey hair, with a camel-hair coat worn over the shoulders. Brent felt a lump come into his throat and he suddenly forgot all about Eleanor.

Out of the corner of his mouth he called to Maxine: 'Shine . . . sparkle!' Then to Pansy: 'Pansy! Shine . . . sparkle!' Then to all of them: 'Ooze personality, everybody! Pretend you're stars.'

Maxine cast a sideways glance at Pansy. They both seemed to understand what was required and, as Kenny counted them into the next number, each gave a wiggle and a dazzling, eye-sparkling smile. Pansy sang 'The Music Goes 'Round and Around' heart and soul, leading Toots into some intricate trumpet playing.

Band members are always aware that, for no accountable reason, their standard of performance can vary from show to show. Sometimes, any difference is imperceptible to listeners but, to the players, it is manifestly obvious. And when they are playing below par, their spirits sink also and they do not project themselves well on stage. A lacklustre performance is hard to turn around. Conversely, when a band is playing well together, when the rhythm and timing are tight, when the sound and the playing is slick and effortless, then they smile more easily and project themselves well. So it was that night. The Owls and the Pussycats were running with the precision of a well-oiled sewing machine in perfect working order; and it showed.

Every song was a delight and, when they slowed the tempo and Maxine sang 'Where or When', couples clinched on the dance floor and the mood was one of romance. After it, everyone applauded, including Bill Brighton and his expensively dressed companion, Brent noticed with satisfaction.

Before long it was time for a break. Brent gathered together the band before letting them loose into the auditorium and the bar.

'Unless I'm very much mistaken,' he said, 'there's somebody very important out front come a long way specially to hear us. I haven't mentioned it to you before but Bill Brighton, the music scribe from the local rag said he would contact somebody called Seth Cohen and bull us up a bit. I wasn't sure he would, so I said nothing. But he's here tonight with somebody and I'm certain it's this Seth Cohen.'

'So who is Seth Cohen?' Ginger asked.

'A big, important entertainment agent. If he likes us he can get us into places creep-oil couldn't get. I'm going over to have a chat. I want you to come with me, Maxine . . . and be specially nice to . . . to both of them, but especially to Bill Brighton.'

Maxine shrugged. 'Aren't I always? I'll just go and tell Howard I'll be a while . . .'

'Okay, but hurry up.'

Howard, of course, did not mind spending the band's break time with Pansy, Toots, Ginger, Charlie and Kenny, while Maxine did her diplomatic stuff alongside Brent. It was for the good of the band; and Howard could accept that.

When she located Brent at the bar he had already been introduced to Seth Cohen. Indeed, it *was* the great man, and he had travelled by train from London just to see and hear them; on Bill Brighton's recommendation.

'Ah, here's Maxine now . . . Maxine, Mr Cohen – Mr Cohen, Maxine Kite.' Seth Cohen swapped his cigar to his left hand before they shook hands. 'You've met Mr Brighton before, of course.'

'Yes. Hello, Mr Brighton, she said familiarly. 'We're still looking for somebody to play the runcible spoon. Any ideas?'

Bill Brighton laughed good-naturedly. He, too, was smoking a cigar. 'You're not going to let me forget that, my dear, are you?' He explained the private joke to Seth Cohen who seemed to appreciate it.

'Great name, The Owls and the Pussycats,' Seth said in an accent that Maxine did not recognise. Accents were not her strong point and those she did recognise she'd picked up only on the wireless. 'Great name. Great band, too. Great sound. Clean and tight. You look great, too.' He turned to Bill. 'You're right, Bill. They could go far.'

'Can you do anything for them?' Bill asked.

'Maybe, maybe. First, I'd want the band's assurance that they're committed. To a man. I have to insist. I can't afford to place a band and find they've broken up when showtime comes round. My reputation, you see. Are you fully professional, Brent?'

'Why, yes, Mr Cohen. That's so, isn't it, Maxine?'

Maxine felt she had no alternative but to say yes. 'Yes, that's so,' she said. Well she was fully professional. It was no lie. She was a CBO professional. 'What sort of shows do you have in mind, Mr Cohen – and where?'

'There's things happening all the time. For instance, we might have notice of an American outfit doing a series of concerts up and down the country. For the first half of the show we'd want a comic and an English band as a support act. There's nightclub and ballroom work – plenty of it in London. Society balls. Out-and-out jazz venues. Broadcasting, even. The list is endless. But you really need to base yourselves in London.'

'How about something on the *Queen Mary*?' Brent suggested. 'I've harboured a desire to play on that new liner since it went into service.'

Seth Cohen sucked cigar smoke through his teeth and shook his head pensively. 'Everybody who's anybody wants to play the *Queen Mary*,' he said. 'Ever since Henry Hall and his band played it on its maiden voyage . . . I couldn't promise you the *Queen Mary* . . . That's not to say you're not good enough – you are – but I couldn't promise you that.'

'You mean you've got no contacts for the *Queen Mary*, or are you saying it's a closed shop?'

Seth Cohen seemed to resent the inference and Brent wondered if he'd gone too far. 'I've got several acts booked on the *Queen Mary*, son. It's not a closed shop to me. I'm a big face where Cunard White Star is concerned.'

'So what are our chances?'

'I wouldn't want to raise your hopes. You ain't big faces, you see, son. Besides, the *Queen Mary*'s entertainment is fully booked. For two years at any rate.'

'Good business for you, though, eh, Mr Cohen?'

'For me, son, good business. But let me give you a bit of advice . . .' He drew on his cigar. '. . . In this business – entertaining – you need a modicum of patience already. You're nobody till you're somebody, see. Then, all of a sudden, you find you're a somebody. And when you're somebody, you're everybody. Remember that. Have patience, and someday you might be a somebody. Someday you might be a big face.'

Brent sensed that this was perhaps a reprimand. But he was intent on pushing himself. 'Thanks for the advice. In the meantime, what can you offer us?'

'You don't mince words, do you, son? Maybe I can offer you

quite a bit now I've heard you and been impressed. When I get back to my office I'll check what's available. If there's something we can agree on maybe we can sort out a contract. What sort of money would you want to work, say, in London – or in Paris, Berlin, Amsterdam?'

'The going rate – at least. We're a great band, Mr Cohen. Your own words.'

At that Seth Cohen's rumpled face creased further into a grin. But Maxine wasn't certain she liked where this was heading, for London was a long way away. Paris and Berlin were further . . . much further. And she was in love . . . While she pondered being parted from Howard by such vast distances, Brent and Seth Cohen conversed more, probing the possibilities more deeply; till Bill Brighton side-tracked her.

'Er . . . can I buy you a drink, Maxine?' he asked, exhaling a cloud of smoke.

'It's all right, thank you, Mr Brighton. My young man has already got one for me.' Brent had asked her to be 'specially nice' to this man. But what did 'specially nice' mean? She had been polite, said thank you. Had he been implying something more? 'Some other time, maybe,' she added as an afterthought. Maybe that qualified as 'specially nice'.

But Bill Brighton seemed encouraged at that. 'Yes, why not, eh? Some other time.' He put his cigar to his lips and drew on it again. 'How about a night out, you and me? I know how to entertain a young lady, you know. Especially a beautiful young lady like you. Brent suggested you might be available for a night out.'

'Did he, by Jove?' At that snippet of information Maxine fired a savage glance at Brent. The very idea! Their eyes met but his gave nothing away. He was engrossed in furthering his career while she was torn between an outright refusal and ruining any chances the band might have. She had to tread a very narrow path here.

'Er . . . At some time, yes, perhaps . . . Bill . . . May I call you Bill?' Maxine responded with deliberate sycophancy.

'I should say so. So when? When's the best time for you, Maxine?'

'It's difficult to say right now,' she edged. 'I'm ever so busy – the CBO and everything. I'm sure you understand. Why don't I call you?'

'Promise?'

She smiled sweetly. 'Oh, I promise. I always keep a promise.'

Bill Brighton gave her a business card. 'Better not call me at home, though, eh?' He winked at her. 'Call me on the office number.'

Maxine summoned a smile and her face was a beautiful mask of complicity. 'I understand,' she said, then glared at Brent again and excused herself.

When she got back to the others Howard handed her a drink and she sat down next to him.

'What was all that about?' he asked.

She explained about Seth Cohen and that he was willing to find them work. However, she made no mention that the work might be in London or even the capitals of Europe nor that such work would almost certainly entail resigning either from the CBO; or, if she preferred to be with Howard, from The Owls and the Pussycats. She had never really believed that she might ever be faced with such a dreadful decision.

Kenny tapped her arm. 'When's that sister of yours coming to see the band again?'

'My sister?'

'The one who came last night.'

'You mean Alice. I've no idea. Why? What's she to you?'

'She's a bit tasty. Runs in the family, does it?'

'I don't really think Alice is your type, Kenny. She's very sullen and self-centred. If you take my advice you'll avoid her . . . God, what am I saying? You're married. I reckon she should avoid you.'

'So I'm married. So are a good many women I go out with. So what?'

195

'So where's Rose tonight?'

'Rose? Her husband was due to come back home today for a few days. He's in the merchant navy. He sails between New York and London via Rotterdam.'

Maxine was still preoccupied with the problems of working far away and still simmering at Brent. Later, as she walked to the stage for the second part of the show, Maxine caught Brent by the arm. He turned round to face her.

'Please don't ever expect me to be *specially nice* to men in this business on your behalf,' she said acidly. 'I am not a prostitute and I'll never prostitute myself for you or anyone else in this rotten business. Do I make myself clear?'

'Excuse me?'

'Bill Brighton said you'd told him I might be available for a night out. Well I'm not. I'm not interested in Bill Brighton and you've got a damn nerve suggesting I might be.'

'Oh, Maxine,' he said, and adopted his pathetic look. 'I . . . only intimated it . . . It was a spur of the moment thing. He was doing us a favour . . .'

'He might have been doing you a favour, Brent. He wasn't doing me any.'

'I didn't mean it like *that* . . . Maxine, I wouldn't . . . I'm crazy about you.'

'Really? It certainly rings true,' she said with justified sarcasm. 'If you're so crazy about me how come you offered me to somebody else?'

On the Tuesday at rehearsal, the orchestra broke for lunch and, as some musicians dispersed, others remained in their places opening packets of sandwiches. A hum of subdued conversations and laughter rippled around the hall. The slanting sunlight from a high window was drenching Maxine as Brent sidled up to her, and tentatively took the adjacent chair that was still warm from Gwen Berry.

'How are you, sweetheart?' he asked gingerly.

'Fine, thanks. And you?'

'Oh, I'm okay,' he answered dismissively.

'Have you heard from Eleanor?'

He shook his head. 'I don't expect to.' He put on his little-boy-lost expression. It was enormously useful to have a range of pathetic facial expressions in one's repertoire when one was seeking forgiveness. It was his experience that women seemed particularly susceptible.

'Are you looking after yourself properly since she's gone?' Maxine asked, immediately softening. 'Are you eating?'

'I can cut a sandwich and boil water for tea . . . What more do I need?'

'Can you clean? Can you wash up? Change a bed?'

'If I have to.'

'Oh, Brent . . . What are we going to do with you?'

'Do I have to spell it out? You know how I feel . . . Maxine, I'm sorry about . . . you know . . . that Bill Brighton thing.'

She sighed heavily. 'It just doesn't add up, Brent. You say one thing and do something else that suggests you're a liar. How was I supposed to react? It was plain stupid. Anyway, I'm not yours to give – let's face it.'

'I know, I know. It was bravado – nothing more. You know how it is when you've had a drink and somebody's doing you a favour . . . You feel obligated. Of course I didn't *mean* it.'

She regarded him tolerantly. He was going through a difficult time without Eleanor. He needed Eleanor. He was falling to pieces without her.

'Oh, Bill Brighton's harmless enough,' she remarked with forbearance. 'But he'll wait forever for a telephone call from me . . . Anyway, what was the outcome of your chat to Seth Cohen?'

'He'll find us work, Maxine, but most of it will be in and around London. We could work on the Continent if we wanted. Frankly, I'm all for that . . . The chance to get away. I quite fancy Berlin . . . those sleazy nightclubs.' He grinned waggishly, his manner changing completely. 'Seth suggested we all get passports ready.'

'I've thought about it a lot, Brent, working away,' Maxine said, reaching for her thermos flask. 'And I have to tell you that I couldn't be part of the band if that happened. I'm not prepared to move away . . . because of Howard. I'm sorry, Brent. I'd just have to resign.'

Brent looked shocked. 'But Maxine, the band's nothing without you.'

'Well, that's just not true. Pansy's just as capable as me on piano and vocals.'

'No she's not. Nowhere near.'

'Well I think she is. And anyway, you could always recruit somebody else.'

'Maxine, I don't want to recruit anybody else and I'm not going to. Without you the band can't exist. If you're not in it, there'll be no Owls and Pussycats. It's that simple.'

'That's just not fair, Brent. You can't sacrifice your own career and the careers of the others just because of me.'

'I think that's up to me to decide.'

'But I'd feel responsible. It's just not fair.'

'Anyway, we've had no offers yet.'

'Well, if you do,' she said calmly, 'and if you accept, you must realise I'll have to resign.'

'I didn't realise you two were as serious as that.' His tone held an icy resentment.

'Well, it is serious. And I ask you to respect that.' She took the top off her thermos flask and poured herself a drink. 'Would you like some tea?'

'If you can spare one.'

She passed him the cup and watched him sip it. No doubt he hadn't brought himself a drink. No doubt he'd had no breakfast, nor brought any lunch either.

'Brent . . .' He looked up at her over the rim of the cup 'Getting back to Howard, I'm deeply involved with him. Please don't try to distract me . . . It wouldn't work. You'd only be wasting your time. Turn your attentions to somebody else.'

'*You're* the one I want, Maxine.'

'But it's only because of Eleanor. Don't you see? It's only because she's gone. You just feel the need to replace her. You feel vulnerable and unwanted. I understand. It's natural, I suppose. You're on the rebound, Brent.'

He drained the cup and handed it back to her. 'It's nothing to do with Eleanor. I've wanted you a long time. I can't believe you weren't aware of it.'

She refilled her cup from her flask. 'You've made me aware of it. And I was interested in you once, as you know. But your being married . . . I could never . . . You know me better than that by now.'

'Eleanor and I are not married, Maxine.'

Maxine looked at him in open-mouthed astonishment. 'Not married? I don't believe you.'

'It's true. We just lived together.'

'Lived together? You mean, you lived in *sin*?' She waited disdainfully for a reaction from him, a sign of bad conscience, but none came. He merely shrugged. 'That's terrible, Brent. You lived together without being married?'

'But it means I'm free, Maxine. Don't you see?'

'I don't know what to say . . . Do you suppose Stephen knows you're not married?'

'I doubt it. There's no need for you to let him know either . . . If you don't mind. So don't tell Pansy. Please?'

'In case Stephen marries her? You don't want Stephen to marry her, yet you wouldn't marry her yourself? How hypocritical! Don't you think you made it easy for her to leave you by not marrying her? . . . What if she'd become pregnant?'

'She didn't, did she?'

'I don't know, Brent. You have no kids. That doesn't mean she never got pregnant.'

'Actually, she did get pregnant once . . . but she got rid of it. We didn't want any kids, so after that we took precautions.'

'You took precautions? But not till after? Not till after you let her have an abortion?' Maxine gasped with indignation. 'Brent, that is the most horrible – the wickedest – thing I ever heard of.'

'What, taking precautions?'

'Oh, don't be so flippant. No, stupid! Letting her have an abortion. I'm flabbergasted. I'm surprised at you. I'm really disappointed in you.'

'It was her decision.'

'But you just said you didn't want kids either. You must have influenced that decision.'

He shrugged again. 'Maybe I did. I can't remember.'

'Huh! How very convenient when you can't remember such things . . .' Maxine sighed. She'd had her say and her indignation was abating. She finished what remained of her drink and screwed the top back on to her thermos. From her basket she withdrew a pack of sandwiches wrapped in greaseproof paper, opened it and offered Brent one to demonstrate her enduring friendship. He took it sheepishly.

'I'll bring some extra tomorrow. Save you bothering. At least, that way you'll eat. But it's more than you deserve.'

'You're an angel, Maxine.'

Chapter 16

Brent Shackleton lit another cigarette and puffed smoke into his kitchen that already looked as if a whirlwind had ravaged through it. He turned over a page of his notepad, nudging a pile of dirty crockery against a mound of opened mail and musical arrangements to make room, then drew hard on his cigarette again. Just what sort of a band would he have if Maxine resigned? And all because of that bloody stupid Zadoc the Priest. What did she see in him? He wrote her name on the right hand side of the page. A definite no. The band would miss her.

Pansy Hemming. He wrote her name on the left-hand side. Pansy would be happy to go to anywhere. All she wanted was to be a professional musician with The Owls and the Pussycats. Pity Maxine wasn't more like her. Pansy would have to fill in on Maxine's vocals. Fair pianist, too.

He flicked cigarette ash onto one of the dirty plates in front of him and wrote 'Toots' below Pansy in the left-hand column. Toots and his trumpet would go to London if Pansy had made her mind up to go; he wouldn't want to be left behind with half the young men in London ogling her.

Charlie Holt, the double-bass player, had no real attachments. He was a draughtsman, designing pressure vessels on decent pay. Charlie might think twice about giving that up. He must have a word with Charlie, paint a rosy picture, promise the earth. Charlie should be okay.

Ginger Tolley would be okay, too. He had no woman to hold

him back, except his mother. He loved his mother. He loved the band, too and hated his job. Ginger would be no trouble. His name went in the left-hand column.

Now – Kenny Wheeler, the drummer. Brent's first inclination was to write his name in the left-hand column but he felt that might be wrong. Kenny was married, his wife had a baby to nurture. Kenny would not leave them in Birmingham while he went to work in London, no matter how many spare women were about. He might want to, but his sense of responsibility would not allow him to go that far. He might be reluctant, but he would almost certainly leave the band. The second name on the right-hand side – two names too many.

They could feasibly get away without a replacement for Maxine, since Pansy was so versatile. She could not sing anywhere near as well as Maxine and, while she was playing piano, she couldn't be playing her clarinet or her saxophone. But they might get away with it . . . No. On second thoughts, Maxine would need to be replaced. Kenny certainly would.

Two new band members . . . It would take a while to break them into the style and repertoire of The Owls and the Pussycat – one Pussycat, damn it – weeks, even. Better if they weren't offered anything yet in the way of London work. But what if tomorrow brought an urgent request from Seth Cohen to do a season at the Lyceum Ballroom say, or tour the country with Django Reinhardt and the Hot Club Quintet? On the other hand, what if Seth offered them nothing and he'd already let both Maxine and Kenny go? That would be dire.

Brent stubbed his cigarette out in an old eggshell, put his head in his hands and groaned. So which came first? Bloody eggs, or bloody chickens? Bookings in London or new band members?

That Saturday night saw the band playing at Tipton Baths instead of the Tower. Recently they'd been offered lots of other work for Saturday nights and Brent was inclined to accept it. First, they did not want to risk getting stale at the Tower, but secondly, and more relevantly, these other venues were offering more money. The acoustics were not exceptional at the baths, but so what? The punters wouldn't mind. Dancing was the nation's favourite pastime and wherever they played the place was sure to be packed, and folk turned away at the door if they hadn't got a ticket.

During the evening Brent spoke to the band about the possibility of working in London and they all agreed that they would love to do it, with the exception of Maxine and Kenny. Brent had been right about Kenny. Whilst he would have liked to have gone, he could not he said, because of his wife and child and Maxine thought how noble of him.

'I don't understand you,' she told him afterwards while they were packing up their instruments. 'You're off with other women all the time, but you obviously care about your wife and baby enough to stay here.'

Kenny grinned boyishly. 'I worship the bab, Maxine. Just because I like a bit on the side, don't make me all bad, does it? Anyway, I've never met one woman yet who could cope with me. I'm after it all the time, I am.'

'Oh, for God's sake . . .'

'I ain't braggin', Maxine, honest. My wife can't cope with me and she knows it. Do you fancy applyin' for a part-time position?'

'No,' Maxine laughed, shaking her head and collecting sheet music into a pile.

'Pity. I fancy you rotten.'

'And I thought you fancied my sister.'

'I do. I fancy your sister as well. She's nearly as pretty as you.'

'She'd be a lot prettier if she smiled a bit.'

Kenny stuffed two cymbals into a black cardboard case. 'I bet I could put a smile on her face.'

'I really don't know what you mean, Kenny,' Maxine said, feigning uppishness.

'Well you smile a lot. I can only presume old Howard over there is suiting you well. Your sister – what's her name again?'

'Alice.'

'She told me her telephone number but I've forgot it. Just remind me what it is, Maxine.'

'No, why should I? You're a married man.'

'God, you're a bloody spoilsport, you are.'

'You work for the GPO telephones. You find it. Do some detective work.'

'If I'm to be a sleuth I'll need a clue, won't I? Can't you even give me a clue, Maxine?'

'Here's one – you won't find her listed in the telephone directory.'

'That's some bloody use.'

The following Saturday night, The Owls and the Pussycats were due to play at Dudley Town Hall, sharing the limelight with Jack Bradney and His Band. Lately, work was coming in from everywhere. Soon they were due to play at West Bromwich Baths, Brierley Hill Town Hall, Stourbridge Baths, Sutton Coldfield Town Hall and even further afield, many of them midweek bookings.

The band, with the exception of Maxine and Brent who would be late due to a CBO concert, had arrived early to set up. That done, they had called at the Saracen's Head before returning to the Town Hall to await the arrival of the other two. To Kenny's surprise and delight, he saw Alice looking a picture in a new dance dress, standing alone in the foyer looking as if she was waiting for someone. When she saw him, her face lit up.

'Alice! Fancy seeing you here. You look really nice.'

'Hello, Kenny,' she replied pleasantly. 'How are you?'

'Fine.'

'Where's Rose?'

'I dunno. She ain't here at any rate. Where's your fella?'

'I dunno,' she mimicked. 'He ain't here either.'

Kenny was thrilled at the prospect of getting her alone. 'You on your own, then?'

'Yes. I thought I'd see our Maxine and her chap here.'

'I expect they ain't arrived yet. Fancy a drink while you wait?'

Alice followed Kenny as he pushed past others to get to the bar. It was crowded in there, noisy, and trying to get served tested your patience. But Kenny did not mind being pressed against Alice – nor did she – while they waited and talked.

'So where's Rose tonight?' Alice ventured to ask.

He shrugged. 'I didn't think to ask her over here. Anyway it's not as if we're courting or anything – she being married and that.'

'You stopped in the car park at the Tower long enough the other night.'

'Hark who's talking,' Kenny parried and he could not help grinning. 'I spotted you with your car windows all steamed up.'

'How d'you know I didn't stay just to spy on you?' Alice fenced, pleased that he should have noticed after all.

'My only disappointment was that you and me was in different motors,' he baited. 'So what are you doing after?'

Alice clasped her handbag in front of her swaying coyly, like a little girl holding a rag doll. It was a pose that usually got her what she wanted with men.

'I ain't doin' nothin' in particular,' she confessed. 'What you got in mind?'

When the dancing was over, Kenny had stacked his drum kit, his pride and joy, in a pile of boxes at the foot of the stage and asked if anybody would like to give him a hand to load his van. Alice and Maxine each took a box they thought they could easily manage, and the lads helped, carrying their own instruments out too.

'Do you want Howard and me to give you a lift home, Alice?' Maxine asked.

'Oh, no, it's all right. Kenny's taking me, Maxine.'

Maxine had guessed as much but felt she should offer anyway. 'Okay. Tell Mother I'll call round tomorrow.'

'Shall you stop for your Sunday dinner?'

'Yes, okay.'

'See you tomorrow, then.'

Maxine held Howard's hand while she watched Alice get eagerly into Kenny's Post Office van. 'I hope she knows what she's doing,' she said to Howard as she waved goodbye to her sister. 'He is a married man, after all.'

'She's a grown woman, Maxine,' Howard advised. 'She has her own life to lead.'

'Let's go that way home. Let's just see if they are going straight to the dairy house. Somehow I doubt it.'

Of course they didn't. Kenny drove straight past Willowcroft and Alice directed Kenny through a gate into a dark, secluded spot off the unlit Oakham Road near Dudley Golf Club with its undulating hills and hollows. They found themselves on the golf course itself, at the top of a downward slope near one of the tees. Through the windscreen, the view over Halesowen and Cradley Heath was spectacular. The furnaces of a hundred forges and the cupolas of a hundred foundries glowed yellow in the distance and, when a load of molten slag was tipped at the Round Oak Steel Works in distant Brierley Hill, the horizon bloomed as if God had switched a light on. The bright moon, too, hovering like a luminous balloon, afforded them plenty of light.

Kenny stopped the engine.

He looked into Alice's eyes. 'I fancied you, Alice, the moment I saw you.'

'I know,' she replied and stroked his hand. 'I could tell.'

'So what are we gonna do about it?'

'What do you think we should do?'

He put his arm around her and drew her to him. Their lips met unhesitatingly and they kissed, their ardour increasing rapidly, for they both knew where they were headed with no time to waste. Kenny's free hand roamed first to Alice's breasts and, experiencing no resistance at all, soon ventured boldly up her skirt. She parted her legs obligingly and he began teasing her between her thighs, to instant sighs of pleasure.

'Let's lie on the grass,' he whispered, trying to visualise the splendour of unfettered horizontal activity on this their first encounter. 'It's hopeless in here, unless we open the door and stick our legs out.'

'But it's too cold,' Alice protested, imagining the chill night's wind whistling around her bare backside. 'We'll freeze.'

'I've got two blankets in the back. One to lie on, one to put over us. It'll be better than trying to outdo Houdini in here.'

It meant starting the rigmarole all over again, but it would be worth it; like lying in bed under the stars.

'Oh all right.' Nobody could ever accuse her of being unadventurous where sex was concerned. She got out of the van, took off her best coat and tossed it inside.

In the darkness, Kenny fumbled around in the back of the van for his blankets while Alice stood and shivered in her sleeveless dancing dress. At last he placed the blankets on the grass at the side of the Post Office van and invited her to join him. When he spread the top blanket over them, she snuggled up to him for warmth.

'Brrr! That's better,' she said. 'Do you always keep some blankets in the van?'

'Usually. To cover my drum kit.'

'I hope you thought to bring some French letters as well. I don't want to get into trouble.'

'Never use 'em. Waste o' time.'

'Maybe I shouldn't let you then. How do I know you'll be careful?'

'Don't worry, I'll be careful – I don't need hassle. Now shut up and kiss me.'

While they kissed, he slid the hem of her dress above her waist and she unceremoniously raised her bottom so that he could take her knickers off easily.

'Now get your trousers off.'

'I'm trying . . .'

'Here, let me help . . .'

Eventually, they had his trousers and his underpants off. She submitted to him readily as he shifted on top of her. Without further ritual she felt him enter, thrusting into her gently, a bit further each time till he was inside her to the hilt, filling her up. She groaned with the pleasure of it till he found her lips again, and she tasted him with delight. She forgot about the cold and, as she clung to him, she first fondled his neck, then gripped his buttocks to pull him harder into her. She looked up at the stars and the moon and saw they were moving, oscillating in time with their rocking bodies. An owl shrieked eerily overhead and she thought she heard something scuffing across the fairway of the golf course, like a fox dragging its quarry. But Kenny was zealously active inside her and that addictive glow deep in her groin was already growing brighter, promising extreme pleasure, urging her to press herself even closer to him. She heard the scrunching on the grass again, further away this time, and tilted her head to see what it was. Odd that Kenny's Post Office van was not there any more. She could have sworn . . . Then, with effortless detachment, she saw it rolling away. God alone knew where it might end up . . . Turning her attention back to Kenny, she thrust up to him, grinding against him harder and harder, for relief was imminent. In time with their movements, the van uttered a quickening, rhythmic squeak as it rolled away, gathering pace.

Kenny heard it too, turned and watched his van disappear down the hill. 'The bloody van!' he cried in disbelief.

'Sod the van,' Alice retorted fervently, and held him hard into her to forestall any inclination he might have to dismount and run after it.

They were at that ecstatic point when she couldn't stop. But he wouldn't dream of foregoing her eternal admiration for such a monumental performance either. The world could cave in under them, the sky could fall in on their heads, but they could not stop. Not at that moment.

At last she cried out: 'Bloody hell, Kenny! . . . Oh, my God! . . . Jesus . . .'

He gave her a few seconds before he spoke. 'You done already?' he queried prosaically.

She nodded, breathless. 'Ooh, I needed that . . . Thank you, Kenny . . . It was smashin'.'

'One hundred percent effort, me. Tell all your friends, eh?' He looked around. He could not see the van at all.

Then, they heard an almighty crash.

In a panic, he made to get up and investigate but she grabbed him between the legs and made sure she held on to him. He was still rock hard, and seemed as thick as her wrist. Impressive, she thought.

'You didn't let go inside me, did you?' she asked, still getting her breath back.

'No. I still haven't.'

'Good. I'll do it for you, eh?'

'But the van . . .'

'That van ain't goin' nowhere else now, Kenny. Relax a bit . . . Relax . . .'

'Okay,' he muttered submissively, 'but quick as you can . . . No, don't squeeze him too tight . . . Gently . . . That's it . . .'

She finished him off and he squirmed with pleasure, holding his breath, his whole body rigid as he climaxed.

'Come on now, let's find the damned van.'

As unceremoniously as it had begun, it ended. He found his trousers, she her knickers, and they dressed themselves in silence. Alice stifled a giggle at the absurdity of the whole thing.

'Your van's rolled into the quarry, I think,' she informed him tentatively, then burst into whoops of uncontrollable laughter.

'Quarry? What damned quarry?'

'There's a quarry. Just over that bump . . .' She pointed in the darkness, shivering without the protection of the blanket. 'Good job we weren't still in the van.'

'Why didn't you tell me there's a quarry?'

'You din't ask.'

'Oh, Christ! The bloody van! Me drum kit!' He went to walk towards the edge to find out if he could see anything.

'Keep away,' she yelled, 'else you'll end up down there with it. You won't make out the edge in this light. It's a sheer drop.'

'But me drum kit, Alice. The van.'

Alice shrugged. 'It'll still be there in the morning. Come on, we'd best get to our Henzey's house, I'm frozen. It's only just down the road. With any luck we might catch Howard there still. He'll be able to give you a lift back to Brum.'

Chapter 17

Next day an outbreak of mirth brightened Sunday dinnertime at the dairy house. Maxine was expected and she in turn had invited Howard to eat with the family after Matins, knowing her mother would have roasted a large joint of beef with ample Yorkshire pudding and fresh vegetables for everybody. While they ate, Maxine and Alice exchanged secret looks and tittered like schoolgirls. Their amusement gathered momentum until they could contain it no longer and they burst into fits of unrestrained giggling. Howard knew, of course, that the cause of all this hilarity was the thought of Kenny's van plunging into the quarry last night while Alice and Kenny were spread-eagled on the grass beside it. But they could not let on to Lizzie or Jesse, of course.

'I wish I knew what was tickling these two,' Lizzie remarked inquisitively. 'They must each have a feather in their drawers. What are they laughing about, Howard?' At least the clerical collar he was wearing suggested to Lizzie that he could not lie.

'I'm sworn to secrecy I'm afraid, Mrs Clancey,' he replied, trying to smother his own laughter and finding it difficult while trying to eat. 'The confessional ethic, you understand.'

'Good job you weren't in the way, our Alice, else you'd have been flattened,' Maxine commented mischievously, inducing more giggles from her sister.

'Well, whatever happened, it's perked our Alice up no end,' Lizzie said innocently. 'I've never seen her chuckle like this.'

Recalling what Kenny had said about putting a smile on Alice's face, Maxine broke out into squeaks of unbridled laughter that everybody found infectious. And so it went on, throughout the whole sitting. Although Lizzie and Jesse had no idea why they were laughing so much, they all enjoyed the merriment.

After dinner, when the washing up had been done and the others were taking their ease in the sitting room and entertaining the children, Alice, Maxine and Howard huddled together on the verandah quietly discussing the events of last night. It was the first opportunity since calling for help at Willowcroft that Alice had had to question Howard about what happened.

'Was Kenny all right when you gave him a lift home?' she asked, serious now. 'Did he seem upset?'

'He was fine,' Howard said. 'I think it was only just beginning to dawn on him what had happened by the time I dropped him off at home. After we'd taken you home, we found the track to the quarry workings. Fortunately, they're only quarrying into the side of the hill, so the workings aren't deep. We got to the van anyway – what was left of it.'

'Was it bad?' Alice said.

'A mess. The bonnet was flattened when it hit the ground and the wheels were splayed out as if the whole thing had been made of Plasticine. It just missed a wooden building as it landed – the explosives store, I think.'

'How far was the drop?' Maxine enquired.

'About a hundred and fifty feet I would think. It was the luckiest thing in the world you weren't still sitting inside the van.' He shook his head at the awful thought.

'Yes, our Alice. If you'd been doing it in the van, you'd never have noticed it moving till you hit the bottom of the quarry . . . You were doing it, weren't you?'

'God! What do you think we was doin' there in the dark? Pickin' blackberries? I told you, we was under a blanket on the grass . . .' She suddenly regarded Howard with apprehension. 'Oh, I bet you think I'm a right one, don't you Howard?'

Alice had temporarily overlooked Howard's calling – as they all seemed to do – then remembered. The better they got to know him, the easier it was to forget he was a curate of the Church of England, and speak to him as if he was one of the family. Certainly he had shown himself to be broad minded and there were no constraints on what they discussed with him these days.

Howard avoided Alice's question. Red hot, was how Kenny had described her on the way back home. 'Anyway, his drum kit was all right,' he remarked. 'We managed to get that out and load it into my car. Then I took him home. I think he left some tools and things in the van but he intended to retrieve those tomorrow with some of his workmates. By the way – I have your coat in my car, Alice.'

'Oh, thank God! Me best coat!' Alice exclaimed. 'Oh, I bet he'll get into terrible trouble, that Kenny. You'll see him tonight at the jazz club, won't you, Maxine?'

'I expect so.'

'Will you give him a message . . . Will you tell him from me that I hope he don't get into too much trouble over it . . . at work or at home?'

'Yes, I'll tell him . . . I take it you're not coming to the jazz club tonight?'

'I wish I was but I'm seeing Charles.' Alice rolled her eyes scornfully.

Maxine and Howard decided they would take a walk that afternoon. It was the only chance they would have of being alone till late that night. The row of terraced houses opposite threw long shadows that were climbing the front wall of the dairy house in the afternoon sunlight. It was warmer today than it had been for a couple of weeks; ideal weather for a stroll to the town centre. They found themselves gazing into shop windows hand-in-hand. Furniture stores seemed to grab their attention with enticing displays and ideas for homes. Occasionally, a fine dining room suite would seize their imagination and fire images in their separate minds about how they would like their own home furnished.

'I like that three-piece suite, Howard,' Maxine said.

'Yes, it's rather nice.'

'And isn't that a lovely standard lamp? That would go nice with it, don't you think?'

'Admirably.'

'You see that mirror over there?' She pointed to a huge example in a hefty gilt frame. 'Isn't it lovely? I can just see that over a fireplace with this three-piece suite set around it.'

Howard realised she was furnishing an imaginary home. A good sign.

'If you could take your pick of anywhere in this country to live, where would you choose?' he asked as they carried on walking with arms linked towards Top Church.

'Here, in Dudley,' she answered without hesitation. 'Why should I want to live anywhere else?'

'What about the seaside, or out in the country, for instance?'

'I like the seaside,' she said simply. 'And the countryside, but *I* could never live there. So why should I even think about it?'

'I wondered whether you prefer aesthetic beauty or somewhere that you feel comfortable. I know how you love the countryside. But you obviously feel at ease living in Dudley.'

'Because it's familiar. Because I know it. The folk are kind and friendly. It's drab in places, I grant you, but I love it nonetheless . . . And it's quite close to you. Quinton isn't so far.'

He smiled his acknowledgement of the fact.

'And you'd be even closer if you were vicar of Top Church here, or St John's,' she added.

'Why? Is there a vacancy?' he asked with sudden interest.

She shrugged. 'I wouldn't know. I don't go to church here to find out. I come to you.'

At Top Church, with its tall granite spire, they felt they had walked far enough and turned around to go back. A tram, travelling on the single track towards the Market Place, whined to a halt and waited at the passing place while another approached from the opposite direction.

'I fancy an ice cream, Howard,' Maxine said with a sudden urge to taste something sweet. 'There's a shop down here we can get one. Do you fancy an ice cream?'

'I'd love one.'

So Howard went into the shop, purchased two ice-cream cornets and they ambled on, first holding hands, then with their arms about each other. It was a spontaneous display of affection. They were in love and so what if the world could see. They had nothing to hide. Masses of folk were swarming towards them on their way to the Regent cinema and nearly all looked twice at this happy young couple, she as fresh as a spring morning with her dark hair ruffling in the breeze, he soberly dressed in his clerical collar and dark suit.

'I've been meaning to say, Howard . . . this thing with the band and that Seth Cohen who came to listen to us . . .' She licked her ice cream and looked up at him intently. 'I haven't mentioned it before, because I haven't really known what to tell you, but he says he's going to find work for the band in London.'

'Oh? . . . Actually, I heard some of the others talking about it. I decided not to mention it, preferring that you did.'

'Well now I have. It would mean living there, Howard . . . But not just London, either. Amsterdam, or Paris or Berlin, if we want to work there.'

'Paris or Berlin?' Maxine saw a look of disquiet in his eyes. 'He reckons you're that good?'

'So it seems . . . But don't worry – I won't be leaving you.' She gave him a squeeze and looked into his eyes with a smile of devotion. 'I've told Brent I don't want to be included. I've already said I would leave the band if they were booked to play away from home. I don't want to live in London or anywhere else. I don't want to be away from you, Howard. It might be

215

for months – a year or more. I couldn't stand to be away from you that long.'

'Are you sure? Are you certain you'd want to give up the opportunity to advance your career in jazz just for me?'

She licked her ice cream again and flicked her tongue around her lips. 'We love each other, don't we?' she said, as if it was the most logical reason on earth. 'What would be the point of us being apart? What would we gain? Only long, miserable periods, missing each other like I don't know what. I want to be with you, Howard – as much as I can. I don't want to have to miss you. Besides, all this jazz is just a lark really . . . A bit of fun . . . I'm a serious cellist by profession, remember.'

He gave her a hug. He was fortunate indeed to have the love of this woman. She was kind, thoughtful, articulate and immensely talented. She was an angel and yet, thank God, a sinner. Her sinning was her most desirable quality.

'I'd still have the CBO. I could even find work in another band if I wanted – a big dance band maybe – I've had offers already. It doesn't mean I have to give up my career. In any case, I don't want to give up my career yet.'

'So I'm competing with your career, Maxine? So . . . if you had to choose . . . between me and your classical music . . . which would you choose?'

'I would have thought it obvious since I just told you I would give up the band to stay close to you. But in any case, I don't see why you need to ask. You wouldn't want me to give up my cello as well, would you?'

'Of course not. I was just trying to establish in my own mind what your priorities are.'

'You seem to be trying to establish quite a lot this afternoon, Howard. What part of the country would I like to live in? Would I give up my cello? Are you sure there's not something on your mind? Is there something I should know?'

He gave her a reassuring squeeze and bit into his ice cream. 'No. I was just curious.'

'Hmm,' she uttered thoughtfully, superstitiously trying to avoid the cracks in the pavement as she walked. 'There's nothing quite as puzzling as a curious curate.'

The postman that delivered mail in the area of Handsworth that Brent Shackleton inhabited was generally early with his deliveries. At shortly after half past seven on the morning of 5th October, the same day that the Jarrow jobless began their march to London, Brent heard mail being shoved through his letterbox as he lay in bed. Yet it did not inspire him to get up straight away. His mind began to shed the effects of sleep, however, and he began to think about the band.

Eventually, he lugged himself out of bed and wondered when Seth Cohen was going to phone him to tell him he had some regular work in London. He could do with the money. The rent on his house was overdue, bills remained unpaid and his expensive car needed some attention. A new trombone wouldn't come amiss either, for the one he had now was getting dented and scratched with overuse.

He lumbered to the bathroom. It was a mess. A filthy ring of scum dwelt around the inside of the washbasin and the soap took on a repulsive mushiness, having lain steeped in a cracked soap dish half-full of murky water for days. The mirror was spotted with toothpaste, the towels were soiled, while fluff, hairs and smatterings of talcum powder embellished the floor. Brent's comb looked disgusting. And the lavatory . . .

He relieved himself in it, flushed it, washed his hands and face using the pulpy soap, and then cleaned his teeth. He shaved, Brylcreemed and combed his hair using water to stick down those errant strands that would not willingly lie down, and returned to his bedroom to dress.

On his way to the kitchen to boil the kettle for his first cup of tea, he picked up the post from the floor in the hall and fanned it out in front of him. Bills, booking confirmations. But one immediately took his notice. The address was typewritten but the postmark had been smudged, so he could not discern where it had come from. He tore open the envelope and drew out a letter. As he read it he was conscious of smiling, of euphoria growing rapidly within him. Maybe he was still in bed dreaming that he was reading this. So he pinched himself hard to make certain that he was indeed awake, and yowked as he experienced the pain he was able to inflict on himself. He was awake all right. He scanned the letter again, danced around the kitchen, boyishly yelling, 'Yippee! Yippee!' as loud as his vocal cords would allow.

On the Tuesday, just after Charles had delivered her home from work, Alice received a telephone call. It was Kenny. It had been a week and a half since their eventful encounter over the fairways of Dudley golf course.

'Alice, I've got to see you.'

'That'd be nice,' she responded, excited that he considered her worthy of a further encounter, flattered that he sounded so keen. 'Where are you playing on Saturday night and I'll try and get over?'

'No, I can't wait till then. I've gotta see yer before then.'

And she had thought it was just a one-off thing . . . 'I dunno. I daresay I could manage tomorrow night if you like. I can always put his nibs off.'

'Okay. Put him off then.'

'You got a new van already?' She smiled to herself at the thought of what had happened to the old one.

'Yeh, I got a new van. I'll come and pick you up – about eight. I think I can remember where you live.'

Brent Shackleton sat himself beside Maxine Kite in the rehearsal rooms of the City of Birmingham Orchestra. She passed him a pack of sandwiches she'd prepared for him, wrapped in grease-proof paper.

'Boiled ham and tomato.'

'Thanks, Maxine,' he said. 'What would I do without you?'

'Starve, most likely. Here, have a cup of tea.' She unscrewed the cap off the new large thermos flask she'd bought specially to cater for him and poured him a cup. 'So what are you so happy about, Brent? You look like the cat that got the cream.'

He grinned as he took the plastic cup from her. 'I've had a letter.'

'Oh? Somebody left you some money?'

'Better than that.' He took it from his inside pocket and handed it to her. 'Read it.'

While she read it he studied her reaction. He watched a beautiful smile render her lovely face even lovelier as she digested the contents.

'That's brilliant!' she exclaimed, happy for him. 'Are you going to accept?'

'Accept? I should say I'm going to accept. It's been my dream to play on the *Queen Mary* ever since they laid the bloody keel. Now that Seth Cohen, God bless him, has come up with this offer I'm not going to turn it down.' He opened his sandwiches and took a bite. 'And you're coming too. No excuses.'

'Oh, Brent, I can't come . . . I already told you. You know my reasons.'

'I think your reasons are pathetic, Maxine. This offer is for eight weeks. An eight-week contract to play the *Queen Mary*, to see New York and, while we're there, go and listen to some of the finest jazz and swing musicians of our time. We'll be fed and watered like lords – free – and be paid for the pleasure. Maxine, it'll be like being on holiday and getting paid for it – good money, too.'

'Yes, I can see that.'

'But eight weeks, Maxine . . . Surely you can stand to be away from Zadoc the Priest for eight weeks? Eight weeks is nothing.'

'Eight weeks or eight months, Brent, it doesn't make any difference. I gave Howard my word. And stop calling him Zadoc the Priest.'

'You mean he extracted a promise from you not to work away? Jeopardised your career?'

'It wasn't like that, Brent. Not at all. Howard has never pressured me to do anything I didn't want to do. I volunteered not to work away – because I want to be close to him. He didn't ask me to. If I wanted to go I'm sure he'd be okay about it . . . It's just that I don't want to be away from him and miss him, because I would . . . terribly . . . I love him, Brent. He's my world now.'

Brent sighed and bit another lump out of his sandwich. 'Such a damned waste of talent . . . I need you on that ship, Maxine. Without you the band can never be the same.'

'And what about Kenny?' she asked. 'Have you tried to get a replacement for him?'

He shook his head. 'I was hoping this stint on the *Queen Mary* would whet everybody's appetite. It's such a wonderful opportunity, Maxine. Who knows what could come of it? Some of the world's greatest people travel on that damned ship – royalty, lords and ladies, Hollywood film stars, film producers. Who knows who might hear us?'

'Dreams, Brent.' She sipped her tea.

'Dreams, maybe. But I've got a feeling about this contract, Maxine. It's a God-given opportunity. It *means* something. We're going to do well out of it. We're going to make a lot of money – we're going to make our fortunes. I can feel it.'

'Good. I hope you do. You deserve it. You've worked hard.'

He shook his head. He did not seem to be getting through to her. This could change their lives, he was certain. But she did not care. She was completely unmoved.

'You haven't got much time to get organised, Brent,' Maxine remarked. 'Four weeks tomorrow, you sail, according to this.'

'I know . . . And I'm going even if you won't. I shall write to Seth when I get home, accepting his offer. When the contract comes through I'm resigning from the CBO . . . Listen, I've been working on some new arrangements. Do me a favour and run through them with me when we've finished this afternoon?'

She shrugged. 'Here?'

'No, at my house. It's a pity you won't come on these cruises, Maxine . . . We'd have time together to start writing. I'd love to start writing songs with you . . . I reckon that creative streak you have could be channelled into writing some great songs.'

'Yes,' she replied, suddenly thoughtful, 'I'd like to try my hand at writing songs. Perhaps while you're away.'

This offer to play the *Queen Mary* had made such a difference to Brent, Maxine thought, sitting beside him as he drove her to his home in his powerful Mercedes Benz. Gone was the melancholy that had persisted since Eleanor had left him, gone was the edginess. He was different, as if a great weight had been lifted from his shoulders. His only major concern was to find a new drummer. That would not be difficult, especially if he had a contract playing the *Queen Mary* to offer somebody, but finding a drummer who could make the music swing like Kenny could, would be more difficult. He had a minor concern, too, that required more immediate attention.

'I'm in a bit of a spot, Maxine,' he said. 'I need to get some petrol and I'm bereft of cash at the minute. Could you lend me five or ten bob till I can get to the bank tomorrow?'

'Course,' Maxine replied, at once rummaging through her handbag.

'Thanks. I've been running on fresh air for days.'

'It's okay. Let me pay anyway,' she suggested. 'You run me round a lot.'

'No, no. Just till tomorrow . . . Here, look. A petrol station . . .'

She drew two half-crowns from her purse and, when they pulled up at the side of the petrol pump, she handed them to him. 'Here, that's all the change I've got.'

'Do you mind? Can you afford it?'

'Better than you by the looks of things,' she replied. 'I don't have a house or a car to run.'

'Maxine, you're a real angel. A totally good egg. Thanks.' He turned and his eyes were warm on her, then he got out to supervise the filling and to pay the attendant.

Eventually, they reached his house and they both alighted from the car.

'The place is a bit of a mess since Eleanor went,' he warned as he opened the front door.

'As long as you've got two clean cups for a cup of tea,' she replied.

'I wouldn't count on that. I might not have any milk, either . . . After you . . .'

'You know, that's the first time ever you've held a door open for me and allowed me in first – anywhere.'

'Nonsense.'

'It's true. I notice these things. You're getting soft in your old age.'

As she entered the house a strange smell struck her; it was a musty, musky aroma, she thought, but with bass notes of *eau de* rotting cabbage. She held her breath momentarily.

'This is the front room,' he said gesturing, 'this is the parlour, and the kitchen's through there. I wouldn't go in the kitchen if I were you.'

That in itself was as good as an invitation and she followed him there.

'Brent!' she cried in horror. 'I've never seen such a mess.' At once she returned to the hall, took off her coat and threw it over the bannister. 'How can you live like this?' she said as she returned to the kitchen. 'You can't live like this.' She went to the sink, removed a pile of dirty dishes coated in rotting food that were causing much of the smell. 'Do you have hot water?'

'The geyser. But you haven't come here to wash my dishes.'

'Brent, I can't put up with this while I'm here. This lot stinks. Can't you smell it? Run the water for me. Let's do some washing-up. It's just too disgusting. Got any soap powder?'

'There used to be some under the sink. I'll get it.'

Water began to flow hot from the geyser and, with a shake of caking soap powder, a reassuring foam started to form in the sink as she filled it. She immersed the food-encrusted crockery and the cleaning began. Brent discovered a clean cloth with which he could wipe everything dry and store it where he thought it belonged, making a joke of the whole episode. When she'd washed the crockery, the cutlery, the pots and pans, she wiped every surface with a dishcloth and scraped more burnt-on food from the hob of the stove.

'If you try and keep everything clean as you go along, Brent, it'll be much easier,' she tried to explain as she folded the dishcloth and put it to rest neatly at a spot at the side of the sink. 'Now, what about that cup of tea?'

'I'll do it. You go into the front room. The piano's in there.'

She dried her hands and left him to it. The front room, however, was almost as bad as the kitchen. Never had she seen a room so untidy, so dirty. Trying her best to ignore it, she picked her way over the debris to the piano. She shifted a pile of manuscripts and sheet music from the stool, sat down and played a few chords. At least the instrument was in tune. The first few bars of a new number the band had been rehearsing spilled out through her fingers: 'Summertime'. . . But it was no good. She couldn't concentrate on music with all this distracting mess lying about. She had to clean it up.

When Brent came in with two mugs of tea she was sorting things into piles; a pile for newspapers, a pile for letters and bills, a pile for manuscripts, a pile for printed music, even one for cast-off shirts and socks he'd left lying about. Once she could see the floor, that, too, was a disgrace. No wonder the place stank.

'Brent, how on earth can you allow yourself to live like this?' she asked again. 'The house is a pigsty. I can't imagine that Eleanor would ever let it go like this. You must try to be cleaner – more tidy.'

'I love it when you mother me,' he said with a grin.

223

'Well don't get too fond of it. Do you have a Ewbank or something to sweep the floor with?'

He put the mugs of tea on top of the piano. 'I need a woman.'

'I'm sure you could advertise for one,' Maxine responded seriously.

'I don't mean a cleaning woman,' he scoffed. 'I mean a *woman*. A woman to live with me . . . You, for instance.'

'Where are those arrangements you wanted to go over?' she asked, wishing to change the subject.

'Probably in that pile of manuscripts you've scooped up.'

'Oh. Sorry . . .'

'I'll have a look. Want to help?'

They stooped down together over the pile of hand-written music, facing each other as they searched. Her hair, cascading over her face, brushed his face and tickled him. He looked up at her and their eyes met.

'Oh, Maxine . . .'

'Yes?' she answered softly, tucking her hair behind her ear.

'Maxine, I want you . . .' he breathed. 'I . . .'

Deliberately, she stood up, determined to side-step this beguilement. 'You want somebody to keep house for you, Brent, that's what you want,' she proclaimed dismissively.

'No . . .' He stood up, side-stepped the pile of music and faced her, their bodies almost touching.

They were so close that she could feel the warmth radiating from his body.

'I know who I want, Maxine . . . Not to keep house for me, but to . . .' He hesitated deliberately.

'To what?' she prompted, driven by a perverse wish to hear him say it.

'To be lovers . . .'

But she had not come here for this. She should have known . . . She went to turn away but his hands went to her waist, halting her.

'Maxine, I can't stop thinking about you. Christ, you're so

bloody *beddable* . . .' He looked at her lips. They looked so soft and inviting and her teeth, so even and clean, made her mouth all the more enticing. 'Let me kiss you.'

'Stop messing about, Brent,' she complained. 'Why should I?' But her throat had gone dry and her heart had started beating faster.

'Because it might not be so bad . . . I've had quite a lot of experience at kissing.'

'I can imagine,' she said feigning disdain.

He bent his head but she turned her face away from him.

'Brent, stop it!'

'No, I'm going to kiss you.'

'No, you're not.'

'Yes, I am.'

It was turning into a game. He lifted her chin and gently brought her face to his. Her resistance was token and, when he placed a kiss on her lips fleetingly, she collected it with concealed pleasure for she had often wondered how it would feel to be kissed by Brent Shackleton.

'There,' he said, with a smile of triumph. 'Was that so bad?'

'It's not that it was unpleasant, Brent,' she conceded, blushing, with an appeal to his better nature in her eyes. 'But you should have more decency than to take advantage. And I shouldn't let you. I have Howard to consider.'

'It's too restricting to have a conscience, Maxine. I learnt that a long time ago.'

'I take it then that you don't have one.'

'No, I don't have a conscience. And nor should you. It's not as if you're engaged or anything.'

Having kissed her once, he moved to kiss her again. This time, she met him halfway, her lips parted ready, waiting to receive him.

He was right, of course. She was not engaged.

Encouraged, his kiss grew more intense, lingering, savouring the pleasure of her lips, the delicious taste of her. She knew it

225

was wrong, against all her principles, but it was so toe-curlingly pleasurable. Of course, it could not go on . . . well, for no more than a second or two at any rate . . . She could not allow it to go on . . . At least, she shouldn't . . . Then, she realised that her own arms were around his waist, that she was participating almost whole-heartedly in a romantic embrace with this man when she had Howard to consider. But this one kiss wouldn't hurt. Like he said, she wasn't engaged . . .

He pressed himself against her and to feel him rock hard against her belly was the ultimate compliment. Hungry for her, his mouth searched for hers more urgently, his hands wandered to her bottom . . .

'*No!*'

She wrenched herself away from him decisively.

'God! How can I live with myself?' she groaned, realising how far she had let him go, realising how far she had let herself go. 'I'm sorry, Brent. I shouldn't have . . .' She turned away in shame and guilt, her head in her hands. 'I don't want you to get the wrong idea or think I'm easy, Brent, because I'm not . . . But you shouldn't have . . . Please don't take liberties with me again. You're supposed to be my friend. I came here trusting you. I didn't come here to be seduced.'

'Don't worry, I won't tell Zadoc if you won't,' he said, and she could not decide whether he was angry or mocking.

'It's all right for you, with no conscience at all, but I feel I'll have to tell him,' she said, 'to salve mine.'

'Then more fool you, Maxine. If you tell him he won't trust you ever again. He won't see it as my fault, but yours. Still, that's up to you . . . *I* can live with the consequences.'

'You're an absolute rotter, Brent Shackleton. A cad. Did you know that?'

A grin spread all over his face.

'Now you're making fun of me. Stop it!' She turned to pummel his chest with her fists in her disillusionment, but he took them and held them firm.

'You know,' he said in a whisper, his mouth only inches from hers, poised, threatening to kiss her again. 'I'm pretty certain you'd come to bed with me . . .'

'Not if your damned bed's in the same state as the rest of the house, I wouldn't. Will you let go of me *please*?' He let her go. 'Now, do you still want me to go over those arrangements with you before I go?'

Chapter 18

Kenny Wheeler arrived to collect Alice Harper from the dairy house at five past eight. Whilst she was sitting waiting, all dressed and ready to go in a stylish yellow linen dress with a dirndl skirt and tight bodice that conveniently buttoned down the front, she heard the sound of a motor's engine in the street. As she flounced through the entry to meet him, her heart beat faster in anticipation of another evening of lusty, exciting love-making that was free of commitment. Kenny was certainly different to Charles. He was relatively uninhibited and only interested in her for pleasure. That was fair enough. It was entirely mutual.

She waltzed round to the passenger side of his van. 'Blimey, this is a posh new van,' she commented admiringly as she got in beside him.

'I don't know about posh,' he answered morosely, pulling away from the kerb.

'Did you get into trouble over it?'

'Not really. Accidents happen. I reported it as an accident.'

She thought how intense he seemed. The bright-eyed roguish look that had drawn her to him in the first place had disappeared.

'Din't nobody ask how it fell into a quarry?'

'Yes, but I said I'd taken my missus on a picnic. I said we got out to enjoy the view and the next thing I knew the perishing van was rolling away and I had no chance to stop it before it

228

toppled over the edge. It seemed to satisfy the transport manager
. . . Which way do we go for somewhere quiet, eh? Somewhere
where we can talk.'

'Talk?' She hadn't put alluring new underwear on just to talk.

'There's something I've got to tell you.'

'Oh. Did you get into trouble with your wife, then?'

'You could say that.'

Alice felt a sudden surge of alarm. 'Did she find out about
me then?'

'No, not you, Alice . . . Rose. She found out about Rose.'

She breathed a sigh of relief. 'How did she find out about *her*?'

'That's what I need to talk to you about. Where can we stop
where it's quiet?'

'I dunno. D'you want to stop in the van an' talk, or walk an'
talk?' She thought that sounded quite amusing but suppressed
any laughter; this evidently was not an appropriate time for
jokes, judging by the serious expression on his face.

'We'll stop in the van. I don't want to risk this one rolling off
without me.'

He had driven down Cross Guns Street and they were at the
junction with Dixons Green which was lined with trees, and
impressive houses where the prosperous professionals of the
borough lived. The Fountain public house was on the corner.

'We could go for a drink if you like,' Alice suggested. 'This
pub here, or the Shoulder of Mutton just along the road.'

'Better not,' he said glumly.

'If you carry on over this road into Bean Road then, there's
Buffery Park down there at the bottom. We can find somewhere
quiet, or walk in the park.'

Eventually they pulled up at the edge of Buffery Park in a
select backwater called Selbourne Road. A street lamp picked out
a man walking a dog, apart from whom, the road was deserted.

'So, what is it you've got to talk to me about?' Alice enquired,
on tenterhooks by this time. She was beginning to fancy that
any chance of lovemaking was slipping away.

Kenny shuffled and delved into his pocket for a packet of cigarettes. He opened it and offered her one.

'I don't smoke,' she said, her glumness beginning to match his.

He put a cigarette to his lips and lit it. As he inhaled the smoke, he wound down the side window a few inches and sighed heavily. 'I don't really know where to begin.'

'Start with Rose, if it's all to do with her,' Alice suggested logically.

'Damned Rose!' he groaned and shook his head in despair. 'My missus found out about damned Rose.'

'You said.'

'Trouble is, it affects you as well . . .'

She rolled her eyes. 'Here we go. How, for God's sake?'

'You know her husband's a merchant seaman, don't you? Well he gave her the bloody clap when he came home on leave. Picked it up in Rotterdam, she reckons. Anyway, as you can probably guess, she passed it onto me and, guess what . . . I passed it on to my missus.'

Alice gasped and began to tremble.

She knew what was coming next; of course she did.

But she could not speak.

And it seemed like another hour before Kenny confirmed what she feared most.

'So that means I've passed it on to you as well, Alice. God, I'm so sorry . . .'

'Christ!' Alice uttered and her voice was low, suddenly hot and frightened as she accepted the inevitable.

'I feel such a swine. I wouldn't pass that on for the world – not to you, not to anybody – not knowingly.'

'Oh, Jesus Christ!' Her eyes swivelled to the roof of the van then became fixed on her lap, staring vacantly at the yellow linen material of her lovely dress. She was looking pale as porcelain now. 'That's just about my flippin' luck, that is . . . Are you certain, Kenny?' She looked into his eyes earnestly, seeking some scrap of hope to cling to. 'I mean, are you absolutely certain?'

'I went to the doctor. I was getting this horrible burning pain when I pee'd. So I looked for more clues and one morning when I got up I noticed I'd got a discharge . . . The doctor told me what it was likely to be, and sent me for some tests . . . It's gonorrhoea, Alice. There's no question. And it takes six weeks to cure.'

She screwed her eyes up and put her hands to her face in horror.

'You know what that means, don't you?' she said angrily, and her tone told him she was blaming him already. 'It means I've passed it on to Charles, poor sod . . . Oh, *Christ*!' She clenched her fists in her anguish. 'The only time I ever let him touch me without a French letter on and you're telling me you'd already given me the clap. Oh, God! I've got to tell *him* now. Jesus Christ, Kenny, he's my gaffer at work. I'll have no job any more. I'll have to leave. He was sorting out my divorce for me . . . *Oh, bloody hell!*'

'I shouldn't say anything to him till you've had it confirmed. It might not have passed to you.'

She shook her head. 'Not with my luck . . .'

'Nor mine, either. But that ain't all . . .'

'Oh, God! What else?'

'The doctor said I'd have to be tested for syphilis.'

'You mean the pox? Christ! Are you sure you ain't got crabs to go with it an' all? God, it's a pity you ain't got flippin' beri-beri or diphtheria you could load on to me as well.'

'Syphilis can take up to three months to show after you've caught it,' Kenny said, ignoring her diatribe. 'And, if you've got it, it takes two years to get rid of it. I've had to have a blood test for it. You'll have to as well, Alice . . . I'm really sorry.'

'Not half as sorry as me.'

'But even if neither of us has got syphilis, it means we can't have sex again for at least three months just in case we have . . . Three months without sex. It'll kill me.'

'Serves you right, Kenny Wheeler. That's all I can say. I'm not sure I want sex ever again after this.'

231

'But it ain't my fault, Alice. And o'course, my missus has chucked me out. I'm gonna have to ask Brent Shackleton if I can doss down with him. Mind you, I reckon he'd welcome a lodger.'

'That's up to him. I know what I'd welcome – a cigarette. Can I have one?'

He felt in his pocket. 'I thought you said you didn't smoke.'

'I think I just started.'

Brent Shackleton possessed no spare bed, so Kenny Wheeler slept on the threadbare settee that had witnessed so much exotic sport between Eleanor and Stephen Hemming. Brent rose early next morning and, while he made bacon sandwiches for his houseguest and himself, he pondered Maxine Kite and how he imagined he had whet her appetite for him with a couple of stolen kisses.

'Breakfast's up!' he called, taking two plates to the table.

'Where?' Kenny queried.

'In here. I'm not waiting on you.'

Kenny lumbered into the kitchen lethargically, rubbed his eyes and sat down. He looked at the sandwiches, lifted the top piece of bread from one and cursorily inspected the interior.

'Have you put any sauce on?' he asked.

'I haven't got any sauce.'

'What, no brown sauce? Some bloody boarding house this is.'

'It'll do for you till we go off to Southampton and the *Queen Mary*.' He rubbed his hands together at the prospect. 'You'll be able to have as much brown sauce as you like on the *Queen Mary*. You'll be able to drown in the stuff. God, I bet you're glad your wife kicked you out, eh, Kenny? Just think, if she hadn't you wouldn't have been able to go. Just think of all those beautiful rich women on that ship. All begging for it. I intend to have me some. That's all they go for, you know – to get laid. Suit you down to the ground.' He bit into his sandwich and they fell silent while they ate.

Kenny had not told Brent that he'd been infected with a

venereal disease. Nor would he. He would confess to nobody. The stigma was too immense. As far as Brent was concerned, his poor wife had learned of his encounter with Maxine's sister because of the van being wrecked in the quarry. Perfectly feasible.

'So,' Brent ventured, 'are you seeing Maxine's sister again?'

'Alice? I doubt it.'

'Why? Wasn't she worth all the trouble?'

He shrugged, avoiding Brent's eyes. 'Depends how you mean. If you're asking whether I would ever have got involved with the girl, the answer's no. If you mean was she worth the effort for one night, the answer's definitely yes.'

'You had her, then?'

'Course I had her. While me poor van was making its way into the blasted quarry.'

Brent guffawed and the memory even raised a grin in Kenny at last. He was beginning to see the funny side. His affliction, though, was not providing him with much mirth at all.

'I'll be bedding Maxine soon,' Brent remarked casually. 'She was here yesterday. She didn't object too strongly to being kissed . . .'

'Bet you five pounds you don't,' Kenny said.

'Okay. You're on.'

'Alice,' Charles said, after he'd finished dictating his last letter, which she had taken down using her own concoction of squiggles and shapes that only she could understand. 'I know you're not given to perpetual smiles – which is a great pity, for when you do smile your whole demeanour improves – but these last few days you definitely seem to have been a trifle preoccupied and even worried. What's bothering you, my love? I've never known you so distant. Can I help?'

Alice tried to quell the tears that were ready to flood her eyes. She looked down at her shorthand notebook that was blurred through the haze and a tear trickled down her cheek unchecked. She screwed her eyes up, releasing more tears and Charles got up from his creaky leather chair and walked round his desk that was piled high with files, to hold her and comfort her.

'What is it, my love? Please, you must tell me. A problem shared—'

'Well, it's a problem shared, Charles, and no two ways . . .' she whimpered.

'Tell me.' He knelt down in front of her and took her hands in his, placing her notepad and pencil on his desk. 'Tell me what it is. I'll help you all I can. You know I will.'

'Oh, Charles!' she cried in a great sob. 'I don't deserve your kindness. I never have. I'm a slut and I don't suppose I'll ever be any different. I *have* got somethin' to tell you an' you ain't gonna like it one bit. In fact, when I've told you I shall go . . . an' you'll never see me again. You won't want to see me again – ever.'

'So what is this calamity?' he asked quietly, rubbing the backs of her hands affectionately with his thumbs, bracing himself for the worst his limited imagination could concoct.

'I've got the clap . . .' She shrugged her shoulders and sighed deeply to emphasise the hopelessness of her despair, while Charles looked at her with open-mouthed incredulity. 'I've been with another chap and he gave me the clap.'

'You're not trying to kid me, are you Alice?'

'Would I kid you about somethin' like this?'

'No, I don't suppose you would. So who is this chap?' He let go her hands as if they were covered in oozing sores.

'It don't matter who he is, Charles. It's done. You can't change nothin'.' She pulled her handkerchief from her sleeve and wiped her eyes.

He got up from his knees and walked back to his chair. 'That means I have it, too, I imagine?'

'It's a racin' certainty.'

He stood by his chair and faced the window, silent for a few seconds, trying to compose himself. 'God, how demeaning. How damned embarrassing. You know, I thought it peculiar this morning when I got up and had a pee. Burned, it did. Awful. That explains it. Have you been to the doctor's?'

She nodded.

'So it's all confirmed?'

She nodded again.

A lorry carrying a load of coal trundled past the window and backfired. Charles barely noticed it, but Alice nearly jumped out of her skin.

'Oh, well . . . That'll put you out of action for a while, Alice. Serve you right, too. I always knew you had to be a bit on the wayward side, but I nurtured the hope that I'd offered you enough to temper your ways . . . Obviously not.'

'I suppose you don't want me workin' here any longer, Charles?'

'Well, it would make things rather . . . strained,' he agreed.

'All right, I'll go. I said I would. I'll go right away. I'll just collect my things. Thanks for not getting angry about it. I thought you would.'

'Not angry? Actually, Alice, I'm bloody seething.'

Plans for the band's season on the *Queen Mary* began in earnest, since the ship was due to sail on Wednesday 4th November. Everybody, with the exception of Maxine, had applied for a passport and Brent had to ensure that their dues to the Musicians' Union were all fully paid up. He had confirmed to Seth Cohen that the band was available, although he deliberately failed to tell him that they would be only a six-piece by the time they embarked, even though the accommodation aboard ship was reserved for seven people. Brent was still hoping to persuade Maxine to join them. He had even considered having a quiet, man-to-man chat with Howard, to get him to release her from her promise to stay close to him. On second thoughts, though, he decided such a request would be hypocritical, since he didn't like the man anyway and only spoke to him under sufferance. To seek favours from him at this late stage, especially favours that would deprive him of his woman, would seem inordinately cavalier, even by Brent's standards.

One rehearsal day, Brent invited Maxine to the White Hart in Paradise Street at lunchtime in a last ditch effort to persuade her.

'The band will be useless without you,' he told her, in an earnest endeavour to appeal to both her vanity and her conscience. 'The rest of them won't have their hearts in it – and not just me. Our performance is bound to suffer. I know it will. I mean, I've never heard anybody play stride piano like you. How do you think we'll sound without that? All that syncopation. There'll be a big hole in the sound. And who'll be able to sing love songs like you?'

'Pansy,' Maxine replied. 'I told you.'

'She can't *do* it like you. I told *you*.' Sitting side-by-side at a table, he took her hand and she made no effort to withdraw it. 'I'll be honest, Maxine, I'm inclined to call the whole thing off . . .'

'No, Brent, that's blackmail. I'm not going to fall for that. Besides, you can't back out now. The contract's signed. You have your passports and all that paraphernalia. And you certainly can't let Seth Cohen down. You'd be blacklisted everywhere the moment you backed out.'

'But there's no point in us going without you.'

'Yes there is, and stop being pathetic. I'm just one member of the band. One member you can actually do without.'

'You're wrong, Maxine. We can't do without you.'

She removed her hand from his. 'I've given my word, Brent, and I won't go back on it. I admit, I would love to go to New York, that it'll be the adventure of a lifetime. If I was unattached I'd jump at the chance, you know I would, but I'm prepared to forego it all for Howard's sake. I'm sorry, Brent. I'm not going to change my mind. Wouldn't I be fickle if I did?'

'So Sunday is going to be the last time you play with The Owls and the Pussycats?'

'Yes . . . Unfortunately.'

* * *

236

And before they knew it, Sunday 1st November had arrived. Howard did not accompany Maxine to the Gas Street Basin Jazz Club because of a diocesan meeting, but he was due to join her when it finished. It was a night of mixed emotions. The rest of the band were excited at the prospect of their *Queen Mary* adventure but sad that Maxine was leaving. She had made her mind up and was not going to be moved.

'Oh, Maxine, we shall miss you,' Pansy pleaded in the dressing room after they had finished. 'I do wish you were coming with us. You'd be my room-mate on the ship. Just think of the lovely time we'd have.'

'But you've got Toots,' Maxine replied. 'If I came, Howard would still be at home and I'd be miserable because I'd want to be with him. I'd miss him terribly, I know I would. It wouldn't be any fun for me, Pansy, and I wouldn't be much fun for you.'

'You've got it proper bad, haven't you, Maxine?'

Maxine sighed and buttoned up the blouse she was wearing. 'Yes, I admit it. But I can't help how I feel. I'm happy. I've never been so happy. Howard is everything to me. And I'm everything to him. Do you understand why I can't go, Pansy?'

'Yes, I think I do,' she answered quietly. 'He's lovely, is Howard, and I think you're very lucky. I don't blame you for wanting to hold on to him.'

'I knew *you'd* understand.'

'Well, wish us all the best of luck, eh, Maxine? I daresay we'll need it.'

'I do. You know I do. But it should be fun.'

Pansy nodded. 'Yes, it should be fun.'

The two girls looked at each other, each certain that the other was going to burst into tears. They hugged each other in a sisterly embrace.

'I wish you all the luck in the world,' Maxine said over Pansy's shoulder, her voice thin with emotion.

'You too, Maxine. Look after yourself.'

'I will. And don't forget to send me a postcard from New York. I want to know everything that goes on.'

'I promise.'

They said their goodbyes and the others, in turn, all gave her a kiss on the cheek as they left her waiting for Howard. Except Brent. Brent stayed with her until Howard arrived. It had started to drizzle and the miserable autumn weather matched Maxine's mood.

'I shan't see you any more,' Brent said poignantly as they stood outside on that cold November night.

She felt tears sting her eyes again. 'I hope we can keep in touch. After all, we've shared a lot together. We've been good friends, Brent. Very good friends.' She took out her handkerchief to stem her tears. 'God, why do I keep crying? I hate saying goodbye.'

He put his arm around her to comfort her and drew her to him. 'It's not too late to change your mind.'

She allowed his show of affection, resting her head on his shoulder, trying hard to stop herself weeping. His consoling gesture only induced her to weep more, however. It was such a sad moment leaving these friends she had got to know so well; these friends whose company she enjoyed, whose musical expertise she admired so much.

'It's breaking my heart to see you all go, Brent.' She raised her head and looked into his eyes and, unemotional as he normally was, her sorrow seemed to touch him.

'Come with us then,' he pleaded.

'I can't. You know I can't.'

He unhanded her at the same moment that Howard's car came into view, turning the corner from Broad Street.

'Look, Howard's here,' she said. 'Write to me, won't you . . . Let me know how you're getting on . . . Goodbye, Brent.' She stood on tip-toe, gave him a brief kiss on the lips and turned to go. She boarded Howard's car and waved to Brent as he walked away.

'Sorry I'm late,' Howard said, effecting a three-point turn. 'But at least Brent's been keeping you company, by the looks of it.'

She looked at him to see if his face showed any resentment of the fact. But all she detected was a self-satisfied expression. Yet he must have seen her kiss Brent goodbye. Then again, Howard was not of a jealous nature.

'Just saying goodbye, Howard . . . Oh, Howard, I feel so sad. I probably won't ever see any of them again.'

'You've been crying . . .' He turned the steering wheel to enter Broad Street.

She wiped her tears again. 'I have. I'll be all right in a minute.'

'It's always so hard to say goodbye to close friends. In any case, you'll keep in touch, won't you?'

'I intend to. Who knows? I might even end up playing with them again when they come back – if they ever come back . . .' She tried to compose herself. 'So how did your meeting go?'

'Oh, brilliant. Brilliant, Maxine,' he said with a smile of self-satisfaction.

'It must have done. I've never seen you looking so smug. So what was it all about? Can you tell me?'

He slowed down to negotiate the junction at Five Ways. 'Yes, I can tell you. I'm going to have to tell you, since it affects you. I've been offered a new living and I've accepted. I'm to become a vicar.'

'A vicar?' She turned to look at him, proud that he should have achieved this step-up so soon. 'That's brilliant, Howard. God, you must be thrilled to pieces.' And didn't it fall just nicely with the cessation of her jazz band activities?

'I am. It'll mean an increase in my stipend, a whole vicarage to live in – a whole new responsibility.'

'Oh, I'm so proud of you, Howard. So how long have you known this was going to happen?'

'A few weeks now.'

'So why on earth didn't you tell me before?'

'I wanted to keep it a surprise until it was all cut and dried. Now it is. I must say, it's all turning into a bit of a rush. I take up my new living a week today.'

'So soon? You'll have your work cut out getting everything ready. Still, I can help. It's not as if you're having to move a whole household. Just you and a few chattels.'

'Even so, it'll take a few trunks to get all my stuff packed.'

'But you'll get it all in your car. If not one journey, then a couple at most.'

'I don't think so, Maxine. Anything I can't take in the car will have to go by rail.'

'By rail? Crikey, where are you going to, for heaven's sake? Timbuktu?'

He changed down a gear to negotiate the Crossroads at Bearwood. 'Remember the fairground over there in Lightwoods Park I took you to, Maxine?' he said. 'The first time we went out together.'

'Of course I remember, Howard . . . So where are you moving to? You haven't answered me.'

'Oh, sorry – Norfolk.'

'Norfolk?' she repeated incredulously. The very word was a dagger stabbing her in the heart, then twisting to aggravate the hurt. 'But Norfolk is on the other side of England, Howard. Miles away.'

'It's not so far.'

'Of course it is. How shall we get to see each other?'

'Well, by train. You'll come and stay whenever you can, I hope, until such time as we can think seriously about getting married . . . I assume we shall get married at some time. I hope so at any rate.'

Contemplating marriage at some time in the future was all well and good, but this news did not augur well for their immediate love life.

'And do you think your parishioners might not have something to say about a young woman staying at the vicarage from time to time with their new vicar? Don't you think your house-keeper would talk? Don't you think something might be said?'

'Gosh, I hadn't thought about that, Maxine,' he responded naïvely. 'Maybe you'd better stay in an hotel when you come.'

They fell bizarrely quiet.

The initial buzz of pleasure she'd felt at his news abruptly dispersed like steam in a wind. She needed to ponder this a few minutes more.

They turned onto the Birmingham New Road. The factory chimneys of Oldbury slipped by on their right, still spewing columns of smoke that were denser than the drizzling night sky. What had brought about this discrepancy in their mutual hopes, in their dreams that were no longer synchronised? Maxine needed a second or two to translate what she was feeling into more coherent thoughts. But her first perceptions were that she felt unwanted, betrayed and apprehensive about their future.

Five minutes later they turned into Gypsy Lane, the steep climb seemed endless by the feeble street lights. In another two or three minutes they would be at Willowcroft.

Still they remained silent.

When the house was in sight, Howard at last reacted to the growing realisation that something had upset Maxine.

'What is it, my angel? You've gone quiet.'

'Yes, I know . . .'

'Why?'

'I'm not so sure that I shall go to Norfolk, Howard.' Her tone told him she was hurt.

'Why ever not?' He drew the car to a halt on the gravel drive, killed the engine and turned to face her.

'Can't you imagine?'

'Because of what my parishioners might say?'

'To hell with your parishioners.' She exploded with a haugh-tiness he'd never believed she possessed. 'Oh, to hell with you, Howard. I'm going in. Goodnight.'

'Maxine!' he clung to her arm to prevent her escape. 'What's this all about? I thought you were pleased for me. I thought my promotion made you happy.'

'I'm not unhappy about your promotion,' she said, incredulous that he could be so insensitive. 'You deserve it. But don't you see?'

'See what? I don't understand.'

'Then go home and think about it. It might dawn on you eventually.' She opened the car door and thrust her legs out.

'Please, Maxine, don't go. I don't understand. You *must* tell me what's wrong.'

'If you don't know, then you have no true feelings for me. It's as simple as that. And if you don't know, my trying to explain it won't make it any plainer.'

'You're upset that you've left the band. I understand that. But why make me suffer?'

'If you remember, I gave up the band for you, Howard. I gave up the opportunity of playing on the *Queen Mary* for you. I gave up the chance of going to New York for you. Why? Because I didn't want to go away and *leave* you. My last gig was tonight. Why? Because I wanted to stay *near* you. Did you hear me properly, Howard? – I said, *near* you. And just when I *need* you more than ever, now that all my friends have all but left the country, you blithely announce that you're going away to live and work in Norfolk – miles away – next week, without so much as a thought for me or what I might feel. Well, thank you! That tells me there's a difference in how we feel about each other, and how irrelevant I must be where your career is concerned!'

'Of course I want to be near you, Maxine. Of course you're not irrelevant. But it's different for me. It's my career.'

'Ah . . . So your career warrants a different set of rules? Your career takes precedence over mine? Your career excuses you to ride roughshod over me?'

'Of course it doesn't, Maxine . . . Look, I love you with all my heart, you know I do. But I have to go where my living takes me.'

'Whereas, I'm prepared *not* to go where mine takes me – for *your* sake – you're not prepared to offer me the same consideration. Howard, that speaks volumes.'

'Maxine, it's not like that. Believe me, it's not like that. You said, if you had to choose, you'd give up your career.'

'So I did, but you also said I didn't need to. Remember?'

'I mean us to be married, Maxine. I want you to be my wife. This is supposed to be a step towards it. If I didn't love you I wouldn't even consider marriage. I wouldn't even have accepted this new living. I accepted it so that we could eventually be married.'

'I'm sorry. I see it differently. I *am* upset about saying goodbye to my friends in the band, but this really is like spitting in my face. I'm so hurt, Howard. I hope someday you'll come to understand . . .'

'But Maxine—'

She wished she could cry now. It might make him realise. But she could not.

'There have only ever been two things in my life really important to me, Howard – my music and you . . . Well, thank God I still have my music . . . Goodbye.'

'I'll see you tomorrow, Maxine. We'll talk about it when you've had time to think about it more.'

'Don't bother,' she retorted acidly as she got out of the car.

She opened the front door and went in the house, without looking back.

Chapter 19

Maxine finished in the bathroom, dressed and went downstairs. To look at her emerging from her bedroom you would think everything was normal and under control. She looked smart, as always; well turned out; her make-up was immaculate and so was her hair. But there was no change of heart, only a resolute determination to defy Howard and everything his decision meant. Only Henzey, hanging Aldo's napkins to dry over a clothes horse, perceived through the polished finish that she was far too preoccupied.

'Is anything the matter?' Henzey asked, with sisterly concern.

'Has Will gone to work yet?'

'He's just about to go. Is anything wrong?'

'I want a lift to Handsworth, Henzey.'

'Handsworth?'

'I'm going on the *Queen Mary* after all. By hook or by crook. I have to know what I should do – what I need. I have to see Brent Shackleton.'

'You'll need a passport anyway, I would've thought. But surely there's no time to get one now if it sails tomorrow? Why? What's brought on this change of heart?'

Maxine explained briefly and Henzey was suitably outraged. Just then, Will stepped back in the house.

'Damned pruning shears! I've just been to the shed to look for them. They're rusty as hell. I reckon I'll have to buy some new ones . . . Is there something wrong?'

'Will, can you give Maxine a lift to Handsworth?'

'Yes, I should think so.'

'She wants to catch up with Brent. She's decided to go on the *Queen Mary* after all and I don't blame her.'

'Oh? What's brought that on?'

'Oh, I'll tell you in the car, Will.'

'Are you ready now?'

Maxine nodded solemnly. 'I'll just get my coat.'

'But you've had no breakfast, Maxine.'

'Don't worry, Henzey. I'll get some at Brent's. Expect me when you see me.'

They left. On the drive over to Brent's house Maxine explained in detail how last night's events had unfolded. Will listened attentively, punctuating her flow with kind words of consolation and advice.

'How could he have been so thoughtless, Will?' she said ruefully. 'How could he expect me to be pleased that he was going away after I had particularly avoided going away myself? Would he have appreciated me more if I'd decided to go on the *Queen Mary* and leave *him*?'

'I understand how you feel, Maxine, but are you sure you're doing the right thing? Are you sure you're not being rather impetuous, dashing off without giving Howard the opportunity to redeem himself? Especially since marriage is at stake?'

'This is not an impulse, Will,' she assured him. 'It's well considered. I've been awake most of the night considering it.'

At last they arrived at Brent's house after some hesitant directions from Maxine.

'This is it, Will,' she said. 'Thanks for the lift. I'll see you when I see you.'

He waited at the kerbside till he saw Brent open the door and let her in. Then he waved and shook his head sympathetically.

'Maxine!' Brent exclaimed with a delighted grin. 'You're the last person on earth I expected to see. How come you're here?'

She stepped inside. 'I want to come with you on the *Queen Mary*,' she said simply.

He could not hide the triumph in his eyes as he shut the door behind her. 'I knew you would. I just knew it. That's brilliant!'

'Have you got a piece of toast or something and a cup of tea? I've had nothing to eat yet. I'm starving.'

'You're in luck, Maxine. I'm just about to create the most wonderful breakfast imaginable.'

She followed him into the kitchen. Again, it was almost as bad as the first time she had seen it. 'Look at the state of this place again. After all the hard work I put into it.'

'Kenny can do it later. Anyway, what's brought this on – this change of mind?'

She explained again and Brent swelled with self-satisfaction.

'I could see it coming, Maxine. I told you what would happen. I always knew Zadoc the Priest would let you down.'

She shrugged. 'Such foresight should qualify you as Nathan the Prophet then.'

'Oh, very funny. Well, I could tell what a ne'er-do-well he was, Maxine. You're best off without him. Stick by your friends, 'cause they'll stick by you.'

'I'm just so angry, Brent,' she told him. 'You can't imagine how angry I am.'

'A woman scorned, eh? Listen, we have to get you a passport – and quick.'

'I know, but how?'

'You'll have to go to London. To the Passport Office. It's the only way.'

'When?'

'Soon as you can . . . Today . . . It'll have to be today. I'd better come with you. Got any money?'

'Yes, I've got some money.'

'Enough for our rail fares and a photo?'

She shrugged. 'I imagine so.'

'Right. We'll have some breakfast quick and dash off to Snow Hill Station.'

*   *   *

That night, Howard called at Willowcroft. He had spent last night wide awake, trying to come to terms with this massive and sudden disruption to a life that had been so ordered, yet so varied and satisfying, but which, all of a sudden, had taken an unexpected turn. Maxine threatened to be no longer a part of it and he did not like it, for he truly adored her and treasured in his heart everything they'd enjoyed together.

'She's not here, Howard,' Will said, 'but please come in if you want to wait.'

'If you don't mind, Will.'

'We're in the sitting room. Go on through.'

Henzey greeted him warmly, not wishing to show any prejudgement. After all, she liked this man. 'Hello, Howard. So what on earth have you two been up to?' Her tone was one of friendly admonishment.

'Oh, Henzey, it seems I've made an awful botch of things.'

'So I hear.'

'Nobody, I swear, could have been more insensitive than I have been. I've come to salvage what I can. When are you expecting her back?'

She put down the newspaper she'd been reading. 'Howard, I haven't the vaguest idea. She went to Brent Shackleton's house first thing. She's intent on joining the *Queen Mary* trip after all.'

'Oh, no . . .' Howard sighed dejectedly. 'But I can't say I blame her . . . after I've been so thoughtless. How can I have been so blind, Henzey? How can I have been so stupid?'

'Anyone fancy a drink?' Will asked. 'I'll put the kettle on if anyone fancies a drink . . . Or have something stronger if you like . . .'

'Coffee would be very nice, Will,' Howard answered. 'Thank you.'

'Me too,' Henzey said. 'Are you prepared for a long wait, Howard? God knows what time she'll get back.'

'I'll wait for ever if I have to, Henzey.'

* * *

247

It was after midnight when Brent Shackleton returned Maxine Kite to Willowcroft.

'Oh, God, Howard's here,' she said when she saw his car parked behind Will's on the drive. 'Wish me luck, Brent.'

'I wish you luck, Maxine. Just don't let him talk you out of going now.'

'He won't. I've made up my mind. I'm going on the *Queen Mary* tomorrow and that's that. See you in the morning. Ten o'clock. Snow Hill Station.'

She bid him goodnight, closed the door of the Mercedes behind her and he sped off. She let herself in the house and saw that Will and Henzey had nobly kept Howard company, but that they looked tired and were probably anxious to get to bed. She bid them goodnight and said she would see them both at breakfast.

'I'm surprised to see you here,' Maxine said coolly to Howard when they were alone.

'I came to make amends.'

'It's a bit late for that,' she said, feeling vindictive for the first time in her life. She took off her coat, tossed it across the back of the settee and sat facing him, her back erect, defiant, her legs crossed. But she was not savouring this situation where she had the upper hand, a situation she had neither sought nor expected. 'I'm leaving tomorrow to join the *Queen Mary*. I have to pack yet.'

'Henzey said you'd decided to go . . . I really can't blame you, Maxine. I'm so sorry, believe me. What I did so thoughtlessly. I didn't pay enough heed to what you'd been prepared to give up for me. Do you think you can find it in your heart to forgive me?'

'I think it's a bit soon to be thinking about forgiveness,' she said evenly. 'I'm just so angry you went ahead and did what you did without even *thinking* of talking it over with me, even when your promotion was just a possibility. We could have made plans. You can't imagine how much you've hurt me.'

'I can see now how much . . .'

She sighed disconsolately. 'But that's only what you can *see*, Howard. What did you think you would gain by not telling me what you intended doing? What did you think I would do? We could so easily have sorted it out without it coming to this – if you'd only discussed it with me.'

He threw his hands out in a gesture of despair. 'I know, Maxine. I know.'

'It just seems that while I was prepared to give you so much, you took it with no comprehension—'

'Believe me, Maxine, it's not like that. I did it so we could be married – as a first step. Marriage was my first thought.'

'But that's not the point, Howard. I would have done anything for you. I would have walked through fire for you. I would have died for you. And how do you repay me? By acting as if I were an irrelevance. How do you think that makes me feel? And now you ask for forgiveness? . . . No matter how much you apologise, no matter what you say, I can't forgive you.'

'Oh, Maxine . . .' He moved to hold her but she shrugged him off and he was visibly affected by her rebuff. 'Am I repulsive, too, all of a sudden?'

'It's not a question of being repulsive, but why should I reward you? What you've done to me is like smacking me in the face for being considerate. Do you expect me to turn the other cheek, like the Bible says I should? Well, I won't.'

'I can only hope that in time you'll forgive me.'

'I doubt I shall.'

The disdain in her voice surprised him. Never had he believed she could be so detached.

'We have eight weeks ahead of us, Maxine. Eight weeks when we shall be apart. Let's see what happens after that, eh? Let's see if we can patch things up when you return.'

She shrugged nonchalantly.

'I suppose you'll forget all about me,' he said, changing tack. 'There'll be so much going on you won't have time to think about me.'

'Quite possibly,' she said with some satisfaction. 'If so, it's of your own making.'

'At least you'll have Brent to keep you company.'

'Well now, there's a thought,' she replied cuttingly.

'Are you sure all this upset isn't because of him?'

Maxine gasped with indignation. 'Have I ever given you reason to think so?' All right, she had allowed him to kiss her, but it had meant nothing.

'You seemed very friendly last night . . . and I suppose you've been with him all day today.'

'Yes, I have, Howard.' She sounded defiant now. 'I've been to London with him, as a matter of fact. He was *thoughtful* enough to go with me, to make sure I could get a passport.' She thought it best not to say she'd paid for his ticket. 'We had a meal together in London.' Neither would she tell him she'd paid for that as well. 'We've only just got back. He very *thoughtfully* dropped me at the door. Does that mean I'm in love with him, do you think?'

'Sarcasm doesn't become you, Maxine. Anyway, I've no wish to argue, especially about Brent Shackleton. I know he's your friend and colleague. I respect that. I meant no slur on either of you. I'm sorry.' Howard was getting nowhere with that line of reasoning, only making matters worse. 'I'll write to you – care of the *Queen Mary* at Southampton. Will you write back? . . . Please?'

'I'll see how I feel.'

She did not sound convincing enough. 'Please, Maxine. You must. We've meant too much to each other to let it be ruined over one thoughtless mistake. I'm distraught at what's happened – at my own crass stupidity.'

'Well, I suppose that's a step in the right direction.'

'The next eight weeks will be a critical time for us, Maxine. I'm really not looking forward to it.'

'I need that time now to think, Howard,' she responded, trying to be rational. 'The damage has been done. I doubt if just eight weeks will put it right.'

'Where there's a will . . .'

'Oh, Howard . . . I don't know whether I can risk being hurt again.'

'I understand how you feel, my love. I really do. But your anger will subside.'

Maybe it would. With time to contemplate she might come to understand better, learn to accept his foibles, her own foibles. Maybe, when this merciless anger had subsided, her love for him might rise to the surface again and triumph over this intolerable hurt.

'So shall I write to you, Maxine?'

'Okay. Write if you want,' she conceded with a heavy sigh. 'Then, let's see what happens after eight weeks.'

'I know how I'll feel, Maxine.'

'But expect no miracles from me, Howard . . . I think you'd better go now. It's late and I have to pack and be up early in the morning.' She got up from the settee and moved to the front door.

He followed her and, as she held the door open, he stepped outside into the cold night air. Bonfire night was only two evenings away and several early firecrackers punctuated the strained silence.

'I won't say goodbye, Maxine. Just God bless you till I see you again.'

The Owls and the Pussycats boarded the *Queen Mary* on Tuesday afternoon, having travelled by rail from Birmingham to Paddington, then crossing to Waterloo Station by taxi for the '*Queen Mary* Special' to Southampton. The journey had been good-humoured, all speculating on some aspect of their cruising. Pansy wondered if they would have to sleep in a cabin no bigger than the privy at the top of their yard and Maxine wondered how they would fare for laundering their smalls. Kenny, subdued, wondered if there would be a doctor on board, and nobody could quite understand why.

The boat train pulled slowly into its special platform alongside the Ocean Dock, prolonging the anticipation. As they spilled out onto the platform carrying their hand luggage, Maxine's first thought was to catch a glimpse of the ship. It was soon in view, dwarfing the transit sheds and towering over the dockside cranes as if they were built from a Meccano outfit. They stood in awe of the three red funnels that crowned the huge black hull and white superstructure that looked far too large to float, let alone achieve high cruising speeds.

They hurried towards the ship. Stewards, smart in their immaculate uniforms, dealt with the increasing bustle and excitement at the quay. They trundled large trolleys stacked with expensive-looking luggage towards the conveyors that would transfer it all inside. Everything was tagged with the owner's name, cabin number, deck and class.

'I'm going to wait till I see my double bass appear,' said Charlie Holt, lingering. 'I don't trust this lot. What if it didn't get put on the boat?'

'Ship,' Ginger Tolley corrected pedantically. 'Don't let anybody hear you calling this monstrosity a boat else they'll have you walking the plank.'

'I'm inclined to wait as well,' Kenny agreed. 'I want to see my drum kit appear before I go inside.'

'Before you board, you mean,' Ginger said. 'On board ship you use nautical terms.'

'I ain't inside yet, so I'll speak landlubber language if you don't mind.'

Maxine and Pansy tutted patiently.

A steward approached them. 'May I see your tickets, please ladies?'

'We're in the band,' Maxine confessed proudly. 'The Owls and the Pussycats. Do we have to go in the same way as the crew?'

'You're part of the entertainment?' the steward asked.

'We are. So do we have a choice?' Pansy asked, tongue-in-cheek. 'Can't we pretend we're First Class?'

252

'We call it Cabin Class, ma'am.' He gave Pansy a cheeky wink. 'You're tasty enough, I grant you. If you all keep together – lads as well – I don't see why not. We're not that busy yet. This gangway, if you please . . .' He waved to a purser waiting by the entrance to the ship at the other end of the gently sloping, covered gangway.

The girls looked at each other, signalling their approval of him.

Inside the ship, they were all instantly taken aback by the Cabin Class's sumptuous main entrance with its ultra-smart shopping arcade. Fine wood panelling surrounded them, they were ankle-deep in soft carpet and everywhere was brilliantly lit. Never had they seen such splendour.

'Good afternoon,' a steward said. 'Welcome aboard the *Queen Mary*. My name is Thomas. This is the main entrance. As you can see, it extends the width of the ship and exits on both sides onto the Promenade Deck.'

'So which way to our cabins, Thomas?' Brent enquired brashly. 'We're on Deck C.'

'May I see your ticket, sir?'

'We're the band,' Maxine said helpfully.

'Ah! So you are Tourist Class. You should have boarded by the Tourist Class entrance.'

Pansy winked at him. 'Your mate at the bottom said we could come in this way,'

'Did he now?' He smiled amiably. 'Then we'll soon have you sorted out.'

Winking seemed to be a useful device on this ship, Pansy thought. It seemed to get you anywhere.

Thomas scrutinised the clipboard he was holding and flipped over some typed pages. 'Ah, yes, seven of you . . . In three cabins. The misses Hemming and Kite . . .' He met their eyes keenly. 'You occupy a two-berth cabin. Messrs Shackleton and Wheeler occupy a two-berth cabin and Messrs Holt, Randle and Tolley, a three-berth. If you prefer to shuffle that arrangement . . .'

He picked up their keys and they all trooped behind him.

'The cabins that artistes and entertainers occupy are equivalent to Tourist Class,' Thomas informed them. 'They're situated in the Tourist Class area, aft of Cabin Class.'

'What's Tourist Class?' Maxine asked, keen to know what she was getting.

They stopped at a lift and Thomas pressed a button to call it, then turned to her. 'Tourist Class is sort of second class but, to be honest, it's only slightly down the scale from Cabin Class as far as accommodation and facilities are concerned on this ship. Moreover, it's better than first class on most others. Third Class passengers occupy the forward part and even that's luxurious compared to other ships.'

The lift arrived and they piled in. As it descended, Thomas asked them about their music and told them that in New York there were great places to hear jazz. He had actually been last trip to a place called the Hotel Pennsylvania in New York and heard Benny Goodman and his Orchestra in concert.

'I'll make a point of coming to listen to you,' he said, 'since I'm a jazz fan. And by the way . . . if you didn't already know, there's a rehearsal room aboard ship – the Studio – specially soundproofed for private practice by our musicians during the voyage.'

'Brilliant!' Maxine said. 'Is there a piano in there?'

'A grand, I believe.'

'Crikey! They've thought of everything.'

The lift stopped and they all piled out.

'This is Deck C. Your cabins are this way. Your luggage should arrive any minute. I suggest that once you've settled in, you explore the ship and its facilities. As artists, you have no restrictions. You are free to enjoy everywhere . . . As long as you are appropriately dressed. Are you booked for a long stay?'

'Eight weeks,' Brent replied.

'You'll be here for Christmas, then. There are some great things planned.'

'Well, at least we'll be home soon after,' Maxine said, reminded of Howard.

'So . . . Here we are. Your cabins.' Thomas opened the doors to each and allowed them to enter. He informed them briefly of sailing time and eating arrangements and answered their questions. 'I do hope you enjoy your time aboard.'

'Thank you, Thomas,' Maxine said, looking round at what the cabin offered. 'We'll look out for you.'

'Bye!'

'D'you think we should have given him a tip?' Pansy asked when he had gone.

Maxine shrugged. 'Maybe. I don't know . . . Well, here we are, Pansy. Home for the next eight weeks. Which bunk do you fancy?'

'I don't mind. You choose.'

So they chose and inspected the wardrobes and drawers. The cabin was larger than either had anticipated. Its white walls and ceiling were relieved by high quality, dark wood furniture and the carpet under their feet was thick. Blissfully, the designers had thought to provide a sink with hot and cold taps, a mirror and even a couple of armchairs. The view through the porthole, which presently overlooked Southampton Docks, would soon yield a vista of the grey, winter Atlantic.

Their luggage arrived and they set about hanging up their dresses and stowing underwear and things in the drawers that they allocated themselves, chatting about this and that, laughing about little incidents that had happened on the journey. Pansy was aware that Maxine was smarting over Howard and she was careful to avoid any reference to him. She knew her friend would open up about him when she was good and ready.

'I wonder where we're playing tonight?' Maxine asked.

'I thought I heard Brent mention something called the Verandah Grill.'

'Till what time, I wonder.'

'Till everybody's had enough, Brent says. Oh, well, we don't have to get up early next morning, do we? Come on, Maxine. Let's go and mooch around. I'm dying to explore. Aren't you?'

'Course I am.'

'Let's see if Toots and Brent are ready.'

Chapter 20

The Verandah Grill, situated at the rear of the Sun Deck, was the most beautiful room any of the Owls and the Pussycats had ever seen. A wide bay window faced aft, overlooking the steely Atlantic and the swirling wake of the ship. Every table wore a gown of crisp, white damask ornamented with lead crystal goblets, sterling silver cutlery and crowned with fresh flowers. A grand piano stood, lid raised, on a dais and adjacent to it was a small dance floor laid in shining parquetry. The band felt it was a privilege to play there on their first night. If you were Cabin Class and didn't want to eat in the main restaurant you could enjoy an *à la Carte* meal in The Verandah Grill, but you would pay an extra premium for the privilege. Meals were served till ten o'clock but it stayed open for as long as passengers wished to revel in the music. The subtle lighting was forever changing colour, enhancing the party atmosphere for it was also the ship's night club. The *Queen Mary*, of course, was still berthed at Southampton and was not due to sail till next morning, but some of the passengers already on board were enjoying the facility, and more would embark tomorrow.

The band gave a good account of themselves but it was a long night. While passengers dined, they played music that was subdued but, afterwards, livened it up with some sparkling jazz and swing. Several new shipboard romances seemed to blossom, with recently introduced couples dancing close to the tender love songs Maxine sang. Some people, at least, were finding romance, however fleeting.

After the show, Maxine was melancholy, having witnessed all this frivolous romance and casual innuendo. She needed to be alone to mull over anew her emotional turmoil. She grabbed the wrap that she had taken up with her and exited the Verandah Grill for the Sun Deck. While the others congratulated each other and chatted to the passengers that were still up, nobody noticed her withdrawal.

She shivered with cold as she walked towards the stern, yet that bitter November morning was no colder than the chill she felt in her heart. She looked up at the sky. The stars shone like pinpricks of light piercing a backdrop of blue-black velvet. *Oh, Howard, what have we done?* She adjusted her wrap and leaned on the biting cold handrail looking out into the night. The remaining lights of Southampton, no brighter than distant candles in the darkness, failed to warm her. The moon, hanging low over the Solent, seemed as heavy as her heart, like a yellow blob of molten lead poised to drop into the icy sea and be instantly quenched. *Howard, Howard, just what have we done?*

Tears stung her eyes. She must be more than a hundred miles away from him already, and by this time next week it would be three thousand. He might as well be on the moon that looked all hazy now through her tears. She felt in her handbag for a handkerchief and blotted them up.

Eight weeks apart. Eight desolate, lonely weeks. How on earth would she endure it? And she would not be able to collect even a letter from him until they returned to Southampton in two weeks. Already, she was wishing she had not been so impetuous, and had forgiven him. Already she was wishing they had become reconciled before he had left her on Monday night.

She walked slowly over to the other side of the ship. On the quay below, people were still arriving. A boat train was disgorging more passengers, even at this hour and stewards were stacking luggage ready to be transferred to the ship. The cold night air was alive with chatter and laughter and introductions made as people traversed the ramp that gave access to the main entrances. What if Howard suddenly took it upon himself to book a passage? Her heart leapt at the thought. Oh, God, if only he would. If only . . .

Another tear formed and quivered for a moment on her eyelashes before running unchecked down the soft curve of her cheek. Then, she felt an arm around her and was startled.

'Here you are,' Pansy said gently. 'I wondered where you'd gone. You must be freezing.' She saw the tears in her friend's eyes and wrapped her in her arms consolingly. 'Oh, Maxine . . . Try not to upset yourself. Everything will work out fine.'

'I've only been away from him five minutes and already I miss him like hell,' Maxine blurted. 'What will I be like when I'm on the other side of the Atlantic?'

'Don't think about it.' Pansy turned Maxine around to guide her back inside, into the warmth of the ship. 'He'll still be there for you when you get back.'

'Yes, in Norfolk.'

'But don't you think he's missing you just as much as you're missing him?'

'I imagine so. God, I hope so. Monday, I was so angry with him. Just one day later and I'm all weepy and sorry and pathetic . . . and I just want to be with him.' Another burst of weeping. 'I think I should get off this ship now and go to him, Pansy. I swear I'll do it first thing tomorrow.'

'Telephone him.'

'At this hour? He lodges at the vicarage, remember.'

'Sleep on it. Do it in the morning. Before the ship sails. There's a telephone exchange on board.'

The thought brought relief to Maxine's tear-traced face. 'Think I should?'

'Yes, I think you should. Clear the air. Tell him how much you love him. Tell him you forgive him. Forget all this stupid nonsense that's making you so unhappy. Swallow your pride.'

'But if I telephone and the vicar answers . . . I don't think he approves of him going out with me.'

'He doesn't have to know. Pretend you're a parishioner he's helping. Pretend you're a relation. Pretend you're God's wife . . .'

Maxine dried her eyes and they walked through the Verandah Grill. She felt happier at the prospect of talking to Howard. By this time, the Verandah Grill was empty except for people clearing up and a maintenance electrician replacing a defective light bulb.

'Where's Brent?' Maxine enquired as they approached the lifts.

Pansy shrugged. 'Gone to bed, I imagine.'

'Did he send you to find me?'

'No. I came looking for you off my own bat. I was concerned about you. I know how upset you've been.'

She felt an illogical pang of disappointment that Brent might not have even considered her. 'And Toots – has he gone to bed as well?'

Pansy nodded.

'Are you and Toots okay?'

'Yes, we're okay. You don't have to worry about us.'

'I hope you realise how lucky you are to be together, Pansy.'

'I suppose we are,' Pansy acknowledged. 'I hadn't thought about it. It's funny how you take some things for granted.'

'Don't . . . You mustn't ever.'

It was after ten when Maxine finally awoke. Maldwyn, her teddy bear, was warm beside her. For a second or two, she was disoriented waking up in that strange room. She looked at the strange clock on the strange wall opposite and realised where she was. God! Was that the time? She looked at Maldwyn and immediately thought of Howard. She was going to telephone him; she must do it now. She was going to leave the ship and go to him. At once she sat up in her bunk and grabbed her handbag to look up in her diary the telephone number of the vicarage. It was not a number she remembered, or even needed to, for she had agreed never to telephone him there except in an emergency.

While she fumbled in her handbag she felt a slight movement, almost imperceptible, and stood up in her nightdress to look out of the porthole. Outside, it all looked different. Land was slipping away from the ship. A peculiar sensation. A town fronted by docks and cranes was sliding rearwards. Portsmouth, perhaps. They were leaving the Solent. The English Channel and Cherbourg beckoned.

Maxine picked up the telephone handset by her bunk and a female voice announced the ship's telephone exchange. Maxine asked to be connected to a Birmingham number, which she recited. It would cost her one pound sixteen shillings for the first three minutes and twelve shillings for each additional minute. Did she still want to make the call?

'Yes, please,' she answered. It would have to be short, though. Eventually, she was connected and it was a very crackly line.

'Hello, hello? . . . Oh, hello. May I speak to Howard, er . . . to Mr Quaintance, please?'

'I'm terribly sorry,' a terribly formal male voice replied. 'The Reverend Quaintance isn't here at present. He's out on parish business. Who is calling?'

'It's a Miss Kite.' Maxine's heart sank.

'Does he know you?'

'Yes, he knows me.'

'Can I give him a message when he returns, Miss Kite?'

'If you would just tell him I telephoned – from Southampton . . . to say sorry . . . Thank you.' She replaced the receiver gently, burdened with disappointment.

'No luck then?' Pansy mumbled from beneath her bedclothes. Her face then appeared over the sheets, her dishevelled hair half covering it in random red strands. She stretched and yawned.

'He's out, Pansy . . . I can't afford to call him again, either. D'you know how much it costs? One pound sixteen for three minutes.'

261

'Blimey, that's a week's wages, Maxine. No, you can't afford to call him again. You'll be broke.' She looked around her, puzzled. 'What's that rumbling noise?'

'The engines,' Maxine responded apathetically. 'We're moving. Look out the porthole.'

'Crikey, we've left Southampton? Oh, smashing! I'm going up on deck to see. Are you coming, Maxine?'

'No, I'm going to stop here and cry myself back to sleep,' she answered in a small voice.

'Aren't you going to have any breakfast?'

'I don't want any breakfast. I want to go home.'

While Pansy prepared herself to face the rest of the ship's company, Maxine snuggled down in her bunk with Maldwyn, feeling deeply sorry for herself. Her last chance to speak to Howard had been thwarted. Her only hope was that the vicar would not forget to tell him she'd called and that, given the message, he would realise why. She could not cry, however. Her thoughts were only of Howard and how much she regretted she was not with him now.

After a while it struck her that feeling morose and melancholy was not going to get her anywhere. She was on board the most luxurious transatlantic liner ever built, whether she wanted to be or not. She might as well shape up and enjoy it. Time would pass infinitely faster if she did. Better to involve herself with life on board and take advantage of everything it offered. Better put a smile back on her face. She was a member of The Owls and the Pussycats on a fantastic, once in a lifetime voyage that she would remember for the rest of her life. What was the point in hiding away and nurturing the blues? Make the most of it, enjoy it, exploit it to the full, meet new people. As Pansy had said, Howard would still be waiting when she returned home. What was wrong with enjoying herself, even though she was missing him? She just had to make an effort to push him to the back of her mind. It didn't mean she didn't love him.

So Maxine threw back the bedclothes, pulled her nightdress

down to cover her bare legs and slipped out of bed, determined to overcome her dejection. She ran her fingers through her tousled hair, put on her dressing gown and headed for the bathroom. She emerged looking infinitely more presentable and, when she was dressed, went up on the Promenade Deck. But the Promenade Deck was teeming with people who had the same idea as Pansy; people who wanted to catch a last glimpse of the English coastline. As she looked starboard through the thick glass wall that protected the Promenade Deck from the elements, she stood for a few moments, this time watching the Isle of Wight receding into the distance. She felt like waving goodbye to it and smiled sadly at a very attractive fair-haired girl, beautifully dressed, about the same age as herself.

'Hi!' the girl said affably. 'I was real sorry to leave England. But now we've gotten underway I'm sure surprised at how keen I am to get on home.'

American. That warm burr, that pleasant drawl.

'I'm just leaving home,' Maxine replied. 'But I know how you feel.'

'You English?'

Maxine nodded.

'All that green,' the girl remarked admiringly. 'I can't get over it. Everywhere's so green, even in November.'

Maxine hadn't really considered it. 'Well, I suppose it's because we have lots of rain.'

'Sure. Enjoy America.'

She smiled politely and moved on, surprised at how easy it was to make new friends, even American friends. If that girl was typical, it seemed American girls had far less reserve than their more reticent British cousins. They didn't stand on ceremony, waiting to be introduced. The boys would find it interesting. They would find *her* very interesting if their paths crossed again.

Aft of the Observation Lounge and Cocktail Bar on the Promenade Deck, Maxine found the sound-proofed artists' practice room, known as the Studio. She tapped on the door politely, lest somebody was using it already, then opened it. All was in darkness. She flicked down the light switch and immediately saw the gorgeous piano; a Bechstein boudoir grand. She walked over to it and ran her hands over it as if it were some sensuous being she'd fallen in love with on sight and needed to caress. She pulled the stool out and sat down to play. Out poured the introduction to 'He's Funny That Way'. At first she merely hummed the tune, then, as she got into it, sang it with all the fervour in her heart. This was Howard's song. This was the song she'd sung for him the night they made love for the very first time. The lyrics somehow applied to them.

Play something else, she told herself. Change the mood. Play something happy, bouncy . . . 'Blue Skies'. But you weren't meant to sing 'Blue Skies' with tears in your eyes . . .

By the time she'd got to the end of it, however, her tears had all but dried. Deliberately keeping her mood neutral, she went on to play 'The Music Goes 'Round and Around', then 'I'm in the Mood for Love'. . .

'I'm in the Mood for Love' was not so bouncy, but it was a beautiful song, sensuous, lilting, casual in its contentment. She played it through twice, savouring the lovely minor sevenths, stressing them. How do people write such beautiful songs?

She began improvising . . . Mmm, an interesting chord sequence. Play it again . . .

That's really nice. Develop it . . .

Now . . . hum a melody . . .

Put some words to it.

What fools we are to offer our love to chance.

Just being hurt shouldn't mean the end of romance.

We turn away from our destiny,

And this is when destiny jests with me.

Hey, that's not bad! It gave her a distinct feeling of achievement.

Do it again . . . Remember it.

Some sheets of manuscript lay on a table near the door. She

rushed over and grabbed one, took the pencil out of her handbag and began jotting down the notes. It was only a chorus, though, and rough at that. She needed a verse. Back to the piano . . . A different chord sequence . . . A bridge . . . Not bad, now work it up.

Because I miss you, I think of you all through the day,
Daydreaming of you and crying the nights away.
Held in your arms is the only place I want to stay,
For this is the moment that destiny jests with me

It took many attempts and a couple of hours of focused work to knock the song into shape, but she was satisfied with it, as far as it went. And by the time she was satisfied, she knew it by heart. Now she had to polish off the lyrics for the other verses. She could do that any time. The first step was to play it to Brent and the rest of the band. Maybe they would like it. If they did, they could include it in their repertoire. She could even imagine Brent introducing it . . . *Now we'd like to play a brand new song, written by Maxine Kite, our gorgeous pianist – 'Destiny Jests with Me'*. She laughed a little at the thought.

But it was her first song! And she felt elated at having completed it. It had not been difficult but it had required intense concentration; so intense that, whilst her troubled romance with Howard had been her inspiration, she had not actually thought about him at all while she was writing it. Maybe she should write more. It was obviously therapeutic.

She left the Studio in a far better frame of mind than she had entered it and went below to Deck C, hoping the others would be in their cabins. They were not. Maybe they would be on the Promenade Deck or the Sun Deck. So back up the lift she went in search of them. She found them on the port side of the Promenade Deck, watching the coast of France creeping closer.

'Maxine!' Brent greeted. 'Where've you been? We looked everywhere for you. We're just coming into Cherbourg.'

265

'Oh? How long shall we be there?'

'About four hours, I think. It depends on the tide. Come and see.'

'I've been in the Studio.'

'Oh? Doing what?'

'Writing a song. I'll play it for you later. Right now I'm starving. I'm going for something to eat. I've had no breakfast. Anybody else coming?'

After she'd eaten, she returned to the Studio and played her song through a couple of times for Brent.

'Yes, I like it. It's good. Have you written it down?'

'I have,' she replied cheerfully. 'But only roughly. I need to polish it up and write it out properly. Do you think it's worth working up an arrangement?'

'Absolutely.'

'Shall we do it together?'

'Why?' he teased. 'Don't you trust me with your song?'

'Oh, it's not that, but I can hear certain riffs going on in my head that I know would work.'

'Then we're halfway there. Let's get on with it . . . What's the song about, Maxine?'

She hesitated to tell him the truth. 'It's just a love song.'

'About you and Zadoc?' he suggested astutely.

'Stop calling him Zadoc. It's just a love song.'

He came round the piano and sat next to her on the stool. 'Shift your bum over.'

She shuffled to the edge of the stool to make room for him.

'It's a smashing song,' he said warmly. 'A great melody. I'm really proud of you, Maxine. D'you know that?' His arm went around her waist momentarily and he gave her a brief squeeze. 'Pass me a sheet of manuscript and let's get on with it.'

She turned to him and smiled, grateful for both his praise and his consideration.

* * *

That night the band's duties were split. They were to play in the Tourist Class Ballroom till about midnight, then at one o'clock in the morning, after a break, they were to relieve for an hour the quartet that usually played in the Verandah Grill. Maxine spotted the American girl she'd met earlier, enter alone. She smiled in acknowledgement from her piano and the girl waved back flashing her lovely even teeth in the same broad smile she'd given before. She took a vacant table close to the stage and asked for drinks to be sent to each member of the band.

They raised their glasses to her and Maxine asked over the microphone if she had a special request that they could play.

'Sure,' she quickly replied. 'Can you play "Honeysuckle Rose"?'

'Okay, "Honeysuckle Rose" it is,' Maxine said and they launched into it.

When they had finished their stint, Maxine went over to say hello and to thank her for the drinks. The girl introduced herself as Dulcie and invited the rest of the band to join her. They pulled up seats at her table.

'Say, you're a great band,' Dulcie remarked. 'I never thought about an English jazz band but, hey, you're really something.'

'Thank you,' said Kenny, aching to get close to her. He'd never been this close to an American girl before and this one really impressed him with her beautiful blonde hair, her big blue eyes and lips that warranted some serious kissing. Damn this curse that was hanging over him.

But it was Brent who positioned himself next to Dulcie, with Maxine at her other side. And Brent seemed to be making the running. Dulcie seemed to be enjoying the things he was saying to her, things Maxine could not hear over the hubbub of laughter and talk from other passengers partying and the resident quartet that had resumed playing. Kenny, however, was not to be outdone and insinuated himself into their conversation, setting up a rivalry with Brent for Dulcie's attention that she evidently enjoyed.

'Would you like to dance, Dulcie?' Brent said.

'Sure, thanks,' she replied and they stepped on the dance floor together.

At that, Toots and Pansy assented to dance as well.

For a time, Maxine watched the couples dancing. Dulcie danced the quickstep well, with beautiful poise and Maxine was surprised at Brent's lightness on his feet, especially when he was so evidently engrossed in charming the girl with clever conversation.

The tempo changed to a foxtrot and Kenny looked at Maxine. 'D'you think you can manage a shuffle?'

'Why not?' When they stepped onto the dance floor, she said, 'I think you fancy this Dulcie, don't you, Kenny? You haven't taken your eyes off her yet.'

'Looks like I'll have to join the blasted queue. Still, I'm not bothered, Maxine. She's no prettier than you.'

'You could have fooled me,' she responded.

'Well, I'm dancing with you and I'm not complaining. I'd happily dance with you all night.' He gave her a squeeze and she smiled coyly. With the easy, boyish charm he exuded, it was easy to see why women seemed to fall at his feet.

Despite herself, Maxine couldn't help but be interested in Brent and Dulcie swirling around the floor. 'See how he's looking into her eyes like a lovesick fool, Kenny?' She was feeling irrationally jealous that Brent should be paying so much attention to this American girl. And yet it was not so irrational. Only recently, he'd stolen kisses from her that she had not disliked and told her how much he wanted her. She had only disliked herself for allowing it. And this very afternoon he had slipped his arm around her waist and cuddled her affectionately.

'You're not jealous, are you, Maxine?'

'Me, jealous? Why should I be jealous? Brent's nothing to me.'

'He thinks a lot of you.'

'Oh, obviously, the way he's mooning over *her* . . . Why? Has he said so, Kenny?'

'I always get the impression that if you hadn't taken up with Howard, the two of you would have got together.'

'What makes you think that?'

'I know he fancies you. There's always been a definite spark between you. I've noticed it . . . Sometimes there's affection, sometimes aggravation . . . I don't know how to describe it.'

'Familiarity. It breeds contempt, they say. We're both musicians, Kenny. I suppose we have this rapport as musicians. But off stage we often rub each other up the wrong way.'

'He's very protective towards you though, Maxine, you have to admit. Look how he still drives you home whenever Howard's not about. More than once he's told the lads in the band to keep their distance – before Howard came along, I mean.'

'Really?' she exclaimed indignantly. 'The cheek! Who does he think he is?'

Kenny laughed at her reaction. 'Maybe I shouldn't have said that. Don't repeat it.'

'Don't worry, I won't. Anyway, he's diverted now.'

'Just his type too – very pretty and very rich. I reckon her being rich is the real attraction. He's just sounding her out, Maxine – testing the ground.'

'Is that what you men do? Test the ground? Sound us women out, to see if we'll let you have your wicked way?'

He grinned. 'What do you think?'

'They say that's all some single women come on these cruises for,' she remarked experimentally.

'To be laid, you mean?'

'If that's how you want to express it, Kenny. Do you think it's true about Dulcie?'

He twirled Maxine around as if she were a doll. 'If I was dancing with her, I'd like to think so.'

'So why don't you make a play for her yourself?'

'Not if Brent's interested.'

'Oh dear!' she sighed theatrically. 'Honour among thieves, eh?

269

So, if I made a play for you, Kenny, you'd have to refuse me? Is that what you mean?'

'Not you, Maxine. I'd jump at the chance with you. I fancy you like hell. I really envy Howard . . . I like Howard though. He's a decent chap.'

She raised her head and smiled into his eyes. 'Thank you,' she said, poignantly reminded of her heartache.

They were silent for the rest of the dance sequence, then, when it finished, they all made their way back to the table.

'I think I'm going to turn in,' Maxine said, not bothering to sit down, 'if you'll forgive me for breaking the party up.'

'Yeah, me too, Maxine,' Dulcie said, much to Maxine's surprise. She picked up her expensive wrap and stood by Maxine. 'It's been a long day, travelling from London since early morning. Gee, I guess I've been up nearly twenty-four hours already.'

Maxine finished her drink, put her glass back on the table and bid everybody goodnight. She and Dulcie left the others and went through the doors.

'Say, why don't I meet you in the morning, Maxine?' Dulcie suggested.

'If you like,' Maxine responded, pleasantly surprised at the invitation. 'What time?'

'Say lunch. Yeah, we could have lunch together . . . In the main restaurant. Say one o'clock? Ask for my table, huh?'

'Okay, Dulcie, thank you. See you then.'

Chapter 21

Whereas the Tourist Class restaurant was chic, the Cabin Class restaurant was ethereal, like some high Art Deco temple with burnished metal pillars. A mellow hardwood veneer relieved by silver bronzed metalwork opulently bedecked the walls. A colourful electronic map, showing the ship's position, occupied the forward wall like a stained glass window.

When Maxine arrived, Dulcie was already at her table wearing a fashionable frock with long sleeves, buttoned to the waist and in a shade of blue that enhanced her eyes. She stood to greet her with the warm smile Maxine had already come to associate with her. She had not yet, however, decided whether this was the sincere smile of a friend or the deceptive smile of an antagonist.

'Please sit down, Maxine. Did you get a good night's sleep?'

'Not bad,' Maxine replied, allowing a waiter to pull out a sycamore chair with a rose pink covering for her to sit on. She thanked him. 'And you, Dulcie?'

'Sure, I slept good . . . till noon. Let me order you a drink.'

'Oh, thanks – lemonade, please.'

'Lemonade? Gee, have something stronger, Maxine. Lemonade's for kids. Say, why don't I order a bottle of wine?'

'Okay,' she assented with a broad smile.

'Are you hungry?'

'Yes, I am. Actually, Dulcie, I must say, it was very nice of you to invite me to lunch. I never expected it. Thank you.'

A waiter hovered and Dulcie ordered a bottle of Meursault. When he'd gone, she told Maxine that this had been her first trip to England. Her father, she said, had established a business connection in London and it was likely she would be visiting the city again in the near future. She lived in New York now with her parents, but had grown up in Massachusetts.

It seemed no time before the wine waiter delivered their wine. He performed the ritual of opening the bottle and asked Dulcie to taste it. When she nodded that it was okay, he filled both glasses.

'Why do people have to go through that rigmarole every time they order a bottle of wine?' she asked rebelliously, handing Maxine a menu. 'It beats me.'

'Tradition? I'm not really sure. I don't often drink wine.'

Maxine studied the luncheon menu for a few seconds while a waiter lingered at a discreet distance, ready to take their order.

'I think I'll have Spanish omelette, please,' she said.

The waiter stepped forward. 'Very good, Madam. No *hors d'oeuvres*?'

The words were familiar but meant nothing. She looked at Dulcie seeking help.

'I'll have marinated herrings to start,' Dulcie said, giving a lead, 'followed by galantine of capon and a mixed salad. Would you also like herrings to start, Maxine?'

'Yes, okay. Thanks,' she said, remembering the delicious pickled herrings her mother used to cook.

Dulcie picked up her glass and took a sip of wine. 'You sure have to watch what you eat on this tub. You could end up like Two-Ton Tessie O'Shea there's so much food.'

'Oh, I don't know, Dulcie. You're nice and trim.'

'Yeah, and I intend to stay that way. You, too, huh?'

'Oh yes. Till I've had six children at least . . . I do like your dress, Dulcie. It's very smart.'

Dulcie laughed generously and thanked her. 'Wool and angora. I bought it in London. Forty-nine shillings and sixpence. You know, I don't think I'll ever fathom your English pounds, shillings and pence . . . Say, tell me about yourself, Maxine? How'd you get into this band of yours?'

Between tastes of wine, which she thought was unnecessarily sour, Maxine gave Dulcie a potted history of her music and everybody connected with it. Inevitably, she ended up telling her about Howard and how she came to be on board the *Queen Mary* when it had not been her intention.

'But I guess I'd have felt the same,' Dulcie said sympathetically. 'It must have hurt real bad.'

'It still does. Every time I think of it my stomach churns. It's just too awful, but I'm determined not to let it spoil my enjoyment.'

'Attagirl! But you miss this guy?'

'Yes.' She smiled wistfully. 'I miss him terribly.'

Dulcie shook her head. 'You got it bad, Maxine and that ain't good. You need some shipboard romance to take your mind off things . . . A bit of a fling . . . Just a temporary arrangement.'

'Oh, I couldn't, Dulcie. I couldn't live with myself.'

'You couldn't? Are you serious?'

'Yes, I am . . .'

While the waiter served their *hors d'oeuvres* Maxine looked with awe at the standard lamps of that otherworldly restaurant. They were like nothing she had ever seen before, substantial, like the great pillars that supported the decks above, but topped with crystal up-lighters that emitted a subtle, subdued light.

'Do you have a sweetheart at home, Dulcie?' Maxine asked, seeing her companion dig into her plate with relish. 'Somebody waiting for you when you get back?'

'Hell, no. My mom's busting a gut to fix me up with the son of one of my dad's wealthy business colleagues. But he ain't for me. The guy's a creep. Say, why don't you get something going with that drummer boy you got in the band?'

'Who? Kenny?' Maxine was taken aback by this suggestion.

'Why not? You were dancing pretty close to him last night,

huh?' Dulcie smiled knowingly. 'He's real cute. He looks like Gene Krupa. Gee, he even plays like Gene Krupa.'

'Oh, I couldn't. Certainly not with Kenny . . .'

'Brent, then, huh? I guess you're real lucky playing in a band with such swell-looking guys. How come you never got off with any of them?'

Maxine shrugged and popped another piece of herring into her mouth. 'I got off with Howard instead.'

'Brent telephoned me when I got back to my cabin last night,' Dulcie said, her voice suitably lowered as she revealed this confidential snippet. 'He wanted to know if he could come to my room for a night cap.'

'You mean, a drink? In your cabin?'

'Room – cabin . . . Yeah, that's what he said. But I guess he meant something more than just a drink, wouldn't you say?'

'Really? You mean . . . ? Do you think so?'

'Hell, I guess so . . . I told him maybe some other time. I was just beat, Maxine.'

'How did he know which cabin you were in?' Maxine asked.

'I guess he asked the telephone exchange. They have a list of passengers. Hell, even I have a list of passengers, Maxine. Cunard White Star like you to know who you're travelling with.'

'Fancy . . .' Maxine said thoughtfully, surprised at how troubled she was by this revelation about Brent. Fancy him trying to tempt Dulcie . . . Maybe she should tell Dulcie some truths about Brent. It might ensure she would never consider entertaining him in her cabin. Yet why should she feel proprietorial? She had no claim on him. She had no claim on him at all. All the same . . .

'I always used to fancy Brent, you know, Dulcie,' Maxine blurted, 'until I found out he was married. Or, rather, I *thought* he was married. It turns out he's not. But he did live with a girl.'

'He lived with a girl? You mean, in *sin*?'

Maxine nodded but her expression registered disapproval. 'I don't admire him for having never married her. Do you?'

'Wow! But don't you think that makes him kinda interesting?'

'But what if she had become pregnant, Dulcie?'

'Then maybe he might have married the girl – who knows?'

Maxine shook her head. 'I don't think so, somehow . . . Anyway, *Eleanor* was certainly interesting. She has the sort of figure men can't stop gawping at and she flaunts it mercilessly. At least she flaunted it at the boyfriend I had at the time – Stephen Hemming. He ran off with her.'

'And now *they* live in sin? Gee! Things really do happen in England after all. And I thought it was all cricket and garden parties. Who'd have thought it? Were you very upset, Maxine?'

'No. I didn't love him.'

'And how about this guy Kenny? Is he married? He's surely not married?'

'I'm not sure about him, Dulcie,' she answered truthfully. 'I really don't know how he's situated.'

'Gee, you could really have some fun with this Kenny guy, Maxine. He really appeals to you, doesn't he? You know, there's a kind of animal attraction about him, don't you think? I've not seen it before in an English guy.'

The weather that day changed. During the bright and sunny daylight hours, the Atlantic was as placid as Rotton Park Reservoir in summer but, come the night, a wild and windy storm brought with it a heavy, rolling sea. Before they even embarked on the ship the band had heard other passengers on the boat train conversing, saying how mercurial the North Atlantic weather could be. That Thursday evening the storm worsened and it became so rough that barely anybody showed up in the restaurants. Most folk remained in the privacy of their cabins, nauseous, unable to face food. Others preferred to stay on deck where they could at least discern something of the intermittent horizon in the murky weather. The ship's musicians were supposed to keep playing, but with nobody to play to, the exercise seemed pointless.

On its maiden voyage, they discovered that the *Queen Mary* had an alarming propensity to roll in heavy seas, and this night was no exception. Most passengers were suffering from seasickness and, as the weather gradually worsened and the pitching increased ever more terrifyingly, absolute fear supplanted mere seasickness.

The Owls and the Pussycats decided that in any case they were due for a break. It was hard enough for Maxine to try to keep up with the untethered grand piano she was chasing as it lurched dangerously from side to side of the stage with the rolling of the ship. She was scared, too, as was Pansy. They needed the succour, the courage and the reassurances of their male colleagues. So, they all decided to sit on the Promenade Deck, which was enclosed and shielded from the elements.

'Try to fix your eyes on a distant point of the horizon,' Ginger Tolley advised. 'I remember going to the Isle of Man once on the ferry and we had a vile storm. Everybody on the ship was sick. But I found it better if I kept me eyes on the horizon.'

'But the bloody horizon keeps disappearing,' Kenny yelled over the din of the crashing seas, clutching one of the substantial deck chairs in an attempt to stop his own sliding about.

The horizon was discernible from time to time, illuminated by frequent lightning flashes. One minute it was up in the air at a terrifying angle on the starboard side of the stern, the next moment it swooped out of sight and all they could see was the sky and its angry lightning. Then, as the ship rolled and the stern dipped, the elusive horizon would reappear on the port side, high in the air again but tilted the other way. And this seemed to be going on all night.

Maxine and Pansy were terror-stricken. Pansy clung to Toots as if her life depended on him, and Maxine was grateful that Brent held her so reassuringly tight, telling her softly not to worry, that it would soon be over. She felt dreadful. Several times she lurched from the deckchair she and Brent were occupying to vomit at a discreet distance from him, and returned pale and utterly miserable to his lap. She welcomed his comforting arm

276

around her and his lips caressing her hair as she rested her head on his shoulder so helplessly.

It was after two in the morning when she opened her eyes. She was still nestled in Brent's arms on the deckchair, but the storm had abated. The sea was no longer crashing against the bulkhead, the thunder and lightning had ceased, the wind had stopped howling and blasting sea spray even as high as the Promenade Deck.

'You're awake,' Brent said.

She shivered with cold and fatigue. 'How long have I been asleep?'

'I'm not sure you were strictly asleep. I think you might have fainted.'

'I think I did. From fear.' She raised herself up and ran her fingers through her hair. 'I've never been so frightened in my life. How long since it's calmed down?'

'An hour, maybe. You've got some colour again now. You were as pale as death.'

She shivered and rubbed her hands over her arms as she looked about her. 'I'm frozen. Where are the others?'

'They all went back to the Verandah Grill. Toots and Ginger and Charlie wanted a drink.'

'Ugh! Not beer? I could drink some water, though.'

'Let's go there then.'

'Looking like this? No, I think I should go back to the cabin. I must look dreadful.'

'You looked beautiful on my lap. Like a kitten all curled up. But if you'd rather go back to your cabin I'll take you.'

'Sometimes, you're too good to me, Brent.'

'I know . . . Steady as you get up. Here, let me steady you. There's still quite a swell.'

The pitching of the ship, though much less severe now, pushed her into his arms again and he relished the additional opportunity to feel the warmth of her body against him in her slinky evening dress.

'You wouldn't think a ship this size would toss about the way it has, would you?' she remarked, detaching herself from him. But, as compensation, she offered her hand so that he could catch her if she lurched again.

'Depends on the sea, I expect,' he commented as they walked to the door into the Cabin Class main entrance. 'But I understand they do have a serious problem with this ship rolling. They're talking about pulling it out of service so they can fix it.'

'It needs it if tonight's anything to go by. I hope we don't have to go through this again. It takes the shine off it a bit.'

Crew were cleaning up everywhere, carrying mops and buckets and cleaning fluid. Brent and Maxine went to the lift and descended to Deck C, still chatting about the ship and the weather. When they reached the girls' cabin, Maxine opened the door. Pansy was already in her bunk.

'Thanks for looking after me, Brent,' she whispered. 'I don't know what I'd have done if you hadn't been there.'

'You're welcome. Anybody would have been glad to look after you.'

'But you were there for me, Brent. Thanks.' She gave him a sisterly peck on the cheek. 'Goodnight.'

'Goodnight, sweetheart. See you in my dreams.'

Although the sea on that crossing never regained the tranquillity it had when they left Southampton, the swell that persisted after the night of the storm was tolerable and things reverted back to normal. The Owls and the Pussycats played in the Tourist Class Lounge for an afternoon concert on the Friday, to enthusiastic applause, and during the evening until midnight. After that, they did their one-hour guest appearance in the Verandah Grill till two o'clock in the morning once more. This spot was gaining in popularity, especially with the younger passengers, and word spread that a cool jazz band from England was performing there every night.

During the day, nobody had seen Dulcie and they assumed

she'd suffered because of the storm but, on the Saturday night, she appeared in the Verandah Grill after midnight with her mother and father. She had insisted, she told the band later, that they come and listen and, she said, they were mightily impressed; and her father knew a thing or two about jazz bands.

The band's relationship with Dulcie was an easy one. None of the lads seemed to make any great play for her, which surprised Maxine since she had believed Brent would, especially as he'd telephoned her in her room one night. But, if anything was going on, she, Maxine, was certainly not aware of it. She did notice, however, that Dulcie was making cow eyes at Kenny frequently and he was flirting with her more. Yet, he seemed to be keeping her at arm's length. Nothing romantic seemed to develop between them; and that surprised her, given Kenny's appetite for girls – especially pretty girls.

As the weekend slipped by everybody was affected in some way by their imminent arrival at New York. On Sunday evening everybody enjoyed a farewell dinner and, after their stint in the Verandah Grill, the band went out onto the Sun Deck in the dark to look for the *Nantucket* Light Ship and the *Ambrose Channel* Light Ship that signalled the start of the shipping lane into New York and the official end of the transatlantic crossing. It was five o'clock on the Monday morning.

Dulcie said her goodbyes to each of them in turn. It might be the last time they saw her, for she really had to go to bed now for a while, at least until the ship docked in New York. She would disembark sometime after breakfast.

'I sure hope you guys are still playing on this ship next time I go to England,' she said tearfully. 'You're great guys and I've had such great fun with you. I love you all.'

The best view of New York is the one you get from the Sun Deck of the *Queen Mary* as you steam majestically up the Hudson River; and it seemed that the whole ship's company was there to witness it that sunny Monday morning of 9th November 1936.

The liner had weighed anchor at the Quarantine Station to await clearance to proceed upstream from Customs, Health and Immigration. Everybody felt the excitement as little tugs with mighty engines then guided her between Brooklyn and Staten Island, past the Statue of Liberty off the port bow. Some folk felt apprehension, perhaps; others felt relief. But there was a buzz everywhere. Immigrants tended to view with fervent hope this new land they saw, spiked with glistening skyscrapers pointing towards the vast New World sky. For them, it was the prospect of a new beginning, another opportunity. Those returning home regarded it with love and pride, for it never failed to invoke gasps and sighs from fellow travellers who had never seen the city before. Manhattan exuded an undeniable beauty as its fabulous mixture of tall Gothic and shimmering Art Deco buildings glinted unashamedly in the sunlight. But those grand monoliths of human endeavour also engendered a kind of confidence and reassurance; those folk were about to arrive in a land of extreme competence, where competence was welcomed and valued for the good it could do.

It was also a land of extremes. There existed inconceivable wealth on one hand and insufferable poverty on the other. Hope and despair lived side by side as did success and failure. The northern states of the Union doled out unbearable cold in winter and the southern ones stifling heat in summer.

The sight of it elicited a smile of admiration on the face of Maxine Kite. New York was some place she had only ever read about. It had no special significance for her before this voyage. Before today, it had existed only in her imagination, mythical, as unreal as Lilliput and as alien as ancient Babylon. But no words could describe what she saw now; no photograph could ever do it justice. Already she could sense the atmosphere. Never mind three thousand miles, it was three million miles from everything she had ever known.

'I'm dying to have a look around, aren't you, Pansy?' Maxine said to her friend as they looked across the mouth of the Hudson

River leaning on the rail. The ship's horn blasted and she put her hand to her ears.

'First thing I'm going to do is go to one of those posh shops and buy some new knickers,' Pansy said. 'I'm just about fed up with the ones I've got.'

'Yes, you could do with some new knickers,' Toots readily concurred.

Pansy looked at him aghast and dug an elbow in his ribs.

'Ouch! What was that for?'

'You're not supposed to know what her knickers are like, Toots,' Maxine informed him judiciously. 'If you do, at least be discreet about it.'

The others sniggered at his *faux pas*.

'First thing I'm going to do is buy a hamburger,' Charlie Holt said. 'I've always wondered what they taste like.'

'I'm going to study the women,' Kenny admitted. 'To see how they're different to English women.'

'Now there's a surprise,' Maxine said.

'But they seem different, American women.' Kenny explained. 'You only have to look at Dulcie. Their hairdos are sleeker as well. Have you noticed that, Brent?'

'Maybe they can afford to have their hair done every week,' Maxine suggested. 'In England, most people can't.'

'They seem more pleasant as well, American women. I like women who smile. I can't stand sourpusses.'

'Looking at all this, I'd say they've got a sight more to smile about. Especially now they've got a new President. Roosevelt says he's going to get them out of the Depression.'

'Look there,' Ginger Tolley said, pointing. 'That's the Empire State Building over there. They say you can go to the top of it. I reckon we should do that.'

'I'm going to buy some new clothes,' Maxine said.

'Knickers?' Brent asked.

'Maybe knickers.' She shrugged, suggesting her knickers were of no relevance to him, for all his attention. 'But I'm going to get a couple of new stage dresses. One of them sparkly with sequins or something – black, maybe. Maybe a silver one – I don't know yet. *And* I'm going to buy a new dress and some trousers for daywear. Have you seen how many American women wear trousers?'

'I know,' Pansy agreed. 'Well-cut ones that clip your bum nicely. Yes, that's a good idea, Maxine. I think I'll look for some trousers as well. And a nice pullover to match.'

'I'm going to buy lots of postcards as well, to send to everybody I know,' Maxine added excitedly. She was engrossed in this vista of New York, in all that it meant to her, in the circumstances that had brought her here. 'I want to let everybody know I'm in New York . . . I can't believe I'm in New York, actually, Pansy. Can you? . . . *New York!* It's something to be proud of. I want everybody to know.'

'I can guess who's top of your list . . .'

'You mean Howard? Yes, course he is . . .' Then an awful realisation struck her, like a spear to her heart. It manifested itself in a look of horror on her face. 'Pansy, I don't know his new address. I don't know where he lives now. It's Monday today. He'll have left Quinton by now.'

'I thought you said he was writing to you, care of the ship, Maxine. You'll know his address when he writes.'

'If he remembers to write at all,' Brent scoffed, 'which I doubt. I told you not to trust him, Maxine.'

'Oh, shut up, Brent,' Pansy said angrily, anxious that her friend should not be upset again, for Maxine seemed to have been tolerating her heartache well . . . until now.

New York was everything that it promised to be. It was late afternoon and dark when The Owls and the Pussycats went ashore, leaving behind the *Queen Mary* berthed at Pier 90. The Customs Hall was clear of passengers by this time and they progressed through quickly. Pansy and Toots wandered along West Fiftieth Street for the first time hand-in-hand, followed by

'I don't want to see naked women flaunting themselves. What do you say, Maxine?'

'Each to their own, I say . . . Have you seen the time, you three? I reckon we'd better get back to the ship. I wonder how the others have got on?'

the other five who alternated their company one with another. West Fiftieth was like no other street they had seen before; long and straight and wide, flanked on both sides at the western end by the warehouses of importers and exporters, factories and cheap chophouses. Charlie realised his first ambition when he tried a hamburger, advertised as the finest on the eastern seaboard by the German owner of the kiosk that sold it. They passed countless blocks of brownstone tenement buildings but, as they progressed eastwards, those gave way to shops and stores and restaurants.

After about three-quarters of a mile, they reached Broadway. Not only was it longer and wider then West Fiftieth, but its thousands of neon lights dazzled, calling attention to the smart shops, glamorous restaurants, bars and theatres. Neither had they seen so many large, curvaceous cars that caused an endless traffic jam, nor heard quite so many people who were not speaking English.

They paused here and there to ascertain which celebrities were appearing at the theatres. As the evening wore on, Broadway seemed to get busier, the neon lights brighter. Street photographers pestered them and they succumbed to one. It would, after all, be a good idea to have one or two photos to send to their families back home. They walked on, blind to victims of the Depression that littered the streets, soaking up the atmosphere, admiring the beautiful clothes the well-heeled New Yorkers were wearing. The clock at the top of the Paramount Building said ten to nine, and they knew they had reached Times Square. They stood and watched with awe and wonder the magically animated neon advertisements that seemed to occupy entire buildings. This was a different world, and they revelled in it.

As they walked on, lingering at this or that window, Maxine found her hand in Brent's. It simply seemed comfortable to hold his hand while they strolled. It did not signal any change of allegiance, merely companionship. She could just as easily have taken the hand of Ginger or Charlie or Kenny – she probably would later – but Brent's was suddenly there. She found it hard to believe that it had been a whole week since she and Howard had last seen each other. A whole week since her anger had erupted. Yet, looking at it from another viewpoint; in only a week she was here in this fantastic city and home seemed light years away. Her anger existed no longer. The voyage and this place had all but blotted it from her mind. If she saw Howard now, there would be no resentment, just pleasure at seeing him again. No animosity. The hurt had gone, too. Now, quite simply, she missed him. She missed the romance, the tenderness, the togetherness and she missed the sheer intimacy and pleasure of lovemaking. Six months ago she would never have believed it possible that she could have missed lovemaking.

Kenny had been missing for about fifteen minutes when suddenly he reappeared from the direction of West Forty-second Street. He made a beeline for Brent.

'I like the look of a place just down here,' he said in a half-whisper and pointing. 'I reckon us lads should go and take a peep.'

'What sort of place?' Brent asked.

'It's a bar, like.' He winked, but his expression was serious.

'I'm game,' Brent said, letting go of Maxine's hand. 'Anybody else coming?'

Ginger Tolley said he would go with them, so long as Charlie and Toots were prepared to stay with the girls. It wouldn't be fair to leave the girls on their own in a strange city.

'Oh, don't worry about us,' Pansy said scornfully. 'We've been known to roam the streets of Brum without you.'

'You don't mind if we split here, do you, Maxine?'

Maxine shrugged, feigning indifference. 'Why should I mind, Brent? Do what you want and we'll see you back on the ship in the morning. Charlie can be my chaperone.' Smiling, she took Charlie's hand and allowed him to lead her in the opposite direction with Pansy and Toots.

'Where shall we go?' Charlie asked, flattered.

'Oh, let's just walk,' Pansy suggested. 'It's fun just seeing the sights. Everything's so different.'

So they walked, and Maxine felt slighted that Brent had decided to take off with Kenny and Ginger. But she soon forgot her pique when, walking back along Broadway on the other side, she noticed a billboard advertising the Benny Goodman Swing Band currently appearing in the Madhattan Room at the Hotel Pennsylvania.

'We must go to that,' she almost shouted. 'We must go and hear Benny Goodman.'

'Well, maybe not tonight,' Toots said, 'but we could find out about tickets from the Travel Bureau on the ship. They'll get tickets for us.'

'For tomorrow, do you think?'

'We can ask.'

They walked on, and Charlie clung to Maxine's hand propri-etorially. After about a mile they saw, on the corner of Broadway and Fifty-third, an old theatre that had evidently been converted. Brilliantly lit letters, at least eighteen feet high, announced the Billy Rose Music Hall. It happened to be an elaborate night club set out like the one in the Al Jolson film, *Wonder Bar*. When they had studied the showcases in the foyer, they decided to go in and be entertained. You could enjoy supper and a show for only one dollar twenty-five cents each. So, hungry by now, they had supper and roared at a comedian called Ben Blue and his stooges, and midgets called Olive and George. A trained seal performed some dazzling balancing tricks, dancers and chorus girls had Toots and Charlie ogling. The finale had the boys ogling even more when footage from the 1919 epic film *The Fall of Babylon* was shown along with a tableau of live nude girls.

'They don't put shows on like this in Brum,' Toots said, incredulous.

'Thank God,' Pansy responded.

'Well, I'm coming here again tomorrow night.'

'Then you'll come on your own,' Pansy replied indignantly

Chapter 22

At breakfast next morning, the band swapped experiences. None of them were up early, since it had been a late night. Toots told the other lads what a great time they'd had in the Billy Rose Music Hall – eaten for one dollar twenty-five – even a tableau of beautiful naked women.

'If you wanted to see beautiful girls,' Ginger said, 'you should have been with us. Wouldn't leave us alone, eh, Brent? Eight or nine women clamouring for us,' Ginger went on. 'And I ain't exaggerating.'

'How come?' Maxine asked. 'They can't be that hard up for men in New York.'

'It was a dime-a-dance saloon,' Kenny confessed. 'You pay the girls to dance with you – ten cents a dance, six dances for fifty cents, or for a dollar the girl's yours for half an hour.'

'If you dance, there must be a band playing.'

'No, Maxine. Just a jukebox.'

'So how much did you spend, Kenny?' Pansy asked.

'Two dollars.'

'You must be mad.'

'Mad I might be, but I didn't half enjoy it. This girl called Blanche seemed to take to me,' he said proudly.

'I expect she takes to everybody,' Pansy remarked, unimpressed.

'You should have seen her, Charlie – blonde, pretty, incredible figure. She was wearing a tight blue dress . . . and I swear that's all she was wearing.'

'How old was she?'

Kenny shrugged. 'Eighteen or nineteen.'

'Disgusting,' Pansy exclaimed. 'Prostitutes. I hope you didn't . . .'

'I don't think she was a prostitute, Pansy. They call 'em hookers here. She wasn't a hooker. I paid her my first dollar and after we'd had a dance – which is when I realised she'd got no knickers on, nor anythin' else – we had a drink together. She told me they work on commission and that's why they almost fight for you when you arrive. They get commission on the drinks you buy 'em, and on cigarettes. You can even buy 'em perfume there and they get commission on that as well. Shame for them, really. They're not prostitutes. Blanche seemed a nice kid.'

'You seeing her again?'

'I might. If we go there again.'

'She'd got no knickers on and you reckon she ain't a prostitute?' Pansy scoffed. 'You're losing your marbles Kenny Wheeler if you think that. Why d'you think she'd got no knickers on? Because it was too warm in there? She'd got no knickers on so's when you danced with her and had a feel round you'd know. When you felt her bum – as you men always do when you dance close to a girl – you'd know she'd got no knickers on. It's to light you up, Kenny – to excite you so's you want to have her, even if you have to pay. How much did it cost to have her?'

'I didn't have her.'

The other lads guffawed in disbelief – all except Brent who remained silent.

'What? That's not like you. How much would it have cost then?'

'Two dollars and fifty cents,' Kenny admitted. 'Two dollars fifty and she would have spent the night with me. But she didn't. She went missing after I'd danced with her.'

'See?' Pansy said. 'Off with somebody else, I expect.'

Maxine glanced at Brent. His eyes had not met hers for ages. He seemed intent on watching the bubbles floating on his coffee as her twirled his cup around in its saucer. He had not spoken, as if he wanted no part of this discussion.

'What was your girl called, Ginger?' Maxine asked.

Ginger blushed to his roots and grinned sheepishly. 'Mona.'

'Mona?' Kenny repeated with derision. 'And *was* she a moaner?'

Ginger shrugged non-committally.

'You ought to know. I watched you go off with her at about midnight.' He turned to Maxine and then Pansy. 'She must have been a right little moaner. He said he didn't get back till after six this morning. Neither did Brent, come to think of it.'

'So you had your two dollars fifty's worth as well, Brent?' Maxine deduced. 'Very nice. So what was yours called?'

'Ignore him, Maxine,' Brent replied huffily.

'Did she have a pretty name too, like Lulu, or Suzie, or Jeanie? Presumably, she'd got no knickers on either?'

'How come you didn't spend the night with this Blanche when you had the chance, Kenny?' Brent asked pointedly, going on the offensive. 'Normally you'd be breaking your neck to bed a woman. Yet, when it's handed you on a plate you shy off. Something the matter down below, is there? Caught a cold in your old man, have you?'

'Mind your own bloody business, Shackleton,' Kenny responded sharply, alarmed and angry at Brent's accurate assessment. He scanned the faces of the others for their reactions but he needn't have worried. Venereal disease was further from their worlds than the planets Jupiter or Neptune. Nobody had any idea what Brent had insinuated. They were simply alarmed at this sudden flare-up which just as quickly fizzled out.

On the Tuesday Pansy and Maxine took a cab and asked the driver to take them to Fifth Avenue, where they gazed in wonder at the fantastic shops. Maxine bought herself a new black stage dress with sequins as she had planned and Pansy, not to be upstaged, bought a new dress as well. In the evening they met up with the others and, having acquired tickets, went to listen to the Benny Goodman Swing Band at the Hotel Pennsylvania. When they returned to the ship afterwards, inspired, they played for passengers who had already boarded early for the voyage to Southampton, determined to be as good and as original as the band they had just heard.

The return crossing was relatively uncontroversial. New faces, more concerts in the Tourist Lounge, a dance in the Third Class Lounge, late night appearances in the Verandah Grill and, by special request of the captain, a concert in the Cabin Class Lounge before lunch on Sunday. It was hard work playing all these hours and so late into the night, yet it was enjoyable enough, for they met and befriended lots of very nice people.

Such intensive regular performing made the band competent. They learned to read each other's musical minds better so that complicated interplay between instruments became second nature. Stimulated by the Benny Goodman experience, Maxine and Brent insisted they practise more, learning new material to enlarge their repertoire and honing to perfection what they already performed. Maxine wanted, and seemed to be getting from everybody, more accurate intonation and more carefully articulated phrasing. They read music of course and indeed, much of what they learned was from arrangements that Brent had written, but she wanted something more expressive. They had to learn the music by heart. She wanted them to play the notes, not just read them. She wanted a style that was tight yet loose, regulated yet liberated, exact and reliable yet open to individual creativity.

She completed the song she had begun, 'Destiny Jests with Me' and the band incorporated it into their repertoire. It was a medium tempo number, which Maxine sang stylishly. Some sparkling riffs from trumpet and clarinet featured, underscored with some growling, poignant trombone passages from Brent. It was beginning to go down very well with their audiences.

Maxine had written it for Howard, about Howard. It symbolised her hopes and dreams that, when these eight weeks of to-ing and fro-ing across the winter Atlantic were over, they could settle down to a steady relationship that would culminate eventually in marriage. Maybe the others realised it, simply by virtue of the lyrics, but nobody other than Brent commented. Although New York and what little she'd seen of its vibrant, abrasive culture had excited and diverted her, she still felt in limbo where Howard was concerned. She knew well her own feelings already. She pined for reconciliation, ached to be in his arms again. He felt the same, she was certain, and this belief comforted her immeasurably. But to be apart when they had so much to put right – when they were both so eager to put it right – was painfully frustrating. Was it her own stupid pride that had driven this wedge between them? Or had the undeniable envy she'd felt, watching her friends joyfully preparing to embark on this chance of a lifetime adventure, prompted her to seek any excuse to join them, even at the expense of Howard? Well, if she had she was sorry. For now, she wanted Howard back.

She waited agonisingly for his letter. Monday arrived and the short stopover in Cherbourg. By early afternoon they were heading towards Southampton. There had been talk that if they were delayed and missed the tide up Southampton Water they might have to wait several hours for the next. Pray that they weren't; she wanted her letter.

There was no delay. The *Queen Mary* tied up at the Ocean Dock, watched by crowds of sightseers, friends and families who had arrived to meet passengers. But after New York, Southampton seemed such a sleepy, parochial town. What on earth would sophisticated New Yorkers make of it, Maxine wondered.

She went to her cabin. No sense in rushing off anywhere yet; let the passengers disembark and clear Customs; allow time for the mail to be brought to the ship.

'I wonder what time they bring the mail on board?' she mused to Pansy.

'No idea. Brent might know. He's always asking the stewards things.'

She stepped out into the corridor and knocked on the door of Brent's cabin. When he answered it, he looked as if he had just woken up from an afternoon nap.

'Brent, do you have any idea what time they bring the crew's mail on board?'

'I haven't a clue, sweetheart, but I'll go and ask for you. You never know, I might even get some mail myself.'

'Will you let me know, then? I'm expecting a letter from Howard.'

He nodded and smiled pleasantly. 'Okay. See you later.' He closed the door.

Maxine brushed her hair and freshened her make-up in the mirror in the cabin she shared with Pansy Hemming. At the immediate prospect of receiving Howard's letter she began to feel nervous. What would he have to say? There would be no gushing sentimentality, that much was certain, for he was not like that. Even after their rift and his desire for them to be reunited quickly, there would be no mushy emotion. He could express his love eloquently enough and she was looking forward so much to his reassurances and confirmation of his commitment to her. She was anxious to know how things were in his new parish, how the move had gone, what the vicarage was like. Did he have a curate working with him? How had his new parishioners received him? What suggestions would he have as to when they might be married? Funny how she was more inclined towards marriage ever since he had mentioned it. It had never before been a concern . . .

'I think I'm ready,' Pansy announced, admiring herself a last time in the mirror. She sighed theatrically. 'It's so difficult to improve on perfection . . .'

Pansy fetched Toots from the cabin he shared with the other lads while Maxine called for Brent. They decided to take a light lunch in the Verandah Grill. From there, they would have a good view over the stern of the hustle and bustle on the quay below.

Besides, it should be quiet with everybody else engaged in disembarkation. After they had eaten, Brent said he was going to the toilet and disappeared. When he returned he waved three envelopes at Maxine with a triumphant grin on his face. Immediately she coloured up and sat on the edge of her chair with eager anticipation.

'Here you are, Maxine,' he said pleasantly, 'three letters for you.'

'Three?' Her face was a picture of joy and relief. 'Oh, thank you, Brent. I wondered whether you'd gone to get them since you were so long.' She studied the envelopes and shuffled them. 'Well, this one is my mother's handwriting . . . this is Henzey's.' A lump came to her throat and she felt hot. 'And this one is . . .' She prised her finger under the sealed flap and opened it. She took out the letter and unfolded it . . . and frowned with bitter disappointment. 'Is this all there was, Brent? This one is from my Uncle Joe and Aunty May. Are you sure there wasn't another one?'

'That's all they gave me, Maxine. You could always go to the bureau to check.'

'I think I'll have to. Howard would have written. I know he was going to write.' She got up from her seat to go.

'Maybe he was too busy,' Brent suggested. 'Especially if he's just moved to Norfolk.'

'He would have found time.'

'Maybe he didn't want to write,' he said tactlessly. 'Maybe he thinks it's all over between you.'

'But it isn't all over, Brent. Of course, it isn't all over.'

'Yes, but does he know that? You told him you weren't going to forgive him. That's what you told me. You know what forgiveness means to a Christian . . .'

'I also know what turning the other cheek means, Brent. I just can't believe he hasn't written. They must still have a letter from him at the bureau. I'm going to check.'

*   *   *

293

There was no further letter. Brent had collected everything there had been to collect. It was the bitterest disappointment of Maxine's life. She returned to her cabin in a daze of misery, hoping to be alone, hoping Pansy would not be there. She was not. Maxine took off her skirt and blouse and, still in her under-slip and her stockings, she slumped into her bunk, buried herself under the covers and wept. She could scarcely believe that Howard had given up hope of a reconciliation so soon and turned his back on her.

But what could she do about it from here? What could she do about it from the middle of the Atlantic? She did not know where he was so she could neither telephone him nor write. The very best option would be to scour Norfolk and all its churches when she returned home. But that would take an age; and it would be another six weeks at the earliest before she could attempt it.

That awful afternoon Maxine knew, for the first time in her life, how acutely the wounds of love could sting. She knew the absolute heartache of being rejected by the one man she earnestly loved. Never had she thought it possible she could feel so miser-able. Never had she felt so unwanted or known such despair. Oh, she had been dumped by Stephen Hemming in favour of Eleanor, but that was farcical compared to this. There seemed to be a lump of ice-cold marble throbbing inside her where her soft, warm heart should be beating. She felt discarded, like an old cardigan that is of no further use.

Was this the punishment love doled out for having principles and sticking to them? Was this the reward she was entitled to for expecting Howard to apply the same standards of consider-ation as herself? Did he feel so damnably little for her after all, that he could nonchalantly ignore her now and not even have the decency to let her know it was over with a few courteous lines?

Her normally sparkling eyes were puffy and red from hot, salty tears. Thank God, the band would not have to perform the other five who alternated their company one with another. West Fiftieth was like no other street they had seen before; long and straight and wide, flanked on both sides at the western end by the warehouses of importers and exporters, factories and cheap chophouses. Charlie realised his first ambition when he tried a hamburger, advertised as the finest on the eastern seaboard by the German owner of the kiosk that sold it. They passed countless blocks of brownstone tenement buildings but, as they progressed eastwards, those gave way to shops and stores and restaurants.

After about three-quarters of a mile, they reached Broadway. Not only was it longer and wider then West Fiftieth, but its thousands of neon lights dazzled, calling attention to the smart shops, glamorous restaurants, bars and theatres. Neither had they seen so many large, curvaceous cars that caused an endless traffic jam, nor heard quite so many people who were not speaking English.

They paused here and there to ascertain which celebrities were appearing at the theatres. As the evening wore on, Broadway seemed to get busier, the neon lights brighter. Street photographers pestered them and they succumbed to one. It would, after all, be a good idea to have one or two photos to send to their families back home. They walked on, blind to victims of the Depression that littered the streets, soaking up the atmosphere, admiring the beautiful clothes the well-heeled New Yorkers were wearing. The clock at the top of the Paramount Building said ten to nine, and they knew they had reached Times Square. They stood and watched with awe and wonder the magically animated neon advertisements that seemed to occupy entire buildings. This was a different world, and they revelled in it.

As they walked on, lingering at this or that window, Maxine found her hand in Brent's. It simply seemed comfortable to hold his hand while they strolled. It did not signal any change of allegiance, merely companionship. She could just as easily have taken the hand of Ginger or Charlie or Kenny – she probably would later – but Brent's was suddenly there. She found it hard to believe that it had been a whole week since she and Howard had last seen each other. A whole week since her anger had erupted. Yet, looking at it from another viewpoint; in only a week she was here in this fantastic city and home seemed light years away. Her anger existed no longer. The voyage and this place had all but blotted it from her mind. If she saw Howard now, there would be no resentment, just pleasure at seeing him again. No animosity. The hurt had gone, too. Now, quite simply, she missed him. She missed the romance, the tenderness, the togetherness and she missed the sheer intimacy and pleasure of lovemaking. Six months ago she would never have believed it possible that she could have missed lovemaking.

Kenny had been missing for about fifteen minutes when suddenly he reappeared from the direction of West Forty-second Street. He made a beeline for Brent.

'I like the look of a place just down here,' he said in a half-whisper and pointing. 'I reckon us lads should go and take a peep.'

'What sort of place?' Brent asked.

'It's a bar, like.' He winked, but his expression was serious.

'I'm game,' Brent said, letting go of Maxine's hand. 'Anybody else coming?'

Ginger Tolley said he would go with them, so long as Charlie and Toots were prepared to stay with the girls. It wouldn't be fair to leave the girls on their own in a strange city.

'Oh, don't worry about us,' Pansy said scornfully. 'We've been known to roam the streets of Brum without you.'

'You don't mind if we split here, do you, Maxine?'

Maxine shrugged, feigning indifference. 'Why should I mind, Brent? Do what you want and we'll see you back on the ship in the morning. Charlie can be my chaperone.' Smiling, she took Charlie's hand and allowed him to lead her in the opposite direction with Pansy and Toots.

'Where shall we go?' Charlie asked, flattered.

'Oh, let's just walk,' Pansy suggested. 'It's fun just seeing the sights. Everything's so different.'

So they walked, and Maxine felt slighted that Brent had decided to take off with Kenny and Ginger. But she soon forgot her pique when, walking back along Broadway on the other side, she noticed a billboard advertising the Benny Goodman Swing Band currently appearing in the Madhattan Room at the Hotel Pennsylvania.

'We must go to that,' she almost shouted. 'We must go and hear Benny Goodman.'

'Well, maybe not tonight,' Toots said, 'but we could find out about tickets from the Travel Bureau on the ship. They'll get tickets for us.'

'For tomorrow, do you think?'

'We can ask.'

They walked on, and Charlie clung to Maxine's hand proprietorially. After about a mile they saw, on the corner of Broadway and Fifty-third, an old theatre that had evidently been converted. Brilliantly lit letters, at least eighteen feet high, announced the Billy Rose Music Hall. It happened to be an elaborate night club set out like the one in the Al Jolson film, *Wonder Bar*. When they had studied the showcases in the foyer, they decided to go in and be entertained. You could enjoy supper and a show for only one dollar twenty-five cents each. So, hungry by now, they had supper and roared at a comedian called Ben Blue and his stooges, and midgets called Olive and George. A trained seal performed some dazzling balancing tricks, dancers and chorus girls had Toots and Charlie ogling. The finale had the boys ogling even more when footage from the 1919 epic film *The Fall of Babylon* was shown along with a tableau of live nude girls.

'They don't put shows on like this in Brum,' Toots said, incredulous.

'Thank God,' Pansy responded.

'Well, I'm coming here again tomorrow night.'

'Then you'll come on your own,' Pansy replied indignantly.

'I don't want to see naked women flaunting themselves. What do you say, Maxine?'

'Each to their own, I say . . . Have you seen the time, you three? I reckon we'd better get back to the ship. I wonder how the others have got on?'

tonight. Thank God, she could cry all day and all night if she felt the need.

And she felt the need.

She took her saturated handkerchief and wiped her nose, wondering if she had been so unrealistic in expecting him to stay around to be with her? Had she been too naïve? By acting the way she had, had she irrevocably turned him against her?

Maybe she had.

But there had been a principle at stake; that basic principle of commitment that she possessed but he evidently did not. That had really caused *their* ship to capsize. He had broken faith with her devotion as if it never existed, as if it was of no consequence.

But he was a man, and men played by different rules.

Even clergymen played by different rules if this was anything to go by.

But she could have sworn . . .

She fell asleep.

It was five o'clock when Pansy returned to their cabin and switched on the light.

'Maxine? Are you awake?'

'Oh . . . Hello, Pansy,' she croaked. 'Gosh, I must have fallen asleep.'

'Oh, Maxine, have you been crying again?' Pansy's voice manifested a wealth of compassion. 'When are you going to learn that men are not worth the heartbreak?'

Maxine tucked her hair behind her ear and sighed as she sat up in her bunk. 'Oh, Pansy . . . I don't know whether Howard's worth it or not.' She sighed again, a deep, heart-rending sigh. 'I always thought he was worth everything. Now I'm not sure any more. I'm just so confused . . . and frustrated that I can't do anything about it. Not stuck in this tub at any rate. Anyway, I've stopped crying now. Where have you been?'

'Ashore.' Pansy threw off her coat and hung it up. 'You should come out with us after. It seems a nice town, Southampton. Nothing like New York, but it's a nice town. There's a dance hall at the start of the pier and it looks as though there are some decent pubs. I think we're all going to explore the pubs tonight.'

'Think I should come?'

'Are you kidding?' Pansy kicked off her shoes and began getting undressed. 'You need company, Maxine. You need somebody to take your mind off things. You're coming out with us tonight and you're going to enjoy it. A few drinks will get you in the mood. It's no good crying over spilt milk any longer. You have to accept things the way they are.'

Maxine shrugged. 'Maybe you're right. I make myself so unhappy dwelling on things . . . on things that might have been. I know I do.'

Pansy unfastened her suspenders and putting her left foot on a chair, slid a stocking down her leg. 'Anyway, I always reckon things happen for a reason. Everything that's happened to you, Maxine, has happened for a reason.'

'I know. To make me miserable.'

Chapter 23

In mid-Atlantic on the second voyage, Maxine rose earlier than the others and breakfasted alone in the Tourist Class dining room on C Deck, just yards from their cabins. To her enormous surprise, she was feeling indifferent to recent events, and thus guilty that her emotions were not as intense as she reckoned they ought to be. She took the staircase to the Sun Deck, drawn by the need for some bracing sea air and to ponder the perplexing phenomenon. As she leaned on the rail with the cold wind blowing through her hair she gazed into the surging sea below and watched how it swirled in endless turmoil alongside the ship. And she was mesmerised by it. Despite the awesome power that could easily lift this eighty-one thousand ton colossus like a cork, despite the crash of enormous waves breaking incessantly against the hull, the sibilant, erratic harmony of the sea was hypnotic and sedating. The heaving ocean stretched away to the horizon and beyond and Maxine felt surprisingly at peace. If this was what being at sea did for you, no wonder those involved with it were so addicted.

But there was something else. Life aboard this luxury liner was good. They had nothing to worry about except performing, and performing was a joy in any case. It was like being on holiday. All the time they were meeting interesting new people, discovering something new about the ship. And New York . . . oh, she couldn't wait to return to New York.

She flicked her hair out of her eyes and turned up the collar of her coat. As she huddled inside it for warmth she felt a presence and turned round. Brent Shackleton was beside her, his hair blowing in the wind.

'Hi!'

She smiled her welcome. 'Brent! Hello. Have you had breakfast yet?'

'Just. Have *you* eaten?'

She nodded and peered into the fermenting brine below.

'So how long have you been here?'

'Ages. I think I could stay here all day. It seems to have a beneficial effect on me.'

'Oh? How?'

'Every day I'm at sea I feel a bit more remote from the real world. It's so peculiar. Everything seems so distant . . . I can't explain . . . I feel like I'm somebody else. I feel, somehow, that I'm no longer the same Maxine Kite who lived in Dudley and played cello in the CBO. It's as if that was another life – somebody else's life . . .' She shook her head. 'It really is peculiar.'

'I feel the same,' he said and stood alongside her leaning against the rail.

'Really?'

'Yes. All that business with Eleanor . . . I know exactly what you mean . . . Detached. As if it really was another lifetime.'

'Fancy that. You as well. It's not that I can't remember Howard, I can, but I can't seem to summon any emotion any more. It's as if he's just a figment of my imagination now. Why should it be? I'm still the same person but I feel completely numb. I should feel guilty that I do, and yet . . . and yet the relief from it more than compensates. I tell you, Brent, this sudden indifference is so much easier to bear than all that anxiety.'

'Then go along with it, Maxine.'

'But that's just it, I am. Nothing's bothering me any more and I can't believe my luck. I keep telling myself it's the ship, the sea, the air, the change . . .'

'It's a whole different world, Maxine . . .'

They fell silent for a while, listening to the crash of waves in the chilly winter Atlantic, and the incessant roar of wind and sea that drowned the low hum of the ship's engines.

Brent said, 'You know, Maxine, I'd like us to be closer, you and me. I see no reason why we shouldn't be closer.'

She looked at him puzzled. 'Aren't we close already?'

'I want us to be closer than we are already.'

'You mean . . . as close as you were with Eleanor?'

'Closer than that, Maxine. Like I said, I've forgotten Eleanor . . .'

'But you must miss her a little bit.'

'Not here. Not on this ship. Certainly not when I'm with you . . . Funny, but I could never imagine you doing to a man what she did to me.'

'No, I don't think I ever could.'

'The longer I know you, Maxine, the more I realise what a treasure you are.'

She laughed. 'I know. Buried treasure,' she replied with typical self-effacement.

Brent laughed too, unstintingly, but another pause developed in the conversation.

'You know, Maxine,' he said presently, 'I did go with a girl from the dime-a-dance saloon . . .' She looked up at him, apprehensive at what he might admit, because she did not really want to know. 'I want you to know, Maxine. But I also want you to know she meant nothing. Nothing at all.'

Maxine shrugged. 'You don't have to confess your indiscretions to me. Why should you want to? What you do with your own money is no—'

'I just want you to know, Maxine. I'd hate you to think I'd normally do such a thing. It was the booze, the place, the moment . . . the loneliness – without you.'

'But you were with me. Right up to the moment you left to go there.' She shrugged at his strange logic.

'But you weren't mine, Maxine. And I needed you.'

'So you went off with Blanche, the beautiful young girl with

299

no knickers, eh? . . . And what about Dulcie?' This seemed as good a time as any to mention Dulcie. 'Did she mean nothing when you telephoned her and asked if you could go to her cabin?'

'Oh, she told you about that?' he asked, surprised.

'Oh, yes. She told me.'

'You weren't jealous, were you?'

'No, not jealous, Brent . . . I was peeved. After you were nursing me in your arms the night of that terrible storm, I think I'd started to believe I was the only one entitled to that sort of attention from you.' She shrugged and uttered a little laugh of self-mockery. 'Stupid of me.' She paused and looked out to sea, at the heavy swell glinting and sparkling as here and there the sun escaped through a lattice of dark clouds. 'I'm not sure whether Dulcie was just trying to sound me out, Brent, when she told me. You know? . . . To see how the land lies between you and me before she made a play for you. She's a very attractive girl, you know, and from a very wealthy family. She's unattached too. Did you know that? She would be a prize catch if you could land her.'

'You think so?' he asked, amused. 'Yes, well . . . Dulcie *is* an attractive girl, Maxine, as you say, and I confess I did fancy her . . . but I think somebody else captured her heart.'

'Oh? Anybody I know?'

'Only Kenny Wheeler.'

'Kenny? You're pulling my leg. And she kept insinuating that *I* should take up with Kenny.'

'To put you off the scent.'

Maxine laughed. 'The crafty monkey! Well, they kept it very quiet.'

'Oh, I don't think anything happened between them, Maxine. In fact, I know it didn't, but there was something going on.'

She chuckled with delight. 'He's a right one, isn't he? I don't know how he gets away with it all the time? And what's going to happen about his poor wife and baby?'

Brent shrugged his shoulders and leaned on the rail again. 'It's his concern, not mine. I've got enough to occupy me . . .'

'Poor you. What problems have you got to occupy you?'

'More like what I haven't got, Maxine . . . You. I haven't got you.'

'Then count your blessings, Brent Shackleton.' She uttered a derisory little chuckle. 'You don't know when you're well-off. You've got all those other girls . . . those in the dime-a-dance saloon. There must be lots of places like that in New York. You could have a whale of a time. Then there's all those other young rich girls that keep making eyes at you while we're playing in the Verandah Grill. And I've seen you making eyes back at them too. The fact that they're dancing with somebody else doesn't seem to make any difference. Just think – you could have a different girl every night of the week. Why should you want to saddle yourself with me?'

'Because you're the only girl I'm really interested in, Maxine.'

'Piffle! You could never be true to one girl.'

He turned to face her. 'Then you don't know me, Maxine,' he said very seriously.

'I know what I see.'

Silence fell between them; a silence filled with the roar of the sea and the bracing wind that from time to time blew fine spray into their faces; a silence that prompted them to ponder each other's feelings.

'Remember how I kissed you when you came to my house that time?' Brent said eventually.

'Did you?' she answered, affecting disinterest by pretending not to remember.

'You know I did. And you didn't dislike it. Well, I'm going to kiss you again.'

'Are you? And if I won't let you?'

He guffawed roguishly. 'It makes no odds. I shall kiss you anyway.' He held his arms out to her.

Unwittingly, she turned and stood with her back to the rail, waiting to receive him. Her arms reached out submissively and she looked into his eyes with a kittenish smile.

'Okay, kiss me before I'm completely out of practice. God knows I've got nobody else to kiss.'

Their lips met in a deliciously long embrace.

The band's time in New York fell into much the same routine as their previous stay. They all trooped along to the Hotel Pennsylvania once more to listen to the Benny Goodman Swing Band and some returned to the Billy Rose Music Hall for the supper show to see again the tableau of naked girls. The lads did not venture near a dime-a-dance saloon this time, as Brent wished to stay close to Maxine. He was at last making some headway and did not want to jeopardise his gains by unnecessary laddish behaviour. On the Tuesday they ventured to the top of the Empire State Building and viewed the rest of the world from the 102nd floor observatory before spending some time drooling over the high class establishments on Fifth Avenue. Later, as they headed back to Pier 90, they happened on a place called the Onyx Club on West Fifty-second Street.

'I've heard of this place,' Brent said. 'It's where all the great jazz musicians hang out. We really must try and get in there one night. Perhaps next voyage, eh? And look – there's the Famous Door Club . . . And the Hickory House is there as well. Oh, this town's unbelievable, Maxine. I want to live here.'

On the Tuesday night, after the band had been playing for early passengers, Brent told Maxine that he was desperately in love with her and asked if she would sleep with him. The suggestion came unexpectedly and Maxine was surprised although, as Pansy told her later, she should not have been. Maxine was not ready to sleep with Brent. Oh, they were chummy enough when they were together in a crowd, even lovey-dovey at times. When they were alone, she enjoyed the tenderness she felt with his arm around her waist, and basked in the contentment his admiration elicited. His attention was enjoyable and far preferable to feeling sorry for herself over Howard Quaintance. Brent could be utterly charming, and he was charming when they walked together hand-in-hand through the streets of New York, or when they sat in a club or restaurant with the others, giggling and whispering syrupy nonsense to each other.

The problem was the night. Although she felt this detachment from real life during the day, the night could be a terse reminder of reality. Her dreams were still about Howard. The rage that she felt before re-emerged night after night, followed inevitably by the sheer sadness and heartache of losing him. She grieved in her sleep and, while she was pleased to awake from it in the morning and leave it behind, it took some time to shake it out of her system once she had woken up. No, she was not ready to sleep with Brent Shackleton and maybe she never would be. In any case, when they arrived at Southampton next time there should be a letter waiting for her. Maybe last time Howard had just missed the post. Because, if it transpired that Howard still wanted her, that was where her future lay. Brent was merely a pleasant diversion.

The Wednesday morning that they were due to sail from New York was one morning when it was not so easy to shut out thoughts of Howard. She had dreamed vividly about him all night and was poignantly reminded of his care and tenderness that first night they made love. Her dream had been totally erotic; she relived his touch, the feel of his lips on hers. She even gasped when he entered her and experienced again the warm glow in her groin, culminating in an intense orgasm that succeeded in waking her up. She turned to hold Howard in her arms before she realised that, apart from her teddy bear, she was alone in her bunk. She was lost in an ocean thousands of miles from him, and began to weep again for her lost love.

The Captain, Sir Edgar Britten, had requested that Maxine give a half-hour concert in the Cabin Class Lounge that afternoon. Some pleasant love songs were required; nothing too demanding of the attention; something easy on the ear to soothe the wealthy passengers after their heady luncheons. She'd insisted that bass and drums accompany her piano playing and it was agreed. Beforehand, she had drawn up a list of suitable songs that would form her repertoire and the time had come when she must sit at the Bechstein on the stage. Already, she had stressed that she wanted no other members of the band there apart from bass and drums.

After Maxine had been introduced, she began with one of her favourites, 'Where or When', which attracted quite some applause. She followed it with 'Making Whoopee' and then, 'I've got my Love to Keep me Warm'. By the time she finished singing 'I'm in the Mood for Love' she had her audience in the palm of her hand. Between numbers she talked to them unpretentiously and made them laugh with little quips. She joked about the awful weather in the Atlantic and announced her next song that she said was very appropriate: 'Stormy Weather'.

Much of what she was playing was unfamiliar to the Cabin Class passengers. Love songs were far removed from the lifestyles of most of these people, but she won them over with a performance that demonstrated her dexterity at the piano, her vocal enthusiasm and her innate charm. She didn't force the music down their throats, but allowed them to partake of it with an open mind as if it were some new wine she wanted them to taste.

'I hope you like this next one,' she said into the microphone. 'I wrote it myself on board this very ship. It's called "Destiny Jests with Me". Here we go . . .'

Each performance she gave of this song was an improvement over the previous one. It was yet still new to her, even though she had penned it herself. But with each performance, her confidence grew and she was beginning to deliver it with panache. It drew warm applause.

Maxine finished her concert with a song that was becoming one of her favourites, 'He's Funny that Way'. As she sang the last chorus she looked up from the piano and saw, to her utmost surprise, a familiar face and couldn't help smiling in recognition. Dulcie Fielding was walking along the edge of the room towards the stage. She stood and watched at the side of the stage while Maxine finished her number and took her bow, then walked directly up to her.

'Dulcie!' Maxine said gleefully. 'This is a surprise. What brings you on board so soon after your last voyage?'

'My father had a cable Monday evening calling him straight back to London,' she said, giving Maxine a hug of genuine affection. 'Some legal problem with a very important contract.' She shrugged and sighed happily. 'Gee, it's great to see you.'

'It's great to see *you.*'

'Won't you come and have tea with me later?'

'I'd love to. Look, Kenny's here and Charlie.'

Kenny left the borrowed set of drums and jumped off the stage to join the two girls, followed by Charlie Holt. Maxine noticed Dulcie's fluttering eyelashes as soon as the boys got close.

'Hi, Kenny! Hi, Charlie! Say, you two look great. Don't they look great, Maxine?'

Both seemed incapable of speaking.

'Are you playing in the Verandah Grill later?' Dulcie asked.

'Yes,' Maxine replied, 'and the Tourist Class lounge before that, if you'd like to come along.'

'Oh, sure, I'd love that. Is that okay, guys? . . . Listen, Maxine, my dad's been listening to you. He wants to meet you. Can I introduce you to him properly? . . . Will you excuse us, boys? I'll be back in two shakes . . .'

Maxine followed her friend to a table towards the back of the lounge. Dulcie's father, whom Maxine had seen before, stood up, offered his hand and invited her to sit.

'And this is my wife, Grace.' Maxine shook her hand and smiled amicably.

'That was some performance, my dear,' Grace Fielding said. 'Wonderful.'

'Thank you, Mrs Fielding. It's the first time I've done a formal sort of concert. I wasn't sure how these people would appreciate it.'

'Hell, I'd say most of these folk don't know commercial music from a lasso,' John said, 'but I guess you really got to them. I'm mightily impressed. Would you like a drink? Let me call the waiter.'

'Thank you, I'd like a glass of water if that's all right. My throat's a bit dry after singing.'

'Sure thing.' John Fielding raised his hand and a waiter instantly appeared.

'Daddy, I'm going to talk to Kenny and Charlie while you and Mom speak to Maxine,' Dulcie said. 'See you later.'

'Sure, honey . . . I don't know whether my daughter's told you anything about me, Miss Kite—'

'Please call me Maxine.'

He smiled benignly. 'Sure. And you call me John. Maxine, I don't know whether my daughter's told you anything about me, but I happen to make my living in the entertainment world.'

'Oh really? She never said.'

'No, well I guess she wouldn't. Anyway, I'm president of an outfit called American Music Producers, better known in the business as AMP. Our business is promoting commercial music throughout the USA – these days in Europe too – which is the reason we're crossing the pond again. And, heck, we make a few bucks, Maxine. Well, ever since Dulcie heard you guys she pestered me to listen to you. She reckons she can tell a great band from a mediocre one. So I listened – on our last return voyage.'

'I remember.' But of course she had had no idea then of the significance of those moments.

'Well, I thought you were pretty darned good. Anyhow, when I knew you were performing in a trio today, Maxine, I wanted to come and hear *you* – without the embellishments of a band. I must say I like your style. I like the way you interpret a song. You don't try and sound exactly like the original artists. It's fair to say you have your own distinctive style which is pretty damned appealing – and you've begun writing your own material – that's swell. Now, I wonder . . . because of what I do, I have many contacts all over the USA who are looking for new artists. So, how would you like to play in New York next time you're over?'

'Gosh, I'd love it. We'd all love it . . . You do mean all of us, don't you, Mr Fielding?'

'John. Call me John.'

The waiter delivered her drink, placed it before her and she thanked him.

'I'm mainly interested in you, Maxine, but sure, if that's what it takes to get you there. However . . .'

'There always seems to be a however,' Maxine remarked suspiciously.

'Well, hopefully, this *however* is no big deal . . . But I might have a problem. You see, unless I can organise work permits for you in time, you might have to work without pay. Temporarily, of course – just one gig. The United States' famous bureaucracy. Would you be prepared to do that for just one gig?'

'I imagine so,' she answered unsurely. 'It depends on the others. It depends what you have in mind.'

'It would definitely be to your benefit. I want you to play for some friends of mine at a place called the Onyx Club on West Fifty-second. Heard of it? . . .' She said she had. 'It's a club that many professional musicians, broadcasters and club owners visit regularly. I'd like to assemble some people there who are influential in the music business. If you come good, it could all come good. Standards are pretty darned high, as you can imagine, but I believe you guys have got what it takes. The punch line is, you're English. We don't get too many English jazz and swing artists in the USA.'

'Isn't it a bit like taking coal to Newcastle?' Maxine commented.

John Fielding was amused at the analogy. 'Sure, but what the hell? Americans love anything English. To us Americans, you're different. That's the difference.'

'I reckon we would do it, Mr Fielding,' Maxine said. 'It sounds like a great opportunity and we'd like to be known in America.

But I think we should confirm it with our agent in London first, if that's all right.'

'Naturally. Who is your agent, Maxine?'

'A man called Seth Cohen.'

'Seth!' John Fielding laughed aloud. 'Gee, honey, Seth is my associate in London. The very guy I'm going to see this trip. He's an AMP guy through and through. Consider it settled, Maxine. I'll talk to Seth Cohen about you guys. You have nothing at all to worry about. Now listen – I've another proposition. Tomorrow's Thanksgiving. I'd like you and your friends to join me and my family for luncheon. Can you make that, Maxine?'

'Oh, that would be great. Thank you. Thank you ever so much, Mr Fielding.'

'Swell. I've hired one of the private dining rooms just for the occasion.'

Later that same afternoon, Kenny Wheeler stole away from the rest of his colleagues and made his way stealthily to the consulting room of the ship's doctor. The sudden appearance of Dulcie Fielding on this voyage had prompted him to seek confirmation that his gonorrhoea had cleared up and advice as to whether he needed to worry any more about the possibility of having contracted syphilis.

'When did your treatment begin?' the young doctor asked.

'The end of September, doctor.'

'And you've seen no discharge since finishing the treatment, nor felt any burning sensation when you've passed water?'

'No, doctor.'

'So where are we now? . . .' He consulted a calendar and counted the weeks. 'Hmmm . . . You'll be cured by now, Mr Wheeler. Any other worries?'

'It's just that when I picked up the gonorrhoea, doctor, I had to have a blood test for syphilis, as a precaution. My own doctor said it can take three months to show.'

'That's so. So it's a sensible precaution, isn't it?'

Kenny nodded. 'The problem is, doctor, I've met a girl on board ship and . . .'

'And you don't want to disappoint her.' He smiled knowingly. 'Of course, I understand. When did you have your last blood test?'

'The end of October.'

'And it was negative?'

'Yes.'

'Then you're due another. I'll take a sample of your blood now and check it out. I can let you have the result tomorrow. How does that sound?'

'Sounds good, doctor.'

'Roll your sleeve up . . .' The doctor went to a cupboard and obtained a syringe, which he assembled. 'Okay, flex your arm to make the vein stand out a bit . . . That's good . . . Don't look if you're squeamish . . . There . . .' The doctor sealed off the phial, labelled it and put it on his desk. 'Call back tomorrow, Mr Wheeler. But listen – a word of advice . . . Just to be on the safe side – if you find you can't keep your hands off each other, do yourselves an enormous favour and use a French letter. French letters provide a wonderful barrier against these nasty germs that cause venereal diseases. I'm forever preaching that advice to the crew.'

'Thanks for the tip, Doctor,' Kenny replied with a broad grin. 'See you tomorrow.'

Chapter 24

In the private dining saloon just off the Cabin Class main restaurant on Thanksgiving Day, ten places were set for luncheon. John and Grace Fielding welcomed Maxine Kite and the rest of The Owls and the Pussycats with an endearing warmth. The seating arrangement was strictly conventional, with John at the head of the table and Grace at the opposite end. Maxine sat at John's right hand with Brent Shackleton next to her, opposite Dulcie. Maxine answered all John's questions about herself; where she lived, where she came from, how she became involved with the band. And he was interested to learn that she was classically trained. Grace was holding court with the lads of the band, who were keeping the waiter busy refilling glasses from the bottles of fine wine that seemed to be in abundance.

'I've always been impressed by the British,' John said benignly, to make them feel comfortable. 'Always coming up with remarkable inventions. This new thing they've recently come up with, though – I'm not so sure . . .' Everybody watched him with anticipation. 'Television, they call it. Moving pictures and sound. Like the movies but transmitted to a receiver in the home. Each set is likely to cost about a hundred guineas in English money. Seems mighty expensive to me.'

'Gee! Really?' Grace uttered. 'Will it catch on? I don't see the point of it. I mean – can you imagine having to stop whatever it is you're doing to look at moving pictures? At least with the radio set you can get on while you listen. I doubt it will ever catch on.'

'What are guineas?' Dulcie asked 'I saw coats and dresses and shoes marked up in guineas when we were last in London. Isn't it the same as a pound?'

'A guinea is twenty-one shillings,' Maxine explained. 'Marking goods up in guineas is supposed to make them seem more exclusive.'

'And gives the shop an extra five percent profit,' Brent added cynically. 'Maybe we should quote our fees in guineas, Maxine.'

Maxine wore a royal blue day dress with a full skirt that she had bought from Bloomingdale's. Its colour contrasted subtly with her thick brown hair that was elegantly piled up and finished in a French pleat. Around her neck she wore a delicate gold cross and chain that Stephen Hemming had once made for her and combined it with small, matching earrings.

The main course was turkey and pumpkin pie, in true American tradition and John had chosen a Côte de Beaune to accompany it. While they ate, conversation was intense, about current events in Europe. Most saw Hitler as a potential threat. However, Ginger Tolley said he did not, but then Ginger liked to wind everybody up.

'But, you see, Hitler has proposed a peace treaty, guaranteeing peace for twenty-five years,' Ginger argued. 'Surely that signals his peaceful intent.'

'And if he showed any respect for previous treaties I'd be inclined to agree with you,' John commented, putting down his knife and fork to gesticulate more effectively. 'But he has no regard for treaties. Look how he defied the treaties of Versailles and Locarno in March by goose-stepping his jackbooted militia into the Rhineland. How can you have any confidence at all in the word of such a goddamn liar?'

'But because of this . . . this suspicion, we must pay an extra threepence in the pound on our income tax,' Ginger said cynically. 'To pay for new tanks, new aeroplanes, new battleships that won't be needed.'

'We can't afford to drop our guard, Ginger,' Charlie replied calmly. 'What do you think we should do? Wait till the Nazis invade before we do anything, then throw stones and pull faces at them? Will that scare 'em off?'

'I think we should talk with Hitler,' Ginger said. 'We should strike a deal that'd make it unprofitable for Germany to be hostile. In any case, I reckon Hitler has no quarrel with us.'

'Maybe you should have a quarrel with him, nonetheless,' John Fielding remarked. 'I understand he has banned the playing of jazz on their radio programmes, because it's reckoned to be performed by blacks.'

'Do you think he'd ban us?' Maxine asked.

'I guess it's all jazz, Maxine. Whoever performs it. I guess he's trying to imply that the whole musical style is degenerate . . . So, guys, whatever happens following your premiere in New York, you can forget Germany as a market for your music.'

Maxine caught Brent's glance as he turned to note her reaction. She smiled with her eyes as she took another sip of wine.

'Who needs Germany?' Brent said. 'What are our chances of success in America, John?'

'Pretty good, I'd say. I would not be investing time and money in you guys if I didn't think it would pay a return. But, like I say, Maxine is centre-stage. It all revolves around her, the way I envisage it. As a singer, she is the focal point. As a pianist, she is an integral part of the band. Hence, there is a place for the band in this enterprise.'

'And what sort of things might we be doing, work-wise?'

'Radio broadcasts, I hope. That's the quickest way to get known. From that should come records. But nightly appearances in clubs and hotels are an important part of the equation. Fans want access to hearing you play in person and seeing you.'

'And shall we have good potential for earning?' Brent persisted.

'The sky's the limit, Brent. There's big money in America. It all depends on you guys . . . and Maxine, of course.'

Brent's eyes lit up at the prospect and he looked covetously at Maxine while John had everybody's glass recharged. The conversation ran on. Waiters opened and served more bottles of wine. Pudding came; cranberry and apple pie with cream, pancakes, compôte of mixed fruits with creamed rice, roll jam pudding, and ice cream. Cheese and biscuits followed. Everybody stayed at the table for ages, talking, enjoying the occasion and each other's company, enthusiastic and grateful for the opportunity to play at the Onyx Club that John Fielding was happy to engineer on their behalf.

When the party broke up Brent took Maxine's hand proprietorially and walked her to the door of her cabin.

'You're going to be a star, Maxine,' he said. 'I'm going to see to it that you are. I've always said you've got star quality.'

'Me a star?' she answered dismissively. 'That'll be the day.'

'John Fielding evidently thinks so as well. Otherwise, he wouldn't bother with you.'

'Star or not, I've still got to sing for my supper tonight.'

'Come into my cabin,' he suggested softly, pressing himself to her as she leaned against the door. 'I'll send for something to drink.'

'I'd better not have anything else to drink, Brent, thanks. I'm tired already. I could use forty winks before we play tonight.'

'Come and have forty winks with me.'

She felt herself blush and lowered her lids. 'I'd best have forty winks on my own.'

'I'm so proud of you, you know.'

She smiled self-consciously. 'Thank you.'

'And you're so beautiful.'

'You won't get me into bed by buttering me up.'

It was his turn to smile. 'Oh, yes I will,' he said confidently. 'So don't say you haven't been warned.'

He put his arms around her and they kissed; a long, delicious kiss that sent the blood coursing through her body.

'I'll see you later,' he breathed when they broke off.

She nodded and let go of him, but not without a little hesitancy.

* * *

313

While her parents were in London, Dulcie Fielding was going to stay on board ship in her Cabin Class accommodation. She would return to New York with the band but was then booked to cruise back to Southampton on the next sailing. Her parents would rejoin the ship two weeks from now for their return home. This arrangement allowed Dulcie to be with Kenny, who seemed to have won her heart; she could enjoy him and The Owls and the Pussycats as her travelling companions. She stuck close to Kenny during the stopover in Southampton and seemed to enjoy the banter while they visited a cinema on the Monday night.

Maxine, having received no letter from Howard on her return to Southampton this time, accepted the lack of any correspondence philosophically. It was evident by now that he was no longer interested in her. It had been a month since last she'd had any contact with him and she was inclined to regard him now as history. In Southampton, the realities of life sprung somehow to the fore again in her mind and Howard's seeming lack of care saddened her. She tried to shake off the fetters of disappointment and not let them show, especially to Brent. Brent, conversely, was becoming more and more attentive. He was somebody she felt she could rely on. In truth, the hurt was nowhere near as painful as it had been a fortnight ago. She had grown used to the idea of being without Howard, and the soporific effect of the sea and sailing, together with Brent's considerate and flattering attentions, helped divert her from the heartache. Rather, she was finally admitting to herself that she was being inexorably drawn to Brent. His manifest affection, his kindness and protectiveness made her feel closer to him than she had ever felt before; and she did not dislike the feeling.

On the Tuesday evening in Southampton, Maxine received a telephone call aboard ship from John Fielding. He confirmed that he had cabled his associates and arranged their showcase concert at the Onyx Club for next Monday when they returned to New York. He was happy to act as their agent in America and Seth Cohen would promote them in Britain and the rest of

Europe. A new contract would be drawn up to cover all promotion in America, which was being despatched by special messenger for immediate signing, and would arrive that night. Meanwhile, John said, it was not possible to arrange work permits till they returned to the USA so they could only appear at the Onyx as long as they were not paid. This situation should apply to one appearance only. Despite this, the band members were excited and speculated on the outcome.

Thus, the band's third entry into New York on 9th December turned out to be something of a landmark in the lives of its members. Maxine and Brent discussed at length their repertoire for the evening, how they were to present themselves. For a start, they would drink no alcohol before, between or during their performances; alcohol led to sloppiness. They discussed what dresses the girls would wear for maximum visual effect. Uncertainties about musical arrangements they sorted out during the voyage, and were content they had done all they could to ensure a smooth and impressive performance.

Snow was carpeting the streets of New York that night and it was bitterly cold. The Owls and the Pussycats, accompanied by Dulcie and their instruments – all except Kenny's drums, for he would use the resident drummer's kit – took two cavernous taxicabs to the Onyx Club and arrived shortly after ten o'clock. The drivers pulled up alongside a line of parked motor cars and deposited them cheerlessly on Fifty-second Street. Maxine looked up with pleasure at the bright neon signs that vied with each other to attract customers to the Open Door Club, The Onyx or the Hickory House, and she beamed brilliantly at Brent. He caught the spirit of her smile, took her hand and squeezed it before he grabbed his trombone from the taxi and paid the driver.

The Onyx Club had started life as a speakeasy during the days of Prohibition and reopened in 1935 after a devastating fire. Dulcie confirmed it was a real cool place to be nowadays and added that it usually posted a 'house full' sign well before midnight, especially at weekends.

The biggest draw there in years had been a trombonist called Mike Riley and a trumpeter called Eddie Farley. In 1935, they recorded the novelty number 'The Music Goes 'Round and Around', the very song The Owls and the Pussycats had taken pains to learn during the summer. To meet them was a treat none of them had anticipated, to watch them perform was an eye-opener, for the two musicians and their Onyx Club Band had developed a wonderful knockabout comedy routine that had everybody in stitches.

As the night progressed, Maxine suspected other elite musicians were dropping by, but frustratingly she didn't know who. Word spread that Art Tatum, the renowned jazz pianist was in the room but she wouldn't have recognised him if he had fallen on top of her. A little later, it was said that Jack Teagarden had dropped by and that Fats Waller was in town again and he was ever likely to show up. The people who mattered to The Owls and the Pussycats, however, were anonymous at that time and the band was totally unaware of them.

At midnight, The Owls and the Pussycats were introduced as a new swing band from England who were currently wowing the rich and famous on the *Queen Mary*, and were the guest band, for tonight only, at the Onyx Club. They stepped into the glare of spotlights and the polite applause of the jazz-orientated audience who did not know what to expect. Nervously, but proficiently, they played their first few numbers. The club was starting to get busy and would get even busier, even on a Monday night. Their nervousness put them on their mettle so they played well. Additionally, their tribute to Mike Riley and Eddie Farley of 'The Music goes 'Round and Around' drew tremendous applause, led by the resident musicians, for the original interplay between Toots on trumpet and Pansy on clarinet. It was well appreciated.

Whoever announced a number spoke informally, intimately

to the audience, as if they were all old friends, and everybody warmed to this. English accents sounded distinctly unusual, especially in the context of jazz, and seemed to elicit greater respect than an indigenous accent might. Maxine's piano playing and vocal technique drew plenty of admiring applause too, but two rather lovely girls with extraordinary talent fronting the band, rendered them all the more fascinating. Those who were well-versed in jazz appreciated hearing it played well. The Owls and the Pussycats were a welcome contrast to the resident musicians who, though competent enough, had come to rely more on comedy and less on music. It was also a revelation to most that an unheard of white band from England could come along and show them how swing should be played. Maybe some even resented it.

After the first set they returned to their dressing room, applause still ringing in their ears.

'I'm glad that's over,' Maxine said to Pansy with relief, and fanned her face with a few sheets of manuscript to cool herself down. 'I think we went down quite well.'

'But what a place,' Pansy enthused. 'It'll be a bit of a let down if we have to go back and play at the Gas Street Basin Club in dear old Brum.'

'Gosh! Brum! . . . I'd forgotten all about Brum.' Maxine shrugged and finished the last of the cola she'd left there before they started. 'Brum seems like another lifetime ago – another life. I mean, just compare New York with Brum. There are clubs like this on almost every street here – theatres, cinemas, restaurants everywhere. And the shops . . . And everywhere's so new and modern and nice. I really love it.'

'D'you think you'll come back then – when the *Queen Mary* thing is over?'

'I hope so, don't you? With the band, I mean. I'm certain Dulcie's dad will do everything he says. Don't you think so? I mean there's so much more opportunity here for the likes of us, especially with him helping us.'

'It would be good, wouldn't it?' Pansy agreed.

'Well, let's see what comes of tonight, eh? Come on, let's find the others, I'm parched after all that singing. And I've finished my drink.'

An intermission pianist was playing, as proficient a player as Maxine had ever heard. She stood listening for a few minutes, admiring his dexterity, at the same time receiving with gratitude and her usual warm smile the compliments of men that came up to say how much they'd enjoyed her performance. The atmosphere was lively by this time and the haze of smoke embraced the incessant symphony of laughter and a hundred conversations. Maxine looked around, trying to locate the other band members. Pansy had gone to find Toots so she was on her own and at the mercy of so many enthusiastic New Yorkers who wanted to stop and talk.

Eventually, she made her way to the bar. Kenny and Dulcie were standing together, arms about each other. A pretty girl of about nineteen with bleached hair and a striking figure was leaning provocatively against Brent and laughing at something he'd said. Brent, sitting on a high bar stool, had an arm around her and Maxine felt a sudden surge of jealousy.

'Have you seen Pansy?' she said, having made a beeline for him in high dudgeon.

At once Brent unhanded the girl and smiled at Maxine with a hint of guilt in his eyes. 'Hi, sweetheart. This is Blanche; Blanche, Maxine. What would you like to drink, Maxine?'

She glanced scornfully at the girl. They'd mentioned a Blanche from the dime-a-dance saloon; the girl with no knickers; the girl who had disappeared after her dances with Kenny. Yes – the girl Brent had spent the night with.

'Nothing, thank you,' she answered in her most peeved voice. 'I'm looking for Pansy.'

She had put about about five yards between herself and Brent when she sensed he was following her.

'What's up with you?' he asked, taking her arm to pull her back.

'Nothing in particular,' Maxine snarled, shrugging him off.

'Come off it, I can see you're nettled.' He said scornfully. 'Is it Blanche?'

'Leave me alone! I've no intention of staying where I'm not wanted. If you'd rather sit with your arms around *her*, then carry on. Don't mind me. Spend the night with her again. Why should I care?'

A man came up to them. 'Say! Just the guys. Great show tonight. Just great.'

'Thanks,' said Brent with a boyish grin, glad of the respite from Maxine's pique. 'Glad you enjoyed it.'

'Sure did.' The man held out his hand to Brent and they shook. 'Teddy Kaufman. Producer of *Saturday Dance . . .*' Brent looked sufficiently puzzled for the man to add: 'You ain't heard of it?'

Brent shook his head.

'Sure, sure . . .' He nodded his understanding and put his hand to his head animatedly. 'Pardon me for being such a dumb-ass. Course you ain't heard of it, you're a Limey.'

'Isn't it a radio show?' Maxine offered.

'How d'ya like that?' Teddy roared and a broad, toothy grin spread across his face. 'The lady knows about *Saturday Dance* . . . Say, honey, I love your voice. I mean I *really* love your voice. Boy, can you sing a song!'

'Thank you,' Maxine said, and quite forgot her pique over Brent and his new friend.

'I had a cable from John Fielding of AMP,' Teddy Kaufman continued. 'Say, can we go talk some place quiet for a minute?'

'Sure,' Brent said, realising he was using the response in the American way. 'We can go to the dressing room . . . Are you coming, Maxine?'

Maxine tagged along and, in the dressing room, the conversation continued.

'Like I say,' Teddy Kaufman continued, 'I had a cable from John Fielding who's in London right now. He suggested I get

319

down here tonight to hear you guys. When somebody from AMP makes a suggestion like that something special is about to break.'

'So tell us about your radio show, Mr Kaufman,' Brent said. 'I'm sorry I hadn't heard of it but in England we don't get to know what shows you have over here.'

'The show goes out every Saturday night, coast to coast. Three whole hours of jazz and swing. I promise, it's a very popular show. We feature the biggest and best bands in the US. Naturally, such exposure can make a band well known and real popular. I'd like you guys to appear for a few weeks.'

'On the wireless?' Maxine said. 'Blimey!'

'You say it goes out across the whole of America, Mr Kaufman?' Brent queried.

'Yep. Coast to coast. From right here in the Big Apple . . . Say, can you guys write some more songs? I dig that one you played that the little lady here wrote – Destiny something. The show is a platform for songs just as much as for artists.'

'We'd love to do the show,' Brent said. 'We have another three weeks before we finish our contract on the *Queen Mary*, though. Then another week to get back here. That's a month.'

'No sweat. That gives us time to schedule you in. So you're agreed?'

'Just arrange it with John Fielding,' Brent answered with one of his boyish grins.

'Sure will! You won't be disappointed. I'll discuss it with John Fielding when he returns. He'll be the one to haggle over your fee, I guess.' Teddy Kaufman offered his hand again to Brent.

'Thank you, Mr Kaufman,' Brent said. 'We'll look forward to it.'

'Sure thing.' Teddy Kaufman then shook Maxine's hand. 'You're really gonna knock 'em dead, little lady. My, oh my! Shame they can't *see* you on radio. Darned shame.'

Mr Kaufman handed Brent a business card and made his excuses. Brent looked at Maxine in disbelief. Then, in sheer joy, they fell into each other's arms.

320

'Oh, Brent. Is this really happening?' she said. 'I can't believe this is really happening.'

Brent picked her up and swung her round, whooping with triumphant laughter. 'Oh, it's happening all right. I knew it would. As soon as I got that letter from Seth Cohen telling us we were booked to play on the *Queen Mary*, I knew. We're going to be famous, Maxine, I know it. We're going to be rich!'

Maxine straightened up Brent's bow-tie, picked a blonde hair from the lapel of his tuxedo jacket and gave him a sideways look that told him she was over her pique. 'Come on. You've dumped knickerless Blanche and her bleached hair now, haven't you?'

'I was only saying hello, Maxine.'

'Okay.' She smiled forgivingly. 'Let's go and celebrate. I'm parched.'

'When we've finished playing. Then we'll open a couple of bottles of champagne . . . If we can scrape up enough money between us. Wait till the others know what's happening.'

Maxine grabbed Brent's hand and led him out of the dressing room, bubbling with vitality. They manoeuvred their way towards the bar again, pushing through the crowd. The intermission pianist was still at it, his endeavours almost drowned out by the noise of the crowd.

'Listen to that guy,' Maxine said to Brent, unaware of the Americanism she had used. 'You'd think people would take the trouble to listen to talent like that.'

Before Brent had chance to reply, another man greeted them and gave his name, although it remained unintelligible in the hubbub.

'I'm from the Waldorf,' he yelled. 'Say, you're a swell band. How'd you like to play a season for us at the Waldorf?'

'Brilliant,' Brent said, looking at Maxine with further incredulity. 'When were you thinking of?'

'Whenever. Are you familiar with the Waldorf?'

'I've heard of it.'

'Great! Xavier Cugat has been performing there.'

'Xavier Cugat!' Brent repeated and gave out a whistle of approval.

'Sure. We hire top bands. You'd be great. The folks in the Waldorf would love you.'

'Thanks. Maybe you'd best talk to John Fielding at AMP. He's handling all enquiries.'

It felt wonderful to be able to say such a thing. Maxine looked up at Brent and beamed and could tell that he was thinking the same. The man from the Waldorf shook their hands again and another man, who Maxine had noticed hovering, waiting his turn to speak, approached them.

'Hi there! I'm from the Roosevelt Hotel on Forty-fifth and Madison . . . Would you be available next March to play a short season for us?'

'It's possible,' Brent replied politely. 'But opportunities seem to be coming thick and fast right now and I can't give you a definite answer. Could you discuss it with John Fielding of AMP? He's looking after things. He returns to New York in a couple of weeks.'

'Sure thing. I know John. I'll be in touch with him. Great show, by the way. The folks at the Grill at the Roosevelt would be knocked out by The Owls and the Pussycats.'

'Thank you.' Brent shook his hand before yet another man accosted them.

'I had a phone call from the Chicago Congress asking me to come and hear you guys.'

'Great,' said Brent with another of his charming smiles and Maxine hoped he would never ration them. 'I hope you aren't disappointed.'

'Hell, no! You're a great outfit. For such a small band you play that big band stuff like it was written for you. Keep it up. I'll put a word in for you at *Down Beat* too. Although, they've probably already heard of you there.'

'*Down Beat* is a music magazine, isn't it?' Maxine queried.

'Yeah. Based in Chicago. Hits the streets monthly . . . Nice to speak with you. I'll put in a good report to the Congress.'

'Thanks. Bye.'

'I can't believe this, Maxine. Pinch me to make sure I'm not dreaming. Have we gone down well, or what?'

'They all want us. It's fantastic. But I'm so thirsty, Brent. I have to have a drink, else I'll never last out the next session.

When they finally reached the bar Toots, Pansy and the others were together, all enjoying themselves. Brent got drinks for himself and Maxine while she told them of the offers they'd had already. The news of the offer for the radio programme excited them and Kenny said he'd had enquiries too from Atlantic City and Boston.

'When we've played our next session we'll get champagne and celebrate,' Brent told them. 'This is the best night we've ever had.'

'And after, there's a party at my house,' Dulcie added. 'With my mom and dad away we'll have the run of the place.'

'Brilliant!' Maxine said. 'How did you manage that?'

'Oh, I called the house staff from the ship and gave them all the night off. Tomorrow, too.'

The next set proved even more successful than the first. The audience listened intently and rewarded the band with enthusiastic applause after every number. The atmosphere was tremendous and Kenny twirled his drumsticks in the air with abandon and a broad grin as he took a bow after his solo.

'Ladies and gentlemen – Kenny Wheeler . . .' Brent proclaimed, holding his hand out to his pal.

Eventually, the compere requested another show of appreciation and the band left the stage to spirited applause, waving goodbye as they went.

'Let's pop those champagne corks,' Brent said as they returned to the dressing room. His handsome face was glowing with elation as he packed his trombone into its case. 'This is definitely a night to celebrate.'

'Definitely a night to remember,' Charlie concurred.

'What time is it?' Pansy asked, fastening the hook and eye at the back of the dress she had changed back into.

'Just after three,' Toots told her. 'The night is young.'

Meanwhile, Dulcie had been fortunate enough to get a table and already two bottles of champagne were standing in ice buckets.

'You open them,' Maxine suggested to Brent. 'I daresay you're used to it.'

With a flourish he popped the cork of the first bottle and filled the glasses.

'Cheers!' they all said in chorus, and drank.

Maxine thanked Dulcie for getting the champagne ready and asked how much they owed her.

'Gee, honey, nothing,' Dulcie replied sharply and Maxine wondered if she had offended her by asking. 'It's my treat. I owe you guys.'

'But we're all going to your house after for a party.'

'Sure. So what?'

'I'm just worried about what it costs, Dulcie.'

'Maxine, let me tell you something. New Yorkers don't worry about what things cost – only about being ripped off. The longer you stay here the more you'll realise that everybody is money mad. That's all they talk about. They love spending it but they sure don't worry about how much anything costs.'

Dulcie's chastising her amused Maxine. 'Okay, I'll try and remember.'

The private party progressed wonderfully and Brent ordered two more bottles of champagne. People around The Owls and the Pussycats caught their infectious high spirits and Charlie Holt and Ginger Tolley drew two other girls, one of whom was Blanche, into the company. Half an hour later, Ginger had his arm around the slim dark-haired one who was called Ellie and Charlie was ensconced with Blanche, though Maxine thought she kept making eyes at Brent, which annoyed her immensely. Come four o'clock Dulcie suggested they move on to her house.

It took ten minutes to organise their departure. Kenny and Dulcie went out into the snow to garner sufficient taxi cabs, while the others collected their instruments and things from the dressing room. Then, having said a hundred goodbyes to well-wishers, they departed, five girls and five boys, to a mansion on Fifth Avenue overlooking Central Park.

Chapter 25

'Welcome to my world,' Dulcie said as she let them into her home.

'Gee, no English butler?' Blanche commented, looking around her.

The entrance hall was imposing with some fine watercolours adorning the green-flocked walls. A chandelier hung low over the ornate staircase that swept up and around them, and a stained glass oriel window by Tiffany looked out onto Central Park. Dulcie flung open the handsome double doors that led into a sumptuous drawing room. An elaborate bar occupied one end and they all headed for it instinctively. Dulcie invited them to help themselves to drinks so Toots, typically helpful, elected himself barman and began serving everybody.

Talk was, of course, mostly about the success of their evening, but the two girls who were partial strangers seemed determined to ask questions about England and what the band thought of New York. Blanche, the blonde girl, seemed to want to monopolise Brent, even though, by default, she was to be paired with Charlie Holt.

'Seems like England might soon get its first American queen,' she commented, seeming to ignore Maxine who was at Brent's side.

'Oh? How's that?' Brent asked.

'Wallis Simpson,' Blanche replied.

'Sounds like a chain of shoe shops,' Maxine remarked with

as much scorn as she could muster and sipped the dry Martini Toots had mixed.

'Yeah? Well your King Edward's mighty sweet on her. He's gonna marry her.'

'But he can't,' Brent replied. 'She's a divorcee.'

'Hell! So what?' Blanche said.

'I don't know much about it. American papers seem to be stirring up quite a fuss about the King and Mrs Simpson from what I can see of it, but there's been nothing in the English press. At least I've seen nothing.'

'You mean you know zilch about it?'

'There've been rumours. Speculation. But it would create a constitutional crisis if the King wanted to marry a divorcee. The government wouldn't allow it.'

'Gee! You sure have some quaint ways in England. What's wrong with being divorced, for Christ's sake? Everybody gets divorced in America. Anyway, who rules the goddamn country?' She shrugged her shoulders and spread her arms to emphasise her point and spilt her drink in the process, which she ignored. 'Anyway, it's great that an American lady's gonna marry an English king. He's real cute.'

'Oh, I don't know about that,' Maxine said, becoming more irritated by the girl and her ignorance of British constitutional niceties, but more especially since she was so obviously after Brent. 'Just think,' she went on, 'he'd have to be King of America.'

'Really? . . . Wow!'

'Yes . . . and with our quaint ideas . . . Still, if he's that cute, you might not mind.' Maxine moved closer to Brent and terri- torially felt for his hand. She gave it a squeeze.

'I used to think all English guys were cute,' Blanche said, looking directly into Brent's eyes, and finally getting the message. 'Trouble is, they don't know when they're on to a good thing. They get sidetracked too damn quick. But hell, I don't kiss ass. There's plenty more fish in the sea.'

Blanche turned her back and joined Charlie while Maxine

regarded Brent through narrowed eyes. She went to move her hand away from his but he held it tight.

'I told you, she meant nothing,' he whispered. 'Hell, you can't complain, Maxine. We weren't . . .'

Maxine sighed frustratedly. He was right, of course. He was a free agent. He could do as he wished. It's just that she felt this jealousy. He always made such a fuss of her and when he made a fuss of anybody else, she didn't like it.

'Okay,' she conceded. 'It's just her attitude . . .'

'It's you I want, Maxine,' he said, and the warmth in his eyes told her he was sincere.

'Okay,' she answered and squeezed his hand. 'I believe you.'

Ellie meanwhile was doing rather well with Ginger, appealing to his more positive side as she gazed into his eyes. 'Do you think I'm cute, Ginger?' she asked in a Brooklyn accent.

Ginger grinned and gave her a squeeze. 'I think you're bloody lovely, Ellie. Here, let's sit down on that sofa.'

Ellie giggled. The alcohol was having an effect. 'He wants to get me on the sofa, Blanche. Think I should?'

'Hell, go to it,' Blanche said.

'Okay, Blanche. If you go to it with Charlie, huh?'

Charlie beamed and Blanche allowed him to lead her away.

Maxine sighed with relief as this arrangement was at last confirmed. It proved to her that there had been nothing to worry about. Brent had shunned Blanche in favour of herself. It proved his love. Besides, an argument about Blanche would have been pointless, and possibly fatal to their relationship. Now Maxine just wanted to take Brent in her arms. She wanted to plant her lips on his and give him one of her most luscious kisses. Maybe she had misjudged him.

She was certain she had not misjudged Blanche, however. Blanche was lying across Charlie in a most provocative way, looking into his eyes, her lips no more than two inches from his. Charlie was evidently mesmerised by the experience.

Brent led Maxine away to the other side of the room where

Kenny, Dulcie, Toots and Pansy were sharing a joke together, about to start playing a gramophone. Dulcie put on a record and Kenny took her in his arms. They began dancing to Helen Ward's 'You Turned the Tables on Me'. Pansy and Toots then started swaying to the easy rhythm. Maxine looked into Brent's eyes and, by an unspoken accord, they fell into each other's arms, moving slowly. When the music stopped they kissed while Dulcie put on another record. It was Duke Ellington's 'The Mooche' – slow, raunchy stuff. The seductive sounds continued for some time. They were all able to relax at last. Till Ginger spoke up from the upholstered depths of one of the sofas.

'Hey, can somebody turn the lights out? It's like the inside of a soddin' lantern here.'

Dulcie burst into laughter. 'Sure!' She moved to the switches and turned them off, leaving on just one table lamp. Then she said quietly to the others: 'Maybe that's our cue to leave, huh? . . . Come on, Kenny Wheeler, you can tuck me up in bed . . .'

'Are we going back to the ship now, Brent?' Maxine asked innocently.

They all heard and their tittering made her realise how naïve she was being.

'Do you want to go back to the ship tonight in all this wind and snow?' Dulcie asked, incredulous.

'No, of course not,' she replied emphatically.

On Fifth Avenue, motor cars left unbroken tracks in the snow while snowflakes rushed into their headlights, drawn like millions of white moths. Central Park wore its pre-Christmas covering like a shroud but the lake looked like a pool of liquid lead. The trees, naked but for the snow that was accumulating on their branches, shimmered as they swayed in the winter wind.

Maxine and Brent stood gazing out of the window of the ornate bedroom that Dulcie had suggested they share. They were in darkness but the fairyland lights of New York reflected a pallid, ghostly suffusion back into the room, enabling them to see each

329

other quite clearly. Dawn was more than an hour away. She turned to face him. He discerned that look of gentleness and trust in her eyes that always appealed to his better nature and gave her a hug. She nestled in his arms as if they had been lovers for years.

'Look how beautiful the park is, even in darkness,' she whispered. 'Oh, I love it here, Brent. I think I could be happy here forever.'

He squeezed her again. 'Yes. I love it too. I'll always be happy here . . . with you.'

For a few minutes, neither spoke more. Maxine continued to gaze out, impassively contemplating what Brent expected of her, what she herself might expect, in this strange rococo bedroom, in this strange grey twilight. She did not mind. She did not mind at all. She would allow her seduction to happen naturally, at its own tempo, for it was time. She would not make the first move; that was up to him. Just because a large accommodating bed was beckoning did not mean she should rush to take her clothes off and jump into it like some sex-hungry nymph. But it would be nice to be loved again. It would be good to make love again, to relive that sweet tenderness and intimacy she had known and enjoyed with Howard. She was missing the warmth and the peace and the closeness of sharing love. Now, the imminent prospect of it thrilled her, yet also filled her with apprehension for, having set her heart on Brent now, she did not want to disappoint him. After all, he was vastly experienced in such things whereas she was a comparative beginner. And yet, she thought, allowing herself a little smile, it's funny how quickly you get the hang of it.

It was as much to her surprise as anybody's that she had someone else to love so soon; someone who had shown his mercurial devotion over many months. At times she had been disconcerted by his wild unpredictability, confused when one day he was all over her, the next ignoring her. In her innocence, Maxine had not considered that it could have been a strategy to generate her interest the more. To her, any inconsistency was because she had not committed herself to him.

She turned and their eyes met once again. Submissively she lifted her face for his kiss. It was tender but frustratingly brief. She buried her face in the warmth of his jacketed shoulder. He smelt of cigarettes and the bleak winter air of New York with a hint of clean, manly sweat and shaving soap added. She gently touched his throat, almost bashfully, with her lips.

Fate had brought them together here. It must be fate that had ensured their hitherto tentative relationship be consummated in this beautiful room in this magnificent house, in this magical city. It was the culmination of many things; their working together; their music; the indisputable attraction they'd always had for each other. It must also be the night, the unbelievable success, the champagne, the moment – this wonderful other world. All had contrived to seduce her.

Brent lowered his head and his lips found hers again in a kiss so tender, so soft, so gentle and yet so unruffled. At any other time she would have considered it half-hearted, but not this night; he was savouring the softness of her lips, perhaps still tasting the champagne and the sweet, fatty fragrance of her lipstick. Funny how she could not help but compare Brent's kisses with Howard's. She enjoyed both and yet they were succinctly different. Brent always tasted different, but that was almost certainly because he smoked. Whatever it was, his lips were scandalously inviting – always had been.

They broke off and she looked up at him, her eyes signalling the warmth and tenderness she felt. Was this affair happening too soon after the hurt she felt over Howard? Should she expose her frail, tortured heart to risk again so soon? Hell, yes. Brent loved her; she was sure of that. And she loved him . . . She knew that now – at long last. She knew it just as surely as she knew the sun would rise next morning. Maybe she had always loved him. Maybe Howard had merely been an enjoyable diversion till destiny contrived this moment for true romance to begin. Maybe

331

she had loved Brent from the moment she first saw him after her audition with the CBO.

Brent's fingers were undoing the hook and eye at the back of her dress. She bent her head forward biddably so that he might have easier access. Then she felt him unfasten one by one the tiny buttons that held her dress together at the back. She stood there impassive, content for him to do it while she continued to gaze out onto Central Park, her head on his shoulder. The city was just showing the first stirrings of life this cold Tuesday morning in December. He peeled the dress from her shoulders and down her arms before he eased it over her slender hips. It fell silently to the carpet that lay thick under her feet.

What would Howard think if he could see her now? Would he care? *Did* he care? Not any longer, evidently. Did he ever really care? He hadn't written and he said he would. He had broken his promise. He must never have cared in the first place.

As if sensing she was fretting over Howard, Brent found her lips again and planted another sweet, lingering kiss, more passionate this time, caressing her shoulders with gentle fingers that sent shivers of delight up and down her spine.

'You have such beautiful skin,' he breathed.

He unfastened her brassiere and it fell from her to the floor. She kicked off her shoes and found herself standing lower against his chest by a couple of inches. His hands went to her waist and traced a line slowly upwards till they were almost under her arms before he moved them round to gently cup her naked breasts. Softly he pressed his thumbs onto her nipples and she felt them harden. Through the huge window she watched with detachment as more cars ploughed the snow on Fifth Avenue below; a man huddled in an overcoat trudged warily lest he slip and slide as he walked to work.

Brent was bending down so that he could kiss her breasts. Suddenly conscious of them, she wondered what he thought of them. They were not large, but she had always considered them adequate and never too much of a burden. Certainly, they were beautifully formed and showed no tendency to sag . . . Howard had said so . . . And it was so invigorating to feel Brent's mouth on them, teasing them each in turn . . .

That poor man outside, battling against the wind and the snow in his winter clothes . . . and she was so warm and glowing in this centrally heated bedroom . . . in America . . . and naked to the waist, God help her. Not that she had the least intention to protest.

Suddenly, Brent was on his knees. He was kissing her rib cage. She ran her fingers through his hair sensitively and felt him pull her underskirt down over her hips and buttocks till it, too, fell to the soft carpet around her. His fingers were stroking her bottom through the legs of her French knickers while his tongue was probing her navel.

It was snowing harder now. The flakes were enormous as they floated past the window, sometimes in a flurry of agitation as the bitter swirling wind caught them. Maxine illogically wondered if it was snowing in Dudley. It must be nearly midday there. What was her mother doing right now? What was Henzey doing? How was little Aldo? Had Alice found another job yet? What was Howard doing?

God! . . . What was Brent doing? Her knickers and her stockings were around her ankles and he was licking between her thighs like a thirsty cat lapping milk. But it was unbelievably nice . . . So she parted her legs a little to allow him easier access and found the effort rewarding for the pleasure was all the more intense. She sighed at her own response to these delectable sensations and was surprised at her lack of resistance and shame at such an outlandish invasion of her most secret place. But why should she resist? Why should she feel shame when it was so, so pleasant? She ran her fingers through his hair with more urgency now and gently pulled his face into her, thrusting her pelvis forward.

Outside, more people were trudging through the snow, more motor cars were negotiating the streets, but gingerly, and one slithered into the kerb as it braked to slow down. Yet, she no longer saw the white, snowy streets of New York, the shimmering trees and the leaden lake. Her eyes were shut tight. Central Park and its white winter overcoat were just part of the unreality as the warm glow in her loins increased and demanded her concentration.

Then Brent stood up and she looked into his eyes again appealingly. He gently scooped her up into his arms as he would a baby and placed her across the massive bed. She lay there expectantly, hungry for him now, while he took off his own clothes. Then, as naked as she, he lay alongside her and their bodies touched. His skilful hands were all over her, touching her breasts, caressing between her legs agonisingly till she wanted to cry out for his weight upon her.

Pray for me, Howard . . . Pray for me . . . Howard . . . Howard . . .

Brent rolled onto her and she gasped with relief and pleasure as he entered her.

They slept till shortly after nine o'clock. It was daylight and through the open curtains Maxine could see that it had stopped snowing. She snuggled up to Brent and almost at once felt him hard for her again. They made love once more, languidly, as if they had always been lovers, then slept again. At midday they were awakened by the sound of giggling.

'Sounds like Dulcie is on the landing,' Maxine whispered.

Then they heard Kenny's unmistakable yelps of laughter.

'Sounds like everybody's up and about,' Brent said.

'Already?' Maxine sounded disappointed. 'I swear, I could sleep on.'

'You'll get precious little sleep from now on, Maxine.'

'Oh?' she uttered innocently.

'Well, I reckon we should alter the sleeping arrangements on board ship . . . Don't you?'

'How do you mean?'

'Well, it's obvious Kenny will be spending his nights in Dulcie's cabin. That means you can move in with me and Toots can move in with Pansy.'

'I see you've got it all worked out.'

'Don't tell me you're objecting . . .'

Maxine smiled bashfully. Her innate modesty inclined her to pull the bedclothes over her naked breasts.

'No, don't cover yourself up,' he complained. 'It's great to see you starkers at last. I always wondered what you looked like starkers . . .'

'Well, now you know. Have I lived up to your expectations?'

'Let's put it this way – you are too good for that Howard Quaintance. I don't think he was capable of appreciating you.'

She turned her face away from him. How could he possibly say that? How could he possibly give an opinion on how much Howard had appreciated her body? Just because he was a clergyman didn't mean . . .

'I'll make you happy, Maxine,' he said as if detecting her resentment. 'You'll not want for sex with me, that's for sure.'

'It's love I want,' she replied softly. But she smiled with contentment, for he had loved her capably enough.

Chapter 26

In the short time he had been in business on his own account in Birmingham's Jewellery Quarter, Stephen Hemming had fared commendably well. The Depression had taken its toll of the area's businesses, but the market had now turned round for the better and demand was healthy once more for the trinkets they produced. Stephen's creative flair led him into designing exclusive and thus expensive jewellery that those manufacturers and retailers that served the more affluent consumers regarded as chic. It was a lucrative niche. Furthermore, it had not taken him long to appreciate that manufacturing these designs himself would be even more profitable, and the new workshop he had established was stacked out with work. Already he was earning a tidy penny and the future looked even rosier with the first commissions appearing as well from top couturiers in London, Paris and Rome.

Eleanor, of course, had watched this meteoric success with a shrewd, calculating regard and increasing admiration. Indeed, her own collection of elegant gems was growing by the week and she was keen to show them off when she escorted Stephen to the theatre and the growing number of dinner parties they were being invited to. This rapidly increasing affluence was reflected in the clothes she was amassing in her wardrobe, in the frequency of her visits to the hairdresser and the motor car they sported – a brand new Alvis Speed 25.

Stephen was turning out to be quite a catch.

Brent had always been debonair and his capriciousness, Eleanor readily understood, rendered him all the more intriguing, especially perhaps to younger women. Stephen on the other hand was predictable, earthy, reliable and, for the most part, relatively forthright. At first she had fallen into the trap of thinking him soft. But Stephen was not soft. He was no pushover and Eleanor had to use all her wiles to get her way when they did not see eye to eye. This quality attracted her now more than ever, for she enjoyed a challenge. Consequently, their relationship tended to be fiery with days on end when they would not speak to each other, usually over some petty disagreement. Generally, Eleanor caved in first . . . when she wanted money to pay for this or that intended purchase. And money was her first love, after all . . .

Stephen seemed to understand this and it inclined him to greater generosity. Whatever she wanted she could have, so long as he first sanctioned it and it did not incur a huge debt. In bed, however, he was demanding, and his sexual appetite surprised not only Eleanor but himself too. To prevent the ignominy of pregnancy, Eleanor had, after a nail-biting false alarm early on, been fitted with a new Dutch cap and there had been no frights since. But although she did not want children, she deemed marriage to Stephen desirable as a means of staking her claim to a share in his phenomenal success; indeed, she had contributed to it in no small measure. Besides, their living in sin could not be countenanced by the more conservative of their peers. It was impeding their advancement higher up the social ladder and thus their opportunities for greater wealth creation.

The problem was, she had always let Stephen believe she was married to Brent and explaining the truth was going to be difficult, if not impossible. However, her need to lay legitimate claim to some of the fortune he was making was blinding her to the potential hazards. Eleanor wanted to raise the issue one night as they were getting ready for bed. Ironically, they had been to a CBO concert at the Town Hall with business friends. It was not really an appropriate time to introduce the subject but impulsiveness and greed was driving her, as it always drove her.

'I thought it seemed strange to be at a CBO concert and see neither Brent nor Maxine on the platform,' she remarked, trying to sound casual as she sat in her dressing gown pulling a brush through her hair repeatedly.

'Really? I hadn't thought about it.'

'You mean she never once crossed your mind while you were listening or watching the cellos playing? I don't believe you.'

'Oh, she might have crossed my mind fleetingly,' Stephen replied nonchalantly.

'See! There you are then.'

'But it's of no consequence.' He was leaning on his pillow, his head resting in his hand, watching her. She was not the vulnerable, demure type he'd always been attracted to; rather she was the complete opposite. But after all these months, he still could not take his eyes off her. She was the complete woman; beautiful, elegant, and such immense fun in bed. He hoped he would never tire of admiring her, of touching her, of making love to her. The only thing he was tiring of was the petty arguments that seemed to flare up all too often, especially at certain times of the month. And one might easily flare up right now if he did not veer away from the subject of Maxine Kite.

'I wonder what they're doing now?' Eleanor mused, persisting with the thread.

'Well, according to Pansy they intend to stay in New York when the *Queen Mary* thing finishes at the end of December.'

'You never told me you'd had another letter from Pansy.' Eleanor stopped brushing her hair and flashed him an annoyed look.

'Does it matter? God! She's my sister. Of course she keeps in touch.'

'Of course she keeps in touch, Stephen. I don't object to that. It's just that you never told me you'd had another letter. You never tell me anything.'

'Actually, I tell you everything, Eleanor. Not always in the same sequence as it happens, I grant you . . . Anyway, some things are too trivial to bother you with . . . Still, I can tell you the band's doing well. They have a series of radio shows booked for a start and long engagements at quite a few of the top night spots in New York. Other cities, too, Pansy says. Chicago and Boston . . . Oh, and Brent and Maxine have quite a thing going for each other now, apparently.'

'You mean . . . do you mean what I think you mean?'

'Reading between the lines . . . I wondered how long it would take. According to Pansy, that vicar chap never contacted her again once she left home to join the *Queen Mary* . . . So Brent muscled in.'

'Well, just fancy . . . Brent and Maxine . . .' Eleanor mused. She slowed the tempo of her hair brushing, pondering the fact. If Stephen had been able to see into her eyes, he might have detected a look of disquiet. 'Who'd have thought it?' she added, as if it were the biggest surprise of her life. 'I never thought she was Brent's type. Never.'

'Oh, come on, Eleanor, don't be so naïve. Any female is Brent's type. He'd lay a female frog if it would stop hopping.'

'God, Stephen! You're disgusting sometimes.'

'Come to bed, Eleanor and stop fiddling with your hair – it's beautiful enough. Come on, I'm as randy as a fiddler's bitch.'

She turned to look at him, put down her brush and took off her dressing gown. 'You're always randy . . . I suppose I should be thankful . . . But I wonder if you'd be as randy if we got married? I mean, it's all stolen fruits at the moment. Aren't stolen fruits supposed to be the sweetest?'

'I don't see as it would make any difference,' he said, his eyes glued to her breasts that were hanging lusciously free as she crawled naked across the bed to join him like a lissom young tigress stalking her prey. 'Why do you mention marriage, though? Have you got the bug just because the King's decided to abdicate and marry Mrs Simpson, or is it because of Brent and Maxine?'

She lifted the bedclothes and snuggled in beside him, borrowing his warmth. 'Neither. Neither has got anything to do with it. The truth is, I've been thinking, Stephen. Us living together unmarried is scaring off a lot of important would-be contacts. It's not tolerated by a good many and won't be seen to be tolerated either, for fear of jeopardising their own good name in society. If we were to get married we'd be thought respectable and we could get to know more people. That way we'd get business that's denied us now . . . Think about it.'

He thought about it – for about ten seconds – while he played with her breasts.

'But how can we if you're already married? Bigamy is a criminal offence, you know.' He scoffed at the absurdity of the idea.

'Oh, Stephen,' she sighed, and paused.

'What is it?'

'Well . . .' She hesitated. 'I'm actually not married to Brent. Nor have I ever been.'

'Not? Why on earth haven't you told me before?'

'Oh, I've meant to . . . a thousand times . . . I swear . . . I—'

'I'm shocked, Eleanor. I'm flabbergasted you never told me.'

'But you believe me, don't you?'

'Well forgive me if I seem a bit sceptical . . .' Stephen moistened his lips. 'If this is true it's going to take a bit of getting used to, let's face it. Are you sure it's the truth?'

'Of course I'm sure. We just wanted people to think we were married because it suited us. There's nothing sinister in that, is there?'

'I suppose it depends on why you wanted to fool people. Well, if it is the truth and we can get married, then, you're probably right . . . We should. If the King couldn't get away with it, I'm damned sure we won't be able to.'

'I know I'm right about us being more widely accepted, Stephen.'

'Then let's do it.'

Eleanor beamed with satisfaction. 'As soon as we can.'

'Let's do this first though . . .' He leaned over her and began by gently biting one of her nipples.

'Ouch!' she yelled. 'Don't do that! They're sore.'

'They're always sore to hear you talk.' He felt between her legs. '*This* isn't sore though, is it? . . .'

She giggled like a schoolgirl and wriggled like an eel. '*That* hasn't been sore for weeks. You must be losing your enthusiasm.'

Usually after he had made love, Stephen Hemming tended to drift into a contented slumber. Not so this night. Eleanor's surprising suggestion that they should marry was niggling him, keeping him awake. Not because he was opposed to marrying her. He would like nothing better. He was the sort of person that thrived on order and convention, but he had always taken for granted that she was already married to Brent Shackleton and, at no time until tonight, had she allowed him to believe otherwise. To any rational person, of course, it would be obvious that if someone proposed marriage, as she had done, then they must, by implication, be free to marry. But why had she allowed him to labour under a false impression all this time? To what purpose?

Eleanor lay in his arms, sleeping contentedly. Funny creatures, women; illogical; unpredictable. They tell you one thing and mean another. Like the night before; she had said, no, she didn't want to make love, but it turned out she was yearning all along to be loved. She'd just wanted him to fuss her first, plead with her. She'd wanted him to tease her into it. At other times she wanted reassurance that this or that new dress she had bought looked good on her. Yet she dressed and presented herself with such confidence and panache that it was obvious that she was going to look good enough to eat in anything. She would look fantastic dressed even in a potato sack; *and* she knew it.

He withdrew his arm from under her and turned over to face the other way. Eleanor licked her lips and grunted softly at this minor disturbance but remained sleeping. He tried to

341

imagine her and Brent making love, unmarried, living in sin, and pictured her lying on top of Brent, her cheeky backside thrusting with the smoothness of a well-oiled pump as she drained him dry. Then his vivid imagination supplanted her with Maxine Kite whose actual naked bottom he'd never had the privilege of assessing. Disturbing images . . . He tried to shut them from his mind. Should he even associate with the kind of girl who was prepared to make herself a target for wagging tongues and contempt by living with a man when she was not married to him, as Eleanor had done and was doing again? He might appear a hypocrite for making it his way of life, but he did not necessarily condone it. Moral standards had slipped since the war. Nonconformists might deliberately flout convention in that way, but respectable society frowned mightily on such lax morality.

Yes. Of course they must get married if she was free to . . .
If.
Then the obvious struck him.
What was he thinking, for God's sake? Of course she must be married to Brent. Why else would she have the same surname? He would tackle her on it . . . But that would end up with yet another argument . . . Maybe he should leave it a day or two . . . perhaps even a week or two. He would bide his time and make no further mention of marriage unless she did. He would make no arrangements for a wedding either. This question had to be sorted out first and he had to pick his time. Unorthodox as this current living arrangement might be, it was thoroughly convenient.

In the meantime, the King had been busy creating a constitutional crisis that only now the British public was becoming aware of. Over lunch with Winston Churchill on 11th December, he renounced the crown so that he could marry Mrs Simpson and sailed into exile in France. His brother, Albert, a dedicated family man, reluctantly assumed the throne as King George VI and instantly afforded much-needed stability to the monarchy.

The Atlantic Ocean, during this time and for the rest of the winter, was the stormiest in living memory. Maxine Kite was grateful she had moved into Brent Shackleton's cabin where he could protect her and reassure her that the ship was not about to sink under one of the massive waves that seemed perpetually to bombard it. On many stormy nights, music was suspended in all of the ballrooms, since only the most resilient of passengers were prepared to venture further than their cabins once they had eaten and thrown up for the umpteenth time.

Maxine received no letters from Howard Quaintance. She was disappointed and surprised that he had failed to write after his ardent declarations of love and his vehement apologies. So, with Howard well and truly part of her past, she applied herself with more commitment to Brent and The Owls and the Pussycats. Her future seemed to lie irrevocably with them now.

So Christmas 1936 came and went in an alcoholic haze of tinsel, crackers and partying. The Atlantic storms abated for a while and The Owls and the Pussycats set off on their final voyage from Southampton on 30th December, working their passage. They arrived at a bitterly cold New York that was still carpeted in snow. In addition to all his other successes on the band's behalf, John Fielding had organised work permits and membership to the New York musicians' union.

At first they occupied three rooms in a cheap hotel in Pell Street on the Lower East Side. It was not the most glamorous of places, especially after the excesses of comfort they'd enjoyed on the *Queen Mary*, but at least it was centrally heated. Maxine continued to share a bed with Brent and he instructed her to get fixed up with a Dutch cap. He hated using those damned smelly French letters. It was like trying to have a bath wearing a mackintosh, he said. Maxine said okay, she would, and sought help from Dulcie as to how and where in New York she might fulfil such a promise.

In mid-January 1937 the band did their first radio broadcast in the USA on the *Saturday Dance* programme that was sponsored by the National Cereal Company. They received rave reviews for it weekly. Maxine wrote more songs especially for the show, for which Brent did the musical arrangements, and these were being picked up by other artists who wished to record them. John Fielding negotiated attractive terms with music publishers for royalty payments, and these were poised to net her a tidy sum of money if the ensuing records sold well.

January also saw The Owls and the Pussycats performing at the Hotel New Yorker and in February they were booked to appear at the Grill Room of the Waldorf for six weeks, at which hotel they were also allocated three bedrooms. Late February also brought the band's first session with Victor Records when they recorded 'Destiny Jests with Me'. It had become the band's most requested number and Victor wanted to release it and promote it heavily. In the middle of March the living arrangements and work moved to the Roosevelt Hotel for six weeks.

As their fame increased, so the money started pouring in. It seemed to come from everywhere. The fees for a season at an hotel threatened to run into five figures, the radio broadcasts made them famous in every state of the Union from California in the west to Maine in the east. By the end of the first thirteen weeks, fan mail was arriving at the rate of five thousand letters a week. Their faces began to appear in every music magazine and fashion magazines were beginning to feature Maxine. Sheet music and record sales boomed and you could hear 'Destiny Jests with Me' blaring from every jukebox in every café and honky tonk in every city and backwater. Other artists began to demand Maxine's songs and the royalty payments from those were due to substantially pile up very soon.

It was in April that Brent proposed marriage. 'Destiny Jests with Me' was both the best-selling record and best-selling sheet music in the United States that week; Maxine's imminent wealth from royalties promised to far outstrip what he himself had accumulated so far. It rendered her all the more attractive. She was an asset he must secure for himself. Since it looked as though they were set to become US citizens he had ideas of buying a house in the city and a holiday retreat at either Rhode Island or Martha's Vineyard. What was the point in having money if you didn't use it? It was also eminently satisfying to spend the bonus money a new wife brought to a marriage, especially a wife who was destined to become outrageously wealthy. Infinitely better, in fact, than having no money at all and running up insurmountable bills, as he had in the past. Besides, he was making new friends every day, fashionable, influential people – musicians, A and R men, movie stars even. He had to impress them, and owning somewhere appropriate to entertain them lavishly would do him and Maxine a power of good.

'So how do we go about getting married in New York?' Maxine asked as they relaxed in the armchairs of their suite at the Roosevelt.

'We just go along to a judge or a priest, I imagine, and ask him to marry us.'

'Won't they want proof of who we are?'

'We have our passports.'

'But what if passports aren't enough? They might want birth certificates and God knows what else. You know what a bureaucratic lot they are, the Yanks. They love paperwork. Papers for this, papers for that.'

He shrugged. 'You may be right. I don't know.'

'You could always ask somebody. You keep telling me you know lots of people now.'

'I don't want to ask people I know.'

'Why ever not?'

'Because that would draw attention to the fact. Our marriage should be a low-key affair. So much the better if we could keep it secret . . . I'm thinking about your singing career, Maxine. You're far more attractive to the American music-loving male as an innocent single girl.'

'Huh!' she exclaimed. 'Innocent is an optimistic adjective these days, especially when applied to me.'

He stubbed out his cigarette in an ashtray and rolled his eyes. 'You're happy, aren't you? We have fun, don't we?'

'Oh, Brent, I've *never* had so much fun. Parties galore, all this adulation from people, playing the music I love for people who really appreciate it. Of course I'm having fun. I never imagined anything like this could ever happen to me. It's a dream.'

'It's a dream that I knew would come true, Maxine,' Brent said seriously. He lit another cigarette. 'You have talent, sweetheart. You have looks and an innocence about you that appeals to these Yanks. I always knew we – you – would make it to the top. We're a good team, you and I. The best. We're on track to make a fortune together. We're a business. Getting married will complete the tie. Drink?'

'Not for me, thanks.'

He got up from his chair and held his cigarette in his mouth while he reached for the bottle and a glass. 'I'm having a scotch. Are you sure you don't want anything?'

'It's too early . . . Don't have too much, Brent. Don't forget we have to play tonight.'

'Oh, leave off, Maxine. I know how much I can drink. I know when to stop.'

'I'm just reminding you . . .' she responded softly.

He recapped the bottle and took his drink with him to his chair.

'Fancy . . .' she said dreamily, 'and I always imagined myself having a white wedding.'

'Did you ever imagine yourself a queen of swing? Did you ever imagine you'd be making thousands of dollars as a singer and songwriter in America?'

'No. Of course not.'

'Well that's happened. You're one in ten million, Maxine. So don't be too disappointed if your wedding day doesn't afford you the glamour and sentimentality you always thought it would. Life's had its compensations.'

She watched motes of dust dancing in a slanted sunbeam that penetrated the window and smiled enigmatically, ignoring the acid sting of his reproach. Every girl dreams of being a radiantly smiling bride in her beautiful white dress and her mother looking proudly on. There was nothing wrong with that. Besides, she could afford whatever wedding she wanted now that money was no object.

'Maybe we should send for our birth certificates, you know, Brent,' she said. 'I bet they *would* want to see them.'

'For proof that we've been born, you mean?' he answered sarcastically.

'For God's sake, stop sneering,' she complained. 'You know what they're like here . . . I'll write to my mother anyway and ask her to send mine. I won't say why, otherwise we'll have no chance of a quiet wedding. My family will be here in droves . . .' Actually that was not such a bad thought . . .

'You won't need a birth certificate, Maxine. What's the point in writing?'

She shrugged. 'All the same . . .'

It had not been a tremendously romantic proposal; not the type of proposal she'd imagined she might be blessed with. He had not taken her in his arms and said, 'Darling, I'm so in love with you and I want to spend the rest of my life in eternal bliss with you.' He had not gone down on one knee and said, 'Will you please marry me?' It had been a more prosaic statement: 'It would make financial sense if we got married, Maxine, in our position'. Well, she was not opposed to it and, whilst she'd agreed, she could just as happily have continued with the present arrangement for all the difference it was likely to make. Lately, Brent had taken to going out with Kenny to sleazy nightclubs in Harlem after their concerts. He'd actually deigned to take her to some. She'd met and talked with Fats Waller, heard him play; a fantastic musician; his records didn't do him justice. Brent said he could introduce her to Duke Ellington; he said he was on first name terms with him at the Cotton Club . . . *Hi, Duke* . . . *Hi, Brent*. He had drunk with Count Basie and Tommy Dorsey, he said. Even Benny Goodman had made himself known when he knew Brent Shackleton of The Owls and the Pussycats was in the Cotton Club one night, he said. Brent assured her that he had to befriend these people. It was not *what* you knew, but *who* you knew that mattered. He could persuade these important musicians to record her songs, he said. Think of the money! 'I'm working for us when I go to these clubs,' he said.

It did not promise to be the cosy kind of marriage she'd always envisaged; a nice house in Oakham Road, like Henzey's, had always been her ideal. A husband who went out to a steady job at eight in a morning and returned at six, like Will, was what she had always anticipated; perhaps two or three children over a span of six or eight years . . . Still, she could hardly complain. The nicest dreams inevitably did not come true. She was living another dream now with money in the bank; the sort of money she'd *never* dreamed of. It would take years of striving to accumulate that sort of wealth if she married an ordinary working guy. And there was no sign of it abating; only increasing. Brent deserved to share it if anybody did. He was the one who pushed her when she was reticent, who protected her when she was vulnerable, who lifted her when she was down. He was the one who loved her when she needed affection and emotional support.

Yes, it made sense to marry Brent. They were indeed partners in business; a highly lucrative business. Swing was the big thing; swing, and all the thousands of dollars that they could make from it. Money was there for the taking. It made a lot more sense to be a hard-nosed businesswoman than a dewy-eyed, small-town girl with pie-in-the-sky fantasies about white weddings in draughty old English churches, and the unpleasant business of having babies.

She and Brent were less romantically inclined these last few months; this *business* and trying to promote it had made them like that. Yet, she still yearned for romance. She had not lost the knack of igniting occasionally that spark of tenderness in Brent, when the muse took her. They had not been sleeping together so long yet that the novelty had completely worn off. True, they did not make love as frequently as they used to at first – sometimes she could not get him going anyway. Some nights he stayed out all night, not returning to their suite till morning, but she did not mind. In some ways, she was thankful. Better than the twice daily exercise he'd taken on her on the *Queen Mary* when she was half drugged by the effects of the sea and the time zones they passed through every day – and in that sleazy little hotel in Pell Street. She had got little rest in those days, having to perform for her audience on stage and for him in bed later. And she needed her beauty sleep.

Well, she was getting her beauty sleep now.

She wondered what her destiny might have been if she'd stayed in Dudley or moved to be near Howard in Norfolk. It's doubtful *they* would have been talking about marriage quite so soon, but it would have happened eventually. She would have become a vicar's wife . . . A vicar's wife! God! How far removed from that was she now? But she would have been happy. She knew, without question, that she would have been very happy. She had loved Howard with all her heart and soul; tenderly; somehow differently to the way she loved Brent. In the frantic and sometimes fraught excitement of life in the music business, in another country, it was so easy to forget that. She tried to imagine herself greeting parishioners at a vicarage she had never seen, dealing with their problems, trivial and profound. She would be arranging the rota for the altar flowers, organising the team of cleaners after every service, attending beetle drives. There would be Young Wives one evening a week, the Mothers' Union. She would have to join the Women's Institute, perhaps even teach at Sunday School. There would have been no end to it. Yet she would have done it all with a glad heart, for Howard.

A lump came to her throat. Did he miss her? Did he ever regret not writing to her? Funny how fate had intervened . . .

No, not funny . . . Sad, really . . . What was Howard doing right this minute? . . .

The band immediately followed up the success of 'Destiny Jests with Me' with a recording of a sensitive love song written by Maxine called 'From Tears to a Kiss'. It had occurred to her that Howard might feasibly hear her music back in England when they released their first record there and, if so, might listen to the words. She hoped he would realise that the message was meant for him, that it reflected the sadness she still felt over losing him. Whether Brent sussed her lingering emotions she did not know, for he made no comment. It was doubtful whether he did; he was too wrapped up in himself, and in his unfailing confidence that Maxine could be besotted with himself only, to realise any different.

The recording session lasted a couple of hours in a small cluttered studio studded with sound-proofing material, wires running along the floor that was strewn with cigarette ends, and a few chairs scattered randomly. The band members and their instruments were placed strategically around a microphone and the distance each member sat away from it determined the balance. Maxine sang into a different microphone and played piano simultaneously, and it took only four full attempts before the most languid, sensuous version of the song was captured in wax. The A and R man, Wes Johnson, could barely contain himself with excitement when they listened to the final playback together. 'From Tears to a Kiss' could not fail to be a smash hit, he told them, as he crooned the chorus along with the recording.

My life has drifted from smiling to sighing,
From sighing to crying,
Please lead me from tears to a kiss.

Lizzie wrote regularly to Maxine. Always, though, she had to refer to Maxine's last letter to check what address she was supposed to mail the next letter to. It was in May that Maxine received a letter, which suggested that Lizzie evidently did not comprehend the financial success her daughter was enjoying. The letter read:

My Dear Maxine,
It's grand to hear you are doing so well in America and I have enclosed, as you will see, your birth certificate as you asked me to and a pound note. I didn't have a clue what I could get you for your birthday, so I have sent you the pound note and hope you won't waste it on softness.

Yesterday, I was all of a tiswas because I heard that record of yours played on the wireless. I was that proud. Straight away I phoned our Henzey and told her to switch the wireless on, but by the time it had warmed up you had finished and they were playing something by Jack Payne which wasn't half as nice. So it looks like Jesse is going to buy a gramophone so we can buy your record and listen to it. I'm writing to the BBC to ask them to play it as often as they can on the wireless. There was a bit in the paper about you and the band and how well you are doing in America as well. The Dudley Herald want to come and ask me some questions so they can print an article on you.

Everybody here is well and they send their love. Our Henzey and Will miss you. The children are fine and they miss you as well but I don't know what's happening to our Alice. She and that Charles fell out some months ago and she doesn't seem to want to go out any more. She doesn't seem interested in chaps any more which is a load off my mind but I hope she's not ailing for something.

How is your new boy friend going on? I hope he's treating you nicely. Henzey tells me he's a nice-looking chap, because she's seen him, hasn't she. She said he was good to you when you was in the orchestra in Brum. I hope as you're keeping away from those gangsters as well. They should lock them all up. By the way, Henzey had a letter from Howard who you used to go out with, wondering if she knew how you were. That was nice of him, wasn't it? I thought he was a lovely chap considering he's a vicar.

It looks as if our Herbert and Elizabeth are going to get married next March. That'll give you plenty of time to organise things so as you'll be able to come to it. They send their love as well.

Well, Maxine, I must close now as I have to get Jesse's tea ready and Richard and Edward are mythering me for a piece of jam and a glass of pop. Look after yourself and keep well and I look forward to getting your next letter.

All the love in the world,

Mom.

So Howard Quaintance had written to Henzey asking about her! Fancy that! After all this time. Maybe he had heard her record. Funny how she kept thinking about him; not that that was significant, of course. After all, you have to think. You can't help thinking. It was hardly surprising he cropped up in her thoughts from time to time, especially since he was the inspiration for her songs. But why did she still feel such a sense of loss when he did?

Brent returned with the news that he had just left John Fielding and that The Owls and the Pussycats had been booked for a month in Chicago at the Congress Hotel.

'Chicago? That will be a change,' Maxine said. 'When do we go?'

'Beginning of July. John's rearranging our schedule. There's also talk of doing some NBC broadcasts from the Congress Hotel. Some tie-up with a big local firm as sponsors.'

'Shall we be married by then, Brent? Or shall we wait till we come back?'

'The sooner the better,' he replied brusquely. 'Let's get it over and done with. And the studio's booked next week at Victor for another recording session. That new song you wrote . . .'

'You mean "It's Not Your Fault"?'

'Yeah, that one. Good job we finished the arrangement early. We can start dropping it into the stage shows already. It's a nice song. Should do well. You're writing some good stuff, Maxine. I'm proud of you.'

'Thanks,' she replied. 'I like it.'

Brent went to the bathroom and Maxine sang the song to herself.

'It's not your fault I love you like I do
It's not your fault I'm lonely without you . . .'

Miss Maxine Kite forsook all others and privately became a June bride in a very quiet civil ceremony on Friday 18th of that month in 1937. Members of The Owls and the Pussycats only were present, plus Miss Dulcie Fielding who acted as witness together with Miss Pansy Hemming. Brent swore everybody to secrecy. Afterwards, the couple entertained their colleagues at a very private lunch at the Ritz-Carlton where champagne flowed in abundance. The new Mrs Shackleton clearly enjoyed herself and was very affectionate towards her husband.

Chapter 27

If she hadn't known that the vast expanse of water she could see through the carriage window was Lake Michigan, Maxine Shackleton would have believed it a sea. Normally you expect to see land on the other side of a lake, but not so any of the Great Lakes. The only give-away was that it was so calm. The sea is seldom as calm. On this hot and sunny day, as The Owls and the Pussycats hurtled towards Chicago by train, skirting the edge of the lake and its sand dunes, they could have been forgiven for thinking they were entering an area of marine rurality instead of a vast industrial city, for through the window on the opposite side were pine trees and brush.

But it was an illusion that was short-lived. They hit the suburb of Gary, actually in Indiana and twenty-six miles from the centre of Chicago. The view of Lake Michigan was cut off by enormous steel rolling mills that produced armour plate, steel tubes and tin plate. They produced girders, from the colossal examples that supported the innumerable skyscrapers of this and other cities to relatively small sections for railway track and angle-iron. All were manufactured in this miasma of putrid haze that was created by blast furnaces that bombarded the clear blue sky with dense smoke. Chicago was a sprawling, industrial mass, all the more amazing since it had been all swamp and prairie a mere ninety years earlier. It was testament to the endeavours and ingenuity of man, if not his regard for wilderness.

'Do you think we'll be troubled by gangsters?' Pansy asked

354

idly as the train passed a huge stockyard with thousands of head of cattle on one side and a canning factory on the other.

'Gangsters?' Maxine repeated. 'Lord, I hope not. My mother warned me to keep clear of gangsters.'

'You should have avoided Brent, then,' Kenny quipped, and the others laughed.

'I doubt if they'll be interested in us,' Ginger remarked seriously. 'From what I know of gangsters they're only interested in making money from brothels and gambling. I shouldn't worry, Pansy. I don't think they trouble normal, decent citizens.'

'They might trouble Brent then,' Kenny wisecracked, and Maxine wondered how much of his joking was serious.

Eventually they arrived in Chicago and took a couple of cabs to the Congress Hotel on Michigan Avenue. It had been a long journey and they were tired. Their priority was to get some sleep so, as soon as they checked in, Maxine unpacked quickly and briefly admired the view from their suite. Grant Park and Buckingham Fountain, which overlooked Lake Michigan, were impressive. Then she lay down and fell asleep. She could sleep for the rest of that day and night if Brent would let her, since their performances weren't scheduled to start till the following night.

Brent woke her up shortly after nine o'clock that evening. He had dressed, put on a fresh shirt and was fastening his tie.

'I'm going out to get something to eat,' he said. 'Are you coming?'

She yawned and stretched, indifferent to him. 'Can't I just stay here and sleep, Brent? I'm so tired.'

'It's up to you, but I'm hungry,' he said grumpily.

'So why not ask room service to bring you something?'

'Because I want to go out. I want to have a look at Chicago and its skyscrapers . . . I don't want to be cooped up in here with you asleep. I'll ask Kenny or one of the others to come.'

'Suit yourself,' she replied heedlessly, and fell back to sleep.

* * *

355

Kenny was of the same mind as Brent. Dulcie too was tired after the journey and he left her sleeping while he spruced himself up to hit the town. In the hotel lobby Brent handed the bellboy a dollar and asked him to hail a taxi cab.

'Take us to a club,' Brent instructed the driver. 'A decent club where we can get some good food and hear some decent jazz.'

The driver deposited them on Chicago's South Side outside a place called Artwork.

'Looks promising,' Kenny said. 'Nice place.'

Inside this shrine to bold American Art Deco design, a show was underway. Six black musicians were playing some of the neatest jazz they had ever heard. Brent handed five dollars to a steward and asked for a table near the stage so they could better see. They ordered beers and listened to the band, enjoying the sounds they were making before asking to see a menu. Soon, four more musicians augmented the band and a bevy of scant-ily-clad chorus girls high-kicked onto the stage from the wings on both sides. Later, a black girl in a sparkly evening dress stepped out of the shadows and approached the microphone. She had a voice like cream velvet and brilliant phrasing. A waiter brought their food and they ate while watching the show.

Kenny fancied one of the chorus girls and had caught her eye. She started smiling coyly back at him in response. The black girl sang 'Crying my Heart out for You' and followed it with 'I Got the Spring Fever Blues'. Then, to Brent's surprise and delight, she sang 'Destiny Jests with Me', written by Maxine Kite. He listened intently as she delivered a creditable performance, different to Maxine's own interpretation. For the first time, it became clear to him the impact The Owls and the Pussycats were having on the American jazz scene. It was a moment to be proud of.

The interval came. Brent sent an invitation for the band to join him at their table. Several did and they chatted matily, swapping compliments. The band was the Chicago Lakesiders, the singer was Evelyn Bright. The chorus girl Kenny fancied was Vanda Lee and one of the band fetched her so that she could be introduced to Kenny Wheeler of The Owls and the Pussycats.

'The Owls and the Pussycats?' she shrieked incredulously. 'Gee! Take me to him fast.' She turned to one of the other chorus girls called Gloria who was her closest friend. 'Gloria, come with me, honey. There are two guys out front from The Owls and the Pussycats – you know, that English band?'

'Sure, I know who The Owls and the Pussycats are,' Gloria replied with a bright grin that revealed a set of even teeth. 'I sure didn't know *they* were in town.'

At the table occupied by Brent Shackleton and Kenny Wheeler, a party atmosphere prevailed. They were introduced to two more men; well-known night owls on the Chicago club circuit apparently; in town again from Hollywood, they said.

Movie men. Important.

'Let's have champagne,' Brent suggested and called for a jeroboam of Bollinger.

'Sorry, the largest we keep in stock is a magnum.'

'So bring two magnums.'

Corks popped and everybody was happy. Brent was especially matey to the movie producer who suggested, with a wink and a tap of his nose, that they join him and his colleague at a friend's place to watch some very interesting movies when the show was over. The girls should come, too – gee, all eight of the chorus girls should come if they wanted. They would be more than welcome. They would all have a real good time.

'Here, try one of these cigarettes, Brent – Kenny . . . You'll enjoy them.'

Brent and Kenny each took a cigarette and the Hollywood producer, whose name was James, gave them a light. It tasted no different to any other American cigarette at first, until they both began to feel light-headed, as if they were drifting.

'Hey, these are good,' said Brent, and asked what brand they were.

The second Hollywood guy, who said his name was Hank, winked knowingly. 'Reefers. You can't buy them in the shops. You never tried one before?'

'Never.'

From then on, they had no concept of time. Before they knew it the show was over and the Hollywood guys were saying it was time to go.

'Wait for the girls,' Kenny said.

Of course they would wait for the girls. They needed the girls.

Six of them decided to come, plus two of the black musicians Brent had befriended from the band. Some piled into James's very elegant Packard and the rest into a taxi cab that was cruising outside plying for trade. They drove further south, to another club that, from the outside, was no more than an anonymous doorway set in a wall. Inside, it was dingy. Seedy-looking men and their overblown tarts danced and drank and smoked God knows what as blues wailed from a jukebox.

'Through here,' their host, who had met them at the door, invited. He ushered them down a darkened passage into another room.

This room was large and elaborately furnished with comfortable settees and divans set around three sides and small tables to accommodate drinks. A thick pile carpet covered the floor and a small bar stood at one end.

'Help yourselves to drinks.'

Kenny and Brent poured drinks for the chorus girls before Kenny eagerly led Vanda Lee by the hand to one of the divans.

Brent escorted Gloria to another divan, sat down and put his arm around her.

'Got any more of those cigarettes?' Brent asked James.

'Sure.' He tossed a silver cigarette case to Brent.

He lit two, one of which he gave to Gloria before tossing the case to Kenny.

'Ever snorted coke?' James asked.

'No, tell me about it,' Brent answered with a grin.

James tossed a small packet over to him. 'Like this, Brent . . .'

Brent watched carefully. 'Gee . . . Makes you feel good . . .'

Brent copied what James did. He inhaled deeply and coughed, then passed the remnants of the package to Gloria.

'Now we're gonna watch a swell movie,' James announced and signalled the host to start the projector that was hidden in a small room behind them.

The lights went out. In a haze of alcohol, marijuana and cocaine, Brent watched spellbound as a strikingly pretty blonde girl of about eighteen appeared on the screen in front of them. At the side of a swimming pool in some vast sunlit garden overlooking the sea, she peeled off her clothes provocatively. Brent could smell her sweet skin. He could hear the sounds of summer, birds calling to each other, the rustle of leaves, the humming of bees, the distant roar of the sea. Splash! The girl dived into the pool naked, swam a length and climbed out elegantly, giving a spectacular view of everything she had. A young man, also stripped for action, built like an Adonis and magnificently aroused, then entered the frame.

Brent drew on his reefer . . .

One morning, early in their residency at the Congress, Maxine, Pansy and Dulcie decided to soak up the sunshine in the formal symmetry of Grant Park that lay between the skyscrapers and Lake Michigan. The idea of wriggling their toes in yellow sand and paddling in the lake at a beach later held tremendous appeal also on this beautiful summer morning.

As they sat on one of the benches placed around Buckingham Fountain, big and spectacularly beautiful, they raised their dresses above their knees to expose their legs to the glorious sun. Lake Michigan, as if to conspire with their well-being, provided a luxuriously gentle breeze that kept them cool. Sitting with their dresses above their knees was, for none of them, an issue. Although two were already famous amongst folk who were versed in commercial music, their faces remained relatively unknown to most people, and they took their anonymity for granted. Rightly, for to passers-by they were just three pretty girls quietly relaxing in the park.

Conversation changed rapidly as they exhausted one subject and embarked on another.

'Fancy Dorothy Round winning the ladies' Wimbledon title,' Pansy said, shifting a strand of her red hair that had found its way to the corner of her mouth in the breeze. 'Stephen said in his letter that everybody was thrilled.'

'Oh, I read about that,' Dulcie said.

'She comes from Dudley,' Maxine proclaimed proudly. 'My home town.'

'Well no wonder the folk back home were thrilled.'

'Oh, I imagine they'll be dancing in the streets. How *is* Stephen, anyway?' Maxine asked. 'And Eleanor.'

'He mentioned about getting married a week or two ago. But didn't say anything in this last letter.'

'Married to Eleanor, you mean?'

'Who else?' Pansy replied scornfully, reflecting her disdain.

'Is there no sign of you and Toots getting married, Pansy?' Dulcie asked.

'What do we need to get married for, Dulcie? We do everything together as it is, including sleeping together. God! If my mother knew she'd have a set of jugs.'

'But don't you ever want children?' Maxine asked. 'I mean when this lot's over . . .'

'You mean when The Owls and the Pussycats thing is over?'

Maxine inclined her face to the sun, shutting her eyes. 'Well, it won't last forever.'

'I suppose not. When it is all over I'd like to have kids. That's when I'll consider getting married. In the meantime I'll keep hoping the Dutch cap don't slip.'

Maxine tittered.

'Dutch caps . . .' Dulcie mused. 'Where would us poor ladies be without them, huh?'

'Up the stick, as they say in Brum, Dulcie. Well and truly.' Pansy adjusted the length of her skirt to expose more of her legs to the sun. 'How about you, Maxine? Do you want kids?'

'You don't get pregnant if you don't have sex, Pansy. In any case, Brent doesn't want children. Me? I'd have a house full.'

Pansy's eyes met Dulcie's.

'You mean you don't have sex, Maxine?' Dulcie asked incredulously.

'Not lately.'

'Crikey, doesn't that bother you?' Pansy said.

'It might have done . . . once . . . Not right now.'

Pansy turned to look at her best friend. Maxine seemed to speak with more than a hint of regret. Or had she imagined it? 'What makes you say that, Maxine?'

Maxine took a moment to answer, first looking at Pansy, then at Dulcie. 'I don't think I want to go through life married but never having a child. It's what marriage is for, after all. Normal peoples' marriages, at any rate. I just don't feel like a normal person these days. But I hope at some time I might . . . When this lot's over.'

'But you're bracing yourself already,' Dulcie suggested.

'Maybe. Maybe not . . . Perhaps it depends who you're married to . . . Did I ever tell you that Eleanor was pregnant once?'

'No.'

'By Brent, you mean?' Pansy queried.

'Oh, yes, by Brent.' Maxine assured her. 'He told me when we were in the CBO. *He* didn't want the child. She lost it, he said. Deliberately. I've often wondered whether he made her get rid of it . . .' She shrugged her shoulders.

'Geesh!' Dulcie exclaimed. 'That's a hell of a thing to wonder about your husband.'

'I know. Don't breathe a word of this, either of you . . . but now I know him better, I reckon he *is* capable of doing such a thing. Do *you* think he's capable of it?'

'How should I know?' Pansy responded diplomatically. 'Maybe he is, maybe he isn't. You know him better than we do. All the same, it's a funny thing for somebody who hasn't been married a month yet to wonder.'

Maxine laughed now; an empty laugh, lacking in humour but flush with irony. 'I'm no fool, Pansy,' she said seriously. 'But sometimes I find it an advantage to let him think I am. That way he thinks he needn't keep up his guard.'

'What about money?' Dulcie asked. 'You don't let him think you're a fool where money's concerned, do you, for Christ's sake?'

'No. He knows I've got my head screwed on where money's concerned.'

Pansy said: 'Blimey, Maxine, am I hearing you right? Do you regret getting married?'

'Well, I'm beginning to wonder if it was the right thing to do . . . so soon after the upset with Howard at any rate. But please don't say anything.'

There remained silence between them for a couple of minutes. The air was filled with the noises of motor cars; so many motor cars, on Michigan Avenue, Columbus and Lake Shore Drive.

'I don't think you're over Howard, are you, Maxine?' Dulcie said, eventually.

Maxine bit her lip to stop it trembling. 'I can't stop thinking about him. At first – when we were in New York – I thought I *was* over him. I didn't think about him that much with everything that was going on and Brent making such a fuss of me. I guess I *was* in love with Brent for a while – or I thought I was, which amounts to the same thing. But now I can't get Howard off my mind . . .'

'Hey, don't upset yourself, Maxine.' Pansy said, concerned for her friend. 'Things'll work out one way or the other. For all you know, he might be married himself by now. You just don't know.'

'Oh, please don't say that, Pansy. I couldn't bear the thought of him married to somebody else.'

'But you're married to Brent now,' Dulcie reasoned. 'Short of divorce, there's little or nothing you can do about that.'

'Even if I got divorced and went back home and found Howard, he couldn't marry me. The Church doesn't allow marriage to a divorcee. I couldn't muck up his life any more.'

'So what's gone wrong?' Dulcie persisted. 'You seemed so happy a short while ago.'

'I don't know . . . Things are just not the same. It hasn't helped living in hotels for the last six months. I miss a home. I want a home. Oh, I love all this . . .' she waved her hands about expansively. '. . . America . . . I love the band, the success and the money, of course, but I miss a home. I miss somewhere I can flop down after a hard day's work and just relax and be myself. Somewhere I could grab my cello and just sit and play it quietly – just for relaxation. You know I haven't played a cello since I left England. Hell, I haven't even seen a cello . . . I miss my cello . . .'

'Then buy one. Buy a house too. Heck, you can afford it.'

'I've suggested a house. We've both suggested a house.'

'And?'

'Oh, Brent doesn't want to buy *one* house, he wants two. He wants a mansion in New York and another in Martha's Vineyard. With *my* money we can afford it, he says. *My* money. But it's always *my* money. Never his. Even before we got married. I'm beginning to think that's all he married me for.'

'That's one heck of an observation, Maxine,' Dulcie commented, but with sympathy in her voice. 'Do you believe it?'

'I'm just saying that's how it seems. Like this morning . . . He's gone out with the other lads to buy a car . . . here, in Chicago. "Why not wait till we get back to New York?" I said. But no, he wants to buy one here. Some big flashy thing, I expect. He just can't wait. If I know him, he won't be satisfied with one – he'll want two. He's probably the same with women, as well . . .'

Uncertainty clouded Dulcie's expression. 'Do you think he has other women, Maxine?' she asked.

'I think it's logical to assume he does, Dulcie. The nights he's out so late . . . The unfamiliar perfumes that waft from him . . . The stray hairs I find on his jackets . . . His history . . . His lack of interest in me now . . .'

'Kenny's out with him, too, usually . . .'

Maxine sighed uncomfortably. 'So maybe you have to make a similar judgement about Kenny, Dulcie,' she suggested plainly. It might appear unkind at first, but she'd had it in mind to alert the girl somehow, if she was not already aware. This was an ideal opportunity. Their relationship was their own affair but, even so, why should poor Dulcie be used? She liked Dulcie. She considered her a close friend; close enough to speak to candidly.

Dulcie sat bolt upright. 'Heck! Tell me more, Maxine.'

Seagulls wheeled overhead, sailing the breeze that was coming from the lake.

'I can't tell you more, Dulcie, because I don't know for certain. But I do know what they're like . . . the pair of them. I've watched them operate.'

'Of course, you've known Kenny longer than I have . . .'

'But not as intimately,' Maxine was quick to point out.

'Sure . . . I know . . .'

They fell into a silence again when the sounds of background traffic mingled incongruously with the screeching of the seagulls above. One landed and waddled towards the wall of the fountain where it pecked at the pavement. Another followed it.

Dulcie said: 'It's funny, now you mention it, Maxine. That could explain a lot . . .'

Maxine shrugged. 'You have to decide. Is he ever unkind to you?'

'Not unkind . . . I'm sure he wouldn't hurt me – knowingly. But already he's less gallant . . . less considerate. Sure, he wants me in bed, but hell, that don't mean all.'

'Right. That don't mean all. Has he told you anything about his past?'

'Sure. I know he's married and all, and that he left his wife

364

. . . I got the impression he's had other women besides – he seemed keen to tell me he'd had a fling with your sister . . . Did you know that, Maxine?'

'Yes, I knew. But it amounted to nothing.'

'Yeah. He said it was no big deal.'

'So what are your plans for the future?' Pansy asked. 'Does Kenny Wheeler figure in them?'

'Long term, I guess not, Pansy. I fell in love with him on the *Queen Mary* . . . but now the magic of that time has gone and something less magical exists now. More exciting for you guys, this fame and all, but less magical for Kenny and me. My feet are firmly planted on the ground now and I can see my relationship with Kenny for what it is. I guess once we're back in New York I'll rethink my position.'

'I think that's sensible,' Maxine said. 'After all, what if his wife came over on the next ship to claim him? She could. I know he idolises his son.'

'His son? Hell, I didn't know he had a son! . . . The son of a bitch never told me that.'

'Just goes to show,' Pansy remarked.

'He never told you?'

'The hell he did, Maxine! Just wait till he gets back.'

'Hang on, Dulcie,' Maxine said. 'Don't tell him I told you. Anyway, why let on that you know? Keep it up your sleeve. It's information that might come in handy some day.'

Dulcie reflected for a few seconds. 'I guess you're right, Maxine . . . The son of a bitch! . . . Can I let you two into a secret? Promise you won't tell?'

''Course,' they said in unison and leaned forward to hear better what Dulcie was about to tell them.

'Just lately, I've been getting real warm signals off Charlie. And you know what? I think he's kinda cute.'

'At least he's decent,' Maxine said approvingly. 'I think he's cute as well. A swell guy, as you Yanks say. You could do worse, Dulcie.'

'Yeah, I got the impression I've already done worse, Maxine,' she said resignedly. 'So how 'bout you? How d'you see your future, since we're being so philosophical – and so honest with each other?'

Maxine shrugged. 'Maybe I just expected too much from Brent. I daresay I'll have to adjust . . .' She sighed poignantly. 'Anyway, whoever heard of a bride being unhappy after just a month of marriage? There's nothing I can do about it now, anyway. I'm stuck with him and he's stuck with me, and that's all there is to it.'

'Sounds like you're no longer in love with Brent.'

'I'm not in love with him, Dulcie. That's certain.'

'He seems to be drinking more,' Pansy said tentatively.

'Drinking more, smoking more and Lord knows what else. And some of those cigarettes he's started smoking . . .'

'Yeah, pot. Kenny, too. I guess they must go to pot parties.'

'The smell makes *me* light-headed. God knows how they make him feel, inhaling the stuff.'

'What a pair of fools!' Pansy proclaimed. 'Have you tried talking to him, Maxine?'

'He takes no notice. Thinks I'm getting on at him. The last thing I want him to think is that I'm a shrew. I have to pick my moments.'

'Men! Who'd bother with them?'

Maxine laughed aloud. '*You* should complain! You're the only one who has a decent love life. Toots is a lovely chap.'

'And I hope he stays that way. I hope this success thing doesn't spoil him. I love him to bits . . . Come on,' Pansy said, to avoid becoming emotional. 'Let's go to the nearest beach. We can buy some sandwiches and some pop and have a picnic.'

'And a paddle,' Maxine added with childlike enthusiasm as she got up from the bench with the others.

'Where can we buy buckets and spades, Dulcie?' Pansy jested, shaking the creases out of her skirt.

Then Maxine noticed something and gave a little squeal of excitement.

366

'Look there!' She pointed to a building next to their hotel. 'What does it say? The Chicago Symphony Orchestra! Hey, they hold concerts there, look – Orchestra Hall. Right next door to our hotel. Shall we go sometime, girls? I've really missed classical music these last months. I might even see a cello. Let's go and see when the next one is . . .'

'Yeah, when we've been to the beach,' Dulcie decreed.

Chapter 28

Brent bought his car; a magnificent yellow Cord 812 with a coffin-nose body and headlamps that disappeared magically into the front wings. It was his pride and joy and he showed it off to Maxine on a demonstration run up and down Lake Shore Drive that evening. The weather remained warm and sunny and, with the hood lowered and the breeze blowing the cobwebs out of their lives, it really could not have been better for a trip out before their performance at the Congress.

'So, do you like it, Maxine?' he asked proudly as they cruised past the recently renovated Greek-like structure that now housed the Museum of Science and Industry.

'Yes, I like it well enough. I just wish you'd tell me how much you paid for it.'

She had a headscarf tied around her head and wore sunglasses. The sun that day had caught her face and arms and she looked, for all the world, like any wealthy young American woman taken out by an aspiring young American male to impress her with a sleek, expensive motor car.

'What does it matter how much it cost?' he replied and, making the big V8 roar, overtook a Chevrolet. 'We can afford it . . . Look how everybody turns to admire the damn thing . . . See? . . . I tell you, I'm looking forward to driving it back to New York. I'll give this four-point-seven litre motor some spade.'

'Well, I won't be with you,' she informed him coolly. 'I shall

368

go back to New York by train. I don't want to end up in a heap with you after you've crashed into something.'

'I won't crash. I know how to handle this beautiful beast. But, hey, I've been thinking, Maxine . . . When I get back to New York I'm going to buy a house. I've decided we're going to stay in America, come what may. We need to be in New York. That's where it all happens. It would be madness to base ourselves anywhere else. I'm going to write to Eleanor as well. I want her to sell the Mercedes Benz. She can send the money for that. Then there's the damned house in Handsworth. I want her to cancel the tenancy. We're never going back there. Ever.' He drew on his cigarette with an air of self-satisfaction.

'I bet the thought of Stephen struggling with all your old rubbish pleases you.'

He grinned. 'It does.'

Over to their left a private yacht, its white sails billowing, was skimming the smooth waters of Lake Michigan.

'See that!' he said. 'I'll buy a yacht as well. I've always fancied myself at the helm of something like that. Look good off Martha's Vineyard, eh?'

'You don't know the first thing about sailing,' Maxine scoffed, visualising even greater plunder of her resources. 'There's more to sailing than meets the eye.'

'I can learn. I'm a quick learner . . . We have the money, Maxine. I intend to use it . . . And talking about money – I'm not sure how American law stands on inheritance, so I want you to make a will leaving everything to me. I'll make one as well, leaving everything to you. We'll see a solicitor, or an attorney, or whatever it is they call them over here, when we're back in New York.'

'Can't I leave something to my folks back home? They're not rich, you know.'

'Maybe a thousand or two, Maxine. No more.'

'That's a bit mean, Brent.'

'I don't see why you should leave them anything, Maxine. I've got nobody, have I? Oh and I've been onto John Fielding about promoting our stuff in Britain. There's no *urgency* about him, you know. He needs a rocket up his backside. After getting on to him for weeks, he's finally assured me that 'From Tears to a Kiss' is due to be released there this month. I can't see the sense in waiting months to release stuff in Britain when it's been successful here. Can you?'

'Not really.'

'They always do it, though. Maddening. Look at 'Destiny Jests with Me'. That's done well there. At last the papers and music magazines over there are starting to get the message.'

'I know. Even my mother says she's heard us on the wireless. And read bits in the paper, saying how well we're doing here.'

'There's a tour on the cards as well, Maxine. In the winter. They're talking about doing eighty or ninety cities across America. We'd net tens of thousands out of that.'

'Ninety cities? But we'd be away three months, living in hotels and dance halls. Must we, Brent? Especially in winter . . .'

'We must. We have to make money while we can. And have you noticed how the music business is not talking so much about The Owls and the Pussycats now, but more about Maxine Kite?'

'But I don't know if that's entirely true, Brent,' she said, typically modest. 'Anyway, it might cause dissension in the band if you spread that about.'

'Who cares? That was John Fielding's idea in the first place. He made it clear at the time. Anyway, you don't think James and Hank are interested in The Owls and the Pussycats, do you? No, they want you and your glamour for their gangster movie. We'll have to push hard for the band to be included in the deal.'

From the point of view of the performances and satisfaction of their audiences, the month at the Joseph Urban Room at the Congress Hotel in Chicago was a brilliant success. The series of NBC broadcasts live from the hotel on Friday nights succeeded in adding to the already glowing reputation of The Owls and the Pussycats. It seemed they could do no wrong. Whilst they were there Brent returned with the news one afternoon that, according to *Down Beat*, their latest record, 'It's Not Your Fault' had sailed to number one in the national record charts and sheet music sales were also buoyant. Another celebration was called for; another celebration they had.

But Brent's relationship with John Fielding had begun to deteriorate. Brent had for some time been of the opinion that John was underselling them. Surely, he could negotiate better money for their appearances in view of their phenomenal success? Surely, he could negotiate even better deals with the music publishers and record companies that were clamouring to use Maxine's material? 'I could do better,' Brent told the rest of the band vehemently. 'I could get us more money.' To Maxine privately, he said: 'Our future lies with you, Maxine. Not Pansy, not Toots, not Kenny, nor any of us. You're the one who'll generate the money, my flower. With me as your manager. Not John Fielding. I can do better than him.'

His chance to prove it occurred when they were negotiating with the two Hollywood guys, James and Hank, whom he and Kenny had first met at the Artwork Club in Chicago. James, having seen and heard the band, wanted Maxine to appear as a singer in a speakeasy in a new gangster film set during Prohibition. Production would commence in early September.

'So we have a deal?' John Fielding said, about to conclude and shake hands on it. 'Maxine sings one number that she's gonna write herself, backed by The Owls and the Pussycats. And ten grand is your final offer?'

'Ten grand is a jumbo deal,' James affirmed. 'You'll get none better.'

'So how soon can you have the contracts drawn up and sent to me?'

'Wait a minute, John,' Brent intervened. 'What's wrong with Maxine writing and performing two songs in this movie?'

'But you heard James, Brent. There's no more money on the table.'

'Who said anything about more money? We'll do it for the same money. But if we have two songs, we'll get twice the money from records and sheet music sales.'

John looked at James and they nodded their agreement.

'Great!' James said. 'We get two songs for the price of one and you get a vehicle for free to promote both. Just add a tree and a fat guy in red and it's Christmas already!'

Eleanor Shackleton was surprised to receive a letter from Brent towards the end of July.

Dear Eleanor,

Just a line to ask you a favour. The band seems to be meeting with a certain amount of success in America and I have decided to become a United States citizen. Because of this, I would be grateful if you would sell my car for me and forward the proceeds. Also, could you please advise the landlord that I wish to give up the tenancy of the house with effect as soon as possible. See if he will do a deal on the rent owing.

The next bit is where the favour comes in: would you and Stephen be so kind as to clear out the house and get rid of all my stuff? There's nothing I need that I can think of, except my old trombone so keep it for me please. The furniture can be disposed of how you will. It's yours after all. I realise this will entail some work, but who else can I turn to? Anything you want for yourself, such as the gramophone or the wireless, please take it or give it away as you see fit.

Meanwhile you can send what's left of the money you get from the car to me care of the Plaza Hotel, Fifth Avenue, New York. You will find the keys to it on the mantelpiece.

Love, as always, and thanks in advance,

Brent.

So, when Stephen returned from his work that evening, Eleanor explained the contents of the letter and asked him to drive her to the house to get an idea of the size of the task. For goodness only knew what state the place would be in after Brent had been living alone there.

That terraced house in Handsworth brought back memories to both, not least how they used to make love on the stairs when Brent was out playing his music. Not surprisingly, the temptation to repeat the exercise for old times' sake was too great to resist. So, having made love, and scuffed the skin off Eleanor's back and Stephen's knees, they began assessing the task in hand. Of course, the furniture that Eleanor always laid claim to was of no value, she admitted, and so shabby that she wouldn't dream of giving it house room any more. An advert in the post office window might attract a buyer. She began to make a list . . . The piano. Pianos were ten-a-penny. Who would buy that? Again, the post office window. The scullery was full of pots and pans, cutlery, crockery. Old curtains and towels abounded, tablecloths, old clothes, old shoes. There were tools of all sorts, a mangle and a maiding tub in the brewhouse that she would never lower herself to use, cupboards full of old sheet music and scores, gramophone records, books, old magazines. On the floors, when you could see the floors, lay rugs and carpets, dingy and dust-laden. Upstairs lived a bed, wardrobes, bedclothes, drawers full of socks, belts, underwear and all manner of unspeakable things. An old sewing machine vied for space in the lumbar room with a wall of tea chests brimming with bric-a-brac and old books from the day they moved into the place. Where to begin? All the correspondence and birthday cards they'd kept over the years had to removed, along with receipts, bills, photographs . . .

'I'll start upstairs,' Eleanor said to Stephen who was opening cupboard doors with a freedom he'd never been allowed before in this house.

Stephen followed her. In the lumber room an ancient hulk of furniture that looked like an ailing Welsh dresser stood against

373

one wall, half hidden by the tea chests. Stephen obligingly shifted a couple to one side so they could open the drawers and rummage through them.

'You can go now,' she said domineeringly. 'Back downstairs.'

He did not go.

From one drawer, Eleanor pulled out a large brown envelope. She opened it and pulled out several pieces of folded paper that looked like legal documents but she quickly shoved them back and shut the drawer firmly. 'Why don't you go downstairs, Stephen, and make a start there? Leave me to sort this out by myself . . . Please?'

'That looked like birth certificates,' he said, immediately suspicious that maybe she was trying to hide something she'd unexpectedly discovered. 'Let's have a look.'

'They're nothing,' she proclaimed dismissively. 'I know what all that stuff is. Just rubbish to be cleared out.'

'So what is it?'

'Nothing. I told you.'

'If it's nothing you might as well let me see,' he said reasonably.

'Oh, just forget it, for goodness sake. Go downstairs and make a start there, else we'll never get done.'

'It's evidently got something to do with you, Eleanor,' he persisted. 'Let me see it.'

'It's nothing to get excited about, Stephen. Just my parents' birth certificates.'

'So let me see.'

'No.' She pressed herself against the drawer so that he could not open it without forcibly shifting her.

Stephen sighed with frustration. 'Eleanor, the way you're acting, it looks to me as if you're trying to hide something. Now if you've got nothing to hide, let me see what's in that envelope.'

Realising his request was perfectly rational and that she had little option but to comply or endure another argument, she conceded. 'Well turn your back first,' she said.

'Oh, don't be so bloody juvenile, Eleanor. Open the damn drawer.'

'Then turn your back . . . please?'

He turned his back.

When she'd opened the draw and he could hear that she was holding the envelope in her hand, he turned round quickly and snatched it off her. She screamed her protest and tried to snatch it back, but he held it out of reach.

'Now, just calm down while I have a look,' he said rationally and took the envelope into the bedroom. Apprehensively, she followed and he sat on the edge of the bed. Again, she tried to snatch it away from him like a petulant child.

'I don't want you to see in there, Stephen. Please?' It was an earnest appeal now. 'Will you please give it back to me?'

'Is it some sort of incriminating evidence?'

'No, of course not. But there's no need for you to see.'

'Well, hard luck, because I'm going to.'

Accepting defeat and preparing herself for the barrage of unwanted questions that would inevitably follow, she allowed him to open the envelope and draw out the papers. He opened out the first one.

'Ah! Brent's birth certificate, by the looks of it.' He read the headings and the entries aloud. '*Name if any – Brent William. When and where born – Thirteenth June 1908, High Street, Chipping Camden. Name and surname of father – Arthur Roland Shackleton. Name, surname and maiden surname of mother – Emma Shackleton formerly Price. Occupation of father – Silversmith* . . . Fancy, Eleanor, Brent's father was a silversmith . . . *Signature, description and residence of informant – Arthur Roland Shackleton of High Street. When registered – Fourteenth July 1908.*' He looked up at her. 'So what's wrong with that?'

She shrugged, a look of defeat clouding her usually defiant eyes, her hair uncharacteristically straying over her face after their struggle.

'Now let's see what else there is in here.'

She snatched at the envelope again and this time she retrieved it. Immediately she darted from the bedroom, ran into the lumber room and tried to lock herself in. With all the strength he could muster, Stephen managed to prise the door open before she could get it closed, for he knew she was headstrong enough to barricade herself in with tea chests. Once in the room he grabbed her wrists hard and firm to prevent her from tearing up the envelope and everything it contained.

'Drop it,' he yelled angrily. 'Drop it, Eleanor or I swear I'll give you such a hiding.'

'Lay another finger on me and I'll kill you,' she screamed and her face was red, her eyes ablaze.

'Drop it, you damned minx!'

He grabbed one wrist with both hands and twisted the flesh till she shrieked with pain and let go of the envelope. As he picked it up she pummelled him, kicked him and screamed, then fell in a heap on the floor, sobbing and complaining that she had never been treated so shabbily in her life and she hoped he would die. Unmoved, he returned to the bedroom and, breathless, sat on the bed once more. He took out the rest of the documents one by one and scrutinised them.

A marriage certificate! Well, how interesting!

As he read it his hands started trembling. It confirmed the marriage on 10th May 1931 of Brent William Shackleton, aged 22, bachelor of Chipping Camden, to Eleanor Christiana Beckett, aged 18, spinster of Evenlode. He ran his sleeve across his forehead to wipe away the bead of sweat that was irritating him and growled in abject disappointment. So she *was* married after all; exactly as he had believed all along.

He was profoundly disturbed and angry that Eleanor had lied to him, but he tried his utmost to keep his anger under control. For a few minutes he sat, trying to consider what it all meant, listening to Eleanor's sobs coming from across the landing. Rationally, he tried to put it all into perspective. The situation was actually no different to that which he had understood it to be before her suggestion of marriage. Merely, Eleanor had lied when she told him she was not married to Brent. It was a lie that could have had far-reaching consequences but, in her desire now to be married to himself, maybe it would not be so difficult to forgive. In fact, he felt flattered that a girl as beautiful as Eleanor was prepared to go to such lengths to have him.

He decided to call her.

'Eleanor!' He deliberately sounded placid. 'I found your marriage certificate. It's all right. So you *are* married after all. It doesn't matter. It was a nice idea that we should wed, but if we can't, we can't. We just carry on like we have been. Let's not fight about it any more. I'm sorry if I hurt you . . . Eleanor . . .'

He got up and went to the lumber room. She was still lying on the floor in the foetal position, unkempt, bereft of dignity with her skirt up revealing her slender thighs. She was quiet now.

'Eleanor, it's all right,' he said kindly, reasonably and stooped down to stroke her arm. 'Come on, get up off the floor. It doesn't matter . . .' He gently stroked her thigh.

She looked up at him with the uncertainty of a thrashed child, her eyes red from crying.

'I mean it,' he went on. 'It doesn't matter. So you're still married. So what?'

She raised herself to the sitting position and pulled her skirt over her legs. 'Oh, Stephen . . . I knew this would happen if you saw that marriage certificate . . .' She gave a great heaving sob and he felt extraordinarily sorry for her. Her elegance had disappeared along with her self-esteem. She seemed so vulnerable that all he wanted was to protect her. 'The truth is, Stephen – and you *have* to believe me – I'm *not* married to Brent . . . Stephen, I swear to God. On my life . . .'

She began to cry again and he wrapped his arms around her consolingly.

'I told you, it doesn't matter, my love.'

'You're not listening to me, Stephen,' she blubbered frustratedly. 'Why aren't you listening to me? I'm telling you the truth,

377

I'm *not* married to Brent.' She broke down again, unable to stem the flood of tears, unable to speak for sobbing.

Stephen took the handkerchief out of his pocket, dabbed her eyes, then handed it to her so she could blow her nose. 'I don't understand, Eleanor,' he said when she had calmed down. 'Your name is on that marriage certificate. It clearly states that you're married to Brent Shackleton, and yet you turn round and blatantly claim you're not. Were you ever divorced?'

She shook her head.

'What does that mean?'

'It means I was never married, Stephen.'

'But it says here you were. There can be no doubt about a marriage certificate, Eleanor.'

'It wasn't me, Stephen. Don't you see? It wasn't *me*.' Another burst of tears . . .

Stephen said: 'Are you saying you are not Eleanor Christiana Beckett?'

She nodded her head against his chest and wept more. 'That's exactly what I'm saying,' she whimpered.

He looked at her with incredulity. 'Then who the hell are you?'

'I wish I could tell you, Stephen . . . I wish I could tell you but I can't . . . Believe me, Stephen, my love, I can't tell you . . . I really can't.'

'So what happened to this Eleanor Christiana Beckett he married?'

'She died.'

'She died? Of what? When? Under what circumstances?'

'I don't know, Stephen. Ask Brent! I don't *know*.'

'So why have you assumed her identity, Eleanor? Christ, how can I still call you Eleanor? Give me a clue as to your real name, for God's sake.'

She was in half a mind to tell him. Get it over with now and be done with it. But she shied away from the truth. She could not tell him. Not yet.

'I want you to still call me Eleanor,' she said in little more than a murmur.

He sighed profoundly and swore to himself as he sat down on a tea chest and ran his fingers through his hair in bewilderment. Exactly what had he stumbled across? He did not like it. He did not like it one bit. But, unless Eleanor deigned to tell him who she really was, he would never know.

'Come on,' he said kindly. 'Let me take you home.'

To some extent, Eleanor's claims that she was never married to Brent Shackleton were so ardent that they set his mind at rest, and he began thinking tentatively once more about instigating arrangements for their marriage. Perhaps he had misjudged her. Certainly, he had been too hard on her recently. Her absolute insistence of the truth of her story, her relentless self-righteousness, were convincing, and he was filled with renewed confidence and affection. He had not been let down or taken advantage of, after all. Despite her other quirks, she seemed to be honest and forthright. That was worth a great deal.

Just one thing; why was she still refusing to reveal her identity? It did not make sense. It made no sense at all. What did she need to hide? Unless she was the daughter of somebody important and well known, of course; the daughter of somebody in the public eye. That would make sense. A judge, maybe; a high-ranking politician or policeman; a bishop or an archbishop. Naturally, he could forgive her for trying to protect the good name of somebody like that. But if she confessed, it would be to him only, and he was not likely to shout it from the nearest church steeple and embarrass anybody; he would be the very soul of discretion. After all, it was in his own interest.

Of course, he wanted to know who she was. He was breaking his neck to know. But this not knowing and her utter refusal to tell him was putting another undeniable strain on their relationship. Deliberately, he had been off-hand with her in an effort to induce her to relent. He had been cold, even turned his back on her in bed, confident that she would acquiesce and confess her roots. But she had confessed nothing. Not so far. Now, it was looking as though she never would.

The problem was, if they were to get married she would have to prove her identity. He even sneaked back to Brent's house alone one day and searched the drawer that had contained those other revealing documents, but he had found nothing. An extended, albeit brief search of the entire house had revealed nothing either. Everything had gone. It was strange, because he would have expected to turn up some old photographs, but there were none. All he could conclude was that Eleanor, in her zeal to hide all evidence, had beaten him back to the house and removed everything while he was busy at work. Perhaps she had destroyed it all, prior to emptying the house in the next week or so.

It was such an important issue and it had to be resolved, but Stephen saw only one way of possibly unearthing the truth. And he would set about doing it within the next few days, when work might allow him a day off.

Eleanor, meanwhile, was incensed that Stephen was treating her so inconsiderately after their traumatic discovery of Brent's marriage certificate. She was telling the truth when she said she had never been married to Brent. She was a single girl, eligible to wed, always had been. The fact that they had always allowed everybody to believe they were a married couple was their business, had always been their business, and nobody else's. Why could Stephen not respect that?

Now he was being perpetually horrible to her. He was rude, insensitive, arrogant even, and she did not like it. It was not the best way to ensure her continued love and admiration. Rather, it provoked her into displays of bad temper and melancholy; moods she was finding harder to overcome. But he deserved to be on the rough end of it with his nastiness and his sarcasm and his continual goading with taunts of who she really might or might not be. She knew who she was. Why did he have to know?

He could love her just as easily. She was still the same person, the same Eleanor he had fallen in love with, even if her real name was not Eleanor. What's in a name, after all? It's just a handle to be turned by, a sound to draw your attention when somebody calls you.

Maybe he had heard that new record by The Owls and the Pussycats on the wireless. She had heard it, a few times. It was a lovely song. Although it peeved her no end to admit it, since the announcer had said it had been written and was performed by Miss Maxine Kite, a beautiful English songstress who was faring remarkably well in America with her band. Maybe Stephen entertained the stupid notion that the song, 'From Tears to a Kiss', was aimed at him. Vain, pompous idiot! Men were like that; believing all the women they had ever known were incurably in love with them for all time. Serve him right if she married Brent or something.

Still, they must be doing well financially if they were famous in the United States. Everybody seemed to have a high old time of it over there if you believed what you read in the papers. Pictures of perpetually smiling women with perfect teeth and wonderful hairstyles. Refrigerators and electric washing machines in every magnificent, spacious home, everybody driving big, gleaming cars, central heating to keep you warm in the winter, perpetual sunshine in the summer.

And look at Brent . . . He wasn't so bad. He was better than most, actually. At least he spoke to her civilly – most of the time. And they did have that gloriously sinful, sexual rapport that was surely lost now, dammit. Maybe she would never capture it again with another man. Certainly, she had never quite attained the same exhilaration with Stephen, for all his prowess, vigour and tenderness.

So what had drawn her to Stephen in the first place, for it was not his looks? Not that looks were so important for a man.

No, it was money.

Of course, it was money. Or, to be absolutely precise, Stephen's potential to make money; his potential to afford her a comfortable, stylish way of life where she could be looked up to and admired, and kept in the manner to which she aspired. That was all she required. And why, with her looks, should she settle for less? In return, she was prepared to offer her body to the ultimate scrutiny, allow him to do things to her that were . . . well, just as enjoyable to her as they were to him, really.

Money had driven her with Brent, too, eventually.

Not at first, though. At first, she had given him her body out of sheer curiosity; a desire to know what having sex felt like. But, having done it once – and she had been an indecently young girl then – she had wanted to do it again. To experiment. And so had he. Before they knew it, they had both become unhealthily addicted. And so the addiction had prevailed, like some incurable affliction that blinded them to reason, to morality and to decency. Afterwards came the money and that was when she bewitched him utterly with her sexual prowess to gain a share of that money. But the idiot had squandered it, left them penniless.

Now Brent had hit on another crock of gold. Who would have believed, when she left him for Stephen, that the fool would turn out to be incredibly successful as a jazz musician in America, when back home he was nothing then but a mediocre trombonist in the CBO with no hope of riches. Did he look back now on those times before he squandered everything and regard it all as pathetically trifling now? Almost certainly he did. For now he must be really coining it in.

But, still obsessed with money when Brent had none, she had prostituted herself with Stephen. No doubt she would prostitute herself again, to the highest bidder, if Stephen carried on belittling her this way.

With hindsight, it had not been a brilliant decision to leave Brent. With foresight, she could have avoided this impossible situation now. For she could not get married to Stephen after all. To do so she would have to reveal her identity.

And that, she finally decided, she could *not* do.

Chapter 29

August in New York in 1937, like in most years, was sweltering, with temperatures into the nineties and humidity that was almost unbearable. At Brent's instigation, The Owls and the Pussycats renegotiated their rates at the Plaza Hotel and, happy that they were getting a better deal than before, resumed living there in apartments on their return from Chicago. Kenny and Dulcie not surprisingly ended their affair and he moved out of the brownstone they had been sharing. In the meantime, Dulcie returned to the family mansion on Fifth Avenue, to her parents' great joy and relief.

The band had no engagements in August. They needed rest. The break afforded Maxine time to concentrate on writing new songs, including the two for the gangster movie. It would also give Brent the opportunity to work out the musical arrangements and the band the chance to rehearse the numbers, in plenty of time for the recording session on the first Monday in September. That was the theory at least.

In practice, it worked out somewhat differently. Maxine completed the songs – entitled 'Does He Ever Think of Me?' and 'Gently, Mend My Broken Heart', but so far Brent had made no effort to work up the arrangements. She reminded him of his responsibility when he returned to their suite one sizzling Friday afternoon. He had been out all day and had been drinking.

She was sitting at the grand piano they'd had brought into their apartment. 'When do you think you'll be able to do the arrangements for the film songs?' she asked, trying to sound casual. It was actually a meaningless question now, but Brent was not aware of that; she had asked it merely to make a point.

'How the hell should I know?' He flopped into a chair and retrieved a tin from his pocket.

Unruffled, she played a few bars of another new song she'd been working on. 'Well it's time you did, Brent. We've signed a contract to supply which is legally binding. I've fulfilled my part. Now we're just waiting for the arrangements. The band has to learn them, remember.'

'I'll get round to it this week.' He was filling a cigarette paper with tobacco. From another tin he took something else that looked like thin strands of tobacco also. Maxine guessed immediately that it was marijuana.

'Don't bother,' she said scornfully. She got up from the piano stool and walked to the window that overlooked The Pond in Central Park. 'I'd rather somebody else did the arrangements.'

'Oh? Why pay somebody else?'

'Because you haven't done them, and the way you keep drinking and smoking *that* stuff, I doubt whether you have the brains left. Actually, we're getting Fletcher Henderson and Duke Ellington. We've talked to them. They're happy to do them.'

As if to say she was a liar, he grinned at her and shook his head while he rolled the strange cocktail in a machine that magically produced a perfectly cylindrical cigarette.

'You? You asked Fletcher Henderson?' He trimmed one straggling end of his reefer with his fingernails, lit it and inhaled. 'He's too busy doing Benny Goodman's stuff to even consider ours. And Duke Ellington? Ha! You're living in cloud-cuckoo-land if you think you can get Duke Ellington.'

'Correction. You're the one living in cloud-cuckoo-land, Brent. You're incapable these days. Just look at you. You're pathetic. Anyway, it's all arranged . . .'

'What do you mean it's all arranged?'

'Do I have to spell it out? Fletcher Henderson is doing the

arrangement for "Gently, Mend My Broken Heart", and Duke Ellington is working on "Does He Ever Think of Me?".'

'Oh, come off it, Maxine. You're pulling my leg.'

'I've never been more serious.' She walked over to a table where an arrangement of flowers stood in a vase and began fiddling with it, for want of something to do with her hands other than throttling Brent. 'Ask John Fielding. He fixed it. He agreed we couldn't afford to wait on you any longer.'

'You mean you've discussed this with John Fielding already? Behind my back?'

She turned and looked at him with defiance in her eyes; defiance he'd not seen before. 'Yes, I've discussed it all with John Fielding – behind your back, if that's how you see it. He does still manage us and, as far as I am concerned, he'll continue to manage us. Dulcie invited me there to lunch today and, in the absence of any such invitation from you, I accepted. Fortunately for us, John was home. When I told him you hadn't done the instrumentation yet, he contacted Fletcher and Duke straight away. He's as anxious as I am that it's ready for the film shoot. These Hollywood people don't mess about, Brent. So he's taking me to meet Fletcher tomorrow morning and Duke tomorrow afternoon to go through them. They promised they'd have the scores ready by the end of the week.'

'You cow!'

Two words.

She had expected more, much more. She had expected some tantrum, some fiery demonstration of his anger and resentment. But none were forthcoming. Instead, he continued to sit in the chair, his breathing heavy, inhaling the smoke from his precious reefer as if his life depended on it. Increasingly, he was descending into a dark world of his own and Maxine realised it. And, in a way, she was not sorry. When he was doped like this he never bothered her. And he was like it increasingly. So far, it had not affected his performances in the band. He was still a trooper, professional, disciplined where playing was concerned. It was the off-duty time that was bringing his problems; time that he did not know how to manage and utilise. His problems were greater than he knew, though, because Maxine realised she did not love him enough to care. She did not even like him any more. She lacked the inclination now to try and nurture him through his addictions. You only get out of love what you put into it, Maxine had always known, and he had put nothing into theirs; so he could expect nothing in return and serve him right. In no time, he had become a stranger, a monster even, somebody she did not recognise any more. He had become cold towards her, off-handed. She resented his cuttingly selfish attitude, his shoving aside all her good intentions when she had tried to reason with him. He could go and pickle his brain in whatever illegal substance he could get his hands on for all she cared now. She was not about to break her heart over him.

She looked contemptuously at him while he was slumped in the chair like some vegetating heap. He looked ugly, hideous, witless. What had she ever seen in him? He was asleep. Of course he was asleep. That's all he was good for.

Suddenly filled with despair, Maxine rushed to their bedroom. What had happened to her life? Had she sacrificed it on a dream that had momentarily materialised but which was now faithlessly turning into a nightmare? Why did she have to be saddled with a husband so mercurial, so mercenary, so unfeeling, so hell-bent on his own destruction and on hers? Why, after only two months of marriage, was she wishing she had never set eyes on him? Their music – his and hers – had been blessed with unbelievable good fortune, had put them on the road to unimaginable wealth and the possibility of living that dream – until they got married. Now it was all inexorably slipping away.

She tried to cry, but no tears would come. She could not weep for Brent Shackleton. He had tricked her. He had diverted her with love that was fickle and tenderness that was sham when she was at her most vulnerable. He had seduced her with soft words and empty promises then beguiled her into marriage with mock pledges and theatrical displays of affection. And for what? For his own financial gain? Surely, it had to be, for *she* could perceive no benefit for herself. He did not love her. How could he when he spent so little time with her? On some days, the only time she saw him was on-stage. What sort of a marriage was that? Yet he was busily looting her bank account, spending her money.

Her money.

His remained in his own account, untouched.

She began to ponder again what might have been. She had made the biggest mistake of her life, leaving Howard to join the *Queen Mary* trips. Was this now her punishment, to be trapped in a loveless marriage to a husband who had become a junkie and a drunkard?

Oh, Howard! *Howard, can you ever forgive me? Can I ever forgive myself?*

It was then that the tears began to flow; tears for herself and tears for the only man she had ever truly loved. If only she could turn back the clock. Please, God, let her return to that first Sunday in November last year – now she had the benefit of hindsight. She would not make the same mistake again. *Please, God . . . Please make it happen . . .*

Eventually, she dried her tears and returned to the sitting room. Brent was dead to the world in his drunken stupor and she looked at him contemptuously as she sat at the baby grand. She made herself comfortable and her fingers trickled over the keys, softly playing the introduction to one of her songs for the Hollywood movie. She thought of Howard. This was another love song for him. At least it was her way of being with him, of reaching out to him. As she began to sing, soulfully, fervently, she hoped with all her heart that he would hear her – sometime . . .

. . . Gently mend my broken heart
When I come home to you . . .

* * *

In Harlem, overcrowding in many apartment buildings was appalling and the rents were often beyond the means of tenants. So, in order to fulfil their monthly obligations to the landlords, Harlemites devised a means of raising the necessary cash and bringing everybody some welcome pleasure in the execution of it.

It worked like this: the tenants of a building would agree to throw a party and would pool their money to spend on food such as pigs' feet, fried chicken and other culinary delights. They set aside more money to buy booze, of course. Other necessities they must pay for were entertainment, usually in the form of a pianist but more usually two, advertising, and the provision of a bouncer in case things got rough. Next, they would distribute cards giving the location, date, menu and names of the 'professors of piano' that would be playing, and spread the word among selected friends and relatives. On arrival at a rent party, guests would pay a small admission charge, buy food and drink at reasonable prices and dance for as long as they and the refreshments held out. It all normally yielded a healthy profit that easily covered the rent.

Brent Shackleton and Kenny Wheeler were introduced to this "chitlin' circuit" by Lips Robinson, a handsome cornet player and Joey Downs, another trombonist, who lived in Harlem. You wouldn't take your woman to these parties, of course, they told them. Hell, there were always enough spare women there in any case. So, both Brent and Kenny quickly developed a taste for the pretty black and mulatto girls that were present in abundance. And because they were respected jazz musicians and perceived to be wealthy celebrities, the girls were eager to be seen leaving with either one of them, for it was deemed to be a feather in their caps. Naturally, Brent and Kenny were delighted to take advantage of the girls' willingness.

Other diversions Harlem offered included a club called Small's Paradise, a 'black and tan' establishment where races intermingled, unlike the Cotton Club where blacks were excluded unless they were waiters, working musicians or visiting celebrities. Brent was fascinated by the free and easy, debauched way of life his two new friends led and allowed them to coach him. They introduced him to a basement club where they regularly held a transvestite fashion display and lewd vaudeville show. It was different. It was a laugh. They took, too, to sampling the goods on offer at a place Joey Downs referred to as 'Ma Froggatt's dicty whorehouse', 'dicty' meaning sophisticated. Okay, they had to pay for their women, but some contenders were well worth the expense. And what the hell! They could afford it. They could afford other things too; things most of civilised society never knew existed.

The day after her meetings with Fletcher Henderson and Duke Ellington, Maxine decided that two more charming men she could not have wished to meet. Because she had witnessed the absolute contrast between those two brilliant musicians and Brent Shackleton, she wondered why her own husband could not be like them. They were proof positive that you could be successful and level-headed, that you could be talented and sane. All it took was self-discipline, common sense and humility. If Brent was too immature to recognise these things, it was madness to continue paying for his philandering. She would not subsidise her husband's drinking, narcotics and womanising habits further. So she went along to her bank and, but for a couple of hundred dollars, withdrew all the money from the joint account he had set up. That money she deposited in a new account under her maiden name and returned to their apartment at the Plaza.

It was gloriously hot weather when Stephen Hemming decided to take a day off work and drive alone to Chipping Camden in the Cotswolds. He left Birmingham's grime behind and found himself travelling through quiet lanes shaded by the lush foliage of oak and elm. He drove past orchards, their trees creaking under the weight of ripening fruit, and fields aglow with the gold of ripe wheat and barley. Sheep grazed the rolling hills with an imperturbability that was enviable. He spotted signposts for villages with beautiful sounding names, like Cleeve Prior, Cow Honeybourne, Weston Subedge and Hidcote Boyce. People stopped and waved, their tanned faces always ready with a smile as he passed them by in his smart Alvis Speed 25.

This unhurried, unhostile rurality influenced his mood, changing it from the tense to the relaxed. He did not have any firm notion of what he would do when he arrived at Chipping Camden. His purpose was to establish the identity of the woman he knew as Eleanor but, to do so, he felt certain he would have to unearth information about Brent Shackleton and unravel the mystery via that route. Brent Shackleton had lived there, had been born there, in High Street, but he did not know which house. He had been baptised at the church of St James. It was something to go on, but what if every person that remembered him had left the area now, or had died?

Stephen realised he had arrived at Chipping Camden when he first had sight of the curved main street through the village. Its charm was instant and breathtaking, as if time had stood still. Exquisite, yellowy buildings lined both sides of the road that broadened out into a wide boulevard, and its gentle curve enticed you to go on and seek more of the same honey-coloured elegance beyond it. Stephen noticed a church with a high tower, overlooking the village. A street on the left looked as if it might lead to it. Cidermill Lane, he noted. It was as good a place as any to start.

As he pulled up outside the church gate, another construction faced him, mostly in ruins but spectacular in design. An arched gateway remained, flanked by a pair of dilapidated lodge houses with stone roofs constructed in the shape of cupolas; a relic of a prosperous bygone age; an age of enlightenment and good manners. An overgrown field of stubble lay behind, dotted with bright wild flowers, adjoining the churchyard on its left and the blue sky above; the grounds of a former mansion. Even what remained was beautiful, and his innate appreciation of things elegant allowed him to admire it the more, and pity its demise.

He stopped the engine and got out of the car. Immediately, he was struck by an awesome tranquillity, an unearthly peace. He had never imagined, being stuck seemingly forever in the seething crucible that was Birmingham, that such serenity could exist, especially after the frenetic peaks and troughs of living with Eleanor. The only sounds he could hear as he passed through the church gate into the cathedral nave of lime trees that sheltered the path, were the calls of blackbirds singing as if for their loves.

Tombstones stood defiant of the ravages of time in the neatly trimmed grass of the churchyard, their surfaces crumbling. Most were indecipherable now. But Stephen inspected some of the later ones, the ones that could still be read, to see if the name Shackleton cropped up. Families of Izods, Trubys, Abbits and Shadbolts were represented, as well as the more common names, but not . . . Then he came upon a headstone bearing the name Price. Brent's mother was a Price, he recalled, though it was a common enough name. It was to the memory of John Price and also his wife, Rhoda; nothing to do with Brent's mother at all. In another part of the churchyard, overlooking the stubble field of the derelict mansion house, were some newer graves. Stephen moistened his lips and ambled over expectantly.

It was after about fifteen minutes or so that he found some evidence of what he was seeking. *To the memory of Arthur Roland Shackleton who passed away suddenly on December 25th 1931. And of Emma Shackleton, his wife, who died February 25th 1932. Rest in peace.*

Brent's father and mother. He was on the right track.

Stephen studied it for a few minutes, trying to picture these two people who had died so close in time to each other – only two months apart. He had died on Christmas Day. It must have been a traumatic time for Brent, for he would have been only recently married. Then to lose his own young wife so soon afterwards. Life dealt some cruel blows. There must be a grave for her somewhere; somewhere close by, among these recent ones.

So he searched. He scrutinised every grave systematically, but found none to the memory of Eleanor Christiana Shackleton.

He wondered whether the parish records might reveal anything. But how did you get a look at them? The sun was hot on the back of his neck and he looked up at the church. Its fifteenth-century perpendicular tower seemed to glow in the high morning sunshine. Maybe if he went inside he might find some clue. In any case, it was bound to be cooler in there. He strolled towards the door, still peering hopefully at headstones as he walked. But these were old; too old.

Inside it was cooler. He bowed to the altar out of a reverence indoctrinated over years as a choirboy. He looked around and saw a clergyman kneeling in one of the pews, but facing the back of the church, using a screwdriver. The man looked up when he heard Stephen approach.

'Good morning.'

'Good morning,' Stephen responded as he walked towards him. 'It's a bit cooler in here than outside.'

'Yes, lucky for me.' The clergyman was young with a ready smile that rendered him immediately likeable; a priceless asset for a man of the cloth. He picked up a brace and bit that had been lying on the pew and began to drill a hole, but inexpertly. When it was to his satisfaction he looked again at Stephen. 'I'm blessed with doing the odd jobs this week, it seems,' he said. 'Trust the sexton to be on holiday when the pew falls to pieces. Normally he would fix it, of course.'

'Handyman, is he?' Stephen commented.

'He is. I'm not. I can't seem to get this screw to bite.'

'Perhaps I can help. If I push against the back of it . . . look.'

'Excellent . . . Thank you so much. If I'd used a longer screw of course, it would've poked out the other side and possibly injured somebody.'

The job was soon finished. The clergyman dusted off his cassock with his hands and collected his well-used tools.

'Thanks indeed,' he said, 'for your timely arrival. I'd have been here till Christmas trying to do it by myself.'

'You're welcome.'

'I don't recall having met you before. You're a visitor here?'

Stephen hesitated, then decided to discover whether the clergyman could help in his quest. 'Yes, I'm trying to trace the death of a young woman round about 1932 or 1933. I believe she was married here.'

'Mmm. I wasn't here then. Only been here a year myself. I'm the curate, actually. Mr Watkins might know, of course, the vicar. Actually, I have a minute or two to spare. Maybe I could look her up in the parish records for you.'

Stephen's heart missed a beat. 'Would you? I'd be ever so grateful.'

'Come with me to the sacristy. One good turn deserves another, I always say.' The young curate led him into the priest's vestry. 'When did you say this girl died?'

'About 1932. Her name was Eleanor Christiana Shackleton – née Beckett.'

'Christiana, eh? Rather a nice name, that.' He flashed his friendly smile and opened the appropriate register. His finger slid down the page as he scanned it looking for the name. 'Is she buried here, do you know?'

'I couldn't find a grave,' Stephen answered.

He looked through the records as far forward as 1936 but found no trace of her death. 'Of course, she might not be buried here. Do you know where she came from? Was it this parish?'

'She was married here, if that's anything to go on, but she came from Evenlode.'

'Evenlode! Then you may have more joy there, methinks. But her death is not registered here.'

'Would the vicar know more?' Stephen asked. 'How long has he been here?'

'Oh, since Adam was a lad, I suspect. Would you like to ask him if he remembers this lady?'

'If he's about. If it's no trouble. He might have some recollection.'

The curate closed the register, put it away and led Stephen out of the church. As they were walking down the path, the vicar himself was coming towards them, an elderly man with grey hair and wise eyes.

'Ah, Vicar!' the curate greeted. 'This gentleman is seeking information on one of our parishioners who passed away about 1932. We wondered if you might remember her.'

'Stephen Hemming,' Stephen said, offering his hand. 'Actually, I'm trying to find information about an Eleanor Christiana Shackleton, née Beckett. I've driven down from Birmingham this morning specially . . .'

'Shackleton? . . .' the vicar mused and rubbed his chin where odd white whiskers that he had missed during his morning shave still sprouted mutinously. 'There was an Arthur Shackleton, I recall . . . a Londoner. Came up with the Guild of Arts and Handicrafts in 1902. Devout Christian as I recall. Worshipped here regularly.'

'You remember him!' Stephen exclaimed and felt his heart beating faster again. 'He was a Londoner, was he?'

'Yes . . . One of Charles Ashbee's craftsmen. Charles Ashbee was a disciple,' he explained, 'if I may use the word in its more liberal sense – of William Morris, the designer.'

'I see. That explains him being a silversmith,' Stephen interjected.

'The whole thing was an exercise in idealism, I think, to arrange the migration of fifty or so craftsmen and their families up to this neck of the woods from London. They integrated eventually, though there was some resentment of them at first, as I recall.'

Stephen, suddenly excited, felt that he was getting somewhere already. 'What else do you know of Arthur Shackleton – his family?'

The vicar scratched his head and his eyes manifested a distant expression as he went travelling back mentally in time. 'Yes, it's coming back to me now. Amazing what you can remember when the old memory is jogged, what? . . . Arthur was a single man when he moved here. However, he met and married a local girl . . . Can't think of her name, though, for the life of me—'

'Emma,' Stephen offered. 'Emma Price.' He witnessed the light of recollection in the vicar's eyes.

'Yes, of course, of course . . . Emma. Pretty girl. Oh, a very pretty girl. Dark hair. In service at Lady Truscott's house, I recall. Yes . . . of course I remember her. They had a son, Brent. He attended the Grammar School. Keen on music, I think . . . yes . . . In fact, he was in the choir here as a boy for a number of years. They had a daughter too, two or three years younger . . . Damned if I can think of her name . . .'

'Sorry, I can't help you there,' Stephen said. 'I didn't know they had a daughter.'

'Pretty girl, too, like her mother . . . The image of her mother—'

'But can you recall the son's wife?' Stephen interrupted impatiently, sensing he was getting close to solving his mystery if only he could keep the vicar's thoughts focused. 'He married in 1931. Surely you remember the occasion if you recalled him as a choirboy?'

'I vaguely remember the wedding. I must have officiated. Don't remember the bride, though . . .' The vicar paused to rack his brains, struggling to recall it. 'No, not for the life of me . . . Don't believe she came from this parish. Otherwise, I'd have known her, I'm sure.'

'She came from Evenlode, Mr Watkins,' the curate prompted, endeavouring to be helpful.

'Ah, that would explain it,' Mr Watkins said. 'Tell me, was there a child? Did she die in childbirth?'

'That's a point,' Stephen said, looking at the curate as if he were also in complicity. 'Actually, I hadn't thought of that. I'm not aware of a child still living at any rate . . . There's no grave for a child here either with the name Shackleton.'

'Then it's almost certain she left this parish before she died. However, I do recall Arthur and Emma passing away quite unexpectedly. She, very soon after him. There was a great deal of sympathy for young Brent at the time. A great deal. Then we saw no more of the lad. Presumably he moved out of the area.'

'Yes, to Birmingham.'

'Well, well! But if you know of his whereabouts, Mr Hemming, why don't you ask him what you want to know?'

'He's in America now, Mr Watkins. If he were in Birmingham I'd ask him, have no fear. Anyway, thanks very much for your help. It's been useful talking to you. Given me some other options to think about. The possibility of a child, especially.'

'Sorry I can't be of more help. But really, you might find it worthwhile to visit Evenlode. St Edward's church. I'm sure the rector could be of help. He's been there some years.'

It had been in Stephen's mind to scout the High Street to see what he could glean from old neighbours. The vicar's suggestion that he visit Evenlode, however, had more appeal. If he met with no success there he could always come back. For the moment, maybe it was better not to draw attention to the past among neighbours who might not have known the Shackletons anyway. And if they did, who knew what hornet's nest he might stir up?

So Stephen drove on through country lanes to Moreton-in-Marsh and then to Evenlode, about seven miles in all. He passed through some of the prettiest villages imaginable and wondered why on earth Brent would want to leave such an idyll. It did not make sense. As long as there was a living to be earned here why migrate? But, perhaps there was no living to be earned. Brent had his heart set on music and the opportunities for music, other than the local Salvation Army band, were most likely very limited.

At Evenlode the road forked and he did not know which one

to take. He consulted his map and saw that it didn't matter, since the road formed a ring around the village. So he took the left option and passed a row of cottages then fields. The lane, overhung with trees, narrowed and twisted to the right. As he drove slowly, peering in every direction, looking for a pub now where he could get refreshment and perhaps a cheese cob, he saw a small church on his left. A few yards from the front of the gate to the churchyard stood a largish tree, and he decided to park beneath it, to take advantage of its shade.

He looked around. The place seemed deserted. It was such a sleepy little village. He peered over the yellow stone wall encrusted with lichens that surrounded the ancient churchyard. The notice board that stood at the gate confirmed it was the church of St Edward; five or six hundred years old, Stephen estimated. He opened the gate, ready to repeat the exercise of looking at the inscriptions on graves. This was a small churchyard. It would not take long to read this lot. And most were so old as to be unreadable.

As he walked between graves he happened on a bunch of freshly cut sweetpeas left lying in brown paper on the ground, alongside a pair of scissors that glinted in the sunshine. Somebody attending a grave had evidently been called away. He would place the flowers on the grave for whoever it was; it would take no effort. Then, out of the corner of his eye, he saw a young woman walking towards him carrying an enamelled grave vase that was dripping with water. She looked at him apprehensively at first then, sensing that he was not unfriendly and, typical of the people of the area, smiled trustingly and wished him good morning.

He greeted her with his friendliest grin, as much to reassure her of his integrity in so deserted a place. 'I was about to place the flowers on the grave,' he said affably, 'till I noticed there was no vase.'

'Thank you,' the young woman replied. 'It was a kind thought.'

'At first, you see, I thought whoever it was, must have been called away.'

'Only by the need to get some fresh water for them.' Her softly spoken voice was refined.

He watched her as she bent down self-consciously and began trimming the stems of the flowers. He tried to think of something to say that did not sound trite. She was in her early twenties, slim and very pretty, with eyes the colour of amethyst and fair, unruly hair that cascaded over her face appealingly as she worked. She wore no stockings and her light summer frock was clean and crisp and, although it was plain and far from new, she looked becoming enough in it.

'I'm a stranger to these parts . . . unfortunately,' he said at last. 'I must say, I do like it around here. It's beautiful . . . and tranquil. Different to Birmingham. I think I could happily settle in the Cotswolds.'

She looked up at him and smiled, and her blue eyes crinkled engagingly. 'Everybody says that who comes here.'

Stephen looked at the inscription on the headstone of the grave she was working on and read it aloud. '*To the memory of Lady Elizabeth Hunstanton who slipped peacefully away January 22nd 1931 aged 72. Rest in peace.*' He paused, expecting her to say something, but she just looked up at him with that pleasant friendly smile. 'Your mother?' he asked.

'No, not my mother,' she replied softly. 'A friend.'

She placed the last of the sweetpeas in the grave vase and adjusted the positions of one or two before she stood up. She was no more than five feet tall in her sandals, Stephen reckoned.

'That's quite an age gap for friends. You must only be in your early twenties.' Out of habit he looked for a ring and noticed she was not wearing one.

'Yes. Early twenties.' She gave him another of her lovely smiles. But the hint of shyness, along with her petiteness, he found very attractive.

'Sorry. I wasn't trying to find out your age. I must seem very ungallant.'

'It's all right.' She smiled again, self-consciously and her long eyelashes swept her cheek as she cast her eyes down. 'I don't really hold with the notion that a woman should try to effect some mystique by withholding her age. Those who do are usually middle-aged and dearly wish they were younger . . . Are you on holiday in these parts?'

He was encouraged by her attempt at conversation. 'No, not on holiday. I've just taken the day off work to do some browsing. What about you? Are you on holiday?'

'No, I live in the village.'

'But you're evidently not at work. It's feasible you could be on holiday, especially as you're not married. I'm assuming you're not married.'

She looked at him questioningly.

'Sorry. There I go again. I don't mean to pry. Really I don't. I design and make jewellery, you see. Instinctively, I always look at a girl's hands to see what rings she's wearing. I see you're not wearing a wedding ring.'

She nodded her understanding without looking at him. 'Oh, it's all right. Please don't apologise. You could say marriage has passed me by.' Her colour rose appealingly as she uttered the words.

'I'm not married either.'

'You say you design and produce jewellery? That sounds fascinating.'

'Yes, when I can't escape to the Cotswolds.'

'So what brings you here?' she asked. 'Is browsing churchyards your hobby or something?'

'Not especially. I'm looking for a particular grave.'

'A very old one? Some of them are illegible.'

'A fairly recent one, actually.'

'Really? Shall I help you look? I might know it.'

'Oh, please. It's not likely to take long.'

'It's all right. I'm not in a particular hurry,' she said.

He managed to divert his eyes from her exquisite profile and scanned the churchyard. 'I'm trying to find out what happened to a young woman that came from this village. It's feasible you might have known her. Her name was Eleanor Christiana Beckett. Have you ever heard of her?'

'What do you want to know?' the girl asked.

'How she died, why she died, under what circumstances . . . Whatever I can find out about her.'

'May I ask why?'

'Personal interest. Somebody I know has assumed her identity and I'm intrigued as to why. I also want to know who the imper- sonator really is.'

His eyes fastened on hers again. He noticed she offered no smile this time. Instead, her expression was one of earnestness.

'I might be able to help you,' she said. 'In fact, I'd like to help you. But you won't find her grave here . . .'

'Oh. So you knew Eleanor?'

'Yes, I knew her. I knew her very well.'

'Well, if I won't find her grave here, perhaps you could tell me where it is. Why not sit in my car under the shadow of that tree there and tell me about her? It'll be cooler there.'

'All right.' She put her scissors in her pocket, screwed up the brown paper from her sweetpeas and tossed it into a bin.

Chapter 30

Stephen reflected on what he had learned in Evenlode with a peculiar detachment as he drove back home to Birmingham. It was the luckiest thing that had ever happened to him, meeting this girl. She was so appealing. Five feet nothing of sparkling blue-eyed femininity that had really turned his head – when, by God, it needed turning. As he drove through Redditch, heading out towards Alvechurch, his thoughts were focused less on the problem of the woman he had always known as Eleanor, more on this other girl. He kept turning over in his mind their conversation, but not just their conversation; he felt from the outset that somehow he appealed to her as much as she appealed to him. He could hardly believe his luck.

'And you're sure this has nothing to do with Brent?' the girl had asked him with a measure of apprehension that was not unnatural in the circumstances.

'Not directly,' he'd replied. 'It's to do with the girl who's been impersonating your friend Eleanor. I thought if I could track down somebody who knew the real Eleanor, then it might shed some light on who this other girl really is.'

'How is she impersonating her?' He could still hear her clear soft voice in his head.

'By living her life, till recently, as Mrs Eleanor Shackleton. She evidently moved to Birmingham from Chipping Camden with him.'

'Birmingham? So that's where he got to. Not so far away,' the

401

girl had commented. 'But you could easily lose yourself, so to speak, in a big city like Birmingham.'

'So do you have any idea who this girl might be?' he'd asked. It was the one question that was burning him up and he could hardly contain himself waiting for her answer.

'Mmm . . .' She had hesitated agonisingly, looking down into her lap where her hands were clasped together. Her thumbs revolved around each other disconcertedly while she determined, it seemed, how much of the truth she should reveal. 'That would be Olive,' she said at last. 'Almost certainly.'

'Olive?' He had never heard of anybody they knew called Olive.

'Yes, they ran away together the night—'

Looking back, he knew he should have asked what night. Instead, like the impetuous fool he sometimes was he had let it go and, instead, jumped in with: 'They ran away together?'

'Yes.'

'So who was she, this Olive?'

'Brent's sister.'

He remembered scoffing in disbelief. Of course, Brent had a sister . . . People had been telling him that all morning. 'But *she* couldn't be his sister,' he'd replied to that lovely girl. 'No, they lived as man and wife . . . With nothing barred – if you know what I mean.'

'Yes, that sounds like Olive . . . I'm sorry.'

There had been a few bewildered moments before he responded to that. It was, after all, a concept that took quite some getting used to. The ramifications finally hit him like the blow from a sledgehammer. He recalled putting his head in his hands in utter disbelief. Was this girl he'd known all this time as Eleanor really Brent's sister, Olive? He felt sick at the thought of all it implied. How could anybody . . . ? It was perverted. It was human nature at its vilest.

'You poor, poor man,' she had whispered, and he remembered the depth of her obvious concern for him at receiving this disturbing information. Then she asked the question that confirmed it as the absolute truth: 'Is she still as stunningly beautiful?'

'Oh, yes, she's still as stunningly beautiful,' he'd answered. 'But only on the outside.' If it were physically possible to purge her depraved soul clean, he contemplated, she could never be a match for that lovely little fair-haired, amethyst-eyed angel that had put him wise.

'Well, I can tell you that Eleanor didn't find out about their incestuous relationship until it was too late,' she had said. 'She was already married to Brent by the time that became evident.' At that, she had bestowed on him a radiant smile that he found extraordinarily comforting.

Stephen should have been sad at what he heard. He should have been angry. He should have felt nauseous at the dark, disgusting secret he had uncovered that day. But he did not. He felt uplifted. He felt relieved. Fortune had unexpectedly smiled on him good and proper this time; not financially, but spiritually. It was entirely because of the lovely girl he had met who was like a fresh breath of springtime ousting a dismal winter fog that conceals ugliness and awful truths. He asked if he could see her again; he had to see her again; he could not lose her now he had found her. And she had said yes. Now he could hardly wait. He laughed to himself, euphoric that something ultimately positive and chaste was unfolding in his life. She had such a wonderful name too, that suited her perfectly. Cassandra, she'd said it was. Cassandra.

'I tried to telephone you today at work,' Eleanor said when he arrived back home in Selwyn Road. She was sitting on a settee in the drawing room with her stockinged feet tucked under her bottom. 'Percy told me you hadn't been there at all. You didn't tell *me* you weren't going to work.'

He grabbed the evening newspaper and sat down on the opposite settee. 'I've been out,' he said in a way that would normally inhibit further questioning, but with a twist of tone that made further questioning essential.

She paused before she asked, for she sensed she was being led into a trap. Yet she could not resist.

'Doing what?'

He opened the newspaper, trying to remain casual. 'Digging.'

'Oh yes? Digging for what? Gold?'

He found a wonderful irony in her comment. 'Not gold . . . I did find it, though, as it happens.' he said, thinking of Cassandra.

'Bully for you, Stephen.'

'Yes. Bully for me.' He peered around the newspaper at her and looked her in the eye. 'Not bully for you, though, I'm afraid . . . *Olive*.'

At once she turned away. 'Olive?' she queried and emitted a derisory laugh.

'Yes. I have to get used to thinking of you as *Olive* from now on . . . But not for long, fortunately.'

'Who the hell is Olive, for God's sake?'

'You are.'

'What on earth are you talking about, Stephen? Has the sun got to you and addled your brain?'

'Very likely it has, but maybe not as much as it's addled yours.' He put down the newspaper. 'Actually, I've been to Chipping Camden today . . . Lovely place, isn't it? It's amazing what people there remember of you, *Olive*, and your brother.'

She looked at him anxiously and got up from the settee. He watched her as she went to the occasional table and fiddled with the arrangement of dried flowers she'd had delivered from Lewis's two weeks earlier.

'Okay,' she responded at last. 'So who told you?'

'A couple of people actually. It doesn't really matter who. It was just a question of putting two and two together . . .'

'So now you know . . .' She sighed, then shrugged, almost as if it was of no significance. 'So what?'

'*So what?*' He could hardly believe her arrogance, her obvious lack of shame. It made him angry, but he did not want to get angry. With anger, you lose self-control and he wanted to retain his. He wanted to remain in charge of this discussion, this final discussion. He breathed in deeply and assumed control again of his emotions. 'You have been having a revolting, disgusting, incestuous affair with your vile brother all these years, and you have the audacity to say, so what? God! You're unbelievable, Olive.' He almost said Eleanor, but corrected himself in time.

'Yes. I say, so what? It's over now. It doesn't matter any more.'

'Is that what you really think? You really think it doesn't matter?'

'It's over, Stephen. Finished. History. Anyway, since when have *you* been such a Puritan?'

'Since I discovered that such immoral, perverted behaviour could actually exist. That's when *I* suddenly became a Puritan.'

She shrugged again.

He shook his head in disbelief. 'You feel no remorse, do you, *Olive?* You have no concept of contrition.'

'Don't look at me like that. Of course I feel remorse. Why do you think I wanted to keep my identity from you?'

He sighed deeply and sat back in the settee, drained of emotion. He had faced her with the truth and he felt relieved for having got it off his chest. But he had more to do and he did not relish having to do it, since it was entirely contrary to his nature.

'Olive . . .' He still found it awkward trying to call her by her real name. 'Olive, it's all over between us. It has to be. I can't go on as we have been and I suspect you wouldn't want to. I can't condone what you've done. Ever. You can't imagine the distaste, the . . . the revulsion I feel. I want you to leave. I want you to go now. You could go back to the house you and he shared . . . There's a bed there.'

'There's a bed here, Stephen. Our bed . . .' Her voice changed to the kittenish tone that always elicited a positive response from him. 'Oh, take me to bed, Stephen and let's forget this nonsense.

Come and make love to me. I'm all wet for you. I've been aching for you all day.'

He gritted his teeth and thought of Cassandra. 'Forget it, Olive. You don't think I'd want to touch you now, do you? Pack your things and go. Tonight. Now . . . I want you to go *now*.'

'Now? Why now, for God's sake?' She was indignant again.

'Just collect your things together and go. I'll take you there.'

'Go? Just like that? How can I possibly? I haven't got any money.'

Of course, she wanted money and he despised her the more. Well, she could have money. She could have all the money he had in the house, which was a decent amount.

'There's about two hundred pounds upstairs. You can have it. I'll get it for you, gladly. Take it. Then get out.'

'Two hundred pounds?' Her eyes signalled her approval. 'Show me the money first.'

Olive left that night. Stephen delivered her to the house in Handsworth, as he gallantly promised he would. The bed was still upstairs, and a table and chairs in the kitchen. She felt utterly humiliated that Stephen had discovered her identity and the scandalous secret that she and Brent had shared over the years. Of course, she knew it had been an unhealthy, perverted relationship, but obsession makes you overlook the morals of such an incestuous liaison that others might find offensive – and she had been obsessed. She loved Brent, not like a brother, but like a lover. She could never get enough of him.

She still craved for those obsessive, lusty hours of deranged passion that she and Brent had shared, if she was honest with herself. There had been nothing like it since, and was unlikely to be anything like it again . . . Unless . . . Well, now she had two hundred pounds . . .

The following week, Stephen received another of Pansy's monthly letters.

My dear beloved brother, (He knew she was being sarcastic.)
In less than a week we fly – yes fly, can you believe it – to
Hollywood to record two new songs and perform them in a
film they're making about Chicago gangsters called "The Loop
Mob". I must say, when we were in Chicago we saw no sign
of any gangsters, but I know some of the clubs were run by
them – a throwback from the Prohibition days and speak-
easies, I guess.

I'm a bit worried that people in the band don't seem to
be getting along as well as they used to. Maxine and me are
fine together, and so is Toots and me, but Kenny's gone all
funny and seems sozzled most of the time. Dulcie, his
American girlfriend, has finished with him as well. She's ever
such a nice person and she's best off without him, that's for
certain. Just lately, Charlie, who plays the double bass, has
been seeing her and that's put jealousy between him and
Kenny, just to make matters worse. So now Ginger Tolley has
palled up with Kenny and Brent and nobody will have
anything to do with them any more socially. The only time
we see them is when we play or rehearse, and at rehearsals
there's sometimes a terrible atmosphere and rows. Pity really.
We have the chance to make all this money and they're all
jeopardising it by being stupid. The problem is, as I see it,
the two drunks in the band don't know how to cope with the
success we've had and all the money we've made. Toots calls
them coke blowers because they sniff cocaine and smoke some-
thing I can't spell.

Something else. It was supposed to be secret, but I'm going
to tell you anyway, Stephen because I know you'll be interested
and I know you'll keep it to yourself. Maxine and Brent got
married in June. It was a civic ceremony and very hush-hush,
but we had a lovely party afterwards in one of the posh hotels
here in New York. The problem is, Maxine is very unhappy.
It just hasn't worked out. And so soon after they got married
as well. She reckons Brent's been trying to bleed her of all the

money she's accumulated since we got here. She's made a lot more than the rest of us because of royalties from her writing songs, not that I begrudge it her. She's earned it. Anyway, at least she's had the good sense to shift what's left so he can't get his hands on it any more. Maxine says he's drunk most of the time or doped on all those illegal narcotics and he's in with a right crowd of wrong-uns, going off with other women and everything, Toots says. Some of the things they've been up to I couldn't bring myself to write down. Maxine doesn't know and I've been in two minds whether to tell her, but I decided against it. She's got enough on her plate right now and she despises Brent anyway. I feel ever so sorry for her. All the time now she's moping over that guy she used to court back home, Howard, the vicar. Do you remember him? He was a nice guy and they suited each other, I reckon. It was rotten of him not to write to her though when he moved to a different part of the country. She married Brent on the rebound and now she regrets it bitterly. Anyway, she's stuck with him. More's the pity I say. And him turning out to be such a swine as well. I'd kill him if he were mine.

I hope Eleanor is OK and that you are treating her well. Don't let her read this letter, though, as I've said such horrible things about Brent. Although, on second thoughts she might agree with me. After all, I suppose she knows Brent as well as anybody, and she left him, didn't she.

Well, I must close now, Stephen, as we are due to practise in a little while. Give my love to Mom and Dad if you see them, although I shall be writing to them as well in a day or two.

Lots of love,
Pansy.

Stephen read the letter again; the relevant bit; just to be sure he'd read it right. Brent had married Maxine and the scoundrel, who patently did not deserve her, was making her life a misery.

Maybe it was time he helped his erstwhile girlfriend. He could not bear to think of her being grossly unhappy with that out-and-out swine when she truly did not deserve it.

Besides, he could help her.

He felt obliged to help.

In Hollywood, filming of The Owls and the Pussycats' contribution to *The Loop Mob* went according to schedule and the director was happy that 'it was in the can'. Maxine enjoyed the experience of working with movie people and appreciated the effort that went into the making of a film. Everything had to be perfect, else whatever it was they were working on had to be done over and over. She had seen the first prints of the speakeasy scenes where she performed the two songs and listened to Duke Ellington's arrangement and her rendering of 'Does He Ever Think of Me'.

Maxine was happy with the song and with the arrangement. The realism of the set they had constructed also struck her, and the atmosphere they'd created reminded her of the Onyx Club in New York. She looked good too, and she sounded good; as did the rest of the band.

So they returned to New York satisfied they had done a good job. None of them enjoyed the flights greatly. The novelty of flying soon wore off by virtue of the unexpected discomforts, although it was interesting to see America as it swept slowly beneath them for the long daylight hours they seemed to hang suspended in the air. They arrived back in New York on 12th September, a Sunday, with a few days off to recover before a week of appearances at the Open Door Club on Fifty-second Street.

Brent and Maxine had occupied adjoining rooms in their Los Angeles hotel for the duration of the filming, although intimacy between them belonged to the past. Following Maxine's stand on the hiring of Fletcher Henderson and Duke Ellington to do the arrangements for her songs, contact had remained cool but relatively civil. Brent, not unexpectedly, complained that the arrangements were weak, that the trombone line did not give him scope to show his capabilities, but everybody else seemed perfectly content. The film crew enthused over the songs and forecast sure-fire hits. In Los Angeles they went to parties, Brent and Maxine, entering as a happy smiling couple who were deemed to be in love. During those times, there did seem to be some accord, certainly enough to fool their hosts, other guests, and the gossip columnists too. But they were celebrities and it was a bluff. In private, the cold aloofness returned, and God knows what Brent got up to in Los Angeles when she was asleep in bed.

The band too, was indeed divided into two camps by this time. Nobody was openly hostile but the atmosphere was strained. The camaraderie and banter they used to enjoy before their success, was gone. Maxine seemed to have a foot in both camps by virtue of her relationship with Brent, although it was less complicated than that in reality. As far as she was concerned, Brent and Kenny could go jump off a skyscraper if they wanted. Dulcie, diplomatically, kept away from the band and their performances, which limited the time she could be with Charlie. Charlie consequently had mentioned to Maxine that he was thinking of resigning so he could spend more time with Dulcie. It all seemed to be falling apart.

Well, Maxine was sceptical about that. He and Dulcie had not been together long enough to consider giving up his career for her. So, next day, Monday, she telephoned Dulcie. She wanted somebody to talk to and this seemed a plausible excuse.

'Maxine! How was Hollywood?'

'Great.'

'Oh, wonderful. How's Brent?'

'Absolutely irrelevant. Have you heard from Charlie yet?'

'Yes, I'm seeing him tonight.'

'Not till tonight? Good. Dulcie, I want to talk to you. Is there somewhere we can go? Maybe we can play tourists. Is there somewhere I haven't been yet?'

410

'The Statue of Liberty?'

'That sounds good. And maybe we can have lunch somewhere afterwards.'

'Sure. Shall I meet you in the Plaza lobby?'

'In about an hour? It'll take me till then to look decent.'

So Maxine told Brent she would be out all day and, wearing a lightweight navy Chanel suit, went down to the opulent lobby to wait for Dulcie. She sat on a sumptuous settee and looked around at the classic pillars picked out in gold leaf. A huge glass chandelier hung sparkling from the elaborate Renaissance ceiling. Only six months ago she wouldn't have dreamt she would ever stay in a place like this. Maxine heard the click of high-heels approaching her on the marble floor and turned to see Dulcie standing and smiling at her, wearing a bright yellow day dress that vied with her blonde hair but complimented her blue eyes. The two girls admired each other's daywear and stepped outside, where a concierge hailed a cab that took them to Battery Park and the ferry terminal. They queued like tourists and it was while they were on the ferry to Bedloe's Island and the huge bronze Liberty monument that Maxine steered the conversation to Dulcie and Charlie.

'How's it going with you two?'

'Charlie and me? Oh, he's sweet. He's so different to Kenny. So reserved, so unassuming. Kenny's so blustery – like a gale-force wind. Charlie's like a gentle breeze.'

'Are you in love with him, Dulcie?'

'With Charlie? Heck, I don't know about *that*, Maxine. I like him. He's a real nice guy. He'd make somebody a decent husband, that's for sure.'

'Do you think you were ever in love with Kenny?'

Seagulls screeched overhead, following the ferry, swooping for scraps of bread that the breeze caught, chucked up for them by enthusiastic children, fascinated that seagulls could be so clever as to catch them in mid-air.

'Looking back, I don't think I ever was,' Dulcie replied.

'Something always held me back – his being married, I guess. And I was never confident of his ability or willingness to be faithful . . . Don't get me wrong, Maxine, I enjoyed being with him. He made me laugh. He taught me a thing or two about sex, too, I can tell you, and I *loved* it. But was I in love with him? I'm not so sure. Then, when you told me he had a son . . .'

'Dulcie, did you know Charlie's considering giving up the band so's he can spend more time with you?'

'No,' she answered simply. 'And I hope he doesn't. That would be crazy.'

'Thank you. I just thought I should let you know. Perhaps you should have a word with him. Reassure him. I reckon it's jealousy over Kenny.'

'He doesn't have to be jealous over Kenny. Hell!'

'Doesn't he?' Maxine chuckled. 'After what you've just told me, I'm not so sure.'

'Sex isn't everything, Maxine,' Dulcie replied in all seriousness.

'No? Try telling that to somebody who's not getting any.'

'You mean you?' Dulcie regarded her friend thoughtfully. She had learnt to read her well. 'You're still grieving over Howard, aren't you?'

Maxine nodded and Dulcie witnessed Maxine's eyes fill with tears. 'I could kick myself, Dulcie,' she said, her voice breaking up. 'I had the best man in the world and I let him slip through my fingers. I must have been mad . . . God! I must have been stark, staring mad . . .'

'He sure as hell struck every note on your keyboard, huh? Why not just go back to him?'

Maxine sighed. She looked down over the rail at the water as it surged along the side of the ferryboat's prow and reminded of being aboard the *Queen Mary*, enjoyed the wind in her hair.

'I'm a married woman, Dulcie – or had it slipped your mind? And he's a vicar in the Church of England. And ne'er the twain shall meet . . .'

'But if you were divorced . . .'

'Especially if I was divorced. Being divorced in England is regarded as worse than being a murderer – especially by the Church. The stigma! Just look what happened to Edward VIII over Mrs Simpson – and he was King. Besides, there's the band to think of – I have responsibilities to the band.'

'Pity some of the band don't share your conscientiousness . . .'

'In any case, Dulcie, it's obvious Howard didn't want me. He never wrote, remember.'

'I know. That's too bad. And I'm so sorry.'

'Not half as sorry as me . . .' She shielded her eyes as she turned and looked out towards Bedloe's Island. 'You know, that's a hell of a statue, Dulcie.'

'Do you want to go to the top? The whole thing is more than three hundred feet high and you'd have to climb more than three hundred and fifty steps.'

'Let's see how we feel when we've reached the balcony at the top of that plinth thing,' Maxine replied, daunted at the prospect. 'That is a balcony, isn't it?'

'Sure, it's a balcony . . . Hey, tell me about Hollywood, Maxine. Did you meet any movie stars?'

'Hey, yes. I met Spencer Tracy,' she replied with sudden enthusiasm and a smile that these days was too rare. 'At a party. And Tyrone Power – *he's* absolutely gorgeous. I swear if Brent hadn't been by my side he'd have propositioned me.'

'And how would you have responded?'

'Who knows? I might even have propositioned *him*. Anyway, he didn't, so that was that. Another romance doomed before it even started. I was introduced to Edward G Robinson and Humphrey Bogart as well.'

'Hey, wow!'

'*And* I met James Whale . . .'

'James Whale?'

'The director. You know. He made those Frankenstein films.'

'Oh, right.'

'He comes from my home town.' Maxine stated proudly then chuckled as she recalled the moment. 'When I told him I came from Dudley he asked me if I knew his sister, and I said, "No, but my mother might." He didn't seem very impressed. But I didn't mean to be sarcastic or anything.'

Dulcie chuckled too. 'You met nobody else?'

'Some, but I didn't know who they were. Oh, I saw Ginger Rogers – from a distance. And Robert Taylor.'

'And did the filming go well?'

Maxine explained that the speakeasy set was in an enormous studio, and that they'd had to do several takes to get the best angled shots. They'd had to mime, she said, because the recording they did earlier was overdubbed onto the soundtrack later.

'So what did you think of Los Angeles?'

'Oh, I loved it . . .'

By the time Maxine had eulogised over Los Angeles, the ferry was tying up at Bedloe's Island.

Of course, they made it eventually to the very top, to Liberty's crown, and peered over at the Manhattan skyline for some time before they decided it was time to come down and seek some lunch.

When they returned to Battery Park, Dulcie pointed out the Shrine of Elizabeth Ann Seton. 'She was the first American to be made a saint by the Catholic Church,' she informed her friend, 'and founded the American Sisters of Charity. After the Civil War, this place became a shelter for Irish immigrant women.'

'What about English immigrant women? Were they excluded?'

'Oh, I guess they all had men to look after them,' Dulcie replied with satirical charm.

'More gallant than the one I've got, I hope,' Maxine commented flippantly.

They had lunch at the Fraunces Tavern on Pearl Street, a place

Dulcie chose. After they had eaten they sat enjoying a beer. They were relaxed and conversation flowed.

'I brought you here because it has historical connections,' Dulcie said. 'Since you're sightseeing today like any English tourist. And the English enjoy history, huh?'

'Well if that's the case,' Maxine chirped, taking in the wood-burning fireplace and the Spartan colonial atmosphere, 'tell me the history of this place.'

'Gee! Don't make life so difficult, Maxine. Heck! All I know is that about thirty years ago, the place was restored to how it was before the Revolution.' She looked around her at the other tourists who had visited the place out of curiosity. 'The place was a meeting point for Revolutionaries. Maybe George Washington used to get stoned here. He's said to have been connected with the place, anyhow. I guess this is pretty much how it must have looked . . . Seems like a man's place to me.'

'I don't mind it being a man's place.' Maxine sipped her drink thoughtfully. 'I have to take a fresh view of men, I think, Dulcie,' she said wistfully. 'I can't see Brent and me being together much longer – at least I hope not. You know, I reckon I'd never be short of offers nowadays . . . if I was of that frame of mind to take advantage.'

'I guess that's true,' Dulcie concurred. 'Heck, you're a real slick chick. Famous too. The guys are always giving you the once-over. I see them. I envy you your looks, Maxine. I guess you could have any guy you wanted.'

'So why do I end up with a man I don't want, Dulcie? I went badly wrong somewhere . . .' She lowered her voice. 'You know, it's refreshing in this country how everybody talks so openly about sex.'

'Maxine, you have to be joking! Women talk about guys, but nobody ever talks about sex. The average American is too conservative and too hide-bound by moral virtues to talk openly about sex. Sure, they might think about it all day long, but talk about it? Never.'

'But you, Dulcie. You're not afraid to talk openly about it. You were saying things to me just a little while ago . . .'

'To you, Maxine. Only to you. You're my buddy.'

'Even buddies don't talk that openly about sex in England. In England women are supposed not to enjoy sex. Society certainly doesn't encourage them to talk about it. And if you have sex before you get married, God forbid you ever admit to it. Why, it's said that most women are so prudish that the men in England never see them with no clothes on. Can you believe that?'

'But people do have sex before they get married in England, surely? I guess they sure do in America.'

'Oh, I suppose most courting couples get round to it eventually. Up against the mangle or the brewhouse door with their underwear round their knees, some of them.' She chuckled at the thought. 'But they'd never admit to it . . . Unless they get a big lump on their belly. That tends to give the game away.'

Dulcie laughed too at the mental picture Maxine's words conjured. 'Doesn't society have some whacky ideas? How did we ever get to that state? I mean, how do you know whether you're gonna love a guy heart and soul if you don't have sex with him first? Hell! You don't buy a new dress without first trying it on . . .'

The analogy amused Maxine. 'I suppose there's good logic in that . . .'

'You bet there is . . . Anyway . . . how was it with Brent?'

'You mean sex?' Maxine blushed, which amused Dulcie.

'Oh, go on. You have to tell me, Maxine.'

'I have to?'

'It's only fair. I told you about Kenny and me.'

She hesitated, wondering how best to describe it without sounding like a well-seasoned whore. Talking about her sexual experiences was not something that came naturally. 'At first it was nice, I suppose,' she began unsurely. 'I thought I was in love with him and he'd been trying desperately to woo me. He was attentive and tender and considerate – and I was flattered. I also needed that kind of attention.'

'So what went wrong?'

'Well, I moved into his cabin when we were on board ship and I reckon he had to prove he was a sexual athlete. I guess he had to prove to me that he was a better lover than Howard was.'

'And was he?'

'Hell, no. He gave me no inner peace. With Howard there was always an inner peace after making love that was wonderful. With Brent, lovemaking lost its tenderness and warmth. We seemed to be doing it just for the sake of it. I felt I was nothing more than a receptacle he could deposit his semen into when the inclination took him. It got to the stage when I couldn't bear him touching me. I was like that before, when I used to go out with Stephen . . . And I kept thinking more and more about Howard . . . I still do . . .' She sighed and turned away momentarily from Dulcie. Already she felt she had told her too much. 'What shall we do afterwards, Dulcie?'

'Well, Maxine. Talking about sex has made me feel kinda horny. Would you mind if I came back to the Plaza with you? I got an urge to see Charlie.'

'I thought you were seeing him tonight.'

'Yeah, but I can't wait.'

Maxine's eyes lit up and she giggled. 'Are you going to . . . ? You're not going to seduce him?'

'Sure. Why not? I gotta get him going sometime. He needs a little encouragement.'

Chapter 31

The girls returned to the Plaza hotel, the structure that, despite its eighteen storeys, was reminiscent of a French Renaissance château. In the lobby, the concierge tipped his hat and a bellboy pressed the lift button for them and received a quarter for his trouble. Dulcie exited at the twelfth floor and Maxine rode on up. At the fifteenth she stepped out and, as she walked along the corridor to their suite, she took the key from her handbag and inserted it in the lock.

When she opened the door she was surprised to hear a voice, a woman's voice, whimpering, weeping, as if she were being hurt. Very quietly Maxine withdrew the key and silently closed the door. She slipped off her shoes and crept along the vestibule.

The sounds were emanating from the bedroom.

The door was ajar.

She peered through the gap at the reflection in the long mirrors on the wardrobe doors that were opposite the door.

Brent was lying on his back while a woman with long dark hair was riding him as if he were a stallion in the Grand National. What Maxine had thought was weeping was actually her groans and squeals of pleasure.

Maxine looked on in disbelief, fixed to the spot. That shining dark hair and the set of the head were disturbingly familiar. She knew that slender back from its poise and elegance. She knew that slim waist from the fancy belts she'd seen tightly adorning it. She knew, from the fashionable trousers she'd seen her wear,

418

whose small buttocks and slim hips were thrusting back and forth as if she were riding a great hunter with the stirrups short.

It was Eleanor.

Maxine gasped. An opened bottle of champagne stood on one of the bedside tables along with two half-empty glasses. Maldwyn, the teddy bear that Howard had won for her was perched upright on the dressing table as if deliberately, to witness this copulatory epic. What should she do now? Should she simply go and let them get on with it? Or should she scream and shout and make an overall unpleasant scene? It was such a ridiculous decision to have to make. After all, if she cared for Brent at all . . .

Then, the decision was made for her; the keys she was carrying slipped through her fingers and jangled metallically as they hit the carpeted floor. Maxine shoved the door open impulsively. At once Eleanor looked around, startled, and was horrified to see Maxine staring open-mouthed at her. She ceased her jockeying and dismounted at once, prompting an instant welter of complaints from Brent who, a moment later, also saw Maxine.

'Jesus!' he exclaimed, and a stupid grin appeared on his face. 'You don't half pick your times, Maxine.'

'Not half as impetuously as you pick your women,' Maxine responded haughtily, still not sure how she should react. But instinct took over. Eleanor was annoying her already with that sullen, scornful look of hers that suggested Maxine was the interloper. 'You, get out!' she yelled. 'However long you've been here, get out and take that pond life with you.'

Eleanor looked for support from Brent, but received none. She slid off the bed and, with a look of silent disdain, unhurriedly picked up her clothes that were scattered around the room.

Maxine grabbed Eleanor's handbag that was lying on the floor near her feet and threw it at her. 'Get out!' she screamed, and picked up a bottle of perfume from her dressing table. She hurled it at her, but it missed and bounced off the bed and onto the floor. Eleanor, more hurriedly now, donned her emerald green underwear, expensive, silk, smooth. Maxine watched, suddenly breathless as the girl slipped her fine emerald green day dress over her head and fastened it. Even in this ridiculous situation she looked extraordinarily cool and glamorous.

'And you!' Maxine shrieked at Brent. 'I've put up with a lot from you, but if you think I'm putting up with any more you can think again. Get out! . . . *Get Out!*' She took a hairbrush from her dressing table and approached him as he lay on the bed. At least he'd had the decency to cover his nether regions with a sheet by now, but his hands went to his head to protect himself as she rained blows on him. 'Get out!' she screamed, 'and don't ever come back. I don't ever want to see you again – either of you. Get out and let me have some peace and contentment.'

Brent wriggled, then darted out of the bed and escaped from her like the coward he was, grabbing his clothes. 'I'm going, don't worry,' he said with a sneer, pulling on his underpants. 'If I ever see your priggish face again it will be too soon.'

'Priggish, am I? Well at least I'm not a junkie. Now go . . . *Go* . . .'

They went. She heard the door click as they left the apartment. Maxine sat on the bed – the bed on which those two had been making love – and began trembling.

What now?

She tried to shed tears but it seemed that tears were off today. She was angry; too angry for tears. In any case, those two weren't worth tears. She caught a glimpse of herself in the wardrobe mirror. Her hair was unkempt as if she'd been in a fight. She tried to tidy it, running her fingers through it. She was beginning to calm down but it had been such a shock. Fancy them . . . Oh, she knew Brent had been up to no good since the day he arrived in New York. The place offered too many distractions, too many temptations. But fancy *her* . . . The nerve! The brassbound effrontery! How long had *she* been in New York? How many times had they . . . ? How had she found him?

Of course, Brent had written to her . . . Presumably, it meant that she and Stephen had parted. Good for Stephen. He deserved better.

Maxine began to feel relieved that Brent had gone, as if some oppressive weight that had been bearing down hard on her had been suddenly lifted. All right, she was still married to him, but this incident had given her the excuse never to be alone with him again, never to live under the same roof. She must even have grounds for divorce. But she would have to meet him on stage and at rehearsals – if the band stayed together. And the prospect of that grew dimmer the more she thought about it. Maybe he would realise he could never face her again and resign from the band. They could soon find another trombonist.

But wait; she was looking at this from the viewpoint of some-body who still had some moral ethics. Brent possessed none. He had the brass-necked nerve to ignore such niceties. He would not suffer from the same embarrassment that she had experienced tonight. It would not unsettle *him*. See how he had leered unruffled at her when she found them together? She could try to forget he ever existed. Meanwhile, she could form a new band, become a solo artiste. John Fielding would help.

And while these thoughts swirled through her head, some logical, some disjointed, one more thought suddenly struck her.

Brent would be back.

He would be back for his clothes, back for his trombone, back for his musical arrangements, back not least to antagonise her. So, to lessen the time it was necessary for him to stay when he did return, she decided to pack up all his things and leave them by the entrance to the suite, ready.

Their suitcases were piled in a cupboard; old ones; and new ones they'd bought to carry the increasing amount of luggage they took with them everywhere nowadays. She grabbed the first two that were to hand, an old one and a new one, and lugged them to the bedroom where she placed the new one on the bed. She would ask the hotel's housekeeper to have this bed changed when she was through; she didn't relish the thought of sleeping on sheets that those two had cavorted on. She opened the suitcase and began filling it with shirts, trousers, underwear, ties, pullovers; anything that presented itself in his drawers and wardrobes. Soon it was full and she pressed down on the lid to close it. That done, she lifted it off the bed and placed it on the floor.

She grabbed the older case. It was one of Brent's. He had used it when they first left Birmingham bound for the *Queen Mary*. As she lifted it by the handle, it flew open and, as it knocked against the bed, she noticed a corner of blue paper suddenly appear from inside the lining that was coming adrift from the side. She righted the suitcase and placed it on the bed as she had done with the previous one, then held back the lining out of curiosity to see exactly what the paper was.

Four blue envelopes.

Maxine pulled them out and looked at each in turn. All were addressed to her, in handwriting that looked agonisingly familiar. She had not seen them before, yet they had already been opened. Suddenly feeling very hot and with a profoundly thumping heart, she opened one, took out the letter it contained and read it.

The Vicarage
Foxham
Norfolk

Friday 13th November 1936

My dear darling Maxine,
After much soul-searching and deliberation I have postponed writing this promised epistle until nearer the time of your return to Southampton. That is to say, I have not rushed to write as soon as you were gone, but nearly two weeks after. That way, I hope I have avoided being overly sentimental at the wretched way we parted that Monday night, having given myself time to ponder everything in greater depth. I must say, I now firmly accept that your reaction to my not telling you

from the outset about my taking the living here in Norfolk was absolutely deserved and I do not blame you in the least for your anger. Experiencing it has been a salutary lesson in affording greater consideration to other people's feelings — specifically yours. Believe me, I am a changed man. But not merely changed: I believe I am changed for the better.

I hope and pray with all my heart that God is keeping you safe and that your nautical adventure is proving enjoyable. These eight weeks are going to drag on interminably before ever I get the chance to see you again and hold you in my arms.

I suppose I have been fortunate in that the move to Norfolk has, to some extent, diverted me from thoughts of you. But not nearly entirely. In my quieter moments, and especially in my big lonely bed at night, I have thought of you constantly. I have ached for the warmth of your body against mine and have scolded myself interminably for effecting this absurd consequence of not having you near. I do hope you are feeling a little more kindly disposed towards me after this first couple of weeks apart.

The whole episode has focused my thoughts even more on the desirability of marriage. I cannot stand to lose you, Maxine, and I urge you to give it your earnest consideration. I wish you to be my wife, my darling, so please consider this my official marriage proposal! I await, of course, anxiously and pray nightly for your positive response.

Maxine, I will close now. I believe I have made my feelings and my intentions absolutely clear. I love you and miss you more than I thought possible. Please be home soon. Please be my wife. God bless you and keep you always.

All my love,
Howard.

She began to weep uncontrollably.

So he had written. He'd written and he still loved her after all . . . then at least. He had wanted to marry her . . . then.

But since she had not replied, what would he think now? That she'd received his letters and decided to ignore them? That she was a fickle, unfeeling vixen?

He was bound to think that.

But Brent was to blame. Brent had callously intercepted them and hidden them away from her like some overbearing father trying to protect a virgin daughter from an inappropriate gigolo.

How could he? What right did he have?

Of course, he had no right. He had no right at all.

She wiped her eyes on her handkerchief and sniffed. So that was the first letter Howard had written. The first of four. She opened another to glean his reaction to not getting her reply.

The Vicarage
Foxham
Norfolk

Friday 27th November 1936
Maxine, my one and only love,
Every morning since the return of the Queen Mary to Southampton, I have rushed in vain to the letterbox here in the vicarage to collect your reply. I can only hope that there is some hitch in the postal system between that great port and Foxham. It wouldn't surprise me, in fact, since this area is quite remote. So I write this second letter in the hope that it arrives safely and that you will reply first chance you get.

I have settled in here quite well. Foxham is a very small town, less than 2000 souls, I believe, yet the church is disproportionately large and grand for such a relatively small population. However, everybody here has welcomed me warmly and they are all very friendly, although some have said how surprised they are to get a vicar so young and one who is unmarried! I have told them that as time goes by both states will be altered, God and you willing! I must say it is very rural, close-knit, and very different to Birmingham.

I don't know whether you will like the vicarage. It is a mausoleum, huge, Georgian, and in desperate need of repair. It is also damp, cold and costs a fortune in fire coal. Maybe I should not tell you this for fear it puts you off coming, but I have determined never to keep anything from you ever again. The grounds are enormous, too, but I suspect that in summer they host acceptable gardens and I understand that provision is made for a gardener as well as the housekeeper and staff I seem to have inherited. No doubt I shall be expected to hold garden parties. Incidentally, there is a strong American connection here, which you will learn about in due course.

Anyway, my darling, my offer of marriage still stands! I love you and miss you far more than you could ever imagine. I can't wait for your first letter to arrive and I long for the day when we are together again. Meanwhile, be happy and safe sailing across the Atlantic, but please don't enjoy yourself too much and forget all about me. I have the unenviable task now of composing two sermons for services tomorrow. God alone knows what I shall preach!

Please write soon and let me know you still love me, because the waiting is unbearable.

Love now and forever,
Howard.

It had been ten months since she had cast eyes on him, ten months since she had heard his voice. It had been ten months since he had written these words and in those ten months his love for her had more than likely expired. In ten months he could have fallen in love with another girl and might even have married, even as she had married. If he had, she hoped his marriage was a success and not the dismal failure hers was. But even if he had not married, even if he remained single, he could never marry her when she eventually became divorced, and risk expulsion from the Church. What strange and cruel tricks life plays on us. She would give everything she owned, everything she'd earned to put the clock back ten months to that weekend before she left him for the incredibly eventful journey to the present day.

She opened another letter, dated 26th December – Boxing Day. His last letter.

My darling,
Writing this letter is likely to be one of the most difficult and heartbreaking things I am ever likely to do. This is my fourth letter to you and I am writing not knowing whether you have received my last three letters or, if you have, whether you are deliberately ignoring them. Just knowing I have your love would make life bearable, but I do not know it any longer. If you have not received my previous letters, I pray you receive this, for I love you more than words can say and look forward to the day you are here to be my wife. If you have received them but are ignoring them, what must I do to get you to reply? I need you, Maxine. Without you, I barely exist. Life is nothing without you and hardly worth the living.

However, I must plod on. I have a job to do here and I am determined to do it and it is only the prospect of work, and events that challenge me every day, that keep my feet planted on the ground.

Write to me, Maxine. Let me know what you feel. If you do not write to me then come to me as soon as you can on your return to these shores. Whatever you do, let me know that you love me.
Yours eternally,
Howard.

With misty eyes she opened the last remaining letter, the one that was his third to her. He reaffirmed his love and his growing concern at a lack of any reply. He enlarged on the community in which he worked and the church itself, but she could tell from his tone that he was growing despondent. He was already living in fear that he might have lost her.

She wept again. Never in her life had she felt so wretched, so unhappy. *She* had lost *him*. She had lost irretrievably the love of her life because she had been deprived of his letters and his love by a callous, heartless brute that masqueraded as a man, when no decent man would ever do what he had done. He had *no* right. She rued the day she ever met Brent Shackleton. How had she ever been so stupid as to be drawn into his dark, degenerate world, into his sordid lair? Why had she ever allowed him to seduce her? His life, his love, his work, his music, his very existence was a sham. How could she ever shake off the fetters of this abhorrent marriage to him? Oh, sure, she might well be able to divorce him – she would get a lawyer onto it tomorrow – but divorce itself would deny her the dream of marrying Howard.

Maxine put the letters safely in her handbag and wiped her tears for the umpteenth time. She needed some fresh air. She needed some space around her. She needed to get out of this stinking room that had witnessed, like her, that act of fornication that merely confirmed that Brent was, and always had been, capable of adultery; not only Brent but Eleanor, too. So, she quickly splashed cold water around her eyes to reduce the puffiness of her tears, tidied her face and headed for the lift that would take her to the lobby and the warm afternoon air of New York city.

Maxine dodged the ever-lurking photographer at the entrance to the Plaza Hotel and turned east onto Grand Army Plaza. The sky was a hazy blue and the sun shone in her eyes as she headed south along Fifth Avenue, one of New York's richest streets, swish and sophisticated. She hardly noticed the dust swirling in the breeze and the constant roar of the traffic. She opened her expensive crocodile skin handbag and took out her expensive sunglasses to shield and hide her eyes. To retrieve them she had to rummage past her expensive Cartier powder compact and her tiny bottle of expensive Guerlain perfume. A thought struck her and, as she looked down at the expensive Chanel suit she was wearing, at the trappings of wealth, she was flabbergasted by their irrelevance.

Money.

She had been manipulated, twisted and emotionally tortured because of money.

She walked on in her solitude and realised she was nothing more than another victim of that great city. For all the wealth she had generated she was as poor as the nearest panhandler; poor, because her treasury of dreams had long since been ransacked.

After about half a mile she passed St Thomas's church. She considered entering and offering a prayer for herself and for Howard; for Brent, even. But why stop when she could pray while she walked? And she needed to walk.

She turned west onto Fifty-second Street. There, like a monument, stood the Onyx Club; the place they had scored their notable success, where the whole of America, it seemed, wanted to engage the services of The Owls and the Pussycats to help swell their own overflowing coffers. There too was the Open Door Club. The band was due to appear there in a few days, but somehow she doubted whether they would make it. Certainly, she doubted whether *she* would make it.

A beggar approached her with dirty clutching hands and shifty eyes and asked if she could spare a dime. She stopped, felt in her handbag and handed over her small change. The poor devil's plight, unfamiliar to her, weighed heavy. She had forgotten about the beggars with their ravaged faces, their washed-up appearances and their reeking clothes, diverted by her life of material splendour at the Plaza. Roosevelt's New Deal was improving life for some, but the down-and-outs were still too numerous.

The swirling dust rose again and she had to shut her eyes to protect them. A heavily pregnant woman accosted her, in rags and tatters and Maxine handed over several dollar bills. The state of the woman touched her heart, but could not dislodge thoughts of Howard, thoughts of Brent. She walked on, faster and faster, preoccupied with the heartbreak he had suffered because of Brent's selfish, unfeeling behaviour, aware, indeed of the heartbreak she herself had suffered and was still suffering. And just what had Brent achieved by his despicableness? Absolutely nothing, bar ruining the lives of two decent people.

Her blouse was sticking to her in the heat and her shoes were making her feet sore as she crossed Broadway, dodging the traffic. The buildings here on West Fifty-second Street were less grand. A drunk confronted her and wanted to know how much a classy dame like her charged. Indignant, she told him he couldn't afford her and continued briskly with her nose in the air. A little way further on, she hid in a doorway while a group of vagrants fought like jackals for the biggest bones and scraps of food plundered from a bin of garbage, in this city she'd grown to love; this, the most dazzling city on earth.

As litter flapped like white birds in the capricious breeze, the sounds of a love song drifted over from a juke joint and Maxine heard her own voice singing 'Destiny Jests with Me'. How pitifully ironic! Was this her destiny? The wretched, derelict life of a once promising young jazz singer, defiled by an avaricious husband who had no more sense than to let himself be ruined by mind-numbing drugs and strong booze, who had no thoughts higher than his groin. She felt an affinity with these destitutes trapped by circumstances over which they had no control and for whom there was no escape.

The scavengers abandoned what remained of their spoils to seek others. Maxine carried on walking, picking her way over bones that had been picked clean, over broken bottles and comatose drunks. Some day, that man she'd married would be one of their number. How low were some folk prepared to sink to?

It was then she told herself she did not have to drift along on this wayward tide. She had the intelligence to determine her own direction. She had been drawn off course by a treacherous undercurrent. Okay, so it was an undercurrent that might maroon a lesser person. But she was not about to be marooned. She would make it back. Without Brent she had no useless freight to weigh her down and hold her back.

She would make a fresh start, reform the band. She would find a new drummer, a new trombonist, a new guitarist; get rid of the troublesome negative element. She would build the new band around Pansy and Toots and Charlie, if Charlie was still of a mind to play. She would write more songs, make much more money . . . But she would give much of it away . . . Think of the poor kids that must have been born to this squalor. Think of that poor, pregnant beggar woman.

Maxine realised she was on Twelfth Avenue and overlooking Pier Ninety. Her heart sank further. The *Queen Mary* was berthed there. Of course. It was Monday. It would have arrived today. It drew her like a magnet and she watched the comings and goings. Thoughts of home brought a tear to her eye. Oh, if only she could get home; if only for a couple of weeks. Did she really want to start a new band after all? Did she really want to risk her heart and soul in another band for it to be ripped apart by puerile, greedy musicians who had the unfortunate knack of latching on to the wrong company and sleeping with the wrong women?

Maybe not. Not yet, at any rate.

She stood gazing at the *Queen Mary* for some time, recalling the couple of months she had spent cosseted by its overwhelming splendour. She pondered how life aboard had tricked her into accepting a different set of values, had deceived her by mollifying the heartache she felt over Howard, had beguiled her into taking a flawed view of love and those who claimed to love her.

Well, it would not deceive her again.

She turned to walk away but her feet were so sore. The heel of her right foot had rubbed against her shoe and it was bleeding; she was not used to walking this far, especially after this morning's outing. So she hailed a taxicab and returned to the Plaza.

Chapter 32

As soon as she arrived back at the Plaza Maxine took a bath. Her walk through New York's dusty streets had made her feel dirty and grubby. She was still pondering the unfortunate individuals she'd encountered. She was still half-hearted about reforming the band and she considered it in the light of the incident with Brent and Eleanor and her ill-starred marriage. She washed her hair, dried it and did it up in a roll. She cleaned her teeth, applied some make-up and began to feel human again. Despairingly, she took Howard's letters from her handbag. She sat down, re-read them and considered again the unnecessary pain and anguish he had suffered. If only she could say how sorry she was. If only she could let him know somehow that she still felt the same way she'd always felt.

But what would she gain? Nothing could come of it but the cruel lacerating of wounds that had never healed. She replaced Howard's letters securely in her handbag and stood up, her head full of his words. Her mouth was dry. She hadn't had a drink since lunch. So she telephoned room service, asked for a pot of tea and meanwhile drank some water.

While she waited, she set about packing more of Brent's things. He had far more now than when they first started sharing a cabin on the *Queen Mary*. Good thing they had these extra suitcases. She cleared out his remaining drawers and his wardrobe, then removed his toiletries from the bathroom and put them in the small travelling case he'd bought for such things.

She was just about to place the bag into one of the suitcases when she heard a knock at the door. Room service? Brent?

She was surprised to see Pansy standing at the door, grinning.

'God, Maxine, where have you been all day? We've called a dozen times to see if you were back.'

'Sorry. I was out with Dulcie this morning and I went for a walk by myself this afternoon. Is something the matter?'

'Brent's not here, is he?' she asked in a half whisper.

'No, thank God. He's gone. For good. I've chucked him out.'

Pansy couldn't help smiling. 'Chucked him out? Brilliant! That's the best news I've heard in a long time. Tell us about it. Can we come in?'

'We?' Maxine queried uncertainly, seeing only Pansy.

'There's somebody here to see you. Close your eyes . . . No, close your eyes, Maxine!' Unknown to Maxine, Pansy gave a signal and two other people came out of hiding and crept towards her. They stood at the door grinning. 'Okay. You can open them now . . .'

'Stephen!' Like the old friends that they were, they hugged each other. 'This is one hell of a surprise.'

'I thought you'd be shocked,' he said warmly. 'Oh, you look great, Maxine. Really well turned-out.'

'And so do you.' She was aware of a girl she did not know hovering in the background wearing an appealing smile. 'So are you going to introduce me?' She at once felt pleased for Stephen that such an appealing and respectable looking girl accompanied him. Maybe she was a new love in his life. She was certainly different to Eleanor.

'This is Cassandra,' Stephen said. 'Cassandra . . . the famous Maxine Kite.'

The girls shook hands and said how pleased they were to meet.

'Oh, please come inside. I've just sent down for a pot of tea. I can always ask them to bring drinks for all of us. What would you like?'

'Maybe a bottle of champagne wouldn't be inappropriate,' Stephen suggested abstrusely.

'Champagne? Are we celebrating something, Stephen?' Maxine asked, glancing at Cassandra who smiled back pleasantly. She was curious about this girl with the intelligent eyes and warm demeanour, especially after Eleanor's unexpected but fateful appearance earlier.

'We hope to be, eh, Pansy? Eh, Cass?'

'Oh? So what are we celebrating? Please sit down and tell me.' Maxine felt the despondency slough off her like a dead skin. 'I can't get over it. It's such a surprise to see you, Stephen. I never expected to see you here in New York. Mind you, having said that, I didn't expect to see Eleanor either . . .'

'Eleanor?' A look of disquiet clouded Stephen's face. 'You've seen *her*? Here? In New York? Are you sure?'

'Oh, I'm sure, Stephen.'

'Hell! I didn't know she was in New York.'

'Oh, she's here all right. Believe me. Large as life, twice as glamorous – as usual – and three times as obnoxious, if you'll forgive me for saying so. She's gone with Brent. For good, I think. I er . . . I got back this afternoon and found them . . . well . . . in my bed, frankly.'

Cassandra smiled sympathetically. So far she had said nothing, but now she spoke. 'Were you upset, Maxine?' she asked, with genuine concern in her clear blue eyes. 'Were you shocked? Are you all right?'

'Shocked, yes . . . And damned angry. But not too upset. I'm afraid Brent demolished any feelings I had for him ages ago. That's true, isn't it, Pansy? Let me order those drinks from room service. What would you like?'

'Tea will be fine, thank you,' Cassandra said.

'But tell them to put that bottle of champagne on ice ready,' Stephen added with a gleam in his eye.

Maxine telephoned for more tea but ignored the suggestion of champagne.

433

'So, tell me what you've been up to,' Maxine suggested.

Stephen smiled benignly. 'Oh, in a minute. Hey, I like that record you made, Maxine – "Destiny Jests with Me". I bought a gramophone just so I could play it. And that other one – "From Tears to a Kiss". Great! They're always on the wireless back home.'

Maxine beamed with pleasure that her records were so obviously popular with her friends. 'Has the new one come out in England yet? "It's Not Your Fault"?'

'Yes. I think I've heard that one as well. Strikes me you must be making a fortune, Maxine.'

'For all the good it's done me . . . So how are your parents, Stephen? Are they well?'

'They were fine last time I saw them . . .' A pause punctuated the conversation, till Stephen added, 'We arrived today on the *Queen Mary*, Maxine. We came all the way to America to see *you* – 'cause I particularly wanted you to meet Cassandra.'

'Well. I'm honoured.'

He looked into Maxine's eyes affectionately. 'We were always close friends, you and I, Maxine. You know I'd never do you a bad turn if I could do you a good one. Well, from what Pansy tells me about your marriage, I reckon you could really do with a good turn.'

Maxine looked at Pansy. 'How much have you told him?'

'Just about everything,' Pansy confessed. 'How unhappy you are. How you married that pig on the rebound. How you're still madly in love with Howard . . . But there's something I've told him that I haven't even told you, Maxine. And if Brent's gone, I think I should tell you anyway . . . Something Toots found out . . . I thought you should know. I mean, I like to think I'm your best friend and I'd hate you to judge me at some time in the future for holding back on something you reckoned you had the right to know.'

'So what is it?' Maxine said, intrigued. 'But I imagine there's nothing you could tell me about Brent that could surprise me now.'

Pansy uttered a little laugh of pity. 'Even so, Maxine, I don't tell you lightly. I've thought about it a lot and I think you should know. I wanted to tell you ages ago but Toots said I shouldn't interfere.'

'Go on then. You can tell me.'

Pansy shuffled her bottom on the richly upholstered seat. 'Well, you remember when we first went to Chicago?'

'I do. Very well.'

'When we arrived, you stayed in bed, didn't you, while Brent went out?'

'Yes, I was dead beat and he was hungry. He went out to get a bite. I think Kenny went with him.'

'Do you know where they went, Maxine?'

'No. And I don't really care. But tell me, if you think it matters.'

'They got a taxi driver to drop them at a nightclub. That was when they met James and Hank, the Hollywood film guys. It was them that introduced them to that funny stuff they smoke, Maxine. And that other stuff.'

'That doesn't surprise me, Pansy. Is that it?'

'Hell, no, there's more . . . These two Hollywood guys took Brent and Kenny Wheeler and a load of chorus girls from the nightclub to a real sleazy dive on the South Side. They'd hired a private room at the back with couches and divans all round the place and they showed blue movies.'

'Blue movies?' Maxine looked from one to the other with a puzzled look. 'What are blue movies, Pansy?'

'Movies that . . . where the actors and actresses do it, you know . . . have sex in front of the camera . . . on screen.'

'My God!' Maxine exclaimed, incredulous. 'Is anybody so lacking in modesty and morality these days as to actually do that on film?'

'Well, they do it for money, I expect – and attention – girls desperate to get into movies. Anyway, Maxine, while they were all watching these films, they were drinking and smoking that funny stuff, and Kenny and Brent had sex with two of the chorus girls. But in the same room as everybody else, Maxine,' Pansy elaborated. 'In full view of everybody . . . They were all at it! It was a right orgy, so Kenny told Toots.'

'I think I want to be sick, Pansy. How low can people stoop?'

'But that ain't the end of it, Maxine. When the film finished they had an interval before they showed another dirty film. Everybody swapped partners. Brent and Kenny had two different girls and they had sex with them as well.'

'Doesn't surprise me, Pansy,' Maxine said phlegmatically. 'Nothing surprises me about those two any more. They're depraved. Capable of anything. I'm just so pleased that Dulcie saw the light and got out.'

'And you as well, Maxine,' Pansy added. 'Apparently Brent's been seeing that Blanche again – regular. He's been having an affair with her.'

'And she's welcome to him,' Maxine responded resignedly.

Stephen reached forward from his seat and placed his hand over Maxine's. 'Things are not as bad as they seem, Maxine,' he said softly. 'Not half as bad.'

'Well at least Brent's gone. That's a start.'

'Something else, Maxine. Let me explain . . .'

So Stephen began his story. He told her that since he had become involved with Eleanor and she'd seen him become successful in business, she wanted to secure him in marriage, but he had always assumed she was already married.

'But Brent told me he wasn't married to her, Stephen,' Maxine interrupted. 'I knew they weren't married.'

'Oh, she told me the same thing, Maxine. But, when we were clearing Brent's house out I found a marriage certificate.'

'A marriage certificate? For Brent and Eleanor?'

'For Brent and a girl called Eleanor Christiana Beckett.'

'I don't understand. Are you saying they *were* married after all?' Maxine queried.

'It's not quite that simple. You see, the girl you know as Eleanor is not the *real* Eleanor at all. The girl *you* know is called Olive.'

'Olive?'

'Yes, Olive. She's actually Brent's sister.'

He allowed a few seconds for this snippet to sink in.

'But . . . but . . .' Maxine stammered. 'If that girl is his sister, what were they doing in bed together stark naked? How come they were—?'

'They had an incestuous relationship, Maxine.'

'Is that what they call it? Doing it with your own sister? God! It gets worse . . . The more I get to know about him the lower he sinks. You know he's a drug addict now as well? And not just marijuana. Did you know that?'

'Pansy said.'

'So who on earth was Eleanor?'

'I'm coming to that, Maxine. When I tackled Olive about it, she told me Eleanor was dead. She didn't tell me how or why she'd died, so I had to find that out for myself. Anyway, when I asked Olive who *she* was – because I didn't know yet that she was Olive, I wasn't sure who the hell she was – she refused to tell me. That meant I had to do some delving. So I went to the Cotswolds where she and Brent originated from and talked to a few people. Cassandra was one of them. She was tending a grave in a churchyard I went to. We got talking and she told me she knew the real Eleanor – better than anybody.' He squeezed the girl's hand affectionately. 'Tell Maxine what you told me, Cassandra. But tell it in the same way you told me . . . You know?'

Cassandra nodded her understanding, and Maxine thought she saw the girl's colour heighten as all eyes focused on her.

'Well,' she began, 'Eleanor was only about seventeen when she met Brent Shackleton in 1930. It was at a fair in Chipping Camden. He was charming and vibrant and very plausible. He told her all about himself, how he loved music, how he wanted to become a professional trombonist in a jazz band. And Eleanor thought that was such a glamorous, exciting thing to be. Jazz mad, he was, but he really impressed her. She fell head over heels and, of course, she told him all about herself.

'She told him that when she left finishing school she was employed as companion to a Lady Hunstanton. Unfortunately, Lady Hunstanton fell ill and became an invalid quite soon after Eleanor went to work for her. Lady Hunstanton was the last in line of an old family and had nobody to leave her money to. So she decided to leave everything to Eleanor, who she said had been so kind to her. But Eleanor made the mistake of letting Brent know she was the sole beneficiary of her will. Anyway, Brent began to show more interest. He told her how madly in love with her he was and how he wanted to spend the rest of his life with her. He was very convincing. *Very* convincing. He made it all sound so romantic. Looking back now, it's obvious that all he was interested in was the money she was destined to inherit.

'So, after Lady Hunstanton passed away on January 22nd 1931, Brent asked Eleanor to marry him. She was crazy about him so she agreed. Her mother was reticent, though. I think she saw it all as girlish infatuation, but she said if that's what Eleanor wanted, then it was up to her. She was quite liberal you see, her mother. Eleanor lost her father in the war, by the way. So, in the May they got married and went to live with his parents and Olive in Chipping Camden. Almost as soon as Lady Hunstanton's money came her way – and it was not really a vast amount, I can tell you – Brent began frittering it away. He bought a very expensive motor car, to impress his friends, and gambled and squandered and drank away the rest of it. Anyway, when Eleanor suggested they buy a house and set up their own home, he was forced to admit that there was precious little money left.

'Then one day, Brent took the day off work. He was working as a clerk then. He said he didn't feel well. Eleanor had gone to Evesham for the day with her mother to do some Christmas shopping. Olive had also taken the day off work. Anyway, his mother and father came home together, quite unexpectedly, and witnessed their wonderful son and lovely daughter on the hearth. They were both stark naked and you can imagine what they were doing. The shock was too great for Arthur, the father. He suffered a heart attack and died on Christmas Day. His heart must have been weak in the first place, of course, but nobody really suspected that was the case before. He was such a good man – a strong churchgoer, a God-fearing man, utterly respectable – and it was just too much for him. He tried to tell Eleanor there were some dark deeds going on in that house but he never spelt it out and she was too naïve to catch on to what he meant. Anyway, Emma, their mother took ill after the funeral and I can only presume that she died of shame and a broken heart, because she lasted no more than two months. Her health started to decline at once, poor woman. In that time she never spoke another word to either Brent or Olive.'

'And Eleanor had no idea what had gone on during this time?' Maxine asked.

'In her heart of hearts, she knew. Brent's mother more or less spelt it out to her while she was so distressed afterwards – rather more graphically than his father did, but Eleanor was inclined to believe they were the ramblings of somebody demented. In any case, her naïvety inhibited her from truly believing it.'

'So when did she finally accept what was going on? I presume she did?'

'You bet, Maxine. In fact, she had a similar experience to his mother and father – a similar experience to yourself. She returned home from work early one day – she had a job in one of the local shops by this time trying to make ends meet – and there they were – at it again. They didn't see her at first and she watched them, mesmerised. She just couldn't believe her eyes. I mean, just try and imagine being in that position. Imagine finding your own husband doing that with his own sister – and with such ardour . . . both of them . . . Well yes, of course, you know, don't you Maxine?'

'And like I said, it was a shock. But poor Eleanor must have been heartbroken.'

'Not by this time,' Cassandra said. 'Only resentful. You see, Brent had a way of making you feel very unwanted when you were of no further use to him. He'd had her money, he'd got Olive for sexual gratification and, by this time, Eleanor was already feeling like an outsider . . . and very resentful of the fact. And it all confirmed what their mother had warned her about. She left him there and then.'

'Good for her.'

'Next day, when she went back for her things, he and Olive had already done a moonlight flit, as everybody called it. Nobody had seen or heard of either of them till Stephen came along asking questions.'

'Did they ever have a child, Brent and Eleanor?' Maxine asked.

'Brent didn't want children.'

'There's a surprise. And she never divorced him?'

'How would she know where to have papers served on him? He'd gone, disappeared, and she really wasn't bothered where. He was a part of her life that was eminently forgettable. A mistake, yes, but a mistake she put behind her.'

Maxine was spellbound by this story. Her eyes never left Cassandra's lovely face. And it was time to ask the same question that had intrigued Stephen.

'So when did Eleanor die, Cassandra? How did she die?'

Somebody knocked again on the door and Maxine, annoyed at the interruption, took a dollar bill from her purse and got up to answer it. It was a waiter with the trolley containing the huge pot of tea and a selection of cakes and sandwiches.

'Thank you, I'll see to it,' she said, anxious to get the waiter out so she could hear the rest of the story. She handed him his tip and wheeled the trolley into the sitting room herself.

'Shall I pour, Maxine?' Pansy said.

'Oh, please . . . So go on, Cassandra . . . How and when did Eleanor die?'

Stephen answered. 'She didn't die, Maxine.'

Maxine looked from one to the other in bewilderment. The implications had not yet registered. It seemed more important to discover what had happened to Eleanor.

'*This* is Eleanor,' Stephen said proudly and put his arm around the girl he'd been calling Cassandra.

'But I thought . . .'

'I know . . . You thought this was Cassandra. Same as I did at first. She told me at first that her name *was* Cassandra.'

'Yes, because you suddenly appearing from nowhere asking all sorts of questions about me put me on my guard. I didn't know you from Adam, although you seemed nice enough. So, Maxine, I told him my name was Cassandra – the original Greek word means "unknown" and I thought it rather appropriate. I merely told him I was a friend of Eleanor.'

'So what should we call you after all?'

'Oh, Eleanor. Please. Stephen calls me Cassandra most of the time but he'll get used to calling me Eleanor soon. And it suited our purpose to hide behind the name Cassandra here, till you knew the full story. No, my name is Eleanor and I'd prefer you to use it.' She smiled amiably.

Suddenly things were falling into place. 'But if Brent married you first and you never divorced him, surely that means you're still married to him?'

'Yes.'

'So his marriage to me must be null and void? . . . Oh, please tell me it's null and void . . .' Maxine's eyes were wide with eager anticipation.

'That's exactly the point, Maxine,' Stephen said, grinning again. 'Your marriage to Brent is illegal, actually. Cassandra – I mean Eleanor – and I came to America just to tell you. It means you're free, Maxine. You're not tied to him any longer. Your marriage means nothing. It doesn't exist. Except that he could face prison for bigamy.'

Maxine did order the bottle of champagne. She asked for reassurance that it was indeed the whole truth and was reassured. Feeling as if a ten-ton weight had been lifted off her, she laughed and joked as they enjoyed the impromptu celebration. She invited them to dinner in the hotel's Oak Room, so they met up again at seven in all their finery, ready to make a night of it. Toots accompanied Pansy by this time and Maxine felt it appropriate to invite Dulcie and Charlie as well. They began the evening with two more bottles of champagne and gossiped about home and mutual friends. They elaborated on the band's activities and generally got up to date on the world they had left behind. During the main course, conversation became serious again.

'So what do you intend to do now, Maxine?' Dulcie asked.

Maxine swallowed the piece of steak she'd been chewing. 'I've been thinking of re-forming the band. Everybody finds it hard to work with Kenny and even Ginger these days. And there's no way I'm ever going to work with Brent again. It means getting hold of some decent new musicians.'

'But are you sure that's what you want to do, Maxine?'

Maxine dabbed her lips with her napkin. 'I have responsibilities to the band, Dulcie. There's Pansy and Toots and Charlie. We have to go on.'

'Not on our account,' Pansy said. 'Toots and I are not really sure what we want to do, are we, Toots?'

Toots shook his head.

'We have enough money put away now to bide our time. We might look for alternative work but, on the other hand, we're inclined to go back to England. We're inclined to go back to Brum and get married – lead a normal life.'

Maxine looked from one to the other and joy registered on her face at the news. 'Really? Honestly? Is that what you want to do?'

'We've talked about it, Maxine,' Toots affirmed. 'We've seen what's been happening to the band – to you and Brent. Despite the success we've had, we've sort of been expecting the band to break up. Pansy and I feel we'd like to get married.' He put his arm around her shoulder proprietorially. 'Anyway, it's time I made an honest woman of her. Besides, I love her to bits . . .'

'Then do it,' Maxine said, overflowing with sentimentality,

'and don't think twice. At least you haven't been put off by what's happened to me.'

'It puts us off being married and trying to sustain marriage living this life. We both reckon it would be best to give up the band to make marriage successful.'

'And I reckon you're right, Toots . . . Blimey! Shall I order another bottle of champagne?' With her napkin she wiped away a tear that had trickled down her cheek and laughed at her own sensitivity. 'Is there anything else we should celebrate while we're at it?'

'We're just concerned about you, Maxine,' Stephen said.

'Well, I'm without a band. Charlie wants to give it all up anyway for Dulcie, who we all adore – and I don't blame him, because she's lovely.'

Charlie nodded his agreement and winked at Dulcie.

'But tell me, Maxine,' Stephen said, his expression serious, 'the way the music business works – whether you continue to perform or not, the records you've made and the songs you've written which other singers record – don't they continue to earn you money?'

'Oh, yes. In royalties. For as long as they continue to sell. Right up to the time the copyright runs out.'

'Which is how long?'

'Lord knows. Fifty, sixty years?'

'So you're made for life, really?'

'Who knows, Stephen? Maybe I needn't ever work again. Maybe enough money will accumulate over the years to see me through my dotage.'

'Then stop worrying about the band.'

'Actually, we still have commitments.'

'I'm sure Dulcie's father will sort everything out, Maxine,' Pansy said. 'He thinks the world of you.'

'He does too,' Dulcie agreed.

Maxine finished her meal, placed her knife and fork on the plate and saw that all eyes were on her. 'You know, I get the strangest feeling you're all ganging up on me.'

'We're just interested in your welfare, Maxine,' Stephen said.

'You've had a raw deal with Brent . . . And we all know you're still in love with Howard.'

'So?'

'So go to him. You're free to.'

Maxine picked up her wine goblet and thoughtfully took a sip. 'I lack the courage, Stephen. What if he's in love with somebody else by now?'

'What if he's not?'

'What if he hates my guts?'

'What if he still loves you as much as you love him?'

'Huh! After not replying to his letters? I doubt it. He'd consider it the ultimate insult.'

'What letters?' Pansy queried and looked at Dulcie in amazement. 'You mean he wrote to you after all?'

'Heck, I forgot to tell you. Today, after Brent had gone, I started to pack up his clothes and things. I found four letters tucked inside the lining of one of his old suitcases. One for each of the four trips we made.'

'You mean Brent had hidden them?'

'Somehow, he'd intercepted them. Oh, he'd read them, of course, and stashed them away. It was only by chance I found them . . . He always went to the post bureau before I did for his own mail. Sometimes he brought me my mail. I thought he was doing me a favour. And I *trusted* him!'

Pansy shook her head in sympathy. 'God! He's capable of anything, that Brent. And what did the letters say?'

'Well, even after that awful row we had that prompted me to go on the *Queen Mary*, he wrote that he loved me . . . and asked me to marry him. Since I never replied, I don't suppose he'd be very impressed if I went to him now.'

'But you *must* go to him, Maxine,' Stephen repeated. 'You've got to. He's most likely languishing, like you. And if you don't, you'll regret it for the rest of your life.'

Maxine took another sip of wine. 'What do you think, Eleanor? What would you do?'

444

Eleanor pushed her plate away and regarded Maxine thoughtfully. 'I would go to him, Maxine,' she said softly. 'It's almost certain he'll still be in love with you. Let's face it, he'll have had plenty of reminders – every time he turned the wireless on. And if he doesn't, at least you'll have satisfied yourself that you tried to make amends. They say there's going to be a war, Maxine, but that wouldn't stop me going back to England for my man. As Stephen says, if you don't try you'll always regret it. But you could be happy for the rest of your life.'

Maxine sighed. 'Oh, that's an enticing prospect, Eleanor . . . War or not.'

'Then do it,' Stephen said. 'You could sail back to England with us on the *Queen Mary* on Wednesday. Think of the voyage as a holiday. You'd be back in Dudley the following Tuesday at the latest. You could be in Norfolk the day after.'

'That would only leave me tomorrow to square things up with John Fielding and settle all my affairs.'

'God! How much time do you need?' Dulcie asked. 'My dad will help you. You know he will.'

'Dammit, I'll do it. I'll make a reservation first thing in the morning. Oh, Stephen, I'm so glad you took the trouble to come to New York. I could kiss you.'

'But only when I'm with him,' Eleanor said with humour in her eyes, and everybody laughed.

Chapter 33

Maxine arrived back in Dudley on Tuesday 21st September 1937. Stephen and the real Eleanor were conscientious travelling companions on the *Queen Mary* and, even when they alighted from the train at Birmingham's Snow Hill station, he was mindful of his self-imposed responsibility to see Maxine home safe and sound. They shared a taxi and made Oakham Road and Willowcroft the first stop. At the entrance to the drive, Maxine told them she would always be indebted to them for what they had done. Stephen, predictably, got out with her and insisted on carrying her suitcases to the front door. Maxine was never so thankful for his gallantry that she used to hold in such huge contempt.

Whilst on board ship she had found the key to the house that in New York she had not needed. In order to surprise Henzey, she determined to use it. Quietly, she inserted the key in the lock and swung the door open. As if she had just returned home from work she called, 'Yoo-hoo,' and was surprised to see a little person in a pale blue romper suit toddle through the kitchen door and stand watching her in the hallway.

'Aldo!' She beamed with delight. 'You're walking! Have I been gone so long?' She bent down and threw her arms open to receive the child, thinking he would run to her. 'Come to Aunty Maxine! Come and give me a big, big hug.'

But the child did not recognise her and turned tail.

She met Henzey, who was coming to see what was going on, at the kitchen door. Absolute joy registered on both their faces and they fell into each other's arms.

'Why didn't you let me know you were coming home?' Henzey asked when they had complimented each other on how well they looked. 'I've never been so shocked in all my life. How come you're back? Will's *bound* to die of shock when he sees you . . . Wait till Mother knows you're back . . . Does Mother know you're back?'

Maxine was amused at Henzey's astonishment. 'I didn't know I was coming myself till the day before the ship sailed. There was no time to write or anything. How is everybody? I could murder a decent cup of tea.'

'Ooh, yes. I'll put the kettle on.' Henzey picked up Aldo who had been hiding behind her skirt. 'Don't you remember Aunty Maxine? . . . Oh, course you don't. You were only eight or nine months old when she left home to make her fortune.'

'He's grown!' Maxine drooled. 'Here. Let me have him. He'll soon get used to me again.'

Henzey handed over the child and filled the kettle. 'Isn't Brent with you?'

'He's still in America, Henzey. We parted . . . Are you ticklish, Aldo, on that little fat belly?' The child chuckled as she tickled him and they were instantly friends again.

'Did you say you'd parted already?'

'It's a very, very long story, Henzey. I'll tell you later. Everything . . . Has he got any teeth yet? Let's see how many teeth you've got, Aldo . . .'

Aldo dutifully opened his mouth for her while she inspected his first teeth.

'So how long are you here for?' Henzey asked.

'Till Saturday. I'm going to Norfolk on Saturday. In the meantime, I'll have to visit Mom and Jesse and Alice and the kids. Everybody. Is everybody okay?'

'Fine.'

447

'And how are Herbert and Elizabeth? At least it looks like I'll be home for their wedding after all.'

'Which will please them no end. So how was America, Maxine?'

'America? Oh, Henzey, I love America. You should go. You should sell up and go and live there. Since Roosevelt's been in office things are picking up fine. Honest, you can't go wrong. You and Will would do great out there.'

'He's not doing so bad here . . . Did you say you're going to Norfolk?'

'I did.'

'Isn't that where Howard lives now?'

'Well blow me! So it is . . .'

The two girls laughed. They understood each other perfectly. Of course, Maxine had to tell her story to Henzey over that cup of tea, and tell it yet again to her mother when she called round to reclaim her long-lost daughter later that day with Jesse. Then, of course, she had to repeat it to Will when he arrived home.

'So what's happened to your singing career?' Will asked, over dinner.

'It's stalled, Will,' Maxine replied. 'I don't have a band any more. It would be a simple enough matter to form another one, though. New York's full of brilliant musicians.'

'So what happened?'

'The Owls and the Pussycats just fell apart. Two of them couldn't handle success and the third followed them like a lamb to the slaughter. Pansy and Toots have decided to get married and lead normal lives, the bass player fell in love with a gorgeous American girl called Dulcie who's my second best friend, and the bigamist I thought I was married to became an alcoholic and a junkie, to add to his impressive list of credentials.'

'But what happens now? I mean, who is looking after your financial affairs in America?'

'We have an agent in New York – a business manager really – Dulcie's dad, and he's taking care of everything. If it doesn't pan out with Howard, I have the offer to go back and resume my career.'

'She's picked up an American accent,' Will proclaimed to Henzey.

'No I haven't.'

'Let's hope she's long enough away next to pick up a Norfolk accent,' Henzey said dryly and wiped Aldo's mucky face with his bib as he sat in his high chair, contentedly plastering himself with food.

Maxine's return to Dudley sparked off a round of impromptu parties and everybody who knew her, it seemed, came to pay homage and congratulate her on her recent success. It was good to see her folks again. It was wonderful to feel safe and secure, wrapped in the warm protective cloak of a loving family; it was a feeling she had almost forgotten; one she had always taken for granted before.

She renewed her love affair with her cello and spent countless hours playing it, brushing up on her artistry of the instrument. Its rich, mellow sounds, the timeless melodies she enticed out of it, were like a salve. She lost herself in the warm vibrato notes that hung in the air for her with the intensity of lovers' promises. She did not think of Brent, nor The Owls and the Pussycats, nor New York, nor anything that had associations of anguish. She did not think of Stephen, nor Olive, nor Eleanor, nor even Howard.

Maxine arrived at Foxham, a small town about fifteen miles from Norwich, on the Saturday evening shortly before six. It had been a long train journey and she felt tired. She had not known where she might find a room, but the taxi driver was confident she would find accommodation at a hostelry called the Dog and Gun.

As he off-loaded her suitcase at the hotel, she noticed a commotion outside the local post office. People were fussing round a young man whom they had seated on a chair that had been brought outside specially. She could see his face contorted with pain and he looked as pale as death as he clutched his arm.

'That poor chap's hurt,' Maxine remarked to the taxi driver. 'I hope it's nothing serious.'

'I'll go over and see if I can help when I've seen you sorted out inside, Miss,' the taxi driver responded.

In the small wood-panelled foyer of the Dog and Gun, Maxine asked for a room. A man who said his name was George told her she was lucky. Visitors from America had taken all but one.

'May I see it?' she requested, certain it would never resemble her suite at the Plaza on Fifth and Fifty-ninth.

George took a key from the board behind him and asked her to follow him upstairs. She was right. The room was nothing like the suite at the Plaza but it was clean and well furnished. It overlooked the Market Place where she could see the final throes of the fuss that was still taking place on the opposite side of the street. The taxi that had delivered her was being used to take away the suffering young man, presumably to the nearest doctor or hospital.

'The room's fine,' she said. 'I'll take it.'

'Right, Miss,' George replied, admiring this well-heeled and personable young woman who was travelling unchaperoned. 'It's eight and six a night. Do you know how long you'll be staying?'

'I wish I knew,' she responded. 'Maybe just one night. Maybe a week. I'll let you know tomorrow.'

'If I could have a deposit, Miss?'

''Course you can . . .' She gave him ten shillings.

'Thank you, Miss. I'll bring your suitcase up shortly. If you could come down and register afterwards?'

'I will. Thanks ever so much . . . D'you think I could have a hot meal in about an hour?'

'I reckon so, Miss. I'll check what's on and tell you when I bring up your suitcase.'

While she waited for her suitcase she peered through the

window again. The crowd was dispersing but a large number of people were heading westwards up the street outside and she watched them disappear round the bend as the orange sun dipped slowly behind the church tower to her right. Her heart skipped a beat at the certain knowledge that this was Howard's church. She felt herself tremble. She must be so physically close to him now; closer than she'd been in more than ten months. She lingered at the window and pondered the good times they'd shared, the tenderness they'd enjoyed, the heartache they'd wrought on each other. If he turned his back on her when he saw her, it would be no more than she deserved. It would be a rightful punishment. And it was half expected.

So this was his world, tranquil now the crowd had scattered, and unashamedly rural. In so small a place everybody must know everybody else, she thought. How utterly different to New York. The setting sun was saturating everything in a dusky red glow and Maxine did not know how long she had been gazing out when she heard a knock on the door. She answered it and George lugged her suitcase into the room.

'You can have game pie, roast lamb or skate wings,' he said with a friendly grin.

'Skate wings?'

'Fish. A bit fiddly with all them bones, but the flesh is sweet enough. I'd go for the game pie meself with some boiled potatoes and fresh Norfolk peas.'

'Oh. I think I fancy the lamb, George, if it's no trouble . . . With boiled potatoes and peas?'

'No trouble at all, Miss. Half an hour?'

'Three quarters. No, make it an hour. I need a bath first and a change of clothes.'

'Bathroom's just down the landing to your left, Miss.'

'Thank you . . . Can you tell me who the vicar is over at the church these days?'

'Oh, that'd be Mister Quaintance, Miss. Young feller. Been here less'n a year.'

'Married, is he?' She could not help but ask.

'Not so far as I know, Miss.'

She sighed with relief. 'So where exactly is the vicarage? Can you see it from here?'

He walked to the window and bid her follow him. As he peered out, he said, 'See the church tower, Miss? The Fakenham Road runs behind it. Opposite side of the road to the church is a big black wrought-iron gate. That's the gate to the vicarage, Miss.'

'Can't you see it from here?' she queried.

''Fraid not, Miss. It's hidden by the church.'

'Oh. Okay . . . Well thank you.'

'You're welcome, Miss. I'll see as your dinner's ready for seven-thirty, Miss.'

'Er . . .' Maxine drew his attention again, curious about the Americans staying in the hotel. Having spent so much time in America, it was only natural to wonder. 'Your American visitors . . . Isn't it unusual to have Americans staying here?'

'No, not here, Miss. It's a sort of annual pilgrimage.'

'Oh, how come?'

'Folk from Foxham in Connecticut,' he said.

'Foxham in Connecticut?' she repeated typically.

'Yes. You see, Miss, sometime in the seventeenth century a lot of folk left this village to make a life in the New World. They founded a settlement there called Fish Bay because it was so rich in fish. But later changed the name to Foxham after their home town here in Norfolk. Well, every year we get some of their descendants coming back. They're very proud of their ancestors – very proud of their roots – and we're proud to welcome them back with a few celebrations and special functions.'

'But how nice to maintain such contact,' Maxine commented.

'Well it's not unique in Norfolk, Miss,' George said. 'Over in Hingham they do something similar, except their visitors tend to come over in August. Ours come for harvest time.'

'So when did they arrive?'

'Some arrived Tuesday evening. Some went to London first and came here later. They all sailed over on the *Queen Mary*, they tell me.'

Maxine marvelled at the coincidence but said nothing. They must have been on the same sailing as her.

'And are they all staying here at the Dog and Gun?'

'Only a few. Local families put up others – those they've got to know over the years or those they're related to. It's getting to be quite a tradition to visit us here. Today there's been a bit of fun for the kids at Tom Wendell's field up the road, and tonight there's a concert over at St James's. Tomorrow there's a harvest fair all day with stalls in the churchyard and Harvest Festival service at Evensong. It'll all keep the young reverend busy, I daresay.'

'Did you say there was a concert in the church tonight?'

'Yes, Miss.'

'An organ recital?'

'No, Miss. They've got an orchestra up from London to play some of that classical stuff. Not my cup o' tea, but there's a good many as seem to like it.'

'I'd love to go. What time does it start?'

'Seven-thirty, Miss. But all the tickets are sold, they say.'

'Damn! I'd have loved to have gone. Is there no chance of a ticket?'

'I'll see if I can find out if anybody's got one, Miss. Would you like your dinner earlier? Just in case.'

'Oh, please. I haven't heard classical music played for ages. I used to be a cellist in the City of Birmingham Orchestra until a few months ago.'

'A cellist? Honestly, Miss?'

She smiled. 'Yes. Honestly.'

'You must have been good.'

'I wasn't bad at all. I'm still pretty good.'

'Did you give it up then, or what?'

'A change of career. I'll tell you about it someday when you've got an hour or two to spend.'

'The day I get that lucky, Miss, the place will probably fall down. Well, I'll leave you to get ready. See you later.'

Maxine took her bath, and got herself ready in double-quick time. Satisfied she looked presentable she went downstairs in a simple sleeveless black dress with a full skirt that she considered suitable for the concert if George had been fortunate enough to locate a ticket.

She sought him eagerly and found him in the bar. Between serving drinks he was talking to two men who were wearing dinner suits and black bow ties. Each had a half-pint of beer in front of him and both were smoking.

'Ah, there you are, Miss,' George said sporting a wide grin. 'We've been waiting for you to come down. These gentlemen would like a word.'

'With me?' She smiled at them apprehensively.

'George here tells me you were a cellist in the CBO,' the taller of the two men said.

'That's right, I was.' She regarded him curiously.

'Allow me to introduce myself. I'm Leonard Beresford, conductor of the City of Westminster Chamber Orchestra. We're giving the concert this evening in St James's church. I understand you wanted a ticket?'

'Yes, I'd love to go,' she answered excitedly. 'Do you have one spare?'

'Well, we might be able to get you in . . .' He looked at his colleague and winked conspiratorially. 'It depends largely on whether you are able to help us out . . . We're in a bit of a pickle, you see. I know it's a bit of an imposition but . . . but our cellist fell and broke his arm earlier . . . I wondered if . . . if you would be prepared, at this very short notice, to stand in for him?'

'I'd be delighted,' she answered sincerely. 'Was it that poor chap I saw by the post office earlier?'

'That was him. You don't happen to have your cello with you, I suppose?'

'Sorry, no.' A shadow of disappointment clouded her face.

'If you wouldn't mind playing his? I'm certain *he* wouldn't mind.'

She glanced from one to the other. 'Okay. So long as he doesn't mind.'

'Normally, we would have two cellists in the orchestra but the other one is indisposed and couldn't even make the trip. We couldn't believe our luck, could we, Charlie, when George told us one of his guests was a professional cellist. Do tell us your name, by the way.'

'Maxine Kite. Pleased to meet you.' She shook hands with Leonard and Charlie.

'Can I get you a drink, Miss Kite?'

'Thanks, but maybe I should stay sober. What's in tonight's programme? It would be nice if I was familiar with every piece.'

'Debussy – Nocturnes, Mozart's *Eine Kleine Nachtmusik*. I'm going to play Bach's *Toccata and Fugue* – they have quite a decent organ here, you know. We're also doing Rimsky-Korsakov's *Capriccio Espagnol* . . . What else are we doing, Charlie?'

'Oh, some Saint-Saëns. All popular stuff. Nothing too demanding on the audience – or the musicians, for that matter.'

'Would it absolutely terrify you, Miss Kite,' Leonard said apologetically, 'if I told you we were also planning to perform a selection from Saint-Saëns' *Carnival of the Animals* in the second half of the programme?'

'Oh, no!' she exclaimed. 'You want me to play solo in *The Swan*? Oh, boy!' She puffed out her cheeks then laughed. 'I should have known there'd be a catch. Hey, I'll try. I know it, but I should tell you I'm a bit out of practice. I haven't played in an orchestra for nearly a year.'

'Oh, you'll cope,' Charlie said encouragingly. 'By the way, did you say your name is Maxine Kite?'

'I did.'

'There's a coincidence. There's a jazz singer called Maxine Kite. English, I believe. Doing very well in America.'

'Fancy!' she responded, amused, determined to admit nothing.

'You've taken a load off my mind, helping us out, Miss Kite,' Leonard Beresford said. 'Maybe we'd best get over to the church and make sure there's a cello still there for you. Shall we go?'

The church was more than half full already and more people were filling the pews. Maxine and her new friends headed for the chancel where seats for the musicians filled the space between the choir stalls, spilling over into the nave. She trembled at the prospect, not only of catching sight of Howard at last, but also because she had committed herself to playing cello in an orchestra she'd never sat with before. Anxiously she looked around, conscious of her heels clicking on the hard stone floor as she walked behind Leonard and Charlie. But she saw no sign of Howard at all.

A cello awaited her, auburn, old, beautifully made, cherished. Perhaps a Bergonzi, she thought. She would handle it with great care. She smiled favourably and Leonard nodded for her to sit down and check the tuning. He clicked a tuning fork against the heel of his shoe and allowed it to resonate through the body of the cello while she deadened the strings.

'C,' he announced.

She drew the bow across each string in turn. C – G – D – A. It was perfect; and the instrument had a beautiful warm tone.

'The best of luck, Miss Kite,' he said. 'And thank you.'

'Thank *you*, Mr Beresford.' She adjusted the tautness of the bow to her liking. 'I just hope I don't let you down.'

The sibilant hum of whispered conversations pervaded the church and the sound of shoes scraping the stone floor of the aisles as it filled with people. Maxine looked around apprehensively while she waited for the rest of the musicians to take their seats. She flipped through the scores on the music stand in front of her. Thankfully, she was familiar with everything. She just hoped her ability to play and sight-read had not deserted her over the months.

The rest of the musicians trooped in and took their seats and she smiled at each in turn as they looked at her quizzically. A double bass player sat by her and expressed his surprise at seeing a strange face, until she explained briefly that she was merely a last minute stand-in for his injured colleague. At last, there seemed to be no more movement in the nave from the gathering audience and an expectant silence prevailed.

Then she saw him.

Howard stood up in one of the front pews and stepped forward to address the people. She noticed he was not wearing his spectacles.

'Good evening,' he began, his back to the orchestra. 'On behalf of the Town Council and the people of Foxham, I welcome you all to this festive evening of music in this, our beautiful old church of St James's. Although I am a relative newcomer to Foxham, I am aware of the close connection this town enjoys with the good people of Foxham in Connecticut, many of whom have made the journey over especially to be with us, as they do every year. Indeed, we welcome them tonight and we always shall. I know we have a feast of music this evening from the City of Westminster Chamber Orchestra. Please enjoy it. But first, let us give thanks . . . *Almighty God, we thank thee . . .*'

He had not seen her. But she was trembling and her heart was thumping so hard that she thought each of her fellow musicians must also be able to hear it. He looked leaner and, typically, needed a haircut but, apart from that, he was the same Howard Quaintance she had fallen in love with. She longed to call out to him; to let him know she was there, to let him know she had come to him at last. But, of course, she could not let him know. Not yet.

He finished his short prayer thanking the Almighty for the gift of friendship, returned to his pew and smiled amiably at the person he was sitting next to. Maxine nearly missed her cue to begin as she craned her neck to see if it was a girl – a rival. But heads were in the way and she could not see. The music took her attention. The first piece was Mozart's *Eine Kleine Nachtmusik*, bright, brisk, and melodious. At once, Maxine was aware she was playing in a smaller ensemble than she'd been used to with the CBO. She had not counted them but only eighteen or twenty musicians formed the orchestra. The sound was less rich but the precision was perfect, proving them competent and it more than compensated. She began to feel the familiar high she'd always felt playing in an orchestra, the sensation of flying on a magic carpet ride. Why had she ever given this up? She must have been mad. This is what she loved. It was so spiritually satisfying.

She risked a glance at Howard. He was watching the conductor. Evidently, he had still not spotted her. But he was still not wearing his spectacles. From where he was sitting he would not be able to recognise her without them. Perhaps it was just as well.

A selection of Debussy's *Nocturnes* followed and Maxine was settling into it well. Once more she risked a glimpse at Howard but still he showed no evidence of having seen her. Naturally, he would not be expecting to see her, she reasoned. When he did eventually, it would be a hell of a shock and she wondered just how he might react. She hoped he would not suddenly turn his back on her and walk out. That would be the ultimate humiliation.

During the interval Maxine put down her bow, rested the cello and breathed a sigh that the first part was over. The bassist was saying something to her but she did not hear him as she watched Howard make his way to the other end of the church for some refreshment. An auburn-haired girl of about twenty-five and two other people accompanied him. Maxine's heart sank, for she knew now there must be a new woman in his life. She sighed profoundly. So she had come all this way for nothing. Still, it was better to find out now than to make a complete fool of herself later. Maybe it was fate that he was not wearing his spectacles. When this was over she could make her exit unnoticed.

'Aren't you coming for a cup of tea?' the bassist asked. 'There are some refreshments available under the tower.'

'No, I'm going to stay here,' she said politely. 'I need to go over the score of *The Swan* before I play it.'

'Are you sure? I bet I could smuggle something back here for you, if you wanted.'

She smiled at him collaboratively through her heartache. 'Okay, thanks. That would be nice. Tea with just one sugar please.'

He winked and joined the throng awaiting refreshments. She was not going to join that horde and risk bumping into Howard there with that girl. It would be just her luck to receive the iciest of cold shoulders just to make her miserable life all the more wretched. No, she would remain where she was, an anonymous blur in his myopic vision, just another musician among those already present.

She read the score to *The Swan* and realised that where Howard was concerned she had lost her nerve. It had been a mistake to come to Foxham on this vague romantic notion that she could win her way back into his heart on sight. She should have written first. Knowing Howard, at least she would have received a reply, if only a polite one. Who knows, maybe he was even engaged now. He would not welcome sight of her if he thought it might upset his future wife. God! What an impetuous fool she had been. The same impetuosity had led her into trouble before by haring off on the *Queen Mary*, marrying Brent. She simply had not thought things through.

The bassist returned with a cup of tea and a chunk of angel cake. She thanked him and he told her his name was Alan. While she ate the cake and drank the tea he conversed easily and it was obvious he was interested in her.

'Do you fancy a drink over at the Dog and Gun after the concert?' he ventured.

She shrugged non-committally. 'Actually, I'm staying at the Dog and Gun . . .'

'Then I'll be happy to walk you back there,' he suggested. 'If you're not too tired we could maybe—'

'Shall we play it by ear?' she replied with a polite smile using an Americanism she'd picked up.

'Pardon me? . . . Oh, I see. Okay. Fine.'

The audience was settling down again and she finished her cup of tea. Gallantly, Alan hurried to the rear of the church again with her empty cup and saucer and plate and returned to her side just in time. All went quiet and the old church shook as the first rousing chords of *Toccata and Fugue* exploded from the organ. Maxine had nothing to do in this, so she sat with her head down, listening to the inspired music created in Bach's inspired mind, competently relayed through the deft fingers of Leonard Beresford. Naturally, she could not resist peering under her eyebrows from time to time at Howard. It was amazing that he had not yet spotted her. It was frustrating too, because she would really love to see his reaction now, favourable or not.

Toccata and Fugue finished and Leonard Beresford returned to the front to take the baton to sustained applause. Maxine turned up the score to Rimsky-Korsakov's *Capriccio Espagnol* and waited for her cue. The piece lasted about fifteen minutes but seemed less.

Next began the selection from Saint-Saëns' *Carnival of the Animals*. Maxine was growing more nervous as her solo vignette grew closer.

At last, the time arrived.

Leonard beckoned Maxine to the front.

With her heart in her mouth she reluctantly stepped forward, carefully lifting the cello over chairs and other players. Alan graciously took her chair and music stand and placed it in the nave in front of the orchestra. She was close to Howard now, but she did not dare look at him and did not know whether he had noticed her. Then Leonard spoke to the audience.

'Before we progress to *The Swan* and the *Finale* from *Carnival of the Animals* I am bound to tell you, ladies and gentlemen, that our regular solo cellist met with an unfortunate accident late this afternoon, which resulted in his breaking his wrist. He has therefore been unable to play this evening. However, Fate has smiled benignly on us and presented us with a late replacement in the form of Miss Maxine Kite, late of the City of

Birmingham Orchestra. Miss Kite fortuitously happens to be staying here in Foxham and, at the very last minute, has very kindly agreed to stand in. I would like to take this opportunity of publicly thanking her for doing so, so redoubtably, at such short notice and without prior rehearsal with The City of Westminster Chamber Orchestra . . . Ladies and Gentlemen, *The Swan.*'

It happened in a flash. She looked again in Howard's direction. He was wearing his glasses now, looking at her agog. She saw him swallow hard and she radiated a warm smile that in no more than a second conveyed everything she had ever felt for him. If he possessed any sentiment at all he would recognise it, but his look of incredulity did not seem to alter.

Since nobody played harp in this orchestra, they were using a piano accompaniment for *The Swan.* Staring at Howard, Maxine missed her entrance, so the pianist seamlessly repeated the introduction till a small cough from Leonard drew her attention back to the music. She smiled apologetically, glanced at Howard again, then drew her bow across the string to form her first note. The familiar, rich melody flowed through her fingers, swooping with intense poignancy that might have reflected her sadness over losing him, only to soar with renewed optimism that was excruciatingly restrained by the accompaniment's interchanging major and minor chords. The first phrases were repeated. She played with a fervour that resonated through the hammer-beamed roof of the ancient church like an incantation, invoking all the magical power that music could summon. The pent up heartache that had existed within her for so long seemed to be released. She had never played *The Swan* like this before. She had never played anything like this before. The cello oozed emotion as she wrung every last drop of pathos from the music. Her eyes became misty with tears and she could no longer discern the score. *The Swan* always had that effect on her.

But she did not need the score. She knew this by heart.

Howard watched and listened spell-bound. He saw Maxine's

beautiful brown eyes glistening with tears. She had not changed. She was no less lovely. Who would have believed that she would appear under his very nose like this, playing the same piece of music that always reminded him so poignantly of her? He had never heard it played so articulately. The vibrato she induced through the fingers of her left hand intoned such emotion and the physical grace with which she played reminded him of so much. What was she doing here now? Had she come to plague him?

The tempo slowed and the piano played its final descent. There was a second's silence, then tumultuous applause. Maxine stood up to take her bow. Instinctively she looked towards Howard and saw that he was on his feet applauding. Before she realised it, he was taking the few steps from the pew towards her.

He reached her.

He took her hand and her heart started pounding more.

He looked directly into her eyes.

Through her haze of tears she saw his gentle smile.

'Brilliant!' he beamed. 'Oh, Maxine, that was brilliant! Thank you for playing it so beautifully.'

She did not know what to say. She did not know what to do. She wanted to incline her head to receive a kiss but that would be too presumptuous. So she smiled at him with uncertainty and bowed again to the audience.

He still had her hand and squeezed it. 'May I see you later?'

'Oh, please,' she replied earnestly, and a tear trickled down her cheek.

Suddenly, she felt quite drained.

Maxine did not know how she would get through the *Finale*; yet she did, smiling throughout its lively jaunt. The full accompaniment of the orchestra, the intricate piano phrases flawlessly played, contrasted vastly with the simple elegance of *The Swan* and she could understand why Leonard Beresford had chosen

Carnival of the Animals. It provided a perfect finish to a vibrant presentation.

When the concert ended, Maxine received the thanks and congratulations of her fellow musicians and the offer of a permanent position in the sinfonia from Leonard Beresford. She wiped the borrowed cello clean of her finger marks and patted it goodbye and Alan said he would put it away in its case for his absent friend. He was sorry when she declined his offer to see her back to her hotel. An old friend had spotted her, she explained, whom she just had to see. So the orchestra drifted away while the audience lingered in conversation, only slowly exiting the church via the South Porch. Maxine gathered her belongings together, retrieved her coat and walked with uncertainty toward Howard who was standing waiting in the aisle.

Her smile as she approached him disguised the commotion inside her head. She was trembling, her stomach was churning uncontrollably with apprehension that perhaps after all, he merely wanted to say hello. But there was warmth in his eyes.

'I can't believe it's you, Maxine,' he said at last. 'You're the very last person I expected to see tonight.'

'You know me, Howard,' she replied flippantly. 'Full of surprises.'

'So when did you return from America?'

'Oh, Tuesday.' She said it as if it had been a decade ago. 'I arrived in Foxham late this afternoon.'

'And what an eventful first few hours you've had. Drafted in to the visiting orchestra straight away . . .'

'I know. I could scarcely believe it when they asked me to play . . . So how are you Howard? How have you been?'

'I believe I've settled in here,' he replied pleasantly, deliberately skirting round her question. 'The locals seem to have accepted me well enough.'

'That's good. But I didn't mean *that* particularly. I meant . . .'

Howard looked about him. People still lingered in the church, talking in lowered voices, some watching him curiously. 'Let's

463

sit in this pew until the crowd has gone, shall we? You and I have got plenty to catch up on, I think.'

'You don't say.' She allowed him to lead her into the pew and sat down on the hard wood. 'How long has it been? Ten months?'

'Nearer eleven, Maxine. Last time I saw you was on the second of November last year. We're almost at the end of September now. I think I've counted every day.'

'But you didn't answer my question. How have you been?' Maxine persisted.

'Need you ask?'

'I do ask, Howard,' she whispered without looking at him. 'I need to know.'

'What do you think? I've missed you . . . in a way I never thought possible . . . I said so in my letters that you never replied to.'

'Oh, Howard,' she sighed. 'I never got your letters. That's why I never wrote. Somebody intercepted them and hid them from me . . .'

'Brent Shackleton?' he suggested.

'Huh! How did you guess?'

'I never liked him, Maxine. And I was always aware he had his eye on you. I suppose he was the only one capable of doing something as underhand as that.'

'I found them, though, Howard. Not much more than a week ago. I thought you hadn't written . . . Don't you see? I thought you didn't want me.'

'Oh, Maxine . . .' He took her hand and turned towards her devotedly. 'I've never stopped wanting you.'

She turned her face up to heaven and closed her eyes with blessed relief. This was exactly what she wanted to hear.

'That's what brought me back from America – the hope that you still wanted me. When I found your letters I just had to come . . . to see if you still felt the same. I couldn't go on not knowing.'

He sighed. A heavy, desolate sigh. 'Oh, Maxine. If you only knew how many times I cried for you. If you only knew how many times I stood outside at night looking up at the moon with tears in my eyes, wondering if you were looking at it too, as if it were some common point of contact, some way of reaching out to you. I spoke to you through the moon. Did you never get those messages?'

'I think I did. I think I must have done. I couldn't forget you, Howard. I'm so sorry . . . that I mucked things up between us . . .' She began to weep again and took her handkerchief out of her handbag to mop up her tears.

'Please don't cry, Maxine . . . You'll start me off too.'

'Can you ever forgive me for what I did? For what I've done?'

'What is there to forgive?'

'Oh, Howard, there's a whole bunch of things. There's too much . . .'

'Look, I'm the one who should be seeking forgiveness. For the way I failed to tell you as soon as I knew I was to move here. That was the crux of it. I was wrong and I should have been horsewhipped.'

'No, Howard, I was wrong in taking the self-righteous attitude I took. It was unforgivable. Like everything else I've done since . . . But I never stopped loving you, you know. Never. You have to understand that. Despite everything that's happened I still love you . . . more than ever.'

He put his arm around her shoulders and hugged her with his infinite fund of affection. 'Oh, Maxine . . . Every day that's dawned I've prayed to God to bring you back to me. I just never thought it would happen, least of all like this. I always imagined meeting you off a train at some smelly railway station . . .'

She tried to imagine it herself, and laughed through her tears. She wiped her eyes and blew her nose.

'Did you ever hear my records on the wireless, Howard?'

'Hear them? I bought the records. I play them constantly.'

'Do you listen to the words?'

'I know them all by heart. Would you like me to sing them to you?'

'Please, no,' she said and laughed, snuggling up to him. 'They were my love songs to you. I didn't know where you were and it was the only way I could think of to let you know how I felt. Did that ever occur to you, Howard?'

'Well, I was able to identify with the sentiments, but I . . . I didn't dare begin to hope that they—'

'Howard, can we try again?' she pleaded, raising her head from his shoulder and seeking his eyes. 'Do you think it's worth risking our poor hearts again for each other?'

'Oh, yes, yes, Maxine. A thousand times, yes.'

She smiled more cheerfully and took his hand. 'I'll make you happy,' she promised. 'I'll make you so happy . . .'

'What do you intend to do about your singing career?'

'All that's behind me, my love. As long as you want me, I shan't go back to it.'

'I want you,' he declared, 'whether you go back to it or not.'

She squeezed his hand, fondling it nervously between her fingers and peered into his eyes through her blur of tears. 'I'll never go back to it as long as I have you . . . Never. Anyway . . . before you commit yourself finally . . .' She sighed deeply. 'There are things I want you to know, Howard. Things you have to know. I don't want any skeletons tumbling out of my cupboard later. You might see me in a different light when I've told you what they are . . . You might change your mind.'

It was his get-out if he felt he needed it; and she felt she owed it him in case he could not come to terms with her recent past. If he did not need an exit, it would indicate the strength of his love. She was risking everything but she had to confess how, when she thought he hadn't written and consequently believed he no longer loved her, she'd allowed herself to be wooed by Brent Shackleton, eventually become his lover and, in secret, been his bride. She told how, after they were married, their relationship had imploded but his interest in booze, narcotics and expensive prostitutes had exploded along with the money she was making; and she saw how Howard's expression changed from elation to despair. She saw how agonised he was when he thought he was too late, how he laboured under the belief that she was married and could never be his. She saw his dejection when he thought his dream could never be realised. But, when she told him how Stephen had suddenly appeared with Brent's existing wife and how it proved that Brent was a bigamist, his face lit up again.

'So you're not married after all?' he said, seeking further reassurance.

'No. Because his first marriage is extant, his marriage to me is invalid.'

'Jesus!' Howard gulped and his whole demeanour changed. 'Well, I think we should keep all that to ourselves, Maxine. We'll make no mention to anybody of a previous marriage, even if it is void.' He regarded her steadily. 'You're sure you don't still love him?'

'Love him? I never *loved* him, Howard. If I *loved* him I wouldn't be here now. I was vulnerable. He was kind to me when I needed kindness and affection. He wooed me through the grief of losing you. Oh, he knew what he was doing. He caught me on the rebound. It was a big, big mistake I made.'

'I forgive you anyway.'

She squeezed his hand tightly and felt tears burn inside her eyelids once more. 'But can you really forgive me . . . knowing you've not been the only one I've . . . ?'

He knew what she meant. She did not need to spell it out.

'I understand, Maxine.' He looked into her eyes with infinite sympathy. 'After all, you're only flesh and blood . . . but aren't we all? I can live with your past. I forgive everything, if there's anything at all to forgive.'

'I've been so worried . . . so worried that you wouldn't be able to accept it,' she said softly. 'I would have understood if you felt you couldn't. Thank you, Howard. Thank you. But . . . but what about you? There was a girl sitting next to you.'

'Oh? Oh, that was Vera.' He patted her hand reassuringly.

467

'Vera is the church secretary. She's engaged to the church-warden's son.'

'So there's nobody else?'

'There's never been anybody else, Maxine. I never wanted anybody else.'

She sighed with relief. 'So d'you still want to give it another try?'

'Maxine, you're still the same lovely girl I fell in love with. I love you still. Why should things you've experienced without me make any difference? I suspect, after everything you *have* experienced, that you're a much better, infinitely wiser person. I reckon you'd make an ideal vicar's wife – you've seen something of life. Ten times more than the average person. The question is, do you think you could stand it here after all the excitement you've had? Do you think you could put up with a sleepy little town like Foxham after the glamour and spectacle of New York?'

'It's not all glamour, Howard,' she said, recalling her trek through the streets of Manhattan, accosted by down-and-outs. 'Believe me, it's not all glamour.'

'Do you reckon you could put up with the constant procession of callers, the committee meetings you'd be dragged into, the personal problems folk would want to share with you, helping run the parish, the being nice to people all the time?'

'I think I'd love it, Howard.' She smiled resolutely, dried away her last tear and shook her dark hair. 'You said in one of your letters that the vicarage was like a mausoleum.'

'Oh, so it is. But I know that with you in residence we could make it a very comfortable home. It's huge, you know. Ideal for raising a family.'

'Raising a family?' She chuckled. 'Now there's a thought.'

'Does it appeal?'

'Oh, you bet. So can I see the vicarage tomorrow?'

'At such short notice?' He laughed. 'How about after Holy Communion in the morning? You'll be my guest for lunch, of course . . . and dinner. So how long do you intend to stay in Foxham?'

'How long do you want me to stay?'

'How about forever?'

'Then I'll stay forever,' she whispered.

'Then we should get married soon. We won't be able to hide your comings and goings at the vicarage before somebody catches on.'

'Couldn't you publish the banns of marriage tomorrow – for the first time of asking?' she suggested.

'Is that your official acceptance of my marriage proposal?'

'If you like.' She smiled joyfully.

'You're sure.'

'Oh, I'm sure.'

He turned round to look over his shoulder. The church had cleared. All the concert goers had disappeared.

'May I kiss you Maxine? Just to set a seal on it. It's been so long.'

She smiled happily and they kissed, a heady, lingering kiss that drained away the ambiguities of eleven unpredictable months and the remaining dregs of doubt. Howard still loved her. Howard still wanted her. She could ask for no better outcome.

'We'd better go,' he said, looking into her eyes. 'Mr Swanton, the churchwarden will be wanting to put out the lights. I'd hate to keep him up. Are you staying at the Dog and Gun?'

She nodded. 'Please don't take me back yet though. Couldn't you give me a moonlit tour of Foxham first?'

'If you like. You'll not see much in the dark though.'

'I'll be able to feel your lips on mine again.'

He smiled contentedly, taking her hand as they rose from the pew. 'I'll get George at the Dog and Gun to take special care of you.'

'Couldn't you take care of me yourself?'

She watched him ponder a moment but she knew he dare not allow her to sleep at the vicarage and she regretted suggesting it.

'I could take a couple of weeks' holiday,' he said earnestly. 'We could go away together. I could soon fix that. Nobody would know us miles from here . . . Shall we?'

She smiled very happily. 'As soon as ever you say the word.'

Rescued from destitution and poverty . . .
but at what price?

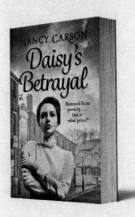

When charming Lawson Maddox asks Daisy Drake to become his wife she jumps at the chance to better herself. But with the honeymoon over he shows his true colours, and Daisy's life descends into chaos.

The appearance of John Mallory Gibson, a sensitive and idealistic painter, offers Daisy the prospect of real happiness, which she finds hard to refuse.

But Lawson will not let go of her, and he embarks on an unscrupulous quest for revenge that threatens to shatter Daisy and her entire family . . .

Only tragedy can save her . . .

When Lucy Piddock meets kind and dependable stonemason Arthur Goodrich, he seems to be the ideal match for her – but he lights no flame in her heart. Lucy dares to dream of love and hankers for Dickie Dempster, the debonair young guard she meets who works on the newly constructed railway.

Prompted by Lucy's rejection, Arthur leaves home to seek a new life in Bristol, leaving Lucy free to pursue her dream of happiness with Dickie.

But when tragedy strikes, Lucy must re-examine where her heart really lies . . .